Carlo Gébler was born in Dublin in 1954. He is a graduate of the University of York, where he studied English Literature, and of the National Film and Television School. His recent work includes the novels *The Cure* (1994) and *How to Murder a Man* (1998) as well as the short story collection *W9 & Other Lives* (1996) and the narrative history *The Siege of Derry: A History* (2005). His version of Strindberg's play cycle *Dance of Death* was published by Lagan Press in 1999 and his adaptation of Arthur Schnitzler's *La Ronde*, re-titled *10 Rounds*, in 2002. *10 Rounds* was shortlisted for the Ewart-Biggs Prize. His most recent play is *Henry & Harriet* which was produced by Kabosh Theatre Company, Belfast, earlier this year. He is also the author of the memoir *Father & I* (2002) and an occasional director of documentary films, including *Put to the Test*, which won the Royal Television Society Prize for Best Regional Documentary in 1999. Currently writer-in-residence, HMP Maghaberry, Co. Antrim, he is married with five children and lives outside Enniskillen in Co. Fermanagh.

By the same author

Fiction
The Eleventh Summer
August in July
Work & Play
Malachy and His Family
Life of a Drum
The Cure
W9 & Other Lives
How to Murder a Man

Non-Fiction
Driving Through Cuba: An East-West Journey
The Glass Curtain: Inside an Ulster Community
Father & I: A Memoir
The Siege of Derry: A History

Children's Fiction
The TV Genie
The Witch That Wasn't
The Base

Young Adult Fiction
Frozen Out
Caught on a Train
August '44
The Bull Raid

Drama
Dance of Death
10 Rounds
Henry & Harriet

Class No. .... Acc. No. ....

A GOOD DAY FOR A DOG

CARLO GÉBLER

Carlos Gébler

LAGAN PRESS
BELFAST
2008

Acknowledgements

Portions of this novel have already appeared, in a different form, in New Writing 9, *Fortnight Magazine*, and the *Dublin Review*. I would like to thank Julian Broadhead, Susan Aurora Irvine and Graham Rawle for the factual information they supplied and Emma Richler, Jason Thompson and Noel 'Razor' Smith for reading the manuscript so carefully and for giving their expert advice on the contents. Hazel Orme prepared the manuscript for publication. All mistakes are my own.

I gratefully acknowledge the assistance of the Arts Council of Northern Ireland whose financial support made it possible to write this novel.

Published by
Lagan Press
1A Bryson Street
Belfast BT5 4ES
e-mail: lagan-press@e-books.org.uk
web: lagan-press.org.uk

ISBN (10 digit): 1 904652 45 X
ISBN (13 digit): 978 1 904652 45 8
Author: Gébler, Carlo
Title: A Good Day for a Dog
2008

Set in Palatino
Printed by J.H. Haynes, Sparkford

This is for Finn

Author's Note

Northern Ireland, Belfast, Omagh and London are real places but Mulberry House and HM Borstal Langham Wood, HM Prisons Carrick, Culcavy and Loanend and the other penal institutions described in the following pages cannot be found on any map. That is because they are invented, as are all the situations and characters described in this novel and they bear no relation to people either living or dead.

1

FIRST HIS MOTHER HAD FIVE GIRLS: then she had two stillbirths, both boys: and then, finally, at the age of forty-seven, in the maternity ward in the County Hospital in Omagh, she gave birth to him. It was 11 February 1957.

He was baptised six weeks later. It was a raw, cold Sunday. His older sisters, who had come home especially for the ceremony, shivered in their frocks as they clustered round the font. He was swaddled in the Melanophy christening robe. According to family tradition, Poor Clare nuns had made this when Queen Victoria was on the throne. It was white linen with an intricate lace breastplate, hem and cuffs.

The priest, Father John, took him in his coarse heavy hands and leant over the font. Beyond the little diamond-shaped glass panes of the nearby window, the sky went black. As Father John intoned, hailstones fell with a whispering sound on the gravestones and the stony path around St Malachi's chapel. They were still falling as the holy water was dashed on his infant forehead. Father John pronounced his name, Stephen Gerard Declan Pearse Melanophy. These were all his father's names. It had been decided, since Mother probably wasn't going to have any more children, to use them all up in one go. As it turned out, this was the correct decision: he was the first, last and only son.

After the service, everyone went back to the family farm in the townland of Tynvalt. Originally, when his grandfather built it, this had been a long one-storey peasant's cottage with a thatched roof and a variety of farm buildings at the side and the back. Then, in 1952, with a grant miraculously extracted from the Stormont administration, the house got a second storey, new windows, a tiled roof and two extensions tacked on to the rear, one housing the scullery and the other the bathroom and the lavatory.

With the dwelling went forty-three acres. In the wetter places at the field bottoms and along the edges, sharp-pointed rushes grew. On the dryer higher land Father fattened cattle and sheep, and there were ten good acres that produced silage. There was also a small garden where Father grew potatoes, carrots and cabbage. There were crabapple trees, too, that produced an abundance of sour fruit for jelly. The family had turbary rights on a local bog that allowed them to cut all the turf they needed for burning.

The farm never made money—it wasn't big enough—so Father had a job. He was a joiner by trade and from Monday to Friday he worked for Henry McDowell & Sons, a shop-fitter in the west of the province. He worked on the farm in the evenings and at weekends and with the income from the joinery supplementing the farm, the family got by—just.

2

STEPHEN WAS A DELICATE BABY, CHESTY, prone to coughing and sneezing, and was diagnosed at three as having asthma. From the age of five, his school reports described him as pleasant if sometimes dreamy.

One Saturday afternoon in April 1966, when he was nine, Father found him in the lounge playing with his plastic soldiers.

'Come on with me now,' Father said. He was a powerful man with long arms and legs, who only shaved on Saturday night and whose face was covered with grey stubble the rest of the week. His eyes were dark and blue, and the one on the left was slightly lower than the one on the right.

'I'm playing.'

'Hatching, you mean.'

'Hatching' was Father's special word for staying inside. It was something Father disliked.

'You need to stretch the legs,' Father said.

Stephen didn't want to go out but that was better than being told to climb up onto Father's lap, which he really didn't like because of how Father pushed at him and made gurgling noises and which, as they were alone now, he might as easily have asked him to do. He followed Father to the scullery.

'Put your boots on.'

He did so and followed Father through the back door. Outside he found the grey tractor standing near the back steps. It was an old Ferguson T20. The seat was painted red. There was no cab.

'Come on,' Father said. 'Hop aboard.' Father hauled himself up onto the metal seat. It was wide and sprung, and it bounced with his weight. 'Don't dilly-dally.'

Stephen clambered up into the link box at the back and crouched in the gully littered with wisps of straw, slips of baler twine and empty Special Brew cans. Father engaged the tractor in gear, rounded the house and rumbled towards the main road.

From his place in the link box Stephen stared back at their house, imagining, as it grew smaller and smaller, that it was a kite and the unfurling lane was the string and the further he moved away so the higher in the sky the wind was lifting it.

Halfway down the lane the tractor lurched sideways onto a muddy track. The ground was soft and its monstrous wheels threw mud and stones into the air. Stephen watched the muck sheeting up and then, when that got boring, he stared at the huge gorse bushes and imagined they were the upturned galleons out of a pirate story lying on the ocean floor.

The tractor stopped. 'Get down and open the gate,' Father shouted.

He jumped out. In front of him was the stone wall with a buckled galvanised gate in the middle. He lifted back the wire keeper and opened it. Father drove through into what they called Dermot's Field and stopped. Stephen shut the gate and got back into the link box.

The tractor moved slowly up the track. There were sheep everywhere, with heavy, grey coats snagged with twigs and bracken stalks. Where were they going, Stephen wondered. Perhaps they were on their way to see a new lamb?

Then he had another thought. Perhaps Father had found an old gun. He knew the IRA hid weapons on the farm in Grandfather Melanophy's day in the 1920s and Father had told him they were still hidden somewhere.

The engine made a new noise as it started up the steepest part of the track, a back to front S with treacherous falls on either side that ran between two huge boulders. On his right, Stephen saw the first. Sometimes, on summer days, he would climb up the spindly ash that grew on the far side and lie on top of it for hours, watching the clouds in the sky. Then the second reared up, bigger than the first, and then, once it was gone, the track straightened out and Father drove on, higher and higher. Stephen guessed they were going to the sheephouse at the top where the ewes went to lamb. So, it wasn't a gun, as he had hoped, but a new lamb he was going to see.

His father stopped the tractor and dragged on the handbrake. This was a fierce noise, like a chain being pulled through a tube. Stephen had a real sense of height now. He could see right down Dermot's Field to the stone wall and the gate they'd driven through. He could see what they called the Lawn and their concrete lane with the cattle grid at one end and their house at the other.

'Get down,' Father said.

He jumped and felt soggy ground beneath him as he landed. Father got down behind him.

'Come on,' he said. 'Don't dilly-dally.' That was the second time he'd used the term. What was the rush? Stephen wondered.

He went round the tractor. The lonely stone sheephouse with its roof of corrugated iron was in front of him with a massive gorse bush on the right. To his surprise, instead of heading for the sheephouse, Father went behind here. He followed. Perhaps, after all, it was a gun he had been brought to see.

Behind the bush, he found Father with his flies unbuttoned and his penis pulled out. It was long and hard, red and swollen. He'd never seen it like this before and he was frightened.

'Now you rub it, son,' Father said.

He didn't want to but this was Father speaking. Father had a temper—he hit Stephen's mother too. He wasn't in a temper now but he could get into one quickly.

Stephen took Father's penis. It was hot and squishy even though it was hard too. He rubbed it and looked at the sky. It was filled with great clouds that were black below and white on top. He could hear the sheep nearby and some were tearing at the grass with their teeth, making a wrenching noise, while others were bleating. His father gave a grunt and there was something warm and sticky all over his hand. He wiped it off with a dock leaf.

Father buttoned himself away. 'Don't mention this to your mother,' he said, 'not unless you want the toe of my boot up your hole.'

Stephen nodded and threw away the dock leaf. It had made a green stain on the back of his hand.

'Did you hear me?'

'I did.'

'Not a soul.'

'Yes,' he said.

'No, you mean.'

'No,' he said.

After that he had to touch Father's penis many more times. Usually this happened behind the sheephouse or in different fields behind gorse bushes though sometimes he had to do it in the bathroom at the back of the house. It was always cold in there and the bleach Mother used to clean the lavatory always caught at the back of his throat and made him feel as he did when he cried.

In his next school report, he was called lazy, obstructive and uncooperative. Mother was puzzled—something was wrong, she was sure of it. Several times she initiated a conversation but she never got an answer from her son. He eluded her when she interrogated him. He had an idea she wanted him to tell her what happened but he wasn't going to. He had promised Father and he knew that if he broke his word the consequences would be terrible.

3

ON THE SATURDAY, AFTER HIS TENTH birthday, the man came to lay poison to kill the rats that ran about the sheds. Mother went out to talk to him. Stephen went to the press in the kitchen and opened it. There was her handbag on the shelf, black and shiny with a yellow brass clasp. He pressed it. The two interlocked arms at first resisted, then gave way with a satisfying click. The bag fell open and the smell of Mother's perfume rose up to his face, a dense, solid scent distantly reminiscent of the lilies in the chapel at Easter.

He reached in and took out her black leather purse. His mind was still. He had made a decision and now he was following through and he knew he must not waste time either with thinking or with considering any doubts he might have about what he was doing.

He undid the zipper and the purse fell open, like an accordion, to reveal three separate pouches: coppers in one part, small silver coins in the next and big silver in the third. That was his mother: always organised.

He took a couple of coppers, a sixpence and a florin, which left some change in each compartment, enough he hoped to ensure that she wouldn't notice. He closed the purse, clicked the handbag shut and returned it to its place in the press. He felt calm as he closed the press door, then incredibly cheerful. He wondered why he'd never thought of doing this before when it was so easy. A few seconds was all it had taken.

With his hand in his pocket, holding the money so it didn't jingle and betray him, he went out of the back door and down the steps. Mother and the rat-man were by the door of the turf shed, talking.

'Just going for a little dander,' he shouted.

'Where?' his mother asked.

'Just down the lane and back.'

'Are you going on the road?' she called.

'I'll be careful,' he said.

He set off. It was a raw spring day. Their concrete lane was rough and scored with dips and lines, and the water that had collected in them was frozen and showed white except where the wheels of the rat-man's van had broken the ice. The sky above was full of ragged white cloud with patches of watery blue behind.

He walked smartly to the end. Here, the spars of the cattle grid were dusted with slippery ice. He crossed gingerly, stepping from beam to beam, until he reached the tarred road. Walking on, he began to count the telegraph poles. There were thirty-eight between his lane and his primary school, St Brigid's. When he got there he went on and kept on counting too. He counted a further six, making a total of forty-four, at which point he reached his destination: Heggartys' shop.

It was set back from the road. There was a greasy forecourt with a rounded kerosene pump and smaller petrol and diesel pumps. The shop was clad in corrugated iron and looked like a toy house, with its centred door and windows on either side. The Heggartys' home, a low building made of stone, lay behind. As usual, all the curtains inside were pulled shut. The Heggartys had a reputation for oddness and this was one of the reasons. Besides running the shop with his old wife, Samuel Heggarty was the caretaker at St Brigid's school.

Stephen opened the door, the overhead bell pinging, and went inside. The shop was dark and smelled of flour, molasses and bacon. There was a wooden counter with a gleaming brass rule behind which old Mrs Heggarty sat on a high stool. She was a heavy woman with a vast bust who gave the impression, owing to her size and weight, that she was sluggish. In fact, she was acute and quick, noticing everything.

'How's Stephen?' she said.

'Fine.'

'What sort of a day is it out there?'

He shrugged.

'Cold, I'd say. What can we do you for today?'

He put all the stolen money on the counter.

'Who's a lucky boy?'

'Me.'

He bought a bar of Fry's Turkish Delight, a packet of crisps, and spent the balance on penny chews. He left with everything in a brown paper bag. He went to the tiny quarry at the side of his school. A century earlier limestone had been mined there but now it was abandoned. There were two huge rocks side by side in the middle of the floor—they were called 'the oul pair' locally—and he put himself behind these where he knew no-one could see him from the road. Then he scoffed everything, taking care to put the wrappers and papers back into the bag. On the way home, he threw his rubbish into the big bin that stood just inside the gates of St Brigid's.

He started counting telegraph poles again but gave up because thoughts started coming. It was wrong to steal, but now he had, he expected to feel something—sad or bad. He did feel something but for a while he wasn't quite certain what it was. Then he realised it was regret. He should have taken more. The crisps had left him feeling thirsty, and if he'd had another coin or two, he could have bought a fizzy drink. He was vexed with himself now that he hadn't.

He reached home, climbed the steps and went through the back door into the kitchen. It smelt of spuds, cabbage water and flour, mixed with the sour ammonia-and-peardrop smell of the rat-man. He was at the table, drinking tea with Mother. He had a sharp face. If he'd whiskers and a tail, as Father often said, he'd have passed for a rat.

Mother looked up. He glanced at her casually. He wanted to see if there was anything about her manner that suggested she knew.

'Did you have a good dander?' she asked.

It was her nice voice. No, he thought, she hadn't noticed. So, he really should have taken more, shouldn't he?

'I did,' he said.

'A boy who likes to walk,' said the rat-man. 'That's as rare nowadays as hens' teeth.'

'Oh, he's a good boy,' Mother said. 'Do you want some squash?' she asked. 'You must be thirsty.'

'I do.'

She got up and put half an inch of orange squash in a glass and added water. She gave it to him and he gulped it down.

'Thirsty boy,' she said. 'That must have been some walk.'

He felt a tiny twinge. He had taken money from this kind woman. Then he remembered what he had bought—the sticky Turkish Delight, the salt 'n' vinegar crisps and the penny chews. He re-experienced the pleasure he had known leaning against the boulder and cramming everything into his mouth. The twinge vanished ...

4

TWO DAYS LATER HE RAIDED MOTHER'S purse again. He didn't take everything because then he would have been found out.

The weekend after he did it again. There was less change than usual, and he could take only enough for a few penny chews. As he crouched in the quarry behind the big stone and devoured them, he realised that he needed to find somewhere else to steal, preferably outside the family. Heggarty's shop, from where he had just come, was an obvious target, but old Mrs Heggarty was always there, hovering and watching. Then he thought about St Brigid's, his school. He could see the buildings from where he was. In the middle of the morning, if he asked to go to the toilet, he would have access to the cloakroom and there wouldn't be anyone around. It had never occurred to him until this moment and it seemed an inspired idea.

The Monday following, just before midday, he put his hand up.

'Yes?' said his teacher, a cross woman with stooped shoulders called Mrs Hardy.

'Can I go to the toilet?'

'Wait until lunch.'

'I can't,' he said.

'Yes, you can.'

'I can't, I really can't.'

'Oh, for goodness' sake, go on but you be sure to come back as quickly as possible or you'll be in trouble.'

'Yes, Mrs Hardy ... '

He sprinted to the cloakroom and started counting.

'One, two, three, four ... ' he began, and as he did he patted the pockets of the coats hanging from the pegs.

Whenever he felt something interesting he stopped and searched. By the time he reached a hundred, which was the point at which he had agreed with himself he would stop and go back to the classroom, he had found a bar of Cadbury's chocolate, a shilling, two halfpennies and a packet of Sweet Afton cigarettes.

He swallowed the chocolate, hid the money and the cigarettes in his coat, then sprinted back to his class.

'You were a long time,' said Mrs Hardy, as he came in. 'What kept you?'

'Number twos,' he said.

There was laughter from the other children.

'That's enough,' she said, 'and you'll do me fifty lines after lunch. "I must not back-answer Mrs Hardy."'

5

OVER THE MONTHS THAT FOLLOWED, HE stole from Mother and he stole from his fellow pupils at St Brigid's. He even stole a few coppers from his father's trouser pockets. No one appeared to notice what he was doing. He grew bolder, and as he grew bolder, he grew covetous. At the end of November, at the Sunday market that straddled the border, to which his father would sometimes take him after Mass, he saw a catapult. The frame was stainless steel with thick yellow rubber strung between and a pouch for the stone of soft black leather. The price was a pound and he wanted it.

The following day, even though there was a whole week to the next market, he went to Mother's handbag and took out her purse.

In at the back, she kept her supply of Free State notes for when she shopped over the border. He found two red ten-shilling notes and a single pound. Which should he take? Such a large note as the single was apt to be noticed, then again without the two ten-shilling notes the space might look so bare that Mother would be alerted to the fact that some of her money was gone. It did not occur to him to abandon what he was about to do and try another day when she might have more notes. He had made up his mind. He must have a pound now.

He decided that the single was the least risky option. He took it out and returned the purse to its place in the handbag, taking care to put it back exactly where he'd found it. Then he crept upstairs and hid the note under his mattress, after which he straightened the covers so it would not look to his mother, if she happened to glance in, as if his bed had been touched.

At the moment that he took the note, he had been faintly troubled by having to make a choice, but now that the note was hidden, he was elated. It was partly the amount he had taken and it was partly the thought of the gleaming catapult that would be his. Confidence followed this surge of joy. It would not be noticed, and even if it were, it would not be found. How would Mother know where to look? All he had to do now was wait.

He had forgotten one thing though. This was November and Christmas wasn't far away. The day after he stole her money, Mother went to Sligo to do some shopping. In Murray's shop, she found a blouse that she thought would be lovely for Hannah, her eldest. It was silk, white and it would lift Hannah's pale complexion, she thought. The price was a penny less than two pounds.

She carried the blouse to the counter. Mr Murray loomed behind. She knew him slightly, having shopped there many times over the years.

'Mrs Melanophy,' he said. He was a man in his fifties with a creased face, and glasses that magnified his eyes, and a white tape measure hanging round his neck.

'I'd like this,' she said, proffering the blouse, 'but I wonder, is two pounds your best price?'

Mr Murray examined the price tag. 'I'll knock five shillings off.'

Mother nodded. He always gave her a good price.

'I've the notes here.' She tugged her purse out of her handbag and pulled out the notes. 'Oh,' she said.

There were two red ten-shilling notes in her hand but the green pound note was missing. A flush spread up her neck and over her face. Did Mr Murray think this was a ploy, that she was presenting all she had in the hope he'd let her have the blouse for that? It was a trick she'd seen others try but she wouldn't stoop to that. 'I could have sworn I had the money,' she said, 'but it seems not to be there.'

'Will we hold it for you?' asked Mr Murray. He didn't seem interested in whether she had the money or not, which was a relief.

'Will I leave ten shillings?' she asked.

'Don't worry Mrs Melanophy.' He threw the blouse onto the shelf under the counter. 'It'll be here when you come back. Even if it's Christmas Eve, it won't go anywhere.'

That night, Mother said to Father, 'Did you take my Free State money?'

They were in the kitchen. Father was sitting on one of the chairs he'd taken out of their old Austin Cambridge and he was pulling on his water boots. It was dark outside. He had been home from work for half an hour but she hadn't been able to talk to him until now because, as he always did when he got home, he had spent the first twenty minutes on the 'throne', as he called the toilet.

'What would I want your money for?' he said.

The chair from the Austin Cambridge was covered with slippery blue leather and his boots were dull black with a grimy, textured, cream lining inside. He was on his way out to fodder the cattle in the byre.

'I have my own money. I don't need to be taking yours.'

'I know that,' Mother said carefully. She didn't want this escalating into a row. 'I just thought you might have borrowed some to pay for something if you were in the south.'

'Such as what?'

'I don't know.'

He got up, stamped one foot and then the other to force his feet down into the boots.

'You're a fucking idiot,' he said. 'If you don't know what I'd have spent it on, you can't know I'd have taken it, can you?'

'I suppose,' she said.

Her husband went out.

6

THE NEXT DAY WAS CLOUDLESS, AND Mother decided she would take advantage of the unexpected fine weather. She would wash the sheets and dry them on the line outside instead of draping them, as she usually did at this time of year, on the rails above the range.

She went to Stephen's room and stripped his bed. When she put on the clean bottom sheet and tucked it under the mattress she felt something under there. It was papery. She lifted the mattress to see what it was and found the note. She guessed it was hers. It had to be. A single Irish pound note— who else could it belong to?

'Stephen took the money I was telling you about,' she said to her husband that night when he got home.

'He fucking did, did he?'

'He doesn't know I know yet,' she said hastily.

'Well, he fucking will now.'

'I wanted to talk to you first.'

'We're not going to do any talking,' said Father. 'When it's something like this you've got to nip it in the bud.'

He pulled Stephen into the yard by the ear and thrashed him with the length of pipe he used to discipline his cattle. As he beat his son, he shouted, 'We don't want no thief in the house. You won't touch your mother's stuff or anyone else's ... do you hear?'

Stephen was vaguely aware that his father was excited and hard as he beat him, the way he was when he took Stephen behind the bushes. But as the pain commanded most of his attention this realisation was on the edge of his thoughts. The same was true of the intuition he had that the beating had heightened his father's expectations, and the next time they were alone, he would demand more of him.

He was right. The next time Father took him to the little dell behind the sheephouse, he did not tell him to touch and hold his penis. This time he had to put it into his mouth.

'I don't want to,' said Stephen, but Father forced it in and a moment later, as Stephen squirmed, his father's stuff was on his tongue. It tasted of fish and sawdust.

7

A FEW WEEKS LATER, WHEN THE Christmas holiday had started, he slipped out of his house one evening and made his way to St Brigid's. He found an old chair with a broken back behind the boiler-house and dragged it to a frosted window. There was a piece of brick on the ground. He picked it up, climbed on the chair, smashed the window and scrambled in. There were sinks on the other side and from there he jumped down onto the floor. The toilet was dark and smelt of stagnant water and wet stone.

He crept along the unlit corridors towards the office of the headmaster, Mr Gormley. He opened the door and went in to the secretary Mrs O'Hara's room. He walked through the next door into Mr Gormley's office and turned on the light. There was a dark wooden desk and pictures of President J.F. Kennedy and the Pope on the wall.

He emptied the desk drawers onto the floor, heaping up stationery and papers but he found nothing of value.

He wanted to pee. He should have used the toilet while he was there, he thought. Well, he wasn't going to walk back. He unzipped and emptied himself onto Mr Gormley's chair. It had a yellow cushion on the seat and as his pee soaked in, the fabric went dark and a warm salty smell drifted up to him. When he had finished, he remembered the cash box. He'd seen it sometimes in the bottom drawer of Mrs O'Hara's desk.

He went to the outer room and, in the bottom right-hand drawer of Mrs O'Hara's desk, he found it. He took it out and shook it. Money rattled inside. The box was locked but it was only made of flimsy metal. He knew he could prise off the lid with one of the screwdrivers in his father's workshop.

He slipped the box under his arm, the coins sliding around (a lovely sound he thought), and opened the door to the corridor. To his surprise, Mr Heggarty, the caretaker, was standing there. In contrast to his wife, who was broad, Mr Heggarty was very tall and thin. He had a long, bony face and a nose with a kink from when it was broken in a football match.

'What are you doing?' said Mr Heggarty. His face darkened. 'And what are you doing with that cash box?'

He went to snatch it but Stephen was too fast for him.

'Don't you arse me around. Hand it over.'

His improbably white false teeth rattled in his mouth and tiny beads of spittle flew into the air.

Stephen took a step back. He was now in the middle of Mrs O'Hara's room. Two more steps and he'd crash into the desk. He glanced at the window. It was closed and the handle was down. He'd have to get out the way he'd come in. But Mr Heggarty was blocking his path.

'You're for the high jump,' said Mr Heggarty. His eyes were very cold and blue. 'Now, don't make things harder for yourself. Hand over the box.'

'Have it then,' shouted Stephen.

He had just decided what to do and now he did it. First, he lifted the box over his head, holding it with his two hands.

Then he hurled it with all his might at the huge old face in front of him. He had a fleeting glimpse of Mr Heggarty's appalled expression as box and face collided. Mr Heggarty cried out, a mix of pain and surprise, then the box hit the floor with a crash.

Stephen lunged past the caretaker's lanky body, dashed out of the door and sprinted along the corridor. Mr Heggarty had turned the lights on, so he saw where he was going. He dived into the toilets.

Had Mr Heggarty followed? He didn't know. All that mattered, though, was that he got out, the quicker the better. He put his foot on the side of the basin in front of the window he'd come in by, lifted himself up and slipped. He saw the window with the jagged glass along the bottom and realised he was falling onto it. He put out his hand to save himself and the glass sliced along the top of his palm. There was no pain, just a sense of soft yielding to hard. He scrambled through the frame, got down onto the chair on the other side and from there onto the asphalt. Then he ran away through the darkness. By now, his hand was hurting. He squeezed it with the other and tried to staunch the blood.

When he got home, he knew it was too risky to go inside. On account of the bleeding there'd be questions. He'd have to wait until it stopped. He slipped into the shed and, heart pounding, chest heaving, threw himself down on the turf pile. Now he remembered it was bad to let turf grit get into a cut because it might have rat's pee on it, which made you sick. He blew away the dust on his hand, and then spat into his palm in a hopeless attempt to clean it.

He heard a car arrive. He didn't recognise it from the sound of the engine. It wasn't his father's van anyway. There was a short period of stillness, then the car drove off.

'Stephen! Stephen!' It was Mother. Her voice crept closer. He saw a line of white light appear at the bottom of the door. That was the torch. It was too late to run and there was nowhere to hide. He was caught. He felt an unexpected surge of recalcitrance. So he'd broken into his school. So he'd thrown the cash box at the caretaker. He'd had a fright, hadn't he? And if he hadn't defended himself, what would have happened?

At the back of his thoughts the idea lurked that Mr Heggarty could have done what his father did. He'd no evidence that he would, only the fear that he might. He wondered if he could tell Mother this? That was why he had thrown the box—to stop Mr Heggarty doing what Father did. Could he tell Mother?

Of course he couldn't. Then he'd have to tell on Father. Mother would be angry and he'd be blamed and Father would be furious because hadn't he said Stephen was never to breathe a word? No, he'd say nothing. He'd just have to take whatever Mother said, and whatever Father said too. He would tough it out, and that was the mark of a man, as his father sometimes said. A proper man always toughed it out.

The door of the shed opened and a white beam caught him in the face as he sat on the sods spitting at his cut hand.

'The police are coming.' Mother's voice was very low and very sad.

8

SHE LED HIM ACROSS THE YARD and in through the back door to the scullery, then to the kitchen. There were scones on a rack on the table, and the flour on the red Formica tabletop below was like a light dusting of snow. The kitchen smelt of turf smoke. The fuel cover on the range had a dent in the edge from the time Father had thrown it at Mother when she let the range go out; ever since then little spurts of smoke would squeeze through the gap. After his sister Hannah was told in school about the Pope's election being signalled with smoke from the College of Cardinals, she had called those puffs 'the Pope's Smoke' and the name had stuck.

At that moment a little one drifted up. 'The Pope's Smoke,' he said, without thinking, then wished he hadn't. She would think he was being boisterous and acting as if he didn't know he was in trouble.

'Come over to the sink,' she said. She'd only just noticed his hand.

He followed her back to the scullery.

Mother turned on the cold tap. 'Put your hand under.'

The cold water dashed into his hand. He saw the blood being carried away and the pink slit that was left behind.

She dried his hand with a clean tea-towel. With cotton wool, she dabbed disinfectant onto the cut. The wound smarted and little beads involuntarily appeared in his eyes.

'There'll be time enough for tears,' she said, 'without fretting over a little cut.'

He could feel a great sob gathering strength deep in his chest. He longed to let it out, and to follow the cry by letting the tears behind his eyes pour down his face. He longed to tell her how sorry he was, for truly he was sorry, and he wished he hadn't done it. He wanted to promise he'd never do it again. He longed to throw his arms up and for her to throw hers round him and pull him to her. He longed to nuzzle against her, to smell her smell, a mixture of perfume, powder and flour. He longed to feel her hand stroking his head and to hear her voice saying, 'There, there, it doesn't matter ... '

He knew, though, that none of this would happen. She was cross, cold and distant. Any sign of weakness from him, any sobs or tears, any indication that he needed her comfort, would produce the opposite effect from the one he wanted. Far from making her feel sorry for him, it would make her even angrier and more disappointed than she already was. She would say he was wheedling. She would call him sly. She would certainly tell Father, and then Father would have yet another excuse to beat him. It was one thing to hurt Mr Heggarty but to be sly was worse in the Melanophy household.

He only had one alternative: to keep the sobs in and to hold the tears back. He had to show his mother a face that wasn't sad.

He swallowed and started to count and, as he did, he blinked to keep the tears at bay.

Mother peeled the covers off the back of the plaster she was holding and covered his cut. 'Go to your room now,' she said.

He went up the stairs and into his room. He did not turn on the light but lay down on the candlewick bedspread. His stomach throbbed with dread. He heard the McDowells' van that Father drove pull up in the yard at the back, then Father stamping in. There was a horrid silence. Father was fetching his hosepipe, he had no doubt, but before he heard him clattering up the stairs, he heard another car and then voices in the hall.

'Come down,' Mother called.

9

HE FOUND MOTHER AND FATHER AND a policeman downstairs. It must have started to rain for the policeman's coat had drops of wet on the shoulders, as did his hat, which he hadn't taken off. The shadow from the peak covered his eyes. Father was smoking a cigarette and glowering.

'We have to go to the barracks,' said Mother.

'You wee bastard,' Father muttered.

The smell inside the police car was male. He sat in the back with Mother and they drove without speaking through the rain with the wipers swishing back and forth. When they got to Crookedstone the light from the street lamps that came in through the quarterlights was sad and yellow.

The barracks was an old stone building with shiny wood floors and rooms that smelled of serge, cordite and gun oil. Every policeman was armed. Stephen found the proximity of the weapons so exciting that his dread receded. He and Mother were brought to a room with green walls and sat down on funny rounded chairs. A man in a suit came in and sat on the other side of the desk.

'One of my men has seen the school caretaker,' he said, 'and he's positively identified your son, Mrs Melanophy, as his attacker. He got sixteen stitches and the hospital says he's damned lucky not to lose his eye.'

Mother turned and struck Stephen twice on the face. 'You'll break my heart if this carry-on continues,' she said. 'That is if your father doesn't kill you first.'

When he got home, Father and Mother went into the parlour to talk. After a few minutes, his father came out looking furious. He found his hosepipe and lit an oil lamp.

Then he dragged Stephen to the shed, hung the lantern on a nail and threw him, face down, onto the turf pile.

'I don't understand you,' Father said. 'We give you all the love and care in the world and this is how you repay us. That old Mr Heggarty, he nearly lost his eye.'

By the pale light of the lamp, he started to beat him with the pipe. Stephen screamed and wept and bits of grit got in his mouth and he wondered vaguely if he'd swallowed rat's pee and was going to die. Then he fainted with the pain.

He came to in his cold bedroom, face down on the candlewick bedspread, with searing pains all over his back, his arms and legs. His father was just slipping out of the room.

10

AS STEPHEN WAS TOO YOUNG TO be brought before the courts, it was decided he should be sent to a residential school for disruptive and violent children.

On a dark March morning in 1968, a month after his eleventh birthday and shortly after Father had left for work, a big green car appeared at the back of the Melanophy house. The driver who got out was a large, bulky woman with a surprisingly small face. This was Mrs McIlveen, the wife of the local Presbyterian minister and a social worker. She went to the back door and knocked.

Mother answered. 'He's ready,' she said.

Stephen and Mother came out, Stephen lugging a plastic suitcase that Mother had bought on Saturday. Mrs McIlveen unlocked the boot. Stephen heaved in the suitcase. The lid closed with a deep metallic clunk.

'We'll go so,' said Mrs McIlveen, who always adopted the diction of the southern Irish countrywoman when she was with clients so they wouldn't think she was posh.

'Be a good boy, won't you, Stephen?' said Mother. She kissed the side of his head.

'I will.' His voice trembled as he spoke and he realised there would be tears unless he left quickly. He clambered into the back of Mrs McIlveen's car. It smelled of perfume, make-up and leather upholstery that had been heated many times in the sun. A yellow tin of travel sweets lay on the front passenger seat with traces of icing sugar on the outside. He wondered if Mrs McIlveen would offer him one. She was talking to Mother. Then she got in.

'Right,' she said. 'Let's make tracks and don't spare the horses until the morning.' She spoke in her normal voice. In Ireland it registered as English, but in England it registered as Irish. In fact, it was an amalgam of the two.

She turned the key in the ignition. The engine started and the car trembled faintly. 'Now, Stephen, don't look back at your mother. It'll only make you sad and you can't afford to be sad. Not after the way you've carried on. Keep looking at the back of my head, do you understand?'

'Yes.'

'Are you looking now?'

'Yes.'

'What can you see?'

'Your hair.'

'Good boy.'

She released the clutch and drove down the lane. He heard the ping as a hard tyre rolled over a stone. He stared at the back of Mrs McIlveen's head and her dyed blonde hair. As the car moved, the hair swished and swayed. When they rumbled over the cattle grid at the end of the lane, it bobbed up and down like something caught on a wave, driven against the shore.

From the end of their lane Mrs McIlveen drove across the province, and during the journey she offered him travel sweets twice.

Some two hours after they had left his house, she nosed her car through a set of old piers and up a muddy drive bordered with laurels and rhododendrons. At the end she came to a large building, a mix of brick and stone. This was Mulberry House, a boarding-school jointly run by social services and the local education authority. It had a small estate, which included an oak wood and a stretch of sluggish brown river. Pupils were expected to work on the land.

'Let's go.' Mrs McIlveen got out and opened the boot. 'You can carry your own bag,' she said. 'I've got my back to think of.'

11

HE CARRIED THE SUITCASE UP THE steps and into the hall. It was a big empty space with black-painted floorboards that were gritty underfoot. There was a fireplace with a few ashes in the grate.

'Put your bag down there and follow me,' said Mrs McIlveen.

They went through a door and along a passage to what had once been the estate office and was now occupied by the principal. There was a safe with its door hanging open so he could see it was empty inside. One wall was covered with fishing rods supported on wooden pegs.

The man behind the desk did not stand. This was Mr Harrison. He was big and bald, in a crumpled tweed suit. Under the jacket he wore a bulky Aran jersey and above the collar the knot of a green woollen tie showed.

'It's a simple regime we run here,' he said, 'isn't it, Mrs McIlveen? I tell you what to do, Stephen, and you do it. You'll sleep in a dormitory. There'll be seven others in there with you, all your age. You'll have the corner bed beside Kieran Woods. The bell goes at seven. You get up. You wash. You come down to the refectory. Breakfast is at half seven. By eight, you're back upstairs. You make your bed and clean the bathrooms. At eight thirty, you're in the hall for roll-call. You go to class then. Just follow the boys. Lunch at twelve thirty. One o'clock, you go back to the dormitory: you rest for an hour. At two there's the second roll-call in the hall, then games, then a shower and back in the hall for third roll-call at four o'clock. Then back to class. Supper is at six. Free time starts at seven in the association room. The boys will show you where that is. At seven thirty, we have the last roll-call. Then it's hot milk and lights out at eight. We follow the same timetable at the weekend but instead of classes there are games, walks and even, if you're very good, some fishing. One final point. If you think that at night you can get up to any mischief, think again. My assistant, Mr Purdue, sleeps in the bedroom off the dormitory. Any questions?'

Stephen shook his head.

'Good.'

The door opened and a man entered.

'Hello, Donald,' Mr Harrison said.

'Who's this?' said the man. He was a middle-aged Scot with very blue eyes, a pointed chin and luxuriant white hair that flopped about his ears.

'Stephen Melanophy,' said Mr Harrison. 'Say hello to Mr Purdue, Stephen.'

'Hello.'

'No,' said Mr Harrison. 'It's 'Hello, sir.' It's always 'sir' here unless you're allowed to use the surname but as you haven't yet earned that privilege, it's 'sir.''

'Sir,' he said.

'Thank you,' said Mr Purdue.

12

TWO DAYS LATER, STEPHEN WAS IN the woods, competing in a cross-country running competition. He was in a singlet and shorts. As he pounded along a track, he saw Mr Purdue standing under the wide bare branches of an old oak. He wore a green steward's armband.

'Come here,' Mr Purdue shouted.

He ran over.

'You're all hot,' said Mr Purdue.

Mr Purdue kissed his head and neck, then took his hand and put it between his own legs.

'Is that nice?' said Mr Purdue.

He shivered with the cold.

'Do you like a cuddle? I bet you do.'

He said nothing.

'Well, run on then,' said Mr Purdue.

That night he woke with someone in the bed beside him, grinding against him and groaning. It was Mr Purdue. He tried to slip sideways but the man gripped him. 'You're too heavy,' Stephen said. It was all he could come up with.

'So you are awake and there I was thinking you were asleep,' said Mr Purdue. 'You little trickster.'

Mr Purdue shoved and grunted, and eventually let out a cry. Then he slipped out of the bed, picked up the bottom of his pyjamas and padded off. He had left a wet patch behind.

13

THE NEXT DAY, QUEUING FOR BREAKFAST, Kieran, whose bed was next to Stephen's, whispered, 'Scottie got in your bed last night, didn't he?' Scottie was Purdue's nickname.

Stephen said nothing.

'Listen,' said Kieran, 'next time, say you'll tell on him unless you get fags and chocolate. Tell him to put the stuff in your locker.'

Each boy had his own locker—actually a small chest of drawers—at the end of the dormitory with the bed number written on the top in red paint.

The following Saturday Stephen was assigned to work with Alfred, the gardener, a huge man with cracked nails.

They met in the backyard, and from there, Alfred led him along old brick paths to the kitchen garden, then into the greenhouse. It was warm and the air smelled of chalky geranium and damp earth.

'Take this.' Alfred handed him the hose. 'We turn it on here.'

Alfred turned a tap in the corner. Water dribbled from the coupling unit attached to the spout and then, a few moments later, the hose vibrated in his hand and water spattered out.

'All you have to do,' said Alfred, 'is point this at each pot in turn and let the water flow until the soil is damp but not swimming.'

Stephen watered one plant and then another.

'Right, I'm off,' said Alfred. 'Do every plant on this side and then every one on the other side. There's five or six hundred. Don't rush. When you finish, turn off the tap, then come and find me. I'll be on the beds at the front. You'll help me with the weeding.'

The door banged after Alfred. Stephen watered one plant after another. The door opened. He looked round, expecting Alfred, but saw Mr Purdue with his long white hair and bright blue eyes.

'I've told that old fool Alfred we're going for a walk,' said Mr Purdue.

Stephen remembered Kieran's advice and then something his father said. 'Don't bother fretting when you should be doing.' This meant that if there was something unpleasant to be done, it was best to do it without thinking about it.

'I could tell on you,' said Stephen.

'Oh, no, corrupted already,' said Mr Purdue. 'I think I'm going to cry.' He pretended to wipe away a tear. 'And I had such high hopes for you,' he said.

Stephen moved the hose to the next pot and watched as the water soaked in and the earth went brown.

'And who would you tell if you did?'

'Mr Harrison.'

'He wouldn't care.'

'Mother.'

'Oh, "Mother" is it? How middle-class. Tell me, at home do you say "sofa" or "settee"?'

'Settee,' he said. He could have added that they didn't

have one but decided not to in case it gave Mr Purdue the opportunity to say something else.

'So, you are a prole,' said Mr Purdue. 'I'm glad we've cleared that up.'

'In my locker,' he said. 'A packet of fags and a big bar of chocolate.'

'Did Kieran tell you to do this?'

'No.'

'Pull the other one.'

'Are you going to do it?'

'Only if you say "please"?'

'Please,' said Stephen.

Mr Purdue turned off the tap. 'You are exasperating,' he said.

Stephen shook the end of the hose to get the last drops out.

'I suppose you want milk and not dark chocolate,' said Mr Purdue.

'Yeah.'

'Come on then,' he said. 'Let's go for our walk.'

14

AT CHRISTMAS, HE WENT HOME FOR a week. When he was in bed on the first night Mother came in. 'Can I kiss you?'

He shrugged.

She sat on his bed, pressed her knees together and smoothed her skirt. 'I think going to Mulberry House was the best thing that could have happened, don't you?' she said.

'Yeah.'

She kissed his forehead. He kept his eyes open and he saw that hers were closed.

On Christmas morning Father took him to see a newborn lamb in the shed, then pulled out his penis.

He closed his eyes and touched it. The shed smelled of wet wool and the little ram in the pen bleated as he worried at his mother's teats.

Mrs McIlveen drove him back to Mulberry House on 2 January 1969. In the refectory, a few days later, he took his plate of fish-fingers, peas and mashed potato, and carried it to an empty table. A few moments later Mr Harrison and Mr Purdue sat down at the other end.

'I don't know,' said Mr Harrison. 'Do you trust the papers?'

'Why wouldn't I?' said Mr Purdue.

'The marchers turn up at Burntollet Bridge,' said Mr Harrison, 'the police and the B-men stand aside and the mob are given free rein. I really can't believe the police acquiesced to assault like that, can you? There *must* have been provocation.'

'Certainly there was,' said Mr Purdue. 'The People's Democracy marchers were singing "We Shall Overcome", hugely annoying that, and asking for decent housing and one man one vote, also highly provoking to your seventeenth-century puritan. A mob formed who were determined to stop the marchers. The police showed up. The men in the mob had brothers who were B-men or policemen. There was talk. "These marchers are trying to take away our Protestant state. Why don't you let us teach them a lesson?" shouted members of the mob. "They won't be so quick to shout their mouths off when we've finished with them." The police thought, Why not? The order was passed through the ranks. "Stand to." And off the mob went. Can't you see it happening? I can.'

In April, Stephen heard more talk. There were riots in Derry and the police entered the Bogside. The Silent Valley reservoir was blown up and the Prime Minister, O'Neill, whom his father had never liked, was replaced by Chichester-Clark, a man his father hated. In August there were more riots in Derry and the Irish Prime Minister, Mr Lynch said he was going to send the Irish army over the border but he didn't. Mr Purdue described the Irish premier as all mouth and no trousers.

Then in October the Hunt Committee, whoever they were, recommended the abolition of the B-specials. His father, who loathed the B-men, would be delighted and he heard Mr Purdue describe the decision as necessary and long overdue. Mr Harrison wasn't so certain and Alfred, the gardener, who'd been a B-man for years, was adamant it was Ulster's blackest day since the state had been founded. 'You mean since the statelet was founded,' Mr Purdue corrected him.

15

AT THE END OF 1969 HE went home for Christmas. On Christmas Day, after the turkey and the Christmas pudding and brandy butter, Father gave him a five-pound note. Two days later he bought a bowie knife in Bundoran. When he got home, it went straight into his suitcase wrapped in a pair of socks.

In early January 1970, Mrs McIlveen came to drive him back to Mulberry House. She let him sit in the front as he was going to be thirteen in a day or two.

On the next Sunday Mr Purdue took him for one of their walks in the wood. They reached the little glade where they usually went. It was away from the paths and well screened from view. The ground was covered with rotting oak leaves and beechnuts. The trees were tall and dripping with wet, and the trunks had green slime on them.

'I never asked what you got for Christmas,' said Mr Purdue, unbuttoning his raincoat. 'Anything interesting?'

Stephen put his hand into his pocket, pulled out his bowie knife and pointed it at Mr Purdue. 'This.'

'Oh, no,' said Mr Purdue, continuing to undo his buttons. 'Is this goodbye?'

'I want to go back now and I never want to go for another walk.'

'Oh, so it is goodbye.' Mr Purdue began carefully to pull off his coat. 'I never thought I'd hear myself saying this, but do you know what you are? You're a cliché, Stephen. Do you know what a cliché is? No, of course you don't. Well, go and look it up in a dictionary, though that will take some courage, because then you'll have to face what you are if you do.'

Stephen's face felt red. He mightn't understand the detail of what Mr Purdue was saying but he got the drift. He felt the same hot rage that had filled him when he threw the cash box at Mr Heggarty.

'I don't know if you're brave enough. I mean, someone who needs a blade to back him up, is he capable of taking on board the truth? I doubt it. Frankly, Stephen, you haven't the balls.'

Stephen lunged and, as he did, the coat dropped over his head. He was in darkness and, next thing, he felt a thump in his solar plexus. He tasted sick at the back of his throat, his legs buckled and he sank down.

'You bloody idiot,' said Mr Purdue.

He felt the teacher's weight on his body, pushing him sideways and pinning him to the ground. His hand was twisted and he let the knife go. Then Mr Purdue got off him and took away the coat. Stephen felt the light flooding over him as he lay sprawled on the ground.

'You could really hurt someone with this.'

Although he'd been down for only a few moments the damp from the leaves had already penetrated his trousers and jacket.

'Look at the blade! It must be four inches.'

He had to stand or he'd get soaked.

'You know the rules, don't you?' said Mr Purdue. 'I'll have to keep this.'

As Stephen stood up, Mr Purdue put the knife into his raincoat pocket.

'But I'll not mention it to Mr Harrison, not unless you're a bad boy. And you're not a bad boy, really, are you? You're a good boy. Tell me you're a good boy, and then I won't have to report you.'

16

AS 1970 ROLLED ON, HE WAS vaguely aware of events in the outside world. The Irish Republican Army split into two wings, the Officials and the Provisionals. The Reverend Ian Paisley, whom his father hated even more than Chichester-Clark, was elected to Stormont, while Haughey, the only Free Stater who cared a jot for Catholics, his father always said, tried to send crates of guns to the Catholics in Belfast and Derry. In the summer there was rioting and six were killed. It was all quite interesting but more interesting was what was happening to him. He was growing at a phenomenal rate.

When the nurse measured him in the summer, he was found to have grown an inch since January.

'Is that why I ache when I get up in the morning sometimes?' he said.

'Certainly,' said the nurse. 'Those would be the growing pains. So you can tell your parents we must be feeding you right, so we must. You might have been the size of twopence when you came but you'll be big as a half-crown when we send you home, so you will.'

Mr Purdue took to calling him a strapping lad. At Christmas 1970, when he went home, Father slapped him on the back and said to his mother, 'I wouldn't recognise the lad as my own boy, he's grown so much.' He was only home for a few days but during that time Father never asked him to go out for a walk. Stephen understood it was his size: he couldn't be forced any more.

On 11 February 1971, Stephen turned fourteen. He was tall for his age and strong from all the manual work in the garden at Mulberry House. He was fast, too, from the cross-country running. He had a large head. His hair was brown with a tinge of red in it. His eyes were blue and there were a few light freckles on his pale cheeks. His body was sinuous and muscular but not especially dense or heavy. His arms were long and he had big strong hands, freckled like his face. His hips were almost too narrow for his shoulders and his legs, which were long and slim. So were his feet. He was an attractive adolescent, and all the indications were that he would grow up to be an attractive man.

17

THE DAY AFTER HIS BIRTHDAY MR Purdue found him in the greenhouse. 'Let's walk,' he said.

He shook his head. 'I'm watering the seedlings.' He dribbled water from the hose onto one shoot after another.

'Oh, no, he's getting conscientious,' said Mr Purdue. 'Well, there's one way to solve that problem.' He twisted the worn brass handle of the tap. The water spurting out of the ribbed end of the hose stopped.

'Turn it on,' Stephen said.

'Didn't you hear what I said?' said Mr Purdue. 'We're going for a walk.'

He moved back to the door and opened it wide. 'Come on.'

Stephen walked to the tap and turned it in the other direction. He'd opened the tap much more than normal and the water surged from the end. The hose recoiled like a snake.

'Are we having our adolescent rebellion?' asked Mr Purdue.

Stephen put his foot on the hose end to stop it wriggling, then picked it up and began to splash water over the seedlings. Because more water was coming out than usual, he couldn't dribble it onto each plant in turn. He had to hold his thumb over the end and spray it around.

'I suppose that means yes,' said Mr Purdue.

A moment later he heard the greenhouse door slam.

He knew there'd be trouble so he wasn't surprised when Mr Purdue discovered a double-handed split-cane rod and matching reel belonging to the head, Mr Harrison, under his mattress.

The next day, after lunch, when everyone else went to the

changing rooms to get ready for games, he was summoned to Mr Harrison's office. Mrs McIlveen was there.

'I thought we were getting somewhere with you,' said Mr Harrison, 'but you had to spoil it, didn't you?'

He said nothing.

'It's customary to say sorry when you've been caught out.'

'Sorry,' he said, smirking. He didn't care that this was a mistake. On the contrary, it pleased him to think how provoking, to use one of Mr Purdue's phrases, Mr Harrison and Mrs McIlveen would find it.

'We gave you a chance,' said Mr Harrison. 'We tried to help and we taught you some skills. And what did you do? You threw it back in our faces. Barring a miracle, and I can't see one happening in your case, your next stop will be Borstal. And after Borstal, unless I'm very much mistaken, it'll be prison. You're on the slippery slope and you've haven't given me any indication you want to get off it.

'Anyway, before you go, I want to put one thought into your head. The next time you're about to do something stupid, just give a thought to your parents and family. You might think helping yourself to this person's property here and that person's there doesn't matter. But it does, because when you get caught, you acquire a reputation, as a thief— the thief Melanophy. It mightn't matter to you, you might be delighted, and you probably will be because I think you're a perverse little so-and-so. But your poor mother and father, they won't be delighted to become known as the parents of the thief Melanophy.

'Think how horrible it'll be for them when they go into church on Sundays. As they go down the aisle the congregation will be whispering, "Their son is the thief." When your mother goes to the shops or your father to the pub, same thing. Can you imagine how horrible it is to become known not because your son has done something to be proud of, but because he's a little thief?'

'Yes, Mr Harrison.'

'Is that all you can say?'

He stared at a mark on the wall behind and just above Mr Harrison's head.

'Yes, Mr Harrison.'

'Oh, go away then—go and make a mess of your life, and when they lock you up and throw away the key don't imagine I or anyone here will shed a tear. Now don't keep Mrs McIlveen waiting.'

'No, don't,' said Mrs McIlveen.

18

HE WENT TO HIS DORMITORY AND began to fold his clothes into his plastic suitcase. He heard the cries of the boys on the pitch and the dull thump made by the leather football as it was kicked up and down. He should have been out there with them, he remembered, and with that thought, there came sadness. He had grown accustomed to this place. He didn't like it but it was what he knew. He was going home now, where he would have to learn how to live with his parents again. He could tolerate Mother but not his father. Even though now he couldn't try anything, Stephen would have been happy never to see him again.

He closed the lid and pressed the catches home. He picked the suitcase off the bed and carried it outside. Mrs McIlveen was waiting in the front seat. She gave him the keys. He opened the boot and stowed the case. Though she hadn't said so, he knew she wouldn't want him in the front, so he got into the back and passed the keys forward to her.

'You closed the boot properly?'

'Yes.'

'Right, we're off,' she said, smoothing back her blonde hair.

She looked at him in the rear-view mirror. He returned her gaze, scrutinising her face. Her mouth turned down at either corner and she wore pink lipstick. Her eye shadow was a pale purple, the colour of a bruise; her cheekbones had dusky red lying over them. It made them gleam. To his surprise, an image came into his mind.

It was Mrs McIlveen on a bed. She was naked. Her knees were up and her legs were apart. He could see her pubic hair (blonde like the hair on her head) and the red mouth running the wrong way, not side to side but up and down. She wore stockings and a suspender belt, the same as the women in *Carnival* and *Parade*, which some of the older boys had let him see. In the image in his head, he was present too. He was standing nearby, aroused. Mrs McIlveen was moaning. She wanted him to climb up and put it in. At Mulberry House the older boys had explained that what happened when a man went with a woman was what he had seen at home when bulls mounted cows and rams ewes. He felt himself going hard. He tried to imagine Mrs McIlveen naked on the back seat beside him but he couldn't make the image take shape in front of his inner eye.

'What goes on in there?' he heard Mrs McIlveen asking.

'Where?'

She took the lid off the tin of travel sweets on the seat beside her, then put a sweet into her mouth. He heard it clicking like a pebble against her teeth.

'In that head of yours,' she said.

'Nothing.'

She snorted. 'I don't believe that. A great deal goes on in there. The trouble is, no one knows what it is and you're not minded to tell.'

Mixed with the image of Mrs McIlveen, naked and waiting on a dormitory bed, he noticed a little tingling at the side of his tongue. He wanted a sweet. It would be lovely. But he wouldn't let that show on his face any more than he'd let the previous thought show—or any other, for that matter.

If he'd learned anything at Mulberry House, it was how to keep his feelings hidden.

19

MRS MCILVEEN DROVE DOWN THE AVENUE between the laurels, turned onto the road and headed west. He knew this road. He'd made the journey along it to and from home several times over the preceding years. He stared out at the landscape flashing past

The day was murky. There'd been fog earlier and shreds of it remained, swirling round bare trees or trapped in hollows in the fields. After a while they reached the first town. The few people who were about were hurrying along, swathed in heavy coats. A few minutes later the car passed out into the bare country, with fog wisps here and there. This was the pattern for the rest of the journey and the only variation was the two times he caught Mrs McIlveen watching him in the rear-view mirror. He knew from her expression that she was trying to judge what sort of mood he was in but couldn't. This delighted him. He regarded it as a victory.

It was dark when she drove into the yard behind his house. He saw Father's van with his employer's name painted on the side. 'Home sweet home,' she said. She made no attempt to get out.

He opened the door.

'Don't say "thank you",' she said.

'Thank you.'

'You'll need these.' She handed him the keys. He went behind the car and put the key into the lock. The mechanism turned smoothly and the lid lifted. He took out his suitcase and closed the boot. He went round to the driver's side window where Mrs McIlveen had her hand out. Her palm, he noticed, was covered with tiny lines and creases. He put the keys into the middle and she closed her fingers round them.

'I'll be seeing you soon,' she said.

'We'll see,' he said.

'You're too young to be so arrogant,' she said. 'Of course you'll be seeing me, you idiot. It's up to me to sort out what to do next with you.'

She drove away.

He carried the suitcase across the yard and up the steps. He turned the back door handle and stepped into the scullery. The smell that met him was familiar, a mixture of cabbage water, flour and the bumpy rubbery lining of the water boots that lived against the wall.

He passed the sink and went through another door into the kitchen. Father was in one of the car seats by the range with the *Tyrone Constitution* in his hands. 'Am I going to be reading about you in here next week,' he asked, 'on the court page?'

Stephen shook his head.

'Well, I'm warning you, I'd better fucking not.'

He looked down at Father's uneven face, the dark blue eyes staring up at him. Father was surprised—Stephen could see that in his expression. Father was impressed too. Stephen had grown, hadn't he, even since his father had seen him last? Oh, yes, he had. And certainly compared to what he had been when he went away to Mulberry House, he was much bigger, much stronger, and much more powerful. He was as big as Father was, perhaps bigger. Now his father might still like to talk hard but he wouldn't bring out the hosepipe any more, would he? If he tried, Stephen would take it off him and slap him back. There'd been a shift. His father couldn't get him to do what he wanted any more. So, that part of his life was over.

'Where is she?' he asked.

'Up the stairs making your bed,' Father said.

20

HE SAT AT THE KITCHEN TABLE with Mother and Mrs McIlveen. He had been home now for two days.

'Why do I have to go to school?' he asked.

'Because you're not allowed to work until you're fifteen,' said Mrs McIlveen. He looked at her face framed by the blonde hair. He had never noticed before how like a doll's it was. When she was younger, he thought, Mrs McIlveen was probably rather pretty.

'St Brendan's won't have him.' Mrs McIlveen addressed this remark to Mother.

'Oh,' Mother said, alarm in her voice.

'But all is not lost.'

His eyes flicked from Mrs McIlveen to Mother. She had a very different look from their visitor: her hair was grey and she wore it scraped into a bun at the back of her head. There were deep creases round her eyes and lines running down from either side of her mouth. When these filled with shadow, she looked as if she had a drooping moustache. She wore foundation and lipstick that had more brown than red in it. Her big hands rested on the table in front of her, the fingers interlaced. Her knuckles were swollen. She could only get her rings off if she smeared her fingers with butter first.

'My husband,' Mrs McIlveen continued—the Reverend Jeremiah McIlveen, the local Presbyterian minister—'he's a governor of Crookedstone High School.' This was the local controlled state school: most of the pupils were Protestants but there were Catholics too. 'He's had a word with the headmaster. They'll take Stephen.'

'Oh,' Mother said. 'Really?'

Stephen couldn't tell whether she was relieved or troubled. He was on more certain ground when it came to his own feelings. At St Brendan's he would be known. It was more than likely he would be picked on. Mr Heggarty might even have relatives at the school who would have a go. At Crookedstone High, on the other hand, he would be with the other lot, Protestants. He might be ignored. He might get through the year without too much trouble. Then he could find a job and start earning money. It wasn't a bad option.

'When would I go?' He assumed he would start after the Easter holidays.

'Monday.'

'Can't I start after Easter?'

'No.'

Mrs McIlveen began to undo the straps of the briefcase on

her lap. She wore several rings and he didn't imagine she needed butter to get them off.

'But why?'

'You have to go to school starting Monday. Don't argue,' Mother said.

The straps came out of the buckles and the briefcase was opened. 'I've brought you this.'

Mrs McIlveen put a brochure face up on the red Formica table. 'Crookedstone High' was written on the front and there was a coat of arms underneath. 'This explains something about the school, the curriculum and so on.'

Mother turned it gingerly and studied the cover.

'There are three sets,' said Mrs McIlveen, 'and Stephen will start in the third. But if he shows promise they'll move him up.'

'What about the religious service?' Mother asked quietly.

'They have assembly three times a week. Two hymns, the Lord's Prayer and a short address by the head. You can opt out if you want but really, everyone goes.'

'Oh,' said Mother. There was still alarm in her voice but not as much as before.

'The school has a substantial number of Roman Catholics,' said Mrs McIlveen. 'They can't afford to be insensitive.'

'I'll have to talk to my husband.'

'Of course,' said Mrs McIlveen.

Outside a cockerel crowed.

'And there wouldn't be an alternative, would there?' said Mother.

'No,' said Mrs McIlveen.

21

FATHER WAS INFORMED THAT NIGHT. STEPHEN was going to Crookedstone High.

'It's not a Catholic school,' said Father.

'That's because St Brendan's won't have him,' Mother said.

'Whose fault is that?'

'It doesn't matter whose fault it is. They won't take him and he has to go to school. If he doesn't we'll have the police back, and we don't want that, do we?'

Father's eyes went dark. 'Oh, no,' he said. 'We've had enough trouble as it is.' He was sitting, as usual, in one of the old car seats by the kitchen range. He lit a Carroll's Red and threw the match into the turf bin. 'He'd better not get into any more trouble. I've had it up to here with him.' He slapped himself under his chin with the back of his hand. 'Up to here.'

'I hear,' Mother said quietly.

'He'd better make a good job of this school or there'll be trouble.'

'I think Stephen knows that.'

22

THE NEXT DAY MOTHER TOOK HIM to Omagh. She bought him his uniform and then they went to a café for lunch.

'What'll it be?' the waitress asked. She had flour on her black skirt and her hair was tied with a ribbon.

'Irish stew and apple pie,' said Stephen.

Mother ordered a cup of tea and an egg salad sandwich.

'Everything together?' asked the waitress.

'If you don't mind,' Mother said.

His courses came simultaneously. He ate quickly and when he'd finished, he stacked the pudding plate on top of the other.

'That was very good,' he said, in the jocular way Father would sometimes compliment Mother after dinner at home.

'I'm glad.'

She emptied her teacup. 'Do you promise no more trouble—you'll make a go of school?'

'I will,' he said.

'Get some qualifications, maybe.'

'I'll try.'

'You're a good boy really, aren't you?'

'Oh, I'm a good boy,' he said, and she squeezed his hand.

23

THE FOLLOWING MONDAY, 22 FEBRUARY, FATHER left for work at seven. An hour later, Stephen slipped out of the back door and started down the lane. The sky was filled with grey cloud. It had been raining in the night and the lane was wet. Like his uniform his shoes were new and he took great care not to step in any puddles or mud.

At the end he crossed the slippery cattle grid and stopped. He had chosen a spot where the driver of the school bus could see him. He felt alert and apprehensive.

The bus appeared. The door banged open. He went up the steps and turned into the aisle. He was aware of other children on the bus in the same uniform as his but he did not look at them. He went to the first empty seat and sat down. It was made of wood and varnished, slippery and cold. He heard no one shouting. He could detect no one whispering. At least he'd managed to get onto the bus without incident. It was a good omen, he hoped. The door banged shut. The driver engaged the bus in gear and moved off ...

The bus stopped. The driver pulled a lever and the door banged open again. He was closest to the door so he was first off. He found himself on a strip of concrete. There were steps ahead, which went up the side of a low mound on top of which sat the school. It was a square building with a flat roof. The front, which faced him, was comprised of large modern windows, wet inside with condensation.

He fiddled with his tie. All the other pupils who had got off after him now rushed past and not one said a word, either to each other or to him. He watched them climbing the steps and streaming towards the entrance. He considered turning round and walking away. But, then, what would he do all day until he could catch the bus home? He decided to go in and see what happened.

He went up the steps and into the school. He found himself in a dark, square hall with a tiled floor and a huge cabinet with glass shelves on which several silver trophies were displayed. There was an office in the corner with glass windows and a sign saying RECEPTION.

He walked over and knocked.

Inside, the secretary slid one of the panes back. 'Yes?' She held a cigarette and he smelled the smoke wafting around him.

'I'm Melanophy,' he said.

'Oh yes,' she said—there was something in her tone that he didn't like. 'The head wants a word.' She stubbed out her cigarette in the tin ashtray and came out. 'Follow me,' she said.

24

SHE USHERED HIM INTO THE HEAD'S office, a big room with a modern desk. There was a reel-to-reel tape recorder on a table and one of the big iron nameplates from Crookedstone station that had been sold off when the line was closed. Mr Moffat had a grey face, puffy cheeks and very big glasses with black frames. His suit had leather bands round the cuffs and patches on the elbows.

'Who's this, Mrs Douglas?'

'Melanophy.'

'Oh, Melanophy.' There was the same knowing tone in the enunciation of his surname that the secretary had used earlier.

'Thank you, Mrs Douglas.' Her heels clicked and the hem of her skirt rustled. The door closed. They were alone.

'Look down in front of you, Melanophy.'

He did so. A piece of red tape was stuck to the parquet floor.

'Step up to the line,' said the head, 'so I can see you.'

He moved forward.

The head took off his glasses and stared up at him. The whites of his eyes were faintly bloodshot and Stephen detected peppermint on his breath. Trebor mints, thought Stephen, if he wasn't mistaken. Mr Harrison at Mulberry House had liked them too. Perhaps all heads did.

'Listen, Melanophy,' Mr Moffat began, 'I know everything about you. Everything.'

Stephen looked at the picture of Queen Elizabeth hung on the wall. She wore a long black cloak held at the shoulder with a badge.

'I've spoken to Mr Harrison at Mulberry House,' continued Mr Moffat. 'Oh, yes, it's amazing what you can do with a telephone.'

He heard Mr Moffat put his glasses back on.

'I'm going to put this in your own language, Melanophy. You step out of line here, even once, you'll get seven shades of you-know-what kicked out of you. Do you understand?'

'Yes.'

'It's "Yes, Mr Moffat".'

'Yes, Mr Moffat.'

'Right, I'll take you to your class. You're with Mr Peters. You should enjoy that.'

25

HE FOLLOWED MR MOFFAT IN SILENCE along the corridors. The head finally halted outside a door with glass panes set into it. On the other side, Stephen could see a man, Mr Peters he presumed, holding a large red book. He saw a girl of about his own age stand up. The roll was being called.

Mr Moffat knocked cursorily, then threw open the door. As the headmaster, he clearly didn't have to wait for the teacher inside to wave him in. 'Mr Peters.'

The teacher looked up from his register.

'Yes.'

'Someone for you.'

Inside the classroom Mr Moffat turned and beckoned Stephen forward. He stepped over the threshold and found himself in a large square room filled with desks. The windows overlooked an asphalt playground. Someone had wiped most of the condensation off the glass, but at the edges and in the lower corners there were puddles of wet.

'This is Melanophy,' said Mr Moffat.

Stephen sensed everyone staring, including the girl who had stood up just before he came in.

'He can't help it but he's a thief,' said Mr Moffat, 'and don't say I haven't warned you.'

Before Stephen had a chance to react, Mr Moffat went out and closed the door.

Mr Peters was suddenly beside him. 'Come on,' he said. 'You can sit here.'

He pointed at a desk just across from the girl, who was still standing. Stephen's face was reddening slowly with shame and resentment. His first objective must be not to let anyone see.

He moved forward quickly, sat down at the desk and stared at the lid, ensuring only his profile was visible.

'Thank you, Rosemary,' said Mr Peters.

Rosemary, the girl standing up, sat down.

'Paul Finnegan,' he shouted.

A chair scraped back, someone stood and shouted, 'Present, Mr Peters.'

The roll continued. Stephen felt his face resuming its normal colour. It was safe to lift his head. He looked sideways carefully.

Rosemary, as his neighbour was called, was gazing at him across the space between their desks. He straightened his shoulders and looked back at her. Her face was broad and long and the pigment in her skin was much the darkest of any girl in the room. Her eyes were brown, her mouth was extraordinarily wide and long, and the lower lip was much thicker than the upper one. Her crinkled hair was black and spread in a pool below her shoulders. Her appearance reminded him of the Polynesian girls in the ancient copies of *National Geographic* that the boys at Mulberry House had been allowed to look at on Sunday afternoons.

The roll continued. Suddenly Rosemary widened her eyes as if she had only just realised she was staring at him, smiled, and turned away to look at the blackboard.

He studied her profile. Seen from the side her mouth looked even larger than it had from the front and her nose, he saw, had a little upturn at the end that he found appealing. After a moment or two, he shifted his eyes from Rosemary to the other children in the room. He noticed three boys by the windows, slouched in their seats, legs splayed. The hard boys in Mulberry House had sat in the same way. He knew at once that if anyone in the room was going to cause him trouble it was these three. By following the roll, he got their names: Reilly, Sterritt and Tooley.

Mr Peters had finished the roll. He handed Stephen a timetable and a couple of copybooks with the school's name on the cover. 'Follow Rosemary,' he said. 'You've got double English, followed by double RE—a great way to start the week. Then it's break. For the second half of the morning, the class splits. The girls do Home Economics, you have metalwork but Rosemary, you be sure to show him where the workshops are.'

'Yes,' said Rosemary.

'After lunch, back here one-thirty for the afternoon roll. Don't worry about today but you'll need money tomorrow for lunch. How much is it in new money, Rosemary?'

The new decimal currency had been introduced only the previous week.

'Fifty pence a week,' she said. She had a nice firm voice.

'That's tenpence a day or two shillings.'

'Yes.'

'I preferred the old money,' said Mr Peters. 'Class dismissed.'

26

HE TRAILED SILENTLY AFTER ROSEMARY ALONG the corridors to the English class. She took a seat at the front and he sat next to her.

The trio sauntered past, heading for the back of the room.

'Watch out, thief about,' Reilly muttered. He had a big, sweaty, freckled face and a slick of hair that hung down over his eyes.

'Go away with you now,' Rosemary said, 'and don't be causing trouble.'

Sterritt and Tooley clucked like hens.

'Don't pay any attention,' said Rosemary to Stephen. 'The beasts in the fields have better manners.'

He nodded. She had little sleepers in her ears. He wanted to ask what her surname was but felt inhibited. She'd know at once what he was getting at. Anyway, he had her Christian name, and though it was a name used by both communities, it was more usually Protestant, in his experience, which probably meant she was one of them. He liked her though. She had a face he could look at for hours and hours.

The teacher appeared and began to read *A Midsummer Night's Dream*. Stephen found himself listening to the words, and forgot about Reilly, Sterritt and Tooley.

Then it was onto RE. The teacher had bright eyes and lank, greasy hair. She was very young, the daughter, Rosemary told him in a whisper, of missionaries who had worked in India. Miss Jenkins opened her Bible and read from the Gospel of St Luke. Once again, the words filled him up and as in the English class, time passed without his having any sense of its passing.

At the end, a bell rang. In the distance, all over the school, doors could be heard opening and feet scuffling. One or two lusty cries even came through the windows from the playground.

'Break,' said Rosemary.

They stood.

'Where's the toilet?' he asked.

'I'll show you.'

She brought him to a door with BOYS written on the outside.

'I'll go out into the playground.' She pointed at a glass double door on the other side of the corridor. Beyond it, the playground was filled with running figures. 'I'll wait there for you. Have you break?'

He looked at her blankly.

'I've a Kit-Kat.' She pulled the bar from her pencil case. 'I'll split it with you when you come out.'

'Good enough,' he said.

27

HE PUSHED THE DOOR AND WENT in. There were toilets with half-doors along one wall and the urinal was opposite with a ledge in front of it. A third wall was taken up with a row of basins, and a drinking fountain, at which a boy was gulping noisily, occupied the fourth.

He went to the urinal, took a position in the corner and began. At that moment the cistern flushed and water flowed down the china wall to gurgle along the gully, agitating the little white disinfectant balls that were lying there. Why did they put these in toilets? he wondered. They didn't make any difference.

He heard the door bang. Something about the sound alarmed him. This was exactly the situation Reilly and the other two would choose. He didn't know why he hadn't thought of it already. He was letting his guard slip.

He heard a scurry of feet clattering on the tiled floor and someone shouting, 'It's the thief. Time to shower his head.'

He zipped up and turned simultaneously. He glimpsed Reilly's freckled face and swung his head sideways, aiming for the boy's nose, but Reilly ducked back. Sterritt and Tooley were round the other side. He tried to catch one with his elbow but he missed, and then they had one arm and Reilly had the other and they were pulling him off the urinal step.

'Fuck you,' he shouted. He pulled left, intending to punch right, spring from Reilly's grip and make for the door. But they had him held hard and now his feet were kicked, the soles of his new shoes slipped on the tiled floor and suddenly he was being swung upside-down.

'Fuck you,' he yelled again. His head was almost touching the floor and he had a strange reversed picture of, first the urinal, a white sheet with a copper vein along the top, and then, for they had wheeled around, toilets with their fixed wooden seats. There were five and he saw now that they were moving him briskly towards the one in the middle. He kicked furiously but couldn't shake the hands from his knees. He was aware of jeering laughter too, and then the three closing against him to squeeze through the narrow doorway. But there was something to hold onto.

He reached for the bottom of the stall door, found it, squeezed and the headlong motion stopped. Then someone kicked his hands and he had to let go. He flailed and wriggled and shouted again as he felt himself hoisted up. He heard the clatter of a cistern and the gurgle as it flushed. He knew they were about to shove him down. Wildly, he threw his hands forward, hoping to grasp the rim. With one hand, he connected but the other slipped past and plunged into the water.

He knew that next they would let him go—and, sure enough, he was sliding down, his toes touching the wall behind and his shoulders on the toilet rim. His head was in the bowl and water was flooding past as the cistern emptied. And they were gone.

In this position, he couldn't jump back. He brought his hand up from the bottom of the bowl and found the rim. Then he levered himself up. Walking on his hands, he turned himself round. Only when he'd gone through a hundred and eighty degrees was he able to jump down onto the floor and stand up. His hair was wet, his shoulder and arm were soaked. His immediate instinct was to run after them, catch and hurt them. He heard the door from the corridor bang. Had they come back? Well, they wouldn't surprise him so easily this time. He bolted out of the stall, but it wasn't Reilly, Sterritt and Tooley standing by the door. It was Rosemary.

'I saw them running out,' she said. 'They're a pack of bullies.'

His heart surged. He knew what he had to do if not how he would achieve it. He would punish Reilly, Sterritt and Tooley and he would do it as soon as he could. He wouldn't wait. By the end of the day, by the middle of the day, even, he would have paid them back.

At the same time, he knew it wasn't them he really wanted to hurt. That was his father and Mr Purdue. But he saw this only fleetingly and then he turned his inner gaze towards the task in hand, and what he had just seen slipped out of sight.

But it remained, waiting for him in the corner of his mind, so that if he chose to look that way again it would be there for him to see.

'Look at your books,' said Rosemary.

They had fallen out of his blazer pocket when he was upside-down and were lying on the floor. She clacked across to pick them up. They'd been trampled on and the covers were scuffed and creased. She straightened them and then banged them against each other to dislodge any dirt.

'I'm sure Mr Peters will give you new ones.'

'Put them in the bin,' he said.

She threw them into the wire basket by the basins. Then she rinsed his head and hands in cold water. A boy came in, saw her and ran out shouting, 'Ugh.' She patted him dry with the coarse green hand towels that came out of the dispenser on the wall. He closed his eyes as she worked. He remembered that metalwork was coming and he knew this was his chance.

28

ROSEMARY BROUGHT HIM TO THE WORKSHOP, damp but not dripping. There were windows that gave onto the corridor and two huge doors with glass panels in which a grid of wire filament floated.

'Who's the teacher?' he asked.

He could see a man on the other side of the door in a brown coat.

'Mr O'Dwyer.'

'What's he like?'

'All right. He's got a limp. He lost his leg from the knee down. Motorcycle accident.'

Stephen registered this information and thought how nicely everything was clicking together.

'See you at dinner, I hope,' said Rosemary. She squeezed his arm above the elbow. 'Good luck.'

He opened the door and went in. He was aware everyone was staring. They would see he was damp. They would all know what Reilly, Sterritt and Tooley had done. He felt a little flush of red under his chin but that was as far as it got. He reminded himself of what he had to do.

'Who are you?' asked Mr O'Dwyer from the front.

'Melanophy.'

A chorus of muted clucks came from the rear of the workshop.

Reilly, Sterritt and Tooley were in the penultimate row from the back.

'That's enough,' shouted Mr O'Dwyer. 'This isn't a farmyard.'

The clucking stopped.

'All right, Melanophy,' said Mr O'Dwyer, 'get behind a bench. Why don't you take one of the empty ones at the very back?'

Once again, everything was slotting into place.

He moved down the side of the workshop between the benches and the wall. As he passed the first bench, he glanced down to see what had been laid out and he saw: a box with various grades of steel wool, a set of files and a three-foot steel rule, the centimetres and inches marked with little grooves. The same tools lay on the next bench and the one after.

Next, he considered what to use. He might try to stab them with the handles of the files but what if the points weren't sharp enough to puncture the skin? He wouldn't hurt them and they'd fight back. No, he decided, the files wouldn't work.

He reached the back corner, turned and began to go along the rear. It would have to be the steel rule. He'd hold it at the rounded end and use the corner at the square end to do the damage.

He reached the bench behind Reilly, Sterritt and Tooley. He was now at the opposite corner from the door. He would have to be very quick if he wanted to do it and get away. On the other hand, he had surprise on his side.

Mr O'Dwyer was holding up a micrometer and talking. Stephen ignored his voice. He reached forward casually and took the rule in front of him by the rounded end. At the same time he lowered his head but lifted his eyes and focused on Reilly, Sterritt and Tooley. They had half turned when he had appeared behind them but now they were facing forward again. They felt secure. They didn't think he'd dare, not in class, and not on his first day. In which case, there was no better time to do it, he reasoned.

He gripped the rule and glided round the side of the bench. Sterritt was closest. He lifted the rule over his head and brought the sharp end down on the middle of the boy's skull. The corner dug through skin and collided with bone. He felt the vibrations of the impact in his hands and wrists. He pulled the rule out and Sterritt toppled forward. He saw Tooley turning, his face registering a mix of surprise and dismay. He swung the rule sideways. The edge went straight into Tooley's mouth, connecting with gums and teeth. Tooley screamed. In parallel, Stephen sensed movement on the other side of the workshop. Mr O'Dwyer had seen and had started to move. His gait was ungainly. That was the limp. He was slow, but not that slow. The good news, though, was the direction he had taken: he was coming down the side closest to Reilly's bench. This left the door in the far corner unprotected.

Reilly, who had no doubt now what was coming, had started to bolt between the benches. Perhaps he hoped to get to the door, thought Stephen. Well, if that were his plan, he wouldn't make it.

Stephen sprinted after him, throwing the rule sideways as he did. He caught Reilly on the ear with the flat. The blow was so savage he was knocked sideways and collided with the vice of the bench he was passing, which turned him half ways round towards Stephen.

Someone shouted. Mr O'Dwyer had reached the angle where he would turn to come down the side. A couple more blows, Stephen decided, and then away. Any more and he'd be caught in Mr O'Dwyer's big hands.

He grabbed Reilly's hair and pulled him sideways, twisting his body and throwing him down onto the bench. Reilly was now reaching back with his hands, groping desperately for something to defend himself. Stephen brought the rule down with the edge leading. He smashed into Reilly's face in a line that ran from the right forehead, across the left eye and down the left cheek to the chin.

Mr O'Dwyer was close now. Stephen dropped the rule and sprinted away, passing several boys whose mouths hung open with amazement. At the far side he turned and ran to the door, pulled it open and was gone.

29

STEPHEN LEFT CROOKEDSTONE HIGH BY THE front gate and started to walk home. It was still cold and grey and there were puddles everywhere, which he was careful to step around.

Two miles from his lane, a police car overtook him and stopped. Two burly men in green uniforms climbed out.

'Melanophy,' one shouted. He had a moustache and his eyes were brown.

'Yeah?' he said insolently, hoping to give an impression of indifference.

'What the fuck are you doing?'

'Walking home.'

'No, at the school.'

'I don't know what you're talking about,' he said.

For the first time, Mother crossed his mind and he wondered what she would say. Father would be furious, of course, but he didn't care about him.

'We're going to have to take you to the barracks,' said the other policeman.

'Yeah, sure,' he said. The words were out before he could stop them. He shrugged and couldn't stop a little smirk appearing.

'Oh, delighted with yourself, aren't you?' said the one with the moustache.

'No. They asked for it,' he said calmly. It was true and he sincerely believed that once this was explained, his actions wouldn't look so bad. They might even let him off with a warning. Stranger things had happened, hadn't they?

'At least he doesn't deny it.'

This was the other policeman. He had left his hat in the car.

He had a strong face and neat black hair. He looked as if he'd just come from the barber. He was from Antrim, judging by his accent, unlike the one with the moustache who was local.

'Of course he doesn't deny it,' said this one. 'He's delighted with himself. But Borstal will soon wipe that grin off his face.'

'Come on,' said the other one. 'Let's put him in the car and get him back.'

30

THEY TOOK HIM TO THE BARRACKS in Crookedstone. It hadn't changed since his last visit, except it seemed smaller because he was bigger. He was booked and put into a holding cell, a gaunt oblong room with a high barred window and a concrete plinth for a bed. The lightbulb was inside a wire cage attached to the ceiling. He lay down on the mattress. The stuffing was wiry and unyielding, but he didn't care.

There was a grey army blanket with big red stitches round the edge. He unfurled it and pulled it over his body and head. Inside the woollen cocoon, he could hear his own breath going in and out. He could hear the barrack noises in the distance— a radio, male chatter, car engines gunning—but he screened them out and listened instead to his breathing. He was tired, very tired, and he wanted to go to sleep. That was the last thought that crossed his mind until he found himself looking up, a little dazed, blinking in the light, and saw a sergeant standing over him, the blanket a bundle in his big hands.

'Come on,' said the sergeant. 'You're going to be charged and then you'll go home.'

He sat up, swung himself off the plinth and stood. 'Is that it, then?' he asked.

'For now.'

'Oh.'

'You're in trouble, really big trouble, sonny.'

'Oh.'

'Those three boys are in hospital. One's got a fractured skull. One needs stitches to his face and has a bone chip loose in his forehead. And one's got a dislocated jaw. Do you know what this means?'

'No.'

'Oh, come on, you can't be that dim.'

'I'm not.'

'They're going to throw the book at you. They're going to lock you away. It'll be a year or two, three or four. That's not long in the scale of a lifetime, but for a boy of your age ... what are you—fourteen?'

'Yes.'

'For you it'll seem like eternity. So if you've any sense, start praying to Him above and see if He can help. There isn't anyone else who can fix this mess.'

Stephen decided to ignore this remark. 'How will I get home? Will I make the bus?'

'Is that all you can think about? How you're getting home?'

'My mother will be worried,' he said.

'Your mother is here. And she's very upset.'

He received this news in silence. It was better, he thought, to see her now, here, and get that over with than have to go home and tell her.

The sergeant brought him first to a room where he was charged and then out to the dayroom. Mother sat on a bench fixed to the wall that was painted a dark brown. She wore her Gannex mackintosh over a blue dress. Her handbag was on her lap, her knees tight together, and behind her spectacle frames she was pressing a white handkerchief to her eyes.

'Mrs Melanophy,' said the sergeant.

She had heard them coming, Stephen knew, because she'd inclined her head. But she kept the handkerchief over her eyes.

'Mrs Melanophy,' said the sergeant again. He spoke gently and touched the back of her hand. She started and dropped the handkerchief. Her eyelids were swollen and smeared with mascara. The lines surrounding her eyes were wet— tears she hadn't mopped away. He felt an inkling of regret. Mother was in pain because of what he had done. Then he told himself it was not his fault. It was theirs—Reilly, Sterritt and Tooley. They started it.

'Come on,' said the sergeant. 'Let's go.'

31

THEY WERE DRIVEN HOME IN A police car that smelled of gun oil and saddle soap. No one spoke. The car pulled up outside the back door. He was relieved to see that his father wasn't back—there was no sign of his van.

'Thank you,' Mother whispered. She got out and went to the back door. He followed. They went inside to the kitchen.

'Are you hungry?' she asked.

The huge alarm clock on the window that was missing a foot and leant at an angle said seven o'clock. 'Yes,' he said.

She steamed potatoes in an iron pot and opened a tin of

sardines. She put the food on plates and called him to the table. They sat side by side and ate in silence.

The potatoes were floury and the sardines were oily. After he had finished Mother split a match to make two toothpicks and they sat as the light outside collapsed, picking out the bits of sardine bone that were stuck between their teeth.

32

THEY WERE STILL SITTING WITHOUT THE light on when they heard the van draw up in the yard, then Father climb out and slam the driver's door. They heard his footsteps as he crossed the yard, opened the back door and came in.

'Hello,' he called from the scullery. He banged the door behind him. 'Anyone in?'

'We're in the kitchen.'

He came in.

'Have we forgotten how to turn the light on?' he asked. 'Or maybe we're trying to save money. That's a first.'

He flicked the switch and the light hanging down from the middle of the ceiling came on. There was a Coolie shade above the bulb so the light was thrown wide across the room while the painted wooden ceiling above remained in shadow.

'What the fuck's going on? I've never seen such long fucking faces. Has someone died? Bad day at school, Stephen?'

'Sit down and listen,' said Mother.

'He hasn't been thieving, has he?'

'Did you hear me?'

'I did hear you, but did you hear me? I asked a question.'

Father had gone from jovial to angry in a moment.

'No, he hasn't been stealing,' she said.

'Well, that's all right. What could be worse than stealing? He hasn't murdered anyone, has he?'

Mother reported what the police had said to her. He'd attacked three boys in the metal workshop with a steel rule. They were in hospital. Stephen had been charged.

'Actual and grievous bodily harm?' said Father, when she had finished. His tone was admiring.

Stephen saw his chance. 'They stuck my head down the toilet,' he said, 'in break.'

'They what?' Mother said.

'You heard,' said Father. 'Fucking barbarians.' He turned to Stephen. 'So, you were paying them back, were you?'

Stephen nodded. Father extended his hand. 'We've a man in the family at last. Put it there, son.'

He put his hand into his father's and his father squeezed it hard.

'A man at last,' he said. 'Well, you did the right thing. If anyone had done that to me I'd have fixed them too.'

'He'll get Borstal, prison,' Mother said. 'Several years. What are you saying?'

'I'm saying ... if you let bullies away with what they done on him ... they'll be back. And they'll do worse next time and the time after. Forever and ever it'll go on. They love weakness. And the way they know they've found it is when you don't fight back. He did the right thing, so he did. He nipped it in the bud. He taught them a bloody good lesson ... one they won't forget in a hurry. And you want to blame him? Could you tell me what else he could have done?'

'Gone to the teachers?'

Father stood and snorted. 'Or maybe the parish priest, fat Father John.'

Father John, the priest who had baptised Stephen, was still in place.

'These things,' said Father, 'you have to sort them out, man to man. You don't tout. You do and you're finished for ever. You know that, don't you? And if you don't you're a more stupid woman than I've given you credit for being.'

She had the expression she wore when she was hurt but she didn't want anyone to know. 'Where are you going?' she asked.

'Where do you think? Out.' His dark blue eyes shone under the yellow light from the forty-watt bulb.

'I've a rake of sheep to check in the fields.' He'd only got them out of the sheds and into the open a few weeks before.

He swaggered out of the kitchen and went into the scullery, kicked off his work boots and pulled on his water boots. 'I'm away, so.' The back door banged and he was gone.

'I don't know which of you will have my heart broken first,' said Mother.

33

HE STOOD UP, CARRIED THEIR PLATES to the scullery and put them into the sink. Then he filled the big aluminium kettle and put it onto the range for hot water to do the washing-up. Mother had got out her handkerchief and was dabbing at her eyes.

'I'm not a bad boy,' he said.

She threw her handkerchief onto the red Formica table-top.

'Yes, you are!' she screamed, 'yes, you are! How could you do this to me?'

A whispering sigh came from the range. Turf settling as it burned, he thought. A little puff of smoke, the Pope's Smoke, issued from the dent in the side of the fuel cover and floated towards the ceiling.

'I'm not a bad boy,' he said, angrily. His first instinct was to run to his room and not talk to her for the rest of the night.

Then he decided that would be a mistake. It would only antagonise her even more and what purpose would it serve? He needed every ally he could get and he was glad that he seemed to be thinking straight.

He washed up and then he fetched a war comic. He sat in one of the car seats and she in the other. He began to read while she stared at the floor. She was sniffling and this disrupted his concentration but then he became absorbed in the story and forgot his surroundings.

The comic was one of the small square ones. The story concerned a party of intrepid British commandos in Burma who got sent on a perilous expedition behind Japanese lines. For days they marched through jungle, evading traps and capture, until at last they reached their destination—a fuel dump filled with petrol drums.

"That lot will blow sky high," said the sergeant in charge of the unit, "as long as we can lay the explosive properly." He was a square-jawed man called Keith, with a scar on his left cheek, inflicted by a Japanese bayonet in a previous encounter. "The trouble is," he continued, "the Japs are watching the perimeter like hawks. It's not going to be easy to get in."

'Stephen,' said Mother.

He looked up.

'Your daddy's gone well over an hour,' she said. 'He couldn't be looking at his animals all this time, could he?'

'He could,' said Stephen.

'No,' said Mother. 'There's something wrong, there must be. He's never this long. Come on, Stephen, we'll walk up the fields and see.'

He tried to dissuade her but she was adamant. They must go and see.

34

THEY PUT ON BOOTS AND COATS and went out into the night. Mother had a torch that threw out a wavering beam. They walked around the house and set off. As the torchlight raked about, bushes and trees lit up by the beam threw great shadows ahead of them. Stephen heard his feet splashing in and out of puddles.

'I'd better save the battery,' Mother said, and turned the torch off. This plunged them into a world of black, or shades of it. The lane was a slightly lighter black to the grass on either side. The gorse bushes and the stunted trees that grew around them were even darker.

They walked on until they were about fifty yards from the cattle grid. A car approached and its headlights lit the entrance to their lane for a moment. It flashed past, and Stephen heard the rumble of the engine growing fainter. It was headed for Crookedstone.

'Hasn't he the sheep above in Dermot's Field?'

This large rocky field was one of the places Father had taken him when they'd gone on their 'excursions', as

Father called them. It offered plenty of places for sheep to shelter.

'Yes,' he said.

They stepped off the lane and set out across the lawn for the gate to Dermot's Field. The ground was wet. With each step he took, his water boot sank down and he had to take care he didn't leave it behind. Every now and then, he felt the brush of a clump of rushes against his leg.

'Do you hear that?' Mother asked.

'I do,' he said.

It was the tractor engine. The sound was a long way off but it was definitely there.

'Oh my God,' Mother said. 'Could he have had an accident?'

She turned on the torch. The beam punched through the darkness. It lit up the long wet grass, the wiry rushes and the metal gate in the middle of the stone wall. A ewe was looking through the bars. Lit by the light from the torch, the ewe's eyes were a powerful, disturbing yellow. For a moment, Stephen thought that the devil was peering at him from the darkness.

Then his mother said, 'Come on.' She began to move forward, quickly.

He hurried after her but said nothing. Could Father have had an accident? He thought about the back-to-front S that ran between the two vast boulders in Dermot's Field. If there'd been an accident, it had to have happened there. Of course it did—where else? Stephen felt a warm nugget of pleasure deep within him. It would be wonderful if he had had an accident. It would solve all his problems, wouldn't it? Whatever he did, though, he had to keep his feelings hidden from Mother. He had to keep them buried deep inside where nobody, not even God or Satan, could see them.

He passed Mother and got to the gate before she did. The ewe with the yellow eyes bolted into the darkness. He heard bleating and the tractor going. He lifted away the wire loop, then pushed back the gate in the special way that stopped the hinges grating on the lugs.

Mother went into the field and shone the torch around, hoping to find the tractor. He closed the gate and followed her. The field was sloped, filled with bushes and boulders, steep hillocks and sharp valleys. As one feature after another was lit, one great shadow after another fell across the rising ground behind. But there was no sign of the tractor though the reverberation of the engine was louder now. It was coming from the top of the field.

'It's a good sign if the tractor's still going,' he said, feeling he should say something.

'Is it?' She didn't sound convinced.

35

THEY FOLLOWED THE TRACK THAT WOUND up between big stones and gorse bushes towards the summit. Mother went first. The tractor had clearly been up this way because he could feel the great mud welts the tyres had left in the ground underfoot. The ground was slippery but that didn't stop Mother going as fast as she was able. As she climbed, she shone the torch wildly from side to side, catching stunted trees and large sheep with heavy wet fleeces in the beam. The higher they got, the louder the tractor's engine became.

After rising steeply, the track reached a little plateau halfway up. It was dotted with several more gorse bushes and some wind-blown alders. Mother stopped, breathless. She let the arm that held the torch hang down and the light made a puddle on the ground at her feet. He slipped past her and went forward over the level ground. The rumble of the engine was louder still and he was sure he knew what had happened.

On the far side of the level area, the ground rose again, and as it climbed it went between two large boulders; it was the steepest section in the field. Father knew the ground. He'd negotiated it many times in his tractor and hadn't Stephen often ridden in the link box as Father drove up the reverse S? But perhaps tonight, thought Stephen, he had misjudged it.

'Wait,' he heard Mother calling. 'Do you see anything?'

He had reached the end of the level. The first big boulder was on his left.

The track swung anti-clockwise round the foot of the boulder and disappeared from view. The rumble of the engine was very loud now and he knew he was right. It had happened here.

'Do you see anything?' she called again.

'No,' he shouted back, 'but I will soon.'

He began to hurry. The second boulder was away to his right, even larger than the first. As the track swung from anti-clockwise to clockwise, there was a short stretch with a steep gradient that shaded into the gully that ran round the back of the first boulder. He hurried towards it, went to the edge and peered down into the gully. There, upside-down and with its nose pointing away from the summit, was the tractor, engine running, wheels spinning ferociously in the darkness.

'Hello,' he called down. 'Can you hear me?'

'Is he there?'

Mother was beside him now.

'Stevie?' she shouted down. 'Stevie, can you hear me?' She pointed the torch down and ran the yellow beam backwards and forwards. He saw the radiator grille. He saw a small front tyre. He saw the underneath of the chassis with its levers and springs. He saw a huge back wheel turning. And sticking out from under the back, he saw a leg.

'Oh, Jesus, Stephen,' Mother said, beside him. He heard a crumpled noise. For a second he thought she had pitched forward into the gully but, turning, he saw that she had sat down.

'Oh, Jesus,' she said again.

She let go of the torch, which rolled away. It plopped over the edge and landed with a bump at the bottom of the gully. It was still on and now its beam pointed under the tractor. Because of the angle at which the light fell, he saw something he hadn't noticed before. On the end of his father's arm, sticking out from under the tractor, was his cold white hand like a dead fish on a muddy river bank.

'This on top of everything else,' he heard Mother say. 'Oh, yes, you picked your day, son, you really picked your day.'

He registered her bitterness but paid no attention. He was preoccupied with his own thoughts. He had often wished the old bastard dead, and now he was, but he had been killed in a way Stephen could never have imagined. But now that he was, it struck Stephen as logical that he should have died as he had. He was surprised that he'd never thought of this means of death before.

From this line of thought he moved, swiftly, to a new conviction. Sometimes things worked themselves out in the most unexpected way, and in dark times ahead, it would be better to trust that this would happen than seek to force events to go in the direction he wanted. The idea came not as a rounded and well-expressed concept but as an intuition and it stayed at the forefront of his mind throughout the journey back to the farmhouse, as beside him, Mother mumbled and wept.

36

HE WENT UP BEFORE THE ASSIZES at the start of July 1971. The judge, Justice McKeown, was a bald man with a tuft of white hair over each ear and a disconcerting habit of staring without blinking.

'What does the accused plead?' asked the clerk.

On advice, Stephen had entered a plea of guilty.

'Do you have anything to say?' Mr McKeown asked, 'before I pass sentence?'

Mr Doherty stood up. He was a thin, nervous man with a kind face. The Melanophy family had always used his firm.

'My client would like to say,' said Mr Doherty, in his quiet, reasonable voice, 'that although there were mitigating circumstances in his offence—he was assaulted by the three youths whom he subsequently assaulted—he is deeply sorry for the appalling violence in which he was involved. The assaults were a momentary lapse, the product of a fit of temper. Had he reflected on what he was about to do he would not have done it, but having done it, he accepts his responsibility for what he did. He would like to apologise to those whom he assaulted and to their families. He is aware that he has been the cause of considerable anguish as well as physical distress to these parties, and he heartily wishes he had not.

'My client, Stephen Melanophy,' Mr Donaldson continued, 'was fourteen in February, earlier this year. He is the youngest of six children. His mother, Mrs Jane Melanophy, who is in court today, was recently widowed. Stephen has five much older sisters, all married and living away from home. Mrs Melanophy is now dependent on Stephen for help on the farm. There is no other man on whom she can rely to do the work, and I have been assured that Stephen has been doing an excellent job since his father's death. In view of this, and in view of Stephen's genuine remorse, we ask the court to consider whether a custodial sentence that will deprive his newly widowed mother of his much-needed support, would be the right course. We humbly suggest that a lengthy probation order might be the better course. Thank you, Your Honour.'

Mr Doherty sat down.

'Three years,' said Mr McKeown, without blinking.

A policeman took Stephen's arm and turned him towards the door behind the dock.

'Stephen,' he heard Mother cry. 'Stephen.'

He knew she wanted him to look at her. That was why she had called out like that. He also knew that if he saw her sorrowful face it would haunt him for the whole of his sentence, and each time it came back to him he would feel sad and guilty. The years ahead would be hard enough without that and his only thought now was of how to make it easier for himself.

So he did not let himself reply to her but hurried out of the door.

37

ON THE OTHER SIDE, HE FOUND himself in a hall with a flight of stairs. He went down and found himself in a basement. There were two holding cells and offices at either end. One of the cells held several men. They looked depressed and sat on benches smoking. The other was empty. He decided he'd rather the latter and was relieved when the escort unlocked the empty one and swung back the door.

'In you go.'

He wondered if there was a policy of keeping juveniles separate from adult prisoners but he knew better than to ask.

'Will you be all right?' said the policeman.

'Aye,' he said insouciantly.

'There'll be tea and something to eat in a bit.'

The grille swung shut and the key turned. The policeman clipped away. He had metal caps on his heels and toes and they made a sharp noise on the stone-flagged floor. Stephen felt shaky and tearful, but he knew that he must on no account let anyone know how he felt. Particularly those men in the other cell, whom, he was certain, were staring at him. He needed to distract himself. He wished he'd thought to bring a book. The bare floor was littered with cigarette butts, and a line of painted benches stretched along the wall, the surface scored with names and messages. He noticed a newspaper at the end. He strolled over—he didn't want to appear hasty or desperate—sat down and picked it up.

The headline read ASTRONAUTS GO FOR A DRIVE ON THE MOON. Under it a photograph occupied the width of the page, showing an astronaut in a lunar landscape with a strange vehicle that had what looked like an upside-down umbrella attached to the rear. He tried to focus on the picture, then on the article.

'How'd you do?' a voice shouted.

He looked up at a man in the cell opposite. He was tall and had a beard. In his mid-forties, Stephen guessed. His sleeves were rolled up to the elbow and he had tattoos of a Tricolour and a scroll of barbed wire.

'Three,' he said.

'Months, is it?' said the man.

'Years.'

'Oh, it's three years!' The man shrugged his shoulders.

'Yeah.'

'But you'll only do two with remission,' said the prisoner. 'It's bad, but not as bad as it seems.'

He lit a cigarette.

'Smoke?'

Stephen nodded. Of course he did. He had learned how in Mulberry House.

The prisoner kicked a packet of Embassy and a box of matches across the floor to him. He took a cigarette, lit it and kicked them back.

'How old are you?'

'Fourteen.'

'So, you do two, that's a seventh of the life you've already lived. That's not so terrible, is it? A seventh of your life?'

He hadn't thought of it in that way. 'I suppose,' he said.

'You'll be all right,' said the prisoner. 'It'll pass.'

'What about you? Do you have long?' he asked.

The prisoner's face darkened. 'Listen,' he said, 'I'm going to give you some advice. In jail, don't ask questions, ever, and don't ever take cigarettes from strangers.'

'But you gave me one.'

'Yeah, and now I hope you've learned your lesson.'

38

LATER THAT AFTERNOON, ALONG WITH TWO other juveniles, a fifteen-year-old car thief and a sixteen-year-old who had indecently assaulted a nun, he was handcuffed, and brought outside. A prison van was parked up, blue with tiny windows running down each side just below the line of the roof. Inside, it was sub-divided into cells, about eight, he guessed. He was put into one and the door locked. It was four-foot square. The seat was steel and cold. He slipped his hands under his bottom and looked up at the tiny window. It was opaque so there was no point in trying to look through it. The engine turned, the vehicle shuddered and started to move ...

Several hours later, the door of his cubicle was unlocked.

'Let's be having you,' said the officer in the doorway.

When he got out of the transporter, he found himself on a parade-ground with a flagpole. There was a brick building with metal-framed windows, several huts made of wood and sticky with creosote and, in the far distance, a line of Nissen huts with their distinctive rounded roofs. He caught a whiff of salt and heard a seagull cry. HM Borstal Langham Wood was a Second World War army camp on the Antrim coast.

'There's no walking here,' said the escort, 'only marching.'

At that moment a group of boys appeared in the distance, swinging their arms like soldiers, a prison officer bawling, 'Left ... right ... left ... right.'

Stephen and the other two formed a line.

'Straight ahead,' said the escort. 'Quick march.'

They crossed the parade-ground and went into Reception, a room full of officers in ironed white shirts and highly polished shoes. He guessed most were ex-servicemen.

'In front of the desk, toes to the line,' said the escort.

Stephen and the other two went up to the line and stopped. It was red tape stuck to the floor, the same as the one in Crookedstone High.

'Not on the line! Toes to the line, didn't you hear?'

The three shuffled back.

Papers were signed and stamped. The escort left. The man behind the desk looked up. He had a large head and very dark eyes. 'I'm SO Mulligan,' he said. 'Do you know what SO means?'

Silence.

'Senior Officer.'

The boys nodded.

'Who's Melanophy?'

'I am.'

'Your number is BC3232. Go over there.' He pointed at a table. 'Strip. And don't act coy. Everyone has to. Now!' he barked.

He took a bath while an officer read *Reveille*. The White Windsor soap had a slimy, jellied texture. A doctor listened to his chest and examined his body for identifying marks. He was kitted out with a pair of sagging grey underpants, a vest, a striped shirt with no collar, a pair of serge trousers, a donkey jacket, a pair of boots and a pair of socks. Finally, he was photographed in front of a grimy curtain holding a slate with his details chalked on:

Name: Melanophy, Stephen
DOB: 11 Feb. 1957
No: BC 3232

'Take him away,' said Mulligan.

The escort took him outside and marched him off along a

cinder path. The clinker was black with bits of mauve and red mixed in. The colouring reminded him of a bruise. 'Where are we going?' he asked.

'Building straight ahead.'

'What is it?'

'You'll find out.'

He didn't like that answer. What if he was thrown into a room with the boys he'd seen earlier? There was only one thing to do. He pretended to stumble.

'My bootlace,' he said, flopping to his knees.

'For Christ's sake,' said the escort.

He scooped cinders into each palm. He could throw them into the eyes of anyone who tried to attack him. However, when he got inside the building they'd been heading for, he found it was the store: this was where bedding and eating utensils, toiletries and PE kits were issued. There were no dangerous prisoners lurking here.

'Right, mate,' the storeman shouted at him, 'step up to the counter and collect your clobber.' The storeman dumped a bedding roll and turned back to the shelves to fetch some more things.

How was he going to carry everything, wondered Stephen, with his hands full of cinder. He looked around for a bin into which he could throw the cinders but there wasn't one anywhere. There was nothing else for it. He put his hands into the pockets of his trousers, let go, then wiped his gritty palms on the serge fabric of the pocket lining.

'What are your hands doing in your pockets?' the escort shouted. He cuffed the back of Stephen's head. 'You will never have your hands in your pockets. Do you understand?'

'Yes, sir.'

'You're in Borstal now, boy.'

39

OVER THE NEXT FEW MONTHS, STEPHEN was taught how to box and introduced to amphetamines. A year into his sentence, two older boys jumped him in the workshop. They wanted the ounce of Golden Virginia wrapped in the twist of brown paper he had tucked inside the belt he wore inside his shirt. His fists proved no match for the wooden clubs they used. They knocked him down, lifted his shirt and took the tobacco.

That night he melted a toothbrush handle and embedded a razor blade in the end. The next morning he slashed his assailants in the bathroom while they were washing. He cut one on the chin and the other, badly, across his bare back. Their wounds were stitched in the prison hospital.

Stephen's adjudication was in the punishment block. The man from the Board of Visitors who presided was from Cardiff. Because two inmates had required hospital treatment, Stephen was sentenced to two months on the boards, bread and water for the first fortnight, plus loss of a month's remission. He passed the time reading the Bible and the paperbacks an officer lent him, or running on the spot, shadow-boxing and doing push-ups. He wanted to be strong in case he had more trouble when he returned to the prison population.

However, by the time he walked out of the punishment block, his enemies were gone. The story of his attack, though, far from being forgotten had become part of the lore of HM Borstal Langham Wood. He was Stephen Melanophy, the trainee who had slashed the two jumpers. He was a hero whom everyone respected. Even the officers, he noticed, treated him slightly better than they did the other boys. The two months on the boards and the loss of a month's remission seemed a ludicrously small price to pay for the reputation he had secured.

40

HE LEFT HM BORSTAL LANGHAM WOOD in August 1973. Willy Brandt had just made the first visit by a West German leader to Israel. The novelist Nancy Mitford had just died. A loyalist vigilante group, the Ulster Freedom Fighters, was claiming responsibility for a series of sectarian murders. In Derry, the inquest had returned an open verdict on the victims of Bloody Sunday.

He went home. He was sixteen. He didn't have to go to school. He could work. Mr Doherty, the solicitor who had failed to move Justice McKeown at his trial, found him a job with a relative of his, a bricklayer, Albert Smith, who promised to teach Stephen the trade.

For a few days it was interesting being out on a site, mixing cement, humping the bricks and blocks about, making tea. He felt like a man among men. Then he grew restless. He wanted more money than he was being paid. He took to roaming around the country at night. He broke into Heggarty's shop and several houses.

Then, in August, he broke into the GAA club on a Tuesday night after bingo when he knew the takings would be in the till. He was careful to wear Marigold washing-up gloves so he left no fingerprints. Unfortunately, he was not so careful with his water boots. When he was walking away he left a footprint in the soft ground at the back of the club. The local police, who had automatically put him at the top of their list of suspects, took a plaster cast and matched it to his boot. The sum he had stolen was large: forty-four pounds.

He was arrested and bailed. In November 1973 he was given a three-month sentence. This time he went to the Young Prisoners' or YP wing in HMP Carrick, the old Victorian jail on the outskirts of north Belfast.

He got out in February 1974, two days after his seventeenth birthday. He went home. He promised his mother he was finished with jail: he would never do anything else that would have him sent back.

41

THANKS TO MR DOHERTY, WHO INTERVENED again on his behalf, Albert Smith took him back.

He started work on a site outside Omagh. It was a new estate for the Housing Executive. Once again, he spent his days mixing concrete, carrying bricks and blocks. At the beginning, the work so exhausted him he couldn't think about anything else. Then he got stronger and more capable. Now it didn't exhaust him. It bored him. He started stealing from the site, wire and pipe, that he sold on to a scrap merchant in Crookedstone, a wily man with bandy legs called Donnelly.

One evening, he brought Donnelly a sack of pipe ends and got a few pounds. They started talking and Stephen complained about lack of money. He wanted to buy a car.

'I don't take just metal,' said Donnelly.

They were in the overheated hut that served as Donnelly's

office at the back of his yard. Outside a German Shepherd was tethered with a chain to a peg, which clinked as the dog paced up and down.

'I take bricks, piping, toilets and sinks, roof tiles, floorboards, scaffolding joints ... anything really. You bring it, I'll give you a good price.'

'I've no way to shift the stuff,' said Stephen.

'You provide the muscle. I'll provide the transport.'

The next morning, at ten, Stephen sat on a wall beside Albert. It was early May, warm and mild. They drank sweet hot tea. Albert was reading the paper. 'This is a bad business,' said Albert. The Ulster Workers' Council was adamant the power-sharing executive created by the Sunningdale Agreement must go and was threatening strike action.

'What happens if there's a strike?' asked Stephen.

'We shan't be working,' said Albert.

The strike came and work stopped. It was too good an opportunity to pass up. One night, Stephen and Donnelly drove to the site in Donnelly's flatbed lorry. They parked by the watchman's hut and went in. They found Victor, a lonely, half-deaf old man sitting at a table beside a small paraffin heater. Donnelly produced bottles of stout. Victor drank and fell asleep.

'Right,' said Donnelly, 'get the flatbed loaded, but you're to take just a bit of everything, understand? We don't want to be noticed, do we? And we don't want them putting up a fence and getting a new watchman.'

Stephen saw that Donnelly's counsel was sensible. This way, they could go on helping themselves for months.

While Donnelly watched the old man, Stephen loaded bags of cement, bricks and tiles onto the flatbed. They left the site at five the next morning with light glimmering at the edge of the sky. As Donnelly drove off along an empty road between high banks of white hawthorn, he said, 'This could be the start of something wonderful.'

Stephen got twenty pounds for his night's work. He felt elated. 'Lend us a sledgehammer,' he said to Donnelly.

'You're not going breaking in somewhere now, are you?'

'No,' said Stephen. 'Haven't I done enough tonight? I need one for a little job on the farm.'

42

DONNELLY GAVE HIM A TEN-POUND BEAST. He went straight to the graveyard where his father was buried and smashed the headstone. It split into three uneven pieces. Then he went home and got breakfast ready for his mother. He had it waiting, on the table, when she came down.

'If only you could be this good every day,' she said. She picked up a knife and fork and cut the end off her sausage.

Father John appeared at midday, looking troubled. There was ash on his jacket and his back was stooped. 'Your late husband's headstone,' he said. His watery eyes were focused on Stephen's mother. 'It's been vandalised.'

After Father John had left she sat in one of the Austin Cambridge seats by the range and wept. He sat across from her and held her hand. 'It must be Loyalists,' she said. 'Who else but the likes of them would do something like that?'

'You're right,' said Stephen.

It felt good not to be suspected—and the old bastard had deserved it. But he didn't feel clean and empty, as he'd expected. That was going to take more, he realised, than he could manage in five minutes at dawn with a hammer.

43

THE EXECUTIVE COLLAPSED AT THE END of the month and Stephen went back to work. No one noticed the missing materials.

During the summer Stephen was happy. Every week or two, he'd go with Donnelly to the site, and while the older man stayed with the watchman, he would load the flatbed. Stephen also continued to work for Albert, so with his wage plus what he stole, he had plenty of money for the first time in his life.

In July he bumped into Rosemary, the girl with the Polynesian looks, whom he had not forgotten from his one and only day at Crookedstone High. They started going to discos and pubs, and it wasn't long before they were an item. He passed his driving test and bought a Cortina. He and Rosemary went for drives. In lonely lanes and isolated car parks they explored each other's bodies.

In the autumn that followed the summer, life continued as it had been. The only difference was that when he and Rosemary were in the car the windows misted up. It was cold too, and he bought a travel blanket. He would lock the car and they would get onto the back seat and under the blanket. She liked to be undressed. They grew adventurous. He got Rosemary to take him in her mouth but she would not agree to have sex although he always had a packet of Durex with him in case she changed her mind. He was eager and he felt certain he would have his way soon.

44

ONE NIGHT AT THE END OF October, just before Hallowe'en, he and Donnelly were at the Housing Executive site where he worked, stealing again. An off-duty policeman, passing in his car, noticed a light. Suspecting he might have stumbled on paramilitaries, he called his station, and a platoon of the King's Own Scottish Borderers was scrambled. Donnelly heard their Land Rovers approaching. He wiped his prints off the bottles of Guinness he'd brought, slipped out of Victor's hut and walked away. Stephen was too busy loading the flatbed to hear. The soldiers caught him and called the police. They came and arrested him. During questioning, he claimed he had been working alone and had stolen the flatbed from Donnelly's yard. The police didn't believe this but Stephen wouldn't change his story.

He was remanded back to the Young Prisoners' wing in HMP Carrick. Donnelly visited and promised him a new car plus money if he kept quiet. In December 1974, he went up before the Omagh Crown Court. He pleaded guilty and got twelve months: with remission that meant he had six months to do, and as he'd done three on remand, he had only three left. He was released at the end of January 1975.

He went home. Mr Doherty was not inclined to ask Albert Smith to take him on a third time. 'Stephen's had his second chance, not to mention the third, fourth and fifth,' he said.

45

THE ONE GOOD THING IN HIS life was that he and Rosemary started seeing each other again. The night before his eighteenth birthday he went to the pub with her. She gave him a bottle of aftershave and they played darts. Afterwards he said he'd drive her home. The Cortina was gone and he was now driving a Mini, fully taxed and insured. This, along with a hundred pounds, had come from Donnelly. Payment for his silence.

Rosemary lived on a small Housing Executive estate outside Crookedstone. Though the kerbstones at the estate's entrance were painted red, white and blue and a Union flag hung wanly from the first lamppost, it wasn't a staunch estate and Rosemary's parents weren't either. One or two relatives had even married Catholics, so Stephen had no anxieties on that account. He was more concerned not to spoil the evening. So far, it had gone well and he hoped it might get better. He might get a hand job. Rosemary might even let him … No, he thought, he mustn't let himself think that.

He parked outside her gate and got out. There was no one around and the lights were out in the houses. He thought this was a good sign. He took Rosemary's arm and walked her through her gate, along the path and up to the door. It was black and freshly painted.

'Why don't you come in?' she whispered.

'What about your mum and dad?'

'They'll be asleep.'

'I'll lock the car,' he said.

He went to his Mini and came back. She slid the key into the lock and turned it. The door opened and the hall was dark. There was a bunch of plastic lilies in a vase on a table.

'Take your shoes off,' she whispered.

They crept into the living room where a fish tank bubbled. The light inside it lit up the three-piece suite, covered with burgundy velour. Stephen kissed Rosemary, unbuttoned her jeans, then pushed her back on the sofa. He waited a beat to see if she would tell him to stop, but instead she lifted her bottom to make it easier for him. He pulled off her jeans and knickers. Her legs were white in the glow from the fish tank. He pulled off her top and her brassiere. He knew, from their times under the blanket in the back of his Cortina, that it excited her to be naked when he was fully clothed.

He kissed her and took out one of the contraceptives that, as usual, he had in readiness in his pocket. He'd practised so he knew how to tear open the foil wrapper and then, having unzipped his jeans at the front, how to roll it on. They made love and later, when she'd dressed, Rosemary gave him tea and a cheese sandwich in the kitchen. Afterwards she sat on his lap and kissed him.

'Happy birthday,' she whispered.

46

HE SLIPPED OUT AT THREE AND drove home. It was a clear frosty night and a white moon hung in the sky.

The next morning Mother woke him.

'Your breakfast is ready,' she told him.

He would have preferred to stay in bed but knew he couldn't. When he went down to the kitchen, he found bacon and eggs, white and black pudding, potato bread and soda farls waiting for him.

'Happy birthday,' Mother said. 'You're an adult now.'

From that he knew she had something to say. When he'd finished eating he pushed aside his plate and said, 'That was good.'

Mother was on the other side of the Formica-topped table drinking tea.

'You want to talk about something?' he asked.

'I do.'

A long, awkward conversation followed. They agreed that his future probably didn't lie in Crookedstone. He had a criminal record. No one would want to give him work. But Mother had a plan. She had a brother in London, Uncle Sean, who was married to Auntie Kathleen. They lived in Wembley, and Uncle Sean owned a yard in Willesden that sold builders' supplies. She had arranged for Stephen to go and live with his uncle and auntie and work in the yard. In a few years, by which time he would have made some money and the memories of his misdemeanours would no longer be so vivid in Crookedstone, he could come back and take over the farm.

'What about Rosemary?' he said.

'What about her?'

He explained that they were going out together.

'You don't understand,' said Mother. 'You have no future here right now. Nobody will give you work. The farm can't support you. You need a job. That's what Sean is offering.'

'Donnelly will give me work,' he said. It was true. Donnelly had offered him work in his yard, breaking cars.

'The police told me he was with you when you were arrested. You go to him and what'll he have you doing next? Robbing banks?'

Tears welled in her eyes. She pulled a handkerchief from her cardigan pocket, lifted her glasses and dabbed. Then she stuffed it up her sleeve. 'I don't want you to go away. I don't want to say goodbye to the last of my children. I don't want to live here on my own. But after all the terrible things you've done, this is the best we can do. You're not going to Donnelly. You're going to London.'

47

THAT AFTERNOON HE WENT TO THE shirt factory where Rosemary now worked cutting patterns. He was waiting at the gate when she filed out with the other women. She wore a blue work coat and her legs were bare. The sun was shining and there were daffodils in the flowerbed inside the gate, their bright yellow heads bobbing in the wind.

'I have to go to London,' he said.

'Why?'

'To work.' He shook his head and grinned.

'Don't look so happy,' she said.

'I'm not.'

That night in the back of the tiny Mini, he undressed her as he had in her parents' house and made love to her. As he pumped away she guided his hand between her legs and showed him where to touch her. After a few minutes, he was surprised to hear Rosemary moaning while she heaved and shivered under him.

After the spasm passed she whispered, 'Come on. Come on, you.'

Later, when he'd finished, she told him she'd never before felt what she had when he'd touched her.

They made love every night thereafter right up to the night

before he was due to leave. Then, after she had dressed and they lay in each other's arms, she whispered, 'Am I your girl?'

'Am I?' he said, and they laughed. 'You are,' he said.

'Am I to stay your girl?'

'Yes.'

'Promise?'

'Promise.'

'Will you write?'

'Oh, aye.'

He was a good writer. He'd written to his mother from HM Borstal Langham Wood and from HMP Carrick at least every other day.

'You know I'll write,' he said. 'Didn't I always write to my mother?'

Rosemary nodded beside him. She knew this. 'I love you,' she said.

'And I love you.'

48

'WELL,' SAID MOTHER. SHE SAT ON one of the car seats by the range.

'Well.' He sat in the car seat opposite.

A little puff of smoke wafted out of the gap in the stove and rose into the air.

'What time is it?' she asked.

The big alarm clock with the green fluorescent numbers and the missing leg was on the window sill beside the medicine for her heart and her shingles. She had her back to the clock but even if she had turned and squinted at it she couldn't have read the time. She didn't have her glasses on. They were upstairs, under her pillow where she had purposely put them that morning. This deliberate not wearing of her glasses was something that went back to her husband's funeral. On that day, she'd left her glasses in the chapel. When she got to the graveyard, which was the part she dreaded, she couldn't see properly. Everything was a blur—the coffin being lowered, the earth being shovelled on, the unfilled hole being covered with the tarpaulin, and because they were all a blur, they weren't nearly as bad as she'd feared they'd be. Consequently, ever since then, she'd taken to putting her glasses away if something painful was coming—like it was now, for today was the day her son left for London.

Stephen squinted at the clock. 'Coming eleven.'

'Have you everything packed?'

'Aye.'

'The shortbread?'

She had made it herself. It was in a tin inside the suitcase standing by the scullery door—the same case he had taken to Mulberry House.

'Aye.'

'You'll try not to break it?'

'I will,' he said.

'Sean's very partial to his shortbread.'

'I know.'

'You'll be sure to write.'

'I will.'

'Nothing short.'

'No.'

'Detail. What you do, where you go, who you see, what London's like.'

'Detail, aye.'

The range sighed. He glanced at the turf barrel—a cut-down oil drum with brass handles welded on. That had been his father's work. 'I'll get the turf in before I go,' he said.

'Don't be doing that,' said Mother, 'and getting your good clothes dirty. Martin will.'

Martin Feeley rented their land. Mother had let it to him after Stephen's father had died and Stephen was in HM Borstal Langham Wood. Martin worked nights in a factory making golf balls but he came every morning to water and fodder his cattle, then again at midday, seven days a week, and he always called to see if Stephen's mother had any messages: he'd run to the grocer, or fill the turf barrel or do anything else that was required. He was handy that way. He also paid on time, and with the money she'd had a phone put in. 'A good man is Martin Feeley,' she always said.

'You'll miss your father's anniversary Mass next month,' she said now.

That would be at the end of March. The Sunday was circled in red on the calendar from Henderson's Feeds that hung on the dresser. It would be five years since his father had died.

'It's a shame,' she added.

'Yes,' he said.

'But with the best will in the world you can't do everything.' She sighed.

He thought about saying nothing, then he decided to speak. 'You were the one who said I had to go to London as soon as I could,' he said.

'I know, but if you'd asked to stay I'd have let you.'

That was the trouble, he thought. Whatever he did there was no pleasing her.

'You never liked your daddy, did you?'

'He was a bastard,' he said. 'And a brute and an animal.'

Mother let out a cry of shock. 'What are you saying? My heart's broken enough, what is this now?'

Well, he'd started, he thought, and he saw no reason to stop. 'He used to touch me in a bad way,' he said.

'He didn't. He was a good man. What are you saying? You've picked up these horrible ideas in prison, haven't you?'

'He did.'

'I don't believe you.'

Another little puff came out of the stove.

'When you have children with a man,' she said, 'you don't want to hear this.'

She began to cry. She found her handkerchief and rubbed it over her face. He looked at her hair, grey and crinkled. It was like the stuffing that sometimes leaked out of his mattress. She was sixty-five and looked older: it was all the children, it was his father, it was her whole rotten life, and it was his behaviour. Suddenly he wished he hadn't spoken as he had. 'I'm sorry,' he said. 'I shouldn't have said that.'

'Ah, you've said it now,' she said bitterly, 'and you can't take it back. And isn't it as well you're going away now and I won't have to hear any more like that?'

They lapsed into silence.

'Did you smash your father's headstone?' she said.

He decided to say nothing.

'That means yes, doesn't it? Oh, Jesus, Stephen, oh, sweet Jesus, son, there was no call for that.'

He had never heard his mother speak like that before and wondered what to say until they heard his taxi pull up in the yard and the horn sound.

'You're the only son I've got,' she said, sniffling, 'and, oh, the hurt you've done me. Have you any idea?'

He shook his head.

'But I'll miss you all the same.'

Tears rolled down her face. 'I'll miss you,' she whispered again.

'It's not like I'll be gone for ever,' he said, hoping he sounded cheerful. 'I'll only be gone for a bit. I'll do a few months with Uncle Sean and I'll be home.'

He heard the engine turning outside, a diesel engine. The noise it made was a low rumble. 'I have to go.' He got up and put his lips on her forehead. She smelled of shampoo and cabbage. 'If I don't leave now I'll miss my bus.'

She dropped her head and looked at the linoleum, hideous stuff called Tara, all swirling Celtic designs taken from the Book of Kells. His father had put it down. It was the last thing he had done before he died. For such an ignorant man he was surprisingly handy. Whenever time had allowed he had always worked on the house.

'Don't forget your case, will you?' Her voice throbbed as if she were asking about a catastrophe.

'I won't,' though how he could miss it when it was by the back door was a mystery to him. 'I'll write.'

'You do what you want. That's what you've always done. Just the same as you always say what you want without care or concern for the other person.'

That hurt him. 'That's not true.'

'You'd better go.'

'I was telling the truth. I wasn't lying.'

She shrugged. 'Do you think I want to know?'

'Why don't I stay a week? Or wait till next month? We can ring Sean tonight. He won't mind I'm sure whether I come today or next month.'

'Go,' she said. 'Go, go, go, go ... '

He felt a little tug. He was the youngest. He was her boy. He was her favourite—or he had been until he'd started to go bad. The five girls were gone. Now he was leaving. Once the taxi carried him away up the lane, there would be no one, just her, in the old place, and she would be alone.

'So, 'bye then,' he said.

He scooted away. He expected her to grab him but she didn't. She stared at the floor and snuffled. He pulled on his jacket.

''Bye,' he called again.

He heard an anguished sob.

'Okay, I'm off so,' he said.

He'd sounded just like his father, he thought, as he opened the back door.

49

HE WALKED OUT ONTO THE step and felt the wind on his face, moist and surprisingly warm, smelling of old mould, wet stone and, very faintly, of diesel fumes. The taxi stood in the middle of the yard, a line of washing stretched across the mouth of the shed behind it. The illuminated sign on the roof read CROOKEDSTONE TAXIS. The driver sat behind the wheel, reading a newspaper.

He waited, expecting to hear Mother's footfalls as she came up behind. But she didn't come. She was still in the kitchen where he'd left her by the range, crying hard now, great sobs fluttering from her mouth. He could hear them now and he thought that he must ignore them. He must move on.

He closed the door, the weatherboard at the bottom

skimming across the floor as he did so and making its characteristic noise, like a little gasp. The latch clicked. He walked down the two steps and across to the taxi boot. He lifted the lid, stored his case among rags and tools, and closed it. He got into the car. The door shut, clunk. It was such a final noise. It said "departure" so emphatically. He smelt Wrigley's spearmint gum and old tobacco. The ashtray hung open, with half a dozen wrinkled butts inside. The driver was chewing.

'Bus depot?' he asked. He folded the *Tyrone Constitution* and dropped it into the little pocket in the driver's door.

'Aye,' said Stephen.

The man put the car in gear and moved off. The house had concrete all around it, another of his father's legacies. As he'd boasted, it was all muck about the house when he'd started and all concrete when he'd finished. He had been proud of that.

The taxi came out at the front and began to drive up the lane towards the road. The driver went slowly. Stephen wondered why he wasn't rushing. Perhaps he had guessed he was going away (which wasn't hard) and was letting him savour his last moments.

He looked back at the two-storey farmhouse, the rarely used front door, and the small brown windows. He thought he saw the curtains twitching in the good room at the front. Was that Mother? Had she weakened and rushed to watch him drive away? Was she about to pull back the curtain and show herself in her agony to him? That was a sight, he decided, he couldn't bear.

He faced forward. He saw the concrete lane along which the taxi was driving floating out across the ground in front of him. Here and there, he saw great dark gorse bushes and bony cattle grazing. In the distance, he saw the stone wall that ran along the side of the lawn parallel to the concrete lane. He saw the galvanised gate and Dermot's Field, studded with boulders and trees. Right at the top he saw the sheephouse where his father had taken him the first time and many others. He remembered the sawdust and fish taste of his father's semen. Then he heard, in his inner ear, a version of all the threats his father had ever uttered rolled into one.

'Your mother will think you're a liar. She won't believe you. And if you ever dare to tout you'll get the toe of my boot up your arse, and that's just for starters.'

He had believed everything his father had said, of course. He had told no one until just now. He banished his thoughts. He felt a great sense of relief that he was going, even if it meant separation from Rosemary. He had to get away. Otherwise all he'd see for the rest of his life would be gorse bushes and beasts and bad rushy land, and they would only remind him of everything that had happened and he would never be able to forget.

50

AT CROOKEDSTONE, HE BOUGHT A BUS ticket to London.

The next day he got to Victoria Coach Station in London. He went to Baker Street and caught the Bakerloo line to Wembley Central. From there, he walked to Uncle Sean and Auntie Kathleen's place, carrying the suitcase on his shoulder like a sailor with his kit-bag.

He reached his relations' house in the evening. It was a small semi clad in white pebble-dash. The hall smelled of fried onions and burned bacon. A picture of Jesus crucified dominated the lounge. He was given the small back bedroom overlooking the garden. His uncle and aunt slept in the front room overlooking the street, and Chris was in the box-room beside them. Stephen and his cousin weren't introduced but he knew about him, so that didn't matter. Chris was a recluse who believed that somewhere in the world there was a Beatles record that carried the word of God instead of the usual lyrics. He planned to go through every Fab Four record ever pressed until he found the one. Waiting for sleep that first night in London, Stephen was not in the least surprised to hear 'Help' being played over and over again in the box-room.

The next morning he went with his uncle to Willesden, to the builders' yard. He worked all day weighing sand, loading bricks, parcelling screws. It was hateful. When he got in from work, he went up to wash and met Chris on the upstairs landing. His cousin wore enormous spectacles that magnified his eyes, and his long dirty hair spilled over his shoulders. 'Specky,' he whispered mysteriously at Stephen. Then he bolted down the stairs and went out, slamming the front door behind him.

Kathleen came out of the kitchen. 'Was that Chris?' she shouted.

'Yeah, I'd say so,' he called back.

That night 'Help' was again the soundtrack to which he fell asleep. When he woke up on his second morning in London, he felt exhausted and bored by the thought of another day in the yard, followed by another evening with his relations, watching television and drinking tea. The only variation in his routine to which he could look forward—the yard was open from eight to four six days a week—was Mass on Sunday.

51

STEPHEN STRUGGLED ON FOR THREE WEEKS. Then came a Saturday morning. Bennett, the storeman, asked him to make tea. The kettle lived in the office on top of a little fridge. As he came in through the door, he saw the petty cash box on the desk. It was open and there was no one around.

He knew that thinking was fatal when he had the opportunity to steal. Once you hesitated, you blew it. If a chance arose, you had to act immediately or not at all.

He cocked his head. No sound of anyone about. He went straight over and lifted away the coin tray. A sheaf of Bank of England notes lay beneath. As he stuffed them into his pocket, he reminded himself that Sean didn't pay him enough for all the work he did in the yard, so he was only taking what was owed to him really.

He put the tray back into the box and picked up the kettle. He was striding across the room when the door opened and he met Sally, the cleaner, coming the other way with the Hoover. His heart sank. The cash box was on the desk, exactly as he'd found it, with the lid thrown back, and there was no one in the room but him. When the money was found missing, and it wouldn't be long before it was, the first question to be asked would be: who was last in the office? Sally would say he was. But what could he do now? Put it back? He'd have to act innocent and pretend he knew nothing. And he had to get rid of the money as well, and the sooner he did that the better.

'I'm away to get water for tea. Will you have a cup?'

'Tea, oh, yes,' said Sally. 'I'm dying of thirst.'

She was a small woman with a sharp nose, buck teeth and

dyed-blonde hair. She was from Liverpool and spoke through her nose. He liked to hear her talking.

'Well, then, you shall have a tea,' he said.

He went to the yard. His denim jacket was on a nail. He put the money in the top-left breast pocket in one nice quick movement without the storeman seeing him. He filled the kettle from the outside tap, the only source of mains water in the place, then started back for the office, swinging the kettle and spilling little blobs of water as he went. This gave a good impression of innocence, he thought.

He pushed the door and strode into the office. Uncle Sean was at the desk and Sally was using the Hoover. He didn't care for the atmosphere one bit but it was impossible to bolt. When Sally turned off the Hoover and went out, he knew he was in trouble.

'Give it back,' said Sean.

'What?' he said. He fitted the kettle lead and flicked the switch.

'Don't come the innocent with me,' said Sean. 'There was two hundred pounds in this box and you took it.'

Sally must have said something.

'I didn't.'

'You put it back, now, and it'll never be mentioned again.'

'But I didn't take it.'

'Well then, you won't mind turning your pockets out.'

'Sure,' he said. Slowly, he put everything on the desk, then patted his pockets to show they were empty. 'Happy now?' he said.

At that moment, Sally shot in through the door. Oh, fuck, she had his jacket and the money. She gave the wad to Sean. His uncle counted it. From the speed with which he did this, Stephen noted grimly, he was used to handling notes.

'This is the missing cash, all right,' said Sean. 'It was in that jacket, was it?'

Sally nodded.

'That's your jacket, Stephen, isn't it?'

He said nothing.

'Five minutes ago you were in here, alone. The cash box was on the desk, open. You took the money and the kettle, and on the pretext of filling it, you went out to the yard and put the money into your jacket pocket. That's what happened, isn't it?'

They'd planned it, he realised. While Sean had kept him talking, Sally had gone to search his jacket.

'Come on,' said Sean. 'We're going home now.'

Sally gave him his jacket. She was gazing at Sean with a funny expression and suddenly Stephen realised: they were an item, she and Sean. That's why she'd touted on him. It was to prove her love.

52

SEAN DROVE HIM BACK TO THE house in silence. They went inside. His aunt, who wasn't expecting them home at that time, came out of the kitchen.

'What's the matter?'

'Stephen's going,' said Sean.

'Why?'

'Because the less time I spend under the same roof as Chris the crackpot,' Stephen said, 'the better.'

He saw their old faces shrink. He had hurt them. Good, he thought. They deserved it.

'Don't for a second think I'm not going to tell your mother,' said Sean.

'Oh dear, big deal. Now I'm really shaking in my boots.' Let them write to his mother. Let them tell her he was a thief. He didn't care.

'She'll be so upset,' said Sean. 'It'll break her heart. You promised to change. You promised never to steal again. So I took you in. I gave you a job. And what do you do? The first opportunity you get, you're back to your old ways. You steal from me. You steal from your own family.'

'You know Bennett, your storeman? He's been stealing your stock and selling it on to other builders for years.' As a thief, Stephen was quick to recognise another when he saw one. 'Why don't you sack him? I just took a couple of hundred from petty cash. He's taken thousands.'

'Go to your room and pack,' said Sean. 'I don't want to hear another word.'

'You needn't worry. I've nothing else to say to you.'

He went to his room. Through the wall he could hear that Chris still had 'Help' on the turntable.

His suitcase packed, he went downstairs. His uncle and aunt were whispering in the kitchen. He felt like shouting, 'I'm glad I'm going. Who'd want to stay here? Chris is bonkers and you're a vile mean-spirited pair. And listen, Kathleen ... do you ever wonder why Sean never bothers with you? Well, ask him about Sally.'

He went straight out of the front door without saying goodbye. He was walking down the road when he heard his uncle shouting, 'Hey, the key.'

He turned and saw Sean. Stephen had the front-door key in his right-hand jacket pocket. He pulled it out by the bit of string that was tied to it and jiggled it in the air.

'Here,' he said, and he lobbed it into a garden on the other side of the road. Then he walked onto the tube station. There was a newsagent's beside it and he bought a London A-Z.

A few days before he had met some people in a pub. They'd told him they lived in a squat in Rifle Place, between Shepherd's Bush and the Westway. He looked it up. The nearest tube station was Latimer Road.

He took the tube down, and walked to Rifle Place. Outside a house a girl was sitting on the steps. He stopped to talk. She had one blue and one green eye. He told her he'd met these people in a pub and they lived here somewhere and he was looking for them. She didn't recognise them, not that that mattered, though. The whole street was squatted, she explained, and there was space in the house she was squatting in, number twelve.

53

HE GOT A SMALL ROOM AT the top of the house; the walls were orange, the sloping roof was green, the roof timbers were white. It smelt of joss sticks. He fell asleep to the sound of traffic belting up and down to the M40 motorway, a roaring noise, like the sea.

A couple of days later he was in the communal kitchen. A few of the others from the house were there along with the girl with different coloured eyes. 'I want to ask you something,' she said. 'I hope you don't mind. It's a bit personal.'

'All right.'

'Are you a Catholic?'

At home, you wouldn't dare ask this but in England, where nobody cared what you were, everybody did.

'Yes,' he said. Even though he hadn't been to Mass for years, that was what everybody knew him as at home.

'What's it like in Ireland?' she went on. The others in the kitchen were listening now. 'You get a lot of trouble over there, don't you?'

Where he lived near the border, Nationalists were the majority and there wasn't much trouble. Yes, there was always tension during Twelfth fortnight, the holiday period when the Orange Order celebrated the battle of the Boyne and most Protestant businesses were closed, and yes, there were pubs and discos he avoided, but that was the height of it. It was nothing like on television. Yet, he guessed, if he didn't provide the girl and the others with what they expected, they'd feel cheated and, worse, they'd think him a fraud, someone not to be believed, someone untrustworthy.

'Yes, you do get a fair bit of trouble,' he said. 'We'd a heap when I was growing up. We'd Orangemen, marches, parades near our house, police and army. There was always shouting and fighting. I couldn't stand it. That's why I come over here.'

'It must have been awful,' said the girl with the different-coloured eyes.

He slept with her that night, and in the morning, when she was sleeping, he found her purse. He took the change. He reckoned he could sleep with her each night and steal from her in the morning as long as he was careful not to take so much that she noticed.

54

HE WENT TO THE LABOUR EXCHANGE in Shepherd's Bush and registered as unemployed. Afterwards, wondering how he would pass his time, he remembered someone in the squat had told him about the Lord Connaught pub on the Harrow Road where it was easy to pick up casual work.

It was an old building on a corner, painted with peeling beige paint and with traffic thundering past. The inside was dingy and smelled of beer and old horsehair. The varnish on the bar counter was worn away in some places but not in others. Where it was worn, the bare wood was almost white but where it remained, the counter was the colour of treacle. The customers in the Lord Connaught were half Irish, half Jamaican. The pool table was a good one, level and well maintained. He started going regularly.

A couple of days later, early in the morning when there weren't many in, turning over a coin in his pocket and wondering whether to have a practice game alone, a fellow he'd never seen before smiled at him and said, 'Ain't seen you before.' He was sitting in the corner on a high stool, and he was in his fifties, Stephen guessed. He had the thin body of someone who drank all the time but rarely ate. He wore spectacles and there were deep lines all over his face.

The man introduced himself as Archer. He didn't play pool, he said. He offered Stephen a drink.

'Aye, I'll have a pint of Guinness.'

Archer was a Londoner. His spectacle frames were red. They reminded Stephen of Elton John's. After the first pint Archer bought him another, plus a whiskey chaser. Archer was drinking rum and water.

'Let's go and sit at a table,' he said.

Stephen took care to sit away from the older man. He thought Archer might be queer.

After a few minutes, Archer lowered his voice and Stephen had to go closer to hear which made him nervous.

'I've got two places,' began Archer, 'one in Maida Vale, where I live, and this other one down in Marble Arch. I let these two tarts go in there, Lisa and Tanya. They aren't mine. This is a business arrangement. They pay me and I pay the landlord. Really, I shouldn't rent it to them—it's sub-letting and that's forbidden in the lease, but I do. It seems a shame to let a place stand empty. Well, now I wish I hadn't been so bloody nice.'

He poked a bony finger behind the collar of his shirt and scratched his very wrinkled brown neck.

'You're wondering why I'm telling you this? It's simple. Last week the girls told me to get stuffed. They told me they're not going to pay me rent any more. And they're not going to move out either. They're just going to stay there. But I've got to go on paying the landlord, haven't I? I don't want to lose the place. I want to go back there one day. Or else Joe, my son—he's away at the moment, in prison—he'll want to move in there when he gets out. So, now I'm paying the rent for a flat with two working girls that don't give me a penny. It's not right, is it?'

'No,' he agreed, 'it isn't.'

'Tell you what,' said Archer. 'I'll give you forty quid to frighten them, half now, half when you've done it. Tell them to clear off in twenty-four hours, and if they don't you'll cut off their nipples. I'll pay you a hundred if it comes to that but I shouldn't think it would. Tell them you're with the IRA. They'll be terrified. Lisa's brother was a soldier. He got blown up somewhere called Newry. They hear your accent and they'll scarper. Do you know Newry?'

Forty pounds to tell two girls to go. Easy money.

'Bad place?' asked Archer. 'Newry?'

He'd never been to Newry.

"Shocking,' he said. 'The worst.'

'You tell those slags you're from Newry then,' said Archer. 'They'll be like putty in your hands.'

55

ARCHER GAVE HIM TWO TEN-POUND NOTES in the gents, and the phone number and address of the flat. Stephen asked for another five to buy a blade. Archer paid it over. He went to Praed Street and bought a Bowie knife in one of the hardware shops that lined the street. Then he found a phone box near Paddington station, went in and dialled.

'Hello?'

'Is that Lisa and Tanya's?'

'Who's calling?'

'My name's John Maguire,' he said. Maguire was his mother's name before she married.

'Yes, Mr Maguire?'

'I want to make an appointment to see Lisa.'

'Do you know her? Have you ever seen her before?'

Archer had told him what to say. 'No, I haven't,' he said, 'but Heather told me about her.'

It was Heather who had introduced Archer to the girls. They knew and trusted her.

'Heather?'

'Aye, Heather said I should ring. Said Lisa'd fix me up.'

'When had you in mind?'

'Today. Now.'

'Lisa's very busy.'

'What—all day?'

'I don't know ... Let me see.'

He heard paper rustling.

'Oh, yes. She could just fit you in. How would three o'clock suit?'

'Yeah.'

'What had you in mind?'

'Round the World.' He'd got this from Archer too. It meant full sex with everything included.

'Right, Mr Maguire, Lisa will see you at three.'

She repeated the address. He hung up.

56

HE CAME OUT OF THE PHONE booth. Now he had to make himself angry. He thought about his father and Mr Purdue. He pounded the streets. He felt his rage stoking up. When he got to the flat just before three, he was full of it.

He put away the A-Z and rang the bell. A middle-aged woman in a kimono opened the door.

'Oh.' There was a tiny pause. It was his clothes, he knew. He wore a donkey jacket, a woollen hat and flared jeans with white bleach blobs all over them. She thought he looked rough. He didn't want her turning him away.

Gently, he said, 'I rang earlier.'

'Mr Maguire?' As soon as she said his name, he recognised the voice.

'Yes.'

'I'm Lisa.'

But on the telephone she'd pretended to be someone else. What was that about? Why hadn't she said she was Lisa then? And didn't it occur to her that when he turned up and heard her voice he'd realise? She must have heard his accent and assumed he was a dense Mick. Well, he'd teach her. Suddenly he felt angry enough to kill.

'Come in.'

He stepped forward, straining his ears. He needed to know who else was about. He could hear a woman moaning— Tanya—but that was it. Good, he thought.

Lisa led him to a bedroom. There was a poster on the wall—Marlon Brando on a motorcycle.

'Take your clothes off,' Lisa said.

She took off her kimono and folded it over the back of the chair. She wore nothing but stockings and a suspender belt. She lay down on the bed. It was a double with a pink cover. She was quite a big woman with very black pubic hair. He got on to her chest, and pinned her arms down with his knees.

'You're not going to get very far like that,' she said.

He had the knife in its scabbard stuck down the sock on his right foot. He pulled it out now and held up it in front of her face where she could see it.

'I won't, but then I'm not going to fuck you,' he said.

She didn't struggle, just watched him closely. 'Tanya's next door,' she said. 'With her boyfriend, black, a boxer. He'll kill you, you know, he finds you in here, like this.'

'Archer wants you out.'

'Oh, yeah?'

'Or me and my mates'll come back and cut off your tits.'

'Don't make me laugh.'

She aimed to sound unconcerned but underneath he heard

terror. 'I'm with the IRA from Newry,' he said. 'You'd better believe me or you'll be sorry.'

He clambered off her and walked out. In the hall he heard Tanya moan and, he thought, the sound of a telephone being dialled. He went out, closed the door quietly behind him and slipped down the stairs.

In the street, he broke into a slow run.

57

TWENTY MINUTES LATER, HE WAS ON the Edgeware Road. He was walking slowly now. His intention was to go back to the Lord Connaught and to meet up with Archer.

He heard the sound of a vehicle approaching at speed. He looked round in time to see a Commer van brake at the kerb a few yards away. The doors opened and four policemen jumped out. He realised he was their target but it was too late to run. They'd surrounded him. Oh fuck, he thought. Lisa's called them. His heart raced.

'What's your name?' one of the officers shouted. He was a big man with grey eyes and coarse, rough skin. Here and there, it looked as if grit had been rubbed into it.

Stephen screwed up his face as if he didn't understand.

'Your name. Tell us your name.'

The one with the grit in his skin was speaking. He had raised the volume and stretched the words out as if he were speaking to a foreigner.

'Stephen Melanophy.'

'Oh, a Paddy. A bloody Paddy.' The policeman's inflection combined anger and distaste.

'Now tell me, what have you been doing with yourself?'

Stephen looked puzzled.

'Are you here on holiday? Working on a building site, perhaps? Or are you making bombs? Isn't that what your lot are good at? Making bombs and killing innocent people.'

Stephen remembered his uncle Sean warning him about the English and especially the police. The Guildford and Birmingham bombings were still a raw sore and, with his accent, he needed to take care, his uncle had said, as the English would connect him with those crimes. When he was among English people he was to be polite and respectful, Sean said. He was never to discuss politics, and if he was pressed to give an opinion on the IRA or their bombing campaign, he was to condemn them. Standing now in the street, with the policemen, he wondered what he could say to rescue the situation. 'I'm not a bomber,' or 'I don't support the IRA.' They'd only make the policemen think he was hiding something. It was better to say nothing, he decided.

'Any identification?'

His mind was blank, and then he remembered he had a letter, which had arrived at his uncle Sean's a few days before, from Rosemary. He pulled it out of his back pocket. The policeman took the envelope and read out the address on the front. 'Is this where you live?'

'It's my uncle's. I'm not there now. I'm staying in Rifle Place.'

'Search him.'

Another policeman ran his hands round Stephen's upper body, then down his legs. He found the Bowie knife and gave it to the one with grit in his skin.

'What's the knife for?'

'Work.'

'What kind of work do you do?'

'Electrical.'

'With this?'

'Yeah.'

'What do you use it for?'

'Cutting wires.' It was all he could think of to say.

'Cutting wires.'

'Yeah.'

'Do you think I'm an idiot?'

He knew where this was going but there was nothing he could do to stop it.

'You must think I'm a fucking idiot because you'd only try to tell an idiot this was for cutting wires.' The policeman waved the knife. 'You use a wire cutter for cutting wires. You don't cut wires with a blade like this. That's a lie, Paddy.'

He looked at the policeman's sorry skin and the little black specks embedded in it.

'Why do you think you can get away with telling a lie like that?'

He looked over the policeman's shoulder and down the street behind.

'Look at me when I'm talking to you.'

He looked back. The policeman had a large nose that was kinked in the middle and eyes the colour of pebbles.

'You're nicked. Get him in the van.'

The policemen began to haul him across the pavement. He had a vague impression of a teenage girl. She wore torn fishnet tights, and a short red leather skirt. When she was quite close, she shouted, 'Leave the boy alone, pigs.'

'Oh, shut up, you daft twat,' someone shouted back at her.

A hand on his head forced Stephen to bend and double up. Next thing he was pushed into the back of the van. One of the policemen was already in there. Stephen didn't know how he'd got ahead of him. The policeman hit him across the shoulder with his truncheon. He fell sideways. The cuffs went on. The doors closed and it was dark.

'If I hear a peep out of you,' said his escort, 'I'm going to hit you until you stop moving.'

This one was mad, he thought. He decided to stay very still and not say a word. He noticed his shoulder was throbbing fiercely.

58

HE WAS TAKEN TO A POLICE station. He later learned it was Paddington Green. The cuffs were taken off and he was put in an interview room. He got a cold cup of tea from a policewoman. She went out, leaving the door open behind her. There were people talking in the corridor outside. He heard someone saying, 'He has the jeans with the bleach spots and he has the knife. It's got to be him.'

A detective came in, the one he'd heard talking outside, a heavy man with grey eyes. The detective asked him a few questions about the knife, but nothing about Lisa and Tanya. He was charged with breach of the peace, threatening behaviour, resisting arrest, and possession of an offensive weapon. He denied the charges and was taken to a holding cell.

It wasn't very different from the ones at home. It was cold and there was one blanket. He lay down on the pallet and covered himself. When he was warm and calm, he started to think.

After he'd paid his visit, Lisa had called the police. She gave a description. The peelers picked him up. But in his interview, there was no mention of what had happened at the flat. All the charges related to what had happened in the street. There had to be a reason for that.

Next, he remembered the moment when Archer had handed him the money in the toilets. He'd jumped at it, as Archer had guessed he would. He had been greedy. What he didn't know then, but which he guessed now, was that the girls paid the police and Archer knew they paid the police but he wanted them out so badly, he'd decided to have a punt on Stephen. It had cost him twenty up front, with another twenty to follow. If Stephen's accent drove them out, as Archer had hoped, he'd have achieved a result for only a small outlay. On the other hand, if Stephen didn't do the business, well, it wouldn't have cost Archer that much. When he got to the end of this thought, Stephen realised: he'd been conned.

A great black rage filled him. If he met Archer, he would kill him. As it happened, he didn't get the chance. He was remanded into custody and was up before the magistrate a fortnight later. He got twelve months. The English rules, different from home, required a prisoner to do two-thirds of his sentence before he qualified for remission. He was sent to HMP Kingsman, an old Victorian prison in west London.

59

HE STARTED HIS SENTENCE FEELING CONFIDENT, hearty and fit. He'd done jail twice at home. This was the same, he reckoned, but with different accents. As he was under twenty-one he started on the Young Prisoners' wing but after a few days, owing to lack of space, he was thrown in with adults.

The man in the cell beside his was called Ignatius O'Doherty. "Docker," as he was known, weighed eighteen stone and had no fingers on his right hand, just a thumb. Stephen was curious about the man and his hand and one evening, during association, in conversation with a housebreaker called Kenny, he saw his chance.

'What's with Docker's hand?' he asked.

'Hooky's you mean,' said Kenny, 'though never call him Hooky to his face. He doesn't like it.'

Kenny, like Docker, was from Leeds and when he said 'Hooky' the word sounded comical.

'It were a mate's stag,' said Kenny. 'Docker's organising and he books a stripper to come to the house. Let's call her Tracey. During negotiations, Tracey says, she'd suck them all for so much or they could poke her. Docker thought this were fucking brilliant. He gathers money up from each man and has it all in a cigarette box along with the fee for stripping. When Tracey arrives, he shows her the money and the box goes on the mantelpiece.'

Stephen nodded as if he was familiar with the scene but in his world there had never been anything like it.

'Tracey strips. She has huge tits, or maybe she doesn't but they all said she did to make it seem better afterwards, and then they all pile in, one after the next, and fuck her. She's so busy Tracey doesn't notice Docker get her poke money out of the box and give each lad his note back. Afterwards, Tracey goes to the mantelpiece, opens the box, and finds it's only got her fee.

'"Where's the rest of me money?" she says.

'"What money?" says Docker.

'"The rest of me money," says Tracey. "I want me money."

'"What for?"

'"For sex. We agreed."

'"You call that sex? Don't be daft. That wasn't sex. That was crap," says Docker.

'"I want me money."

'"Hey lads, you hear this?" Docker shouts to the boys, who were getting dressed, "Tracey wants money off each of you."

'"I'm not paying," says one lad. "Worst screw of my life."

'"Yeah," says another. "Fuck off, Tracey."

'Then the chorus starts, "Flabby cunt," and Tracey knows she's going to need help. So she fetches her driver and he asks for her money but he's one against twelve blokes and he can't do anything. Tracey gets furious and starts shouting she's going to get them, but these blokes are so drunk they don't care or notice. In the end, the driver takes her away.

'But Tracey doesn't forget. She has two brothers who are bikers. They go to the factory where Docker operates a machine putting the eyes in shoe uppers. One of them gets Docker in a headlock and the other feeds his hand under the punch.

'When Docker wakes up in hospital, he's lost all his fingers. The doctor says he's lucky to have kept his hand. Police come, of course, ask questions but he says he doesn't know what happened. He was rushed from behind, his hand went in the machine, and he passed out. Coppers don't believe him but they couldn't do nothing.

'Eventually Docker gets out. He doesn't even drop his things home. He buys piano wire and goes straight to the bikers' clubhouse. It's outside Leeds, in the country, and he ties the wire between trees. He doesn't get the brothers who done him but he gets an old biker. The wire cuts his larynx out. The fellow never talks again. Docker went to London after that. Had to, no choice, they were going to kill him otherwise.'

Meandering back to the cells after association, Kenny and Stephen reached the bottom of the stairs that led up to their landing at the same time as Docker.

'Docker,' called Kenny, 'can I introduce you to someone? This is Stephen. He's in the cell next to you.'

Docker stuck out the fingerless palm. Stephen knew better than to hesitate. He reached downward, gripped it and felt Docker's thumb pressing down. It was like taking hold of a fleshy hatchet, he thought.

'Stephen,' said Docker. They began to climb the stairs together. 'Irish?'

'Tyrone,' said Stephen.

'Kerry,' said Docker. 'Mum and Dad.'

'Never been,' said Stephen, 'but I always wanted to.'

60

THE FOLLOWING MORNING STEPHEN CARRIED HIS plastic chamberpot out of his cell and took his place in the line of men waiting to empty their own in the recess. Docker was in front of him. After the story he had heard the night before, his bulky neighbour provoked in him a mixture of awe and trepidation.

The queue moved forward briskly. Slopping out was the one job every man was anxious to get done quickly. As he got closer to the recess, Stephen noticed two prisoners he hadn't registered before, standing near the entrance. One was a skinny little fellow and the other was big, with sticking-out ears. He'd no idea who they were or why they were there. Why weren't they slopping out? Were they orderlies? Of course, those were questions he couldn't answer. And until such time as he could, the trick, he knew from his previous sentences, was to be the grey man nobody noticed.

Shuffling forward, he concentrated on Docker's shaven head. It was like a piece of meat sprinkled with pepper.

His thoughts drifted back to the conversation he had had with Kenny. In London, Docker had worked first as a bouncer, then begun to look after girls. He was doing two years for living off immoral earnings. As he trailed along the landing, Stephen wondered if Docker knew Archer. One of the things he'd discovered in jail was that men in the same line always seemed to know each other: burglars knew burglars, pimps knew pimps.

He was a few feet from the recess when he heard talking between the pair he'd noticed.

'Here he comes,' said the smaller one. 'It's the new cunt on the wing,' he continued, while his friend glared at Stephen.

Ah, the slagging test, he thought. Abuse the new boy and see how he takes it. The traditional response was to give as good as you got. 'You fucking so-and-so why don't you fucking dot, dot, dot?' If you spoke back strongly, the abuse should stop. But to do that you needed confidence. You needed to know your way about. You needed allies. He was new. He didn't really know anyone. And there were two of them to one of him. He'd try to make them laugh instead, he decided.

'Oh, tough guys.' He said it nicely, with a bit of a smile and a bit of a roll.

'You talking to me?' said the bigger one. Stephen was now almost level with them.

'Who else? I'm here; you're there. Let's keep it clean, shall we?' he continued. His tone, he thought, was polite but firm. He wasn't going to stand any nonsense but he wasn't intending to start a row either.

He winked and passed on into the recess.

'Oi, you, Mick, ugly mug, I'm talking to you,' he heard behind. 'No speaka da English where you come from? Parlez-vous Anglais?'

There were two toilets and two small low-set sinks, each with a single cold tap. He tipped his pot into a toilet then rinsed it under the cold tap.

He sallied out of the recess. The hecklers were still loitering. He stowed his pot in his cell and came out onto the landing. Docker was just ahead of him. He followed the shaven-headed man down the landing towards where the hecklers stood. As Docker passed, the pair didn't look at Docker, and Docker didn't look at them. It was as if neither admitted the existence of the other. Then the moment was gone and Docker was on his way down the stairs. Now it was his turn to pass. As they approached they stared at him and he stared back. Nothing was said. Then he began to go down the stairs. On the third tread he heard one of them gob, and then he felt something land lightly on his shoulder. He did not react—that would have been a sign of weakness—but Docker, he heard and turned and glanced back at the two at the top of the stairs before resuming his descent.

Stephen got to the dinner hall and joined the queue. Docker was just ahead but he didn't want to ask him, so he turned instead to the man behind, a housebreaker from Dagenham named Manny Davies, whose arm was in plaster.

He had broken it falling from the drainpipe of a house he was hoping to rob and had been arrested in Casualty. The police had had a description from a neighbour and Manny was the only man with a broken arm who answered to it.

'Is there something on my shoulder?' he asked.

'Yeah,' Manny said.

'Is it green gob?'

'It's more brown, mate.'

'Who were the guys outside recess?'

'I'm sorry, mate, I don't know. I didn't see anyone.'

Even giving their names was too big a risk for little Manny with his broken arm to take.

Stephen got to the front of the queue.

'You wouldn't have a bit of scrap paper?' he said to the orderly behind the counter.

'Certainly,' he said.

He tore the label off a can of baked beans and gave it to him. Stephen cleaned his shoulder and threw the wrapper in the slop pail. Then he got his breakfast—cereal, milk, white toast—and turned to walk back to his cell. He spotted Docker just ahead, moving slowly in the direction of the stairs that went up to their landing. Had Docker loitered in order that he could catch up? It looked like it. A couple of steps and Stephen drew level with him. He saw Docker used his good left hand to support his bowl, while his hatchet shaped fingerless hand rested on top, holding the toast down on the plate.

'Could I ask you something?' he said.

'It depends,' said Docker. 'I certainly shan't tell you where the money's hidden.' Like Kenny, Docker had a strong Leeds accent.

'I'd a bit of aggro this morning,' said Stephen quietly.

'Did you?'

'One was skinny and the other had ears a mile wide,' he said.

'Really,' said Docker, his tone was absolutely neutral. Until this moment Stephen had assumed that Docker, who was powerful and strong unlike, say, Manny, would give him their names because he wouldn't be frightened. Now he wasn't so sure. Perhaps Docker would not be helpful in the way Stephen needed. Perhaps, contrary to what he believed, the pair on the landing frightened Docker, or had friends who frightened him. Still, he'd started, Stephen thought, so he may as well continue. What was the worst that could happen? He didn't get an answer. It wasn't the end of the world.

'This morning,' he said, 'who were those jokers outside recess? You know, the ones mouthing off.'

A prisoner passed, heading for the dinner hall. Docker gave the man a nod and the man nodded back. They walked on. When was he going to answer him? Stephen wondered. He decided to push it a bit.

'They must be on our landing,' said Stephen. 'I'll find their cells. I'll look at their door cards.' The cards above their cell doors would show their names. 'I can find out for myself, Docker. Don't worry.' He was shaming him.

'Do you want to have breakfast in my cell?' said Docker.

Stephen nodded.

'Yeah, let's,' said Docker, his tone now breezy and affable.

They climbed the stairs in silence and, as he went, Stephen wondered about his shoulder. Was there a silvery trace of snot on his prison-issue blue shirt? He had been insulted. He would have to pay back the pair who had done it.

Their landing, when they arrived, was empty. They filed along, Docker leading and turned into the older man's cell.

'You're the guest, so you can have the chair,' said Docker.

Stephen sat and put his cereal bowl and plate of toast on the little table. Docker did likewise and sat on the bed. 'You want to know the names of those clowns?' he said.

Stephen nodded.

Docker took his cereal bowl in his left hand, clamped a spoon between his thumb and the palm of his fingerless hand, lifted a spoon of cornflakes into his mouth and began to chew.

'Always work together, them two, and neither would have the gumption to do anything without the other to back him up. Cowards, obviously.'

'Aye,' said Stephen.

'But dangerous, don't forget that. There's always going to be one behind you when the other's talking to your face. That's how they work. They're sneaky.'

Docker took another mouthful. Even without his fingers he managed his spoon with aplomb.

'The pair are called Mitch and Huggy,' said Docker. 'Mitch is the little one.' Then he told Stephen the numbers of their cells and where they worked.

His cereal eaten, Docker buttered a piece of toast using the fingerless hand, the knife held between his thumb and his palm. When the butter was on, he added marmalade, of which he'd a dollop on the side of his plate. It was the tinned, horrible stuff that set the teeth on edge. Stephen never touched the stuff.

'What are they in for, Mitch and Huggy?' he said, reaching for his bowl and taking a first mouthful of cornflakes. They were soggy, having been standing in milk.

'They broke into an oil depot,' said Docker, 'to steal diesel and coshed the night watchman—I doubt he's worked since. Robbery with violence. Fucking amateurs.'

61

AFTER HE'D FINISHED BREAKFAST, STEPHEN JOINED
the detail for the carpenter's shop, where he'd been allocated
work. When he got to the workshop doors, he bent down and
undid his bootlaces. Then, as he filed in with the other
prisoners, he pretended to trip over.

'Oi,' the instructing officer shouted. 'You drunk?'

'My laces,' Stephen called back.

'Don't they teach you how to do them up in Ireland?'

There was weak laughter.

'Do them up. I don't want you tripping in here.'

He moved aside, out of the way of the men coming in. He
was now close to the trolley where the wood scraps went. The
prisoners, he'd noticed, chucked their scrap across the shop at
it, and often the off-cuts went underneath. He slid a hand in,
felt around and brought out a nice piece of dowel about the
width of his palm. That would be his handle. He stuck it
down his sock on the inside of his ankle where it was less
likely to be found when he was rubbed down, then finished
tying his laces and stood up.

'Listen up,' said the instructing officer, banging a mallet on
a bench to get everyone's attention. 'Good morning.'

'Good morning, Mr Jones,' the prisoners chanted back.

'Here are today's instructions ... '

At the end of the morning Jones banged his mallet and
shouted, 'I want a volunteer to sweep up.' The orderly who
usually did the job was at the dentist. Stephen put his hand
up.

'Right, all of you can fuck off except for the volunteer.'

Sweeping the floor, Stephen saw a long nail with the head
missing. He couldn't pick it up in front of Jones so he swept

it up with everything else. Then he tipped the dustpan into the rubbish drum and dropped it.

'I dropped the pan.'

Jones waved. 'Just get it out,' he said.

He reached in, felt around and found the nail. It was about four inches long. He put it into his right hand and folded his fingers around it. Sometimes the officers were so busy trying to be clever when it came to prisoners hiding weapons that they missed the obvious. That was his theory at any rate, and in the event, he was proved right. The officer who rubbed him down on the way back to his landing missed the nail and the dowel in his sock.

After lunch, during lock-down, he made a hole halfway along the dowel. Then he shoved the nail's sharp end into it and banged the head end on the floor, coughing to cover the sound. After several minutes he had got the nail right through. He now had something that looked like an old-fashioned corkscrew, except that instead of a spiral there was a nail. With the dowel in his palm, the nail could stick out between his middle and ring fingers. When he punched with this, he would hurt. To carry it he would hold it so the nail rested against the inside of his hand and wrist. He could bring it into play with a flick of the wrist.

Lying back on his bed, practising the flick, he thought about Mitch and Huggy. They're vicious, vile, hateful, he repeated over and over again. Then he thought about his father and Mr Purdue. A rage filled him.

At last, it was time for afternoon unlock. Keys jangled outside. He had his weapon in his hand, nail lying snug to his wrist. Come on, come on, he thought, unlock my door. There was nothing in his head except that he would get Mitch and Huggy.

Finally, the door swung open.

'What is it? Can't wait to get to work?' said the officer as he shot out.

He looked down the landing. He saw Mitch and Huggy where they'd stood that morning. The only difference this afternoon was that their backs were turned. He wanted to run down and do them straight away. But that would have meant scooting round the prisoners in front of him who were filing along the landing towards the stairs. If he jostled them, they might shout, which would alert Mitch and Huggy. Softly, softly was how he had to go and if he was lucky, by the time he got to the end, they'd still have their backs to him.

He walked forward. He could feel his heart going. He was going to wipe the smiles off their faces. He got closer. When there were just two prisoners—Docker and a man he didn't know—between them and him, he made his move.

He rolled the dowel to bring the nail between his middle and ring fingers, pushed Docker and the other prisoner sideways and got up to them. Huggy, the bigger one, was closest to him. Huggy sensed him coming and instinctively put up his hand as Stephen launched himself at the man's neck. He caught the hand and the nail punched right though Huggy's palm. Stephen felt the point skim past bones and sinews. Huggy screamed. Some prisoners behind, seeing something was happening, jeered and shouted.

He pulled the nail out of Huggy's hand and, as it came away, blood spurted. Mitch was making for the stairs.

Stephen got his foot out and tripped him. Out of the corner of his eye, Stephen could see Huggy holding his hand, blood on his shirt. With Mitch down, he had time to hurt the bigger man again before he hurt the smaller fellow. In one seamless movement he scraped the nail down the side of Huggy's head, catching his ear, then turned and pushed the nail into Mitch's calf until he felt the back of the shinbone. Then he pulled the nail, moved the point and pushed again, only this time Mitch's hand got in the way and he couldn't get the nail as far in as before.

The bell was ringing—it had been going for a while but it was only now that he became aware of it. He heard boots on the stairs as officers scrambled up towards him. He pulled out the nail and registered that his knuckle and cuff were wet. He looked back along the landing towards his cell. There were officers coming that way too but the prisoners were obstructing them. It was heartwarming but they couldn't postpone the inevitable. Soon he'd be collared.

'Give me the weapon,' he heard. It was Docker. Stephen threw it to him and Docker closed his good hand round it, hiding it as Stephen had. Then Stephen vaulted over Mitch and ran down the stairs. Two officers were coming the other way. One smacked him across the side of the head with his baton, a hard blow. He fainted.

62

HE WAS TAKEN STRAIGHT TO THE punishment block and charged. At the adjudication the next day, he denied using a weapon and insisted he'd inflicted the wounds with his nails and teeth. He wasn't believed, but without the weapon, he couldn't be charged with possession, only with assault, which carried a lesser tariff. He got four weeks on the boards, four weeks' loss of remission. Mitch and Huggy, though they protested their innocence, got the same but they couldn't start in the punishment block immediately. They were in the hospital.

Stephen started his sentence with three days' dry bread and water. He had no books except the Bible. Hunger and boredom separately are bad but when they come paired they make each other worse. At the end of the first day, he begged the dinner orderly to bring him something to read.

The next morning the orderly winked at him. 'Good morrow, and how are we, sir?' he said, in a cod actor's accent. Malcolm was an ex-soldier from Manchester whose wife had reported him for indecently assaulting their two daughters. He'd been charged, secured bail and moved into a hostel to await his trail. One night, very drunk, he'd set the family home on fire when his wife and daughters were asleep inside. A neighbour, seeing smoke, raised the alarm and got everyone out. Malcolm was doing six years for the indecent assaults plus eight for the arson and attempted murder, the two running concurrently. 'We trust you slept well?' he continued.

'Oh, fuck,' said the officer who had unlocked the door, a Glaswegian called Sunny Bill. 'We're not in a theatre here, you know.'

Sunny Bill darted away to the next cell and unlocked it. Malcolm produced a newspaper from the bottom tier of his food trolley. Stephen took it and hid it under his mattress. Sunny Bill came back.

'Come on,' he said. 'Stop admiring each other and get on with it.'

Stephen took his jug of water and plate of bread from the orderly.

'Hope you enjoy that, Paddy,' said Malcolm.

'Come on, move it,' said the officer. 'There's hungry men waiting for their breakfast.'

Sunny Bill reached for the door, then stopped. 'Hang on,' he said. 'I've got something to say to you.' Stephen looked into Sunny Bill's face. He felt apprehensive but hoped it didn't show.

'Those two you had your spat with.'

Stephen nodded.

'Well, they've been in the hospital and they've been put back together again and they're coming in here today to start their punishment. It's unlikely you and they will cross paths in here, but if you do and you try any more funny stuff, I'll kill you. Is that clear?'

'Yes,' said Stephen quietly.

'Good. I like a nice obedient Paddy.'

He slammed the door and turned the key.

Stephen sat and waited. He heard the orderly and the officer as they made their way down the wing. When he couldn't hear their footfalls or the trolley's squeaking wheels any more, he got out the paper. It was a *Daily Mirror*, dog-eared, grubby and five days old. Chewing his bread, he started reading at the top left-hand corner on the front page and went forward slowly. On page five, he saw the headline ULSTER BOMB SHOCKER. The accompanying photograph showed burning buildings and billowing smoke. Passport-sized photographs of the dead were arranged round the edge.

He was familiar with such articles. They always followed the same pattern. First, there was a description of where the bomb had been left, its likely weight, and other technical information. Then came a list of who had been killed and their relatives' reactions and at the end of the article there were invariably responses from local politicians and clergymen. These were always critical: the bombers had no mandate; the bombers had shown a callous disregard for human life; the bombers would achieve nothing in a democratic society by the use of violence. Stephen felt disappointed: he'd much rather have had something about an adulterous vicar.

He started reading anyway. It was all he had. The opening paragraphs described the time the car had been abandoned, the coded warning telephoned to the BBC in Belfast, the frantic attempts by the police to clear the street. So far, so predictable. Then, he came to the names of the injured and the dead, among them, "Donald Purdue (55), respected teacher from Mulberry House School".

He stopped. Purdue, Mulberry House, it couldn't be. He read it again.

Still he felt it couldn't be true. He had to have got it wrong. Or there was a mistake. He let his gaze roll up the page, cross the photograph of a street full of glass, mangled signage, smoking cars, and come to rest on the passport-sized photograph, captioned DONALD PURDUE. It was a small black-and-white image, a bit smudged, and showed a man with short dark hair wearing a tie. Was that Purdue? He was young and the man he had known was middle-aged and had white hair. But then he saw that this was the man he had known. The face staring up at him was unmistakably a younger version of Purdue.

He threw down the paper and began to pace up and down his cell. He felt a queer trembling sensation he couldn't identify. It wasn't joy and it wasn't relief. It must be shock, he decided. He went on pacing, waiting to see what else he would feel.

He read the article again. He resumed walking. He read it a third time. Then, abruptly, tears were sheeting down his cheeks. They fell down his front and spattered the cell floor for several minutes and then, as mysteriously as they'd started, they stopped. He felt exhausted. He lay down and fell asleep.

It was evening. The key turned in the lock and the cell door swung open. Stephen was in the doorway facing Malcolm. Sunny Bill was at the next cell, turning the key in the lock.

'I really enjoyed my breakfast,' he said, 'and I wonder if you've got anything smaller but longer.'

The next morning, when Sunny Bill wasn't looking, Malcolm handed him a tattered paperback of *The Loneliness of the Long Distance Runner* by Alan Sillitoe. He read it through the day. The account of a Borstal boy who wouldn't bend to the system was thrilling.

The following day was his fourth on the boards. He was back on a normal diet and was allowed books. He got writing paper and envelopes, a Biro and stamps, too.

Although it had disappeared when he was arrested, he hadn't forgotten Rosemary's letter. He should write to her, he thought. He sat on his bed, spread a sheet of paper on the newspaper, which he still had, and picked up the Biro. But what should he say? Did he tell her where he was? He'd have to. The letter would be stamped CENSORED along with the name of the jail.

He got up and walked round the cell. But he didn't want her to know he was in jail. No. He didn't want to have to explain how he'd come to be there, either. Nor did he want to make promises about the future as he would feel obliged to if he wrote to her.

He saw Rosemary in the lounge at her parent's house, sitting beside the fish tank as she waited for the postman to clip down the path to the front door with a letter from Stephen. He saw her running to the door but there was no letter. He saw her in her work coat, her bare legs goose pimpled, walking through the factory gates with her arms crossed and her eyes red because no letter had come.

It was cruel not to write. He could see that. It was cruel leaving her not knowing what had happened. He could see that too. He wouldn't like it if it were the other way round.

But could he be certain she didn't know anything? His uncle Sean must have sent a message to his mother by now. He must have told her that Stephen had stolen and that he had left the house. And when Rosemary didn't hear from him, she would go to his mother and ask about him. He could be certain of that as well.

However, his mother wouldn't retell his whole story. She'd leave out the stealing. But she'd tell Rosemary he'd left his uncle Sean's. She'd venture that that was why he'd not responded to Rosemary's letter. She might even say he'd probably not got her letter because it had arrived after he left his uncle's.

As for where he was now, his mother would say she had no idea, which was the truth. She would offer this information to Rosemary in the belief that it would comfort her.

Of course, once Rosemary knew he'd vanished, she'd assume he was in prison. In which case, why write to tell her?

At this point his thinking changed. What would writing achieve besides telling her he was in HMP Kingsman? It would make her keen. It would raise her hopes. It would make her believe their relationship had a future. And that was wrong.

It wasn't that he didn't like her. Or even love her. But he was a criminal with a record. There was no way she could come to England when he was released and be with him. And there was no way he could go back to Crookedstone and be with her.

It was best not to reply. Let her imagine he had abandoned her, found another woman, whatever she wanted to think. First, she would be hurt, later she would be angry but then, finally, when she'd met someone else, a decent man who had no record, who would marry and support her, she would be grateful. She would thank him too, later, for not having kept her but for letting her go so she could have a proper life.

Yes, he decided. He would not reply and she would go her own way. She was better off without him. He put the writing-paper away.

He spent the rest of his time in the punishment block reading. The orderly brought him two or three books each morning; they were mostly thrillers by writers like Hammond Innes and Mickey Spillane. Out of all the writers that he read, he liked Eric Ambler best.

63

WHEN THE FOUR WEEKS WERE UP, he was put back into his old cell. The first association he had he went to find Docker. He wanted to thank the man for taking the weapon and saving him from a longer sentence.

He found him playing ping-pong. Docker held the bat with just his thumb. Despite his disability and bulk, he was a considerable player.

The game over, Docker said to his opponent, 'Got to talk to this man here.'

'No worries.'

'Let's go over there,' Docker said to Stephen.

They went to the wall of the Recreation room and leaned against the cream-painted brickwork.

'I owe you,' said Stephen.

'Yeah, you do,' Docker said jovially.

A new game of ping-pong started. They watched the ball fly back and forth over the green mesh net.

Docker turned to Stephen. 'Do you play?'

'No.'

'You should try. Good game. Gets all your aggression out without you having to hurt anyone.'

The man Docker had been playing volleyed the ball over the net. It struck the tabletop, then flew high into the air beyond his opponent's reach.

'Good shot,' said Docker.

'I'll give it a try,' said Stephen.

Docker turned to the wall and Stephen did the same. He was indebted and he didn't know what he was about to be asked.

'Now, listen to me, and listen good,' Docker began. 'You know I'm an orderly in the hospital.'

Stephen didn't but he nodded anyway.

'I'm excused heavy work on account of my hand.'

Docker touched the flesh where his fingers had once been.

'So, when you started on the boards, Mitch and Huggy were in the hospital, being patched up.'

'Yeah,' said Stephen.

'And we had a talk, me and them two.'

He didn't like the sound of this at all.

'They're arseholes and they can't help it,' said Docker, 'but don't you be an arsehole too. It's not worth it. When they come back tomorrow, you'll shake hands, forget any of this ever happened, and so will they.'

'Oh.' Stephen couldn't hide his disappointment.

'You probably want to have another pop at them, don't you?' said Docker.

Stephen couldn't deny it.

'You might win. You might not. But say you put them in hospital again. For a few months you'll be Mr Hard Nut, the mad Paddy who done Mitch and Huggy. But you won't stay at the top. Someone'll push you off your perch because someone always comes along who's harder than you. It's a rule of life. You can't win for ever so don't try it. You got your result, now leave it. Walk away.'

Stephen saw that he couldn't refuse. It wasn't an option. He was grateful too. This had to be better than fighting a vendetta. But he had a question he wanted Docker to answer before he agreed.

'Why?' he asked.

'Why what?'

'Why are you helping me?'

'Why not?'

In the pause that followed, he heard the cries of the prisoners dotted about the recreation room.

'My old man was a Kerryman,' Docker continued. 'Funny accent, you know how they talk, and when he went to jail he had a hard old time until someone took him under his wing. A bloke from the East End, as it happened. Anyhow, after that Dad always tried to do the same, when he was in jail. He was a thief and that, but he had his principles. "If someone does you a favour," he used to say, "pass it on." I've never forgotten it. So what I'm telling you is, you ain't going to win, so walk away and don't think about losing face because you won't. It's sorted. Mitch and Huggy want this finished too.'

'Right,' said Stephen, and with that their agreement was sealed.

The next day Mitch and Huggy returned to the wing. Mitch was still limping and the hair on the side of Huggy's head, where it had been shaved so the wound could be stitched, had still not grown back. During association Stephen went straight up to them and said, 'No hard feelings, I hope.'

The three shook hands silently and never spoke again. For the rest of their time in jail, they were like ghosts in each other's lives.

64

HAVING STARTED READING IN THE PUNISHMENT block, Stephen went on reading back on the wing. Now he could pick the books he wanted from the library. He was desperate to cram his head with words.

A couple of months later, during evening association, he was reading, as usual when a hand wrenched away his book. He looked up and saw an older prisoner, Higgins, a bank robber. He had a mug in the other hand. Stephen was worried about what might be in it, and that it might be dashed in his face, but he couldn't jump up and move away. If Higgins wasn't hostile and he moved, he'd look weak and foolish.

'What are you reading?' asked Higgins. 'Oh,' he said, in a cod camp voice, '*The Pursuit of Love* by ... who's this ... Wanky Mitford?'

'Nancy,' said Stephen, standing. Some wag had altered the name with a Biro to Wanky.

'Nancy, right,' said Higgins. He had a long face and his jowls trembled as he spoke. 'And what sort of a book is it?'

'It's about three sisters—'

'Is it saucy?' interrupted Higgins. 'I fancy a wank later but at my age I need something to start me up. Will it do the business?'

From across the hall, a voice shouted, 'What is it?'

Higgins turned to the far wall where two men were smoking. Stephen recognised them as Higgins's cronies. The speaker, Joe was a sharp-nosed man who had killed a stranger in a pub with a bar stool. He was doing eight years for manslaughter.

'It's *The Pursuit of Love* by Nank someone or other,' Higgins called back.

'Nank, what sort of a name is that?' shouted Joe.

'It's the name of a Nanky boy,' shouted the second, then roared with laughter. This was Amiable Andy. His wife Barbara had famously bad teeth. When he discovered she was having an affair, he'd instructed her dentist to remove them all on the pretext they couldn't be saved. And if the dentist didn't, Amiable said he'd hurt him, his children and his mother. The dentist did as he was told. The lover deserted the toothless Barbara and so did Amiable. He was currently doing ten years for armed robbery.

'Here.' Higgins handed the book back to Stephen. 'What is it then?'

'What?

'Your name?'

'Stephen.'

'That's queer, mate. It's a well-known fact, honest—if you're called Stephen, or Steve, or Stevie, you're a poof. Stevie, it's a poof's name. Are you a poof?'

'No.'

'So why are you called Stephen?'

'My parents—'

'Oh, stop it.' Higgins waved his hand and cut Stephen short. 'What you need is something short and strong. What's it to be?'

Stephen remembered his father's advice, 'Whatever you do, say nothing,' and looked away.

'It's staring us in the face, mate,' said Higgins. 'It's Nank. That's a great name, strong, masculine, and not in the least bit queer. Yeah, Nank, good ring to it, don't you think? Nank like Hank.' Higgins laughed. 'Yeah, that's good. From here on in, you're Nank.'

He stuck his finger into his mug and made a cross on Stephen's forehead in what turned out to be tea. 'I hereby christen you Nank.' He shouted, 'Oi! I just christened this nice boy, Nank.'

'Nice Boy Nank,' jeered Joe and Andy, stamping their feet and clapping.

Then Higgins emptied the slops in his mug over Stephen's head and strolled back to his grinning friends.

Over the days that followed the new moniker chased after him, along the draughty wings, under the streaming shower heads, across the echoing dinner hall, and even into his hard bed when he crept under the brown hairy blankets that smelt of mothballs and sweat.

At first, he refused to answer to it. Then, one day the thought came, unexpected yet unanswerable. In HMP Kingsman he was growing into the proper criminal he guessed he was supposed to become, and as he was a new person, it was right to have a new name. Back home in Tyrone, a local Protestant sect, who practised adult baptism, always gave initiates a new name when they were received into the Church. When a nun took her vows, she got a new name too, the name under which she was married to Christ. Well, when Higgins had splashed the tea on his head, it had been a baptism. He would take this new name.

65

DOCKER AND NANK LEFT HMP KINGSMAN within a few days of one another at the end of March 1976. Outside they kept in touch. A few weeks later Docker had fifty kilos of hash in Rotterdam that he wanted in Southend. Nank agreed to drive it across. He phoned his mother.

'Where are you?' she asked, sounding aggrieved. 'Where have you been?'

'Here and there,' he replied. Then he continued, speaking quickly, 'I've been that busy with one thing and another. Sorry you haven't heard from me.'

'Oh,' was all she said now. It was hard to tell if she believed him or if she knew he had been in jail but had decided to say nothing. She might know, though how she would have found out he had no idea. Still, he was relieved that she wasn't saying anything about it. It made everything easier.

'I've a surprise for you,' he said, his tone jaunty. He wanted to take her to the Netherlands, he explained. His mother accepted.

A few days later he flew her from Ireland and together they travelled to Holland in a white van. Nank told his mother it was borrowed from his employers, a fictitious firm of plumbers. They had two wonderful days in Rotterdam.

The smuggling part of the journey, the return leg, was uneventful. Mother took it upon herself to tell everyone who would listen, including the Customs officers at Harwich, that her adorable son had just taken his poor old Irish mother on a wonderful Dutch holiday. The officers smiled and waved them through, the Irish boy and his garrulous mother. Of course, Mrs Melanophy had no idea what was hidden in the van's panels. Nank got five grand for his trouble. He bought his mother a coat at Harrods before he put her on the plane for Belfast.

The Dutch run was the start of a close relationship between Docker and Nank. It deepened when Docker began to sell to dealers on the north side of Dublin and moved to Redhills in Co. Cavan. It was, he said, a good place from which to conduct his business because the police there hadn't a clue. Nank, now twenty-two, became his regular courier. In 1978, the year Docker moved to Redhills, Nank went to Britain three times and the continent once and came back with heroin, cocaine and marijuana. In 1979 Nank made five trips, and in 1980, seven.

All this work generated cash.

One day, just before Christmas in 1980, Docker said to him, 'Why don't you buy a house or a shop or something?'

'Why would I do that?' He lived at home, except when he was away on business. His mother fed him, washed his clothes and didn't ask questions when he disappeared, sometimes for weeks, even months at a time. 'It would just be a hassle.'

'If it's a house, you have a letting agent. They get the tenants, they sort everything out. If it's a shop, you get a manager. You don't have to do anything.'

Nank was puzzled. 'But I won't make any money.'

'Exactly. The object is to use the money you've got. You make your money when you sell your asset.'

Early in 1981, Nank noticed an advertisement in the property section of the *Tyrone Constitution*. The executors of the estate of Mrs Edith Duggan were selling a shop-cum-garage: it had a few petrol pumps and came with a two-storey dwelling house attached. The property was at Grange Cross, five miles outside Crookedstone and two hundred yards from the border between Tyrone and Donegal, just inside Northern Ireland. Nank bought the property and leased the shop. For a moment he toyed with the idea of living in the house, but then he decided he preferred living with his mother. He would leave it empty for a while.

66

IN THE SUMMER NANK WENT TO the South of France. He had to collect a consignment of heroin from Marseille, drive it across the Italian border and leave it at an address in Turin. When he arrived he called his connection from the airport and was told to wait a couple of days.

He took a taxi to the centre of Marseille, got out and walked around. He chose a hotel with two stars on the brass sign beside the glass double doors. He didn't want to look like someone who had money to spend. He didn't want to attract attention.

His room was square and white. There was a pine wardrobe that smelt of blanket on account of the spare one on the shelf, and a small dark windowless bathroom. There was a balcony too. From here he could see, over the roofs of apartment blocks and houses, all the way to the harbour. On his first night he heard ships' hooters in the distance as he fell asleep.

The next morning he went to a museum filled with everything connected to the sea. He spent the rest of the day in a café and read an entire Robert Ludlum novel. In the evening he felt lonely. He went back to the hotel, where he found a dark-skinned man behind the desk in the lobby.

'Do you speak English?'

The man nodded. Nank started to explain. He was interested in female company, he said, and he wondered where in Marseille he might go to find it. The dark-skinned man looked blankly at him. Nank had his inspiration.

'Masseuse,' he said, and with his hands he kneaded the counter.

The dark-skinned man opened a drawer, took out a card and gave it to him. HEIDI, SWEDISH MASSAGE, HOME VISITS, and a telephone number. Bingo. He rang her number. She agreed to come that evening at eleven.

She arrived fifteen minutes late. She was a small plump girl with coarse red hair and dark holes in her lobes but no ear-rings. She explained her terms in poor English. He paid. She undressed, showered and got into his bed. He got in beside her. They had sex. She made no attempt to get up and dress. He drifted into sleep.

A few minutes later he came to. He could hear Heidi moving about near his clothes. He half opened one eye. She was pulling notes out of his wallet. He had twelve thousand pounds in fifty-pound notes and four thousand francs.

He lifted the covers off quietly. She heard him and turned. He sprang up, swung his arm and struck her cheek. Heidi gave a cry of surprise and pain. The wallet fell and notes flew. He was aware of them swirling in the air, some red, some blue.

She sank down on the floor and pulled her lower lip forward. There was a nasty cut where the soft skin inside her mouth had split.

'What the fuck were you doing with my wallet?' he said.

She started to cry. 'Pick up the money,' he said.

She got onto her hands and knees and began to move around the floor collecting the notes, crying quietly and occasionally pressing the heel of a hand to her eyes or mouth.

Eventually she stood up and handed it to him. Her breasts were small and pointed. He counted the money and as he did so he thought, she probably had somebody waiting in the lobby. The next step in the sequence, inevitably, was that some burly so-and-so, or perhaps several burly so-and-sos, would use the fact that he had hit her as an excuse to take all his money off him. He couldn't let that happen but what should he do? Suddenly, he knew exactly. The thing was not to rush. That way lay fuck-ups.

He put everything back into the wallet except the same amount in francs as he'd already paid her. He handed her this money. 'Again,' he said.

'Again?'

'I want to have sex again.'

'Again?'

'Yes.'

She looked doubtful, then reached out to touch him.

'Hang on.' He looked at her face. 'You need to do something about that lip.' He pointed at the bathroom door. 'Let me get something from the bathroom for you.'

She nodded to show she had understood, then sat down on the bed, holding the money he had just given her.

He got some toilet paper and his sponge-bag from the bathroom. She pulled her lip down and began to dab, with

the paper he gave her, at the blood that had pooled behind
and stained her teeth.

Nank got his holdall from the wardrobe, threw in his
sponge-bag and piled his spare clothes on top.

She watched him shrewdly, then got up and went towards
her clothes. She never reached them. He got between her and
the chair where they were piled. 'I said sex again,' he said. 'I
paid.'

'Are you going to hurt me?'

He shook his head. 'Go on, wait for me in bed,' he said.

She got back in bed, still holding the money, and pulled the
covers up to her chin.

He packed his bag. When that was done he dressed, then
went to the chair where her things were. He took
everything, including her shoes and bag, and put them into
the holdall and zipped it shut. The first fee he'd paid was in
her bag, which he was taking and that was why he'd paid
her again (though she didn't know that yet): he didn't want
her complaining that he hadn't paid. He went to the phone
and ripped the wire out of the socket. Then, for good
measure, he snapped the cable between the cradle and the
handset. He didn't want her to call the desk either. Then he
went to the bathroom and gathered the towels. He went
back to the bedroom and dropped them onto the balcony
below. He pulled the curtains off the rail and they followed
the towels.

'Get up,' he said.

She got out of bed.

'Strip the bed. Throw it over the balcony.'

He mimed what he wanted her to do. She did as he said.
He looked around the room. It looked empty. Then he
remembered the spare blanket in the wardrobe. He fetched it

and dropped it, too, onto the balcony below. There was nothing left in the room for her to use. She'd have to wait until she heard someone in the corridor to call for help. That meant he had several minutes to get away.

He left and double-locked the door. He took the lift to the ground floor and stepped into the lobby. There were potted plants, a fountain and a strong smell of paint. In one corner a man sat on the leather sofa. He was young and had a goatee. He was reading a French paper. Her pimp, Nank thought. He was sure of it.

He went to the side of the counter and put down his bag where the pimp wouldn't see it. The dark-skinned man was gone, replaced by a young white man called Daniel, according to his name tag, who looked at him curiously.

'Yes?' he said.

Nank gave his room number and asked to settle. A bill was produced and he paid cash. The man with the goatee hadn't looked up.

He grabbed his holdall and crossed the lobby. As he went through the glass double doors, he was aware of the goatee standing and going to the desk.

He got to the pavement. He looked up and down. There were no taxis. He glanced over his shoulder. The goatee was crossing the lobby towards the doors. He swung his holdall onto his shoulder and started to run. He heard the goatee shouting something but he had no intention of stopping. He ran until he came to a square where taxis were parked in a line. He jumped into the one at the front. The driver was black. He said something in French.

'I want a hotel,' said Nank.

'Hotel,' the driver echoed in English.

He turned on the meter and eased out. Nank peered

through the back window. There was no sign of the goatee on the dark street.

Later, in his new hotel room, he examined Heidi's bag. Her name was Veronica and she was Maltese. She was studying textiles in Marseille.

Very early the next morning he took a walk. He found a huge municipal bin. He had Veronica's things in a plastic bag. He lifted the bin's lid, threw the bag inside and walked away.

67

NANK PLANNED TO BE AT HOME for a while and had bought a car. He invited Smiler, whom he'd met in HMP Kingsman, to come and stay. Smiler, who lived in Dublin, was supposed to drive up but his car broke down and he had to take the bus.

On Friday afternoon, Nank drove to the depot in Crookedstone to collect him. The first bus to roll in was from Omagh and he watched the passengers getting off. Suddenly he found himself looking at Rosemary, who gazed back at him. He decided he should say something and started to walk towards her but she shook her head, turned away and disappeared through the gate.

A few minutes later the Dublin bus came. Smiler got out, a tall gangling man with a shaved head and a gaunt face. 'Hello Nank,' he said. 'You look terrible.'

Nank didn't doubt it. His heart was racing. 'I just bumped into someone,' he said.

'A ghost from your past?'

'Old girlfriend.'

'They're the worst kind, always unfriendly. Did you dump her? Was she grumpy?'

'No, we never had a you're-dumped conversation. It was worse. I had a letter, got arrested, never wrote.'

'Oh dear,' said Smiler. 'Women don't like that. They'd rather be told. I'm surprised she didn't cut your balls off.'

They got into his car and Nank started to drive. 'I haven't told my mother about being in prison in England, okay.'

'Right,' said Smiler.

'So don't you tell her.'

'No problems mate. Not a word.'

They got to the house and went in. Smiler was introduced.

'Cup of tea?' offered Nank.

'Wouldn't say no, Nank,' Smiler said smoothly.

'What did you just call him?' asked his mother.

'Nank.'

'Nank.' She spoke the name as if she had something horrible in her mouth. 'Nank,' she said again. She looked into her son's eyes. 'What happened to the name I gave you, Stephen? Don't you like it any more?' She was hurt and troubled by what she'd heard. It was all in her voice. As he tried to think how he could explain, Smiler chipped in, 'But Nank's his new name.' He hadn't been told not to use it, only not to mention HMP Kingsman, so he assumed it was all right.

'Stephen, is that so?'

'Yes,' he said to his mother.

'Well, I can't say I like it. Nank ... it sounds like Hank or tank or something. I think Stephen's much nicer. '

After a long discussion a compromise emerged: she would go on calling him Stephen but friends like Smiler could use his new name.

68

ONE NIGHT STEPHEN TOOK SMILER TO Bundoran. They went to several pubs and, around ten, intending to have a last drink before they went to the disco in the Great Northern Hotel, they went into the saloon bar in Dorian's pub. It had a plain interior, mostly painted brown, a few benches and several mirrors advertising defunct brands of Irish whiskey. There was a grate full of ashes and cinders.

They reached the counter but there was no sign of anyone. Nank peered through the door to the public bar, hoping to catch sight of someone. 'Do you think they'd mind if we served ourselves?' he said.

'There might be a bit of disgruntlement.' The speaker was a woman. She stood a few feet along the bar from them. She was short, had brown wavy hair and looked to be in her twenties. Her eyes were brown and her face was long.

'"Disgruntlement", there's a word you don't hear often,' said Nank.

The woman was looking at him oddly. He wondered if he knew her.

'You don't recognise me, do you?' she said, moving closer.

The awful idea that he might have met her in court flashed across his mind. 'No,' he said carefully.

'But I know you,' she said.

'Does he owe you money?' said Smiler. 'Because if so, nobble him now while his wallet's full.'

'No,' she said. 'We used to be neighbours. Obviously, I made a huge impression.'

'Oh, yes,' said Nank.

Her father, Arthur, had had the farm on the other side of the road from theirs and sometimes he'd seen her sitting on her gate or cycling up and down her lane when he was a child but that was the extent of their contact. Her father had died a few years ago and the farm was sold—he remembered his mother telling him. The widow and Jenny, she was an only child, had moved away then.

'You're Jenny Wallace,' he said. 'You used to wear your hair in plaits with coloured ribbons. I remember that because no girl at my school did.' Jenny, of course, had gone to a different school from him because the Wallace family was Protestant.

'I don't wear plaits any more.' She smiled and her brown eyes shone. 'That's one good thing about being a grown-up.'

'And there are lots more, aren't there?' This was Smiler.

'Really?' she said.

'Well, sex for a start,' said Smiler. 'That's something you don't get to have until you're an adult.'

'Not everyone's that lucky,' said Nank.

'Oh, right enough,' said Smiler, 'but sex with a kiddy-fiddler doesn't count.'

'So,' Nank turned to Jenny, 'what happened after the farm was sold?'

'Me and Mum moved to Crookedstone, to a bungalow on the Omagh Road.'

'Are you still ... ?'

'Nosy, aren't we? Yeah, we are.'

'He's just a fellow who likes to know,' said Smiler.

'And I suppose you want to know what I do?'

'Why not?' said Nank.

'I'm in Dunbar's, the garage.'

'I fill up there,' said Nank. 'How come I don't ever see you?'

'I work for the manager,' she said, 'not on the forecourt. For the record, it's dull but the money's nice. Anything else?'

'Have you got a boyfriend?' said Smiler. 'Because I haven't got a girlfriend.'

She caught Nank's eye. 'No.'

'So,' said Nank, 'you're not here waiting on a twenty-stone Border Chief?'

That was the local biker gang, the Border Chiefs, and Bundoran was where they drank.

Jenny laughed. 'Certainly not.'

Smiler again: 'So how come a pretty girl like you ... ?'

'Is in a bar by herself?' said Jenny. 'I was with a hen party but it was so ... I don't know, I wasn't in the mood for it, so I left them to get on with it and came here.'

'Yes, folks.'

It was the barman, a plump man with spots of brown on his white shirt.

'Two pints of Guinness,' said Nank. 'And ... ' He turned to Jenny. He squinted at her glass. There was a finger of something brown in the bottom.

'What's yours?'

'Bacardi and Coke,' she said.

'Two pints and a Bacardi,' said the barman.

The drinks came and they each carried a glass to the table. As they sat down, Nank jogged his and Guinness slopped over the side to form a black puddle on the wood.

'Nice one, Nank.'

'What did you call him?' said Jenny.

'Nank. It's his name,' said Smiler. Then he put his hand to his mouth. 'Oh God mate, am I allowed to say?'

Nank shrugged. It was too late now.

'What did he call you?' Jenny addressed the question to Nank this time.

'Nank.'

'You used to be Stephen.'

'Yeah.'

'And now you're Nank?'

'Yeah.'

'Is it a nickname?'

'Yes,' said Nank.

'You're having me on.'

'It's true,' said Smiler.

'What sort of a name is it, anyway?'

'It's his name now.'

'And I suppose you've a funny name too?' Jenny addressed this question to Smiler.

'Yeah.'

'Go on, then,' she said. 'Make me laugh.'

'Smiler.'

'Why?'

'Because I'm always smiling—well, when I'm stoned.'

'So,' said Jenny, 'if he's Smiler because he smiles when he's off his head, why are you Nank?'

Smiler wriggled. 'I know but I won't say.'

'Are you going to tell me?' said Jenny.

'I'm trying to find the words.'

'You were in prison,' she said quietly.

Nank was astonished. 'What makes you say that?'

'I don't ... I'm just guessing ... Oh, all right, you were in Borstal. I heard that. And then you were in prison, weren't you?'

Smiler looked at Nank who was running his forefinger up and down the film of condensation that had formed on the outside of his glass.

Finally, he said, 'Yeah. And my mother still doesn't know.'

'I can keep a secret.'

There was something about her that made him believe he could trust her. 'I know.'

'So, this is what happens in jail, I suppose,' said Jenny. 'Everyone gets a new name, do they?'

'Not everyone,' said Nank.

'No,' agreed Smiler. 'Nearly everyone.'

'So what am I to call you, then?' said Jenny.

'Call him Nank,' said Smiler.

'Nank,' she said. She pursed her lips. 'Nank. What does your mother say?'

He shrugged.

'Nank,' she said. 'I suppose I'll get used to it. Don't they say you get used to anything?' She picked up her glass. 'Oh, well,' she said. 'Cheers Nank.' She clinked her glass against his, then Smiler's. 'You as well, big boy.'

'Hey, I'm a big boy, yeah,' said Smiler, snorting with laughter.

Everyone drank and put their glasses down.

'So, tell me then how you got your name,' said Jenny to Nank.

He explained how Higgins had caught him reading Nancy Mitford's *The Pursuit of Love* and how this had led to his new name. Then Jenny asked about prison, and the two men, careful not to mention the unhappiness, the loneliness and the occasional violence, told her several funny stories. Jenny laughed a lot, and every now and again Nank noticed her looking at him. He wondered if it was attraction, then dismissed the idea. They'd only just met, other than when they glimpsed one another when they were children. It wasn't possible.

But even as he thought this, desire and lust, affection and tenderness, which he had last felt with Rosemary, were flooding through him. It was incredible to think they had been hidden inside him waiting until now to be released.

Ever since Marseille he had been thinking he needed a girlfriend. Now it seemed he might have found one, or he hoped he had, anyway.

69

NANK AND JENNY BEGAN TO SEE one another. They went to pubs and to the cinema. They went for walks by the sea. One night he went to her bungalow to watch television and to meet her mother, an old woman with liver spots on her hands and fine white hair with a purple tinge.

At the end of the evening Jenny went out with him to the front-door step to say goodbye.

'Listen,' he said, 'there's a nice hotel outside Donegal Town, the Pear Tree.'

She nodded. She had been there for lunch, she said, with her mother one Sunday. 'It's a bit grand,' she said. The waiters had called her and her mother madam, she added, and in between courses they had swept the crumbs off the table with a special pan and brush.

'I thought we could go there next weekend.'

'For lunch?'

'I thought we could stay. For a couple of nights.' He looked at her carefully. All the signs he'd been getting pointed to her willingness to go to bed with him. He thought she would say yes. He hoped she would. He expected she would. But she said nothing, just looked back at him, not blinking. Perhaps he had read her wrong.

She shut the front door and stepped closer to him. 'The thing is,' she said, her voice almost a whisper, 'what do I say to my mother?'

Ah, yes, he thought, he should have thought of that. Jenny's mother monitored all her comings and goings. Of course that would be a problem. But it hadn't occurred to him—well, it wouldn't: his mother exercised no control over him. He came and went as he pleased.

'What's she going to do if she finds out?' he said. 'Throw you out? What about the truth?' It was bold but sometimes that was best.

'Oh, no—no! That won't do with my mother.'

There was another pause. Jenny was thinking. He could see it on her face. She saw him watching her and smiled, the brown eyes shining most beautifully. 'Oh, well,' she continued, 'I'll just have to lie.'

That she was prepared to do that for him made him feel warm and gave him a sense of unexpected certainty. This wasn't just a relationship, he thought suddenly. It had the makings of something deeper and more long-lasting. The idea of marriage came into his head. He thought about it for an instant, weighted it—it felt good—and put it aside. He was getting ahead of himself. One thing at a time. First, they'd go away. Later on, when he'd seen how things panned out, he could think again.

70

THE FOLLOWING FRIDAY HE MET HER at the bus depot. She put her bag into the boot of the car and got into the front seat.

'Hello,' he said.

'Of all the sodding things to happen,' she said, then fell silent.

He drove towards the gate and indicated right. The ticking sound, which normally he never noticed, filled the interior. He wondered what the problem was? Had her mother found out and tried to stop her going? Perhaps she had thrown her out. It crossed his mind that he might have to take her to his own home. He tried to imagine how his mother would react if he turned up with Jenny on Sunday night. He pictured the scene, his mother on the car seat by the range, himself and Jenny standing in the middle of the floor under the light. 'This is Jenny. Can we put her in the spare room?' He saw his mother shrug and get up to make tea. She'd probably just accept it, he thought.

He drove out onto the Donegal Town road.

'My period's just started,' she said.

'And there I was thinking something serious had happened,' he said, and began to laugh. The laughter came from deep down.

That night in the Pear Tree, Jenny came to bed with her knickers on. The following weekend he insisted they went back to the Pear Tree and this time they made love on rough linen sheets. On the Sunday evening he drove her back to the bus depot from where she would ring for a taxi to take her home.

He parked close to the phone box. 'Have you change?'

She nodded.

'Ring them and you can sit in the car until they come.'

She made the call. As she got back in beside him she said, 'Ten minutes.'

'Fair enough.' He felt tired, stretched and happy.

'Are you doing anything?' she said.

'What?'

'Next Monday-Tuesday-Wednesday-Thursday-Friday-Saturday-Sunday? Next month? Next year?' She paused. 'When am I going to see you again?'

It was, he realised suddenly, a declaration of love, or infatuation mixed with love. He also knew for certain that the answer he was about to give, the only answer he had, would disappoint her horribly. He'd made a mistake in not telling her before and now he would have to pay for it.

'I have to go to England,' he said quietly.

The atmosphere changed.

'I have to go to England,' he said again. 'Tomorrow.'

Her eyes looked wet and he thought she was going to cry. Her mouth had shrunk, and he knew she was angry.

'When?' she said.

'Tomorrow.'

'Why didn't you tell me?'

'I didn't want it hanging over the weekend and spoiling it.'

'So you've had your fun, and now you're pissing off.'

'It's just for a few days.'

She rolled her lips, which had lipstick on them. 'Are you going there for work?'

He was. He had to go to Leeds, pick up a consignment of hash and drive it back to Docker in Redhills. He wouldn't be telling her any of that, of course, so he simply said, 'Yeah.'

Jenny sighed and he knew for certain she was going to cry. His last admission was the trigger. Her eyes filled, then tears rolled down her cheeks. He thought he had a tissue in his pocket and reached to find it.

'I can wipe my own tears,' she said.

'Fair enough.'

He took his hand away from his pocket and straightened up. 'It's just for a few days,' he said, 'and like I said, I didn't tell you because I thought it would spoil the weekend.'

She said nothing so he felt he had no alternative but to carry on. The silence was awful. 'I should be back by the end of the week. Friday morning.' He said this in his most confident tone.

'Are you going to do something stupid and get arrested?'

'No.'

'But you are going to do something stupid, aren't you?'

'No.'

'So what are you doing?'

'I can't tell you.'

'You're going to go over, get arrested and I'll never hear from you again.'

'That won't happen.'

The taxi pulled up beside them and the driver honked to attract their attention.

'I have to work. I have to have money.' The implication was that it had paid for the Pear Tree but he wasn't going to say that in case it made her even angrier.

'Well, so long,' she said.

They both got out. He took her bag from the boot and put it into the taxi's boot and she got into the taxi and closed the door. He went to the door and opened it.

'Not saying goodbye?'

'Goodbye,' she said, in a low dull voice.

He closed the door. The taxi reversed and went across the

depot forecourt towards the gate. He stared after it, hoping she would relent and wave goodbye, but her head, which he could see through the taxi's rear windscreen, didn't move.

71

HE GOT BACK TO CROOKEDSTONE FROM Leeds very early on Friday morning. He drove straight to Jenny's bungalow. He parked outside, let his seat back as far as it would go and went to sleep.

He was woken by the sound of knuckles rapping on glass. He opened his eyes. He opened the door and Jenny threw her arms around his neck and kissed him. Her tongue was warm and tasted of tea. 'Come on, I'll drive you to work,' he said.

She circled the car and climbed into the front passenger seat. He started the engine.

'I haven't been able to stop thinking about you,' she said.

'Nice thoughts?'

'What do you think?'

'I should have said,' Nank said quietly, 'not kept it back that I was going away.'

'Hindsight's a fine thing ... '

'Isn't it?'

' ... my daddy always said,' she continued, finishing her sentence.

He wondered if she was busy that evening. He wondered if she might like to do something. He had money. Perhaps they could go to Dublin.

'Listen,' she said.

'I'm listening.'

'Can we have an understanding?'

'Depends what you're offering.'

'No, this isn't a joke. This is serious.'

'Oh, it's serious.'

'If you ... ' She stopped.

'Go on.'

'My parents,' she said.

He wondered where this was going. 'Your parents?' he said.

'They were happy.'

'Yes.'

'Because they talked, all the time, they discussed everything—well, not everything, obviously, but all the important things, the things that mattered. You know, if money had to be spent, big things. "We have some little secrets but no big ones" was what my daddy said. It was the secret of their success.'

'Yes, and what?' he said. 'Is this—'

'Yes,' she interrupted. 'Just tell me what you're doing, and if not what, then tell me when, so I have a fair idea at least of when I should be worrying about you. Just tell me as much as you can. That's the secret that'll make this work.'

'Little secrets allowed but no big ones,' he said.

'Exactly.'

'Okay,' he said.

Her hand came over and squeezed his, which was holding the steering-wheel. 'So that's a deal, is it?'

'That's a deal.'

They reached the garage where Jenny worked. He drove round to the back where the office entrance was.

'Let's go away,' she said. 'Tonight.'

'Dublin?'

'Yeah.'

'Shall I meet you at the bus depot?'

'No,' she said. 'Come to the house say at six and pick me up.'

'What about your mother?'

'She'll have to get used to us,' said Jenny, 'so she may as well start sooner rather than later.'

She kissed him, got out and closed the door. He watched her walk towards the entrance. She waved again and disappeared.

72

IT WAS A SUMMER'S EVENING WHEN Nank and Jenny went to Grange Cross. The shop's tenant waved through the window as Nank drove across the forecourt and he waved back. Then he turned down the side, went along a short lane and stopped at the end near the nice stone house with the small windows and the black front door.

He took the heavy old key from the glove compartment. They got out, and he opened the door. He pushed it back with difficulty because the floor behind was piled with circulars and old letters. They walked down the hallway, which had wooden panels painted brown, and into the kitchen at the end.

This was a big square room with windows that overlooked the yard at the back. There was a range, its doors hanging open. The room smelled of fly-papers and coal dust. There were three more rooms downstairs, four bedrooms upstairs and a bathroom with a huge old bath. They stopped finally in one of the back rooms. It had old pine cupboards and a pine floor painted black. Sunshine slanted in through the window and lit specks of dust that danced in the air.

'Well?' said Nank.

'Yeah,' said Jenny. 'I could live here. It just needs painting and furniture and care.'

That evening Jenny told her mother that Nank had asked to marry her. Ten minutes later, Nank arrived. He was invited into the kitchen and offered a seat at the table.

'Jenny's told me.'

This was Mrs Wallace. She was a thin, bony woman with flesh looping down under her chin and deep lines in her face. She didn't sound too delighted, Nank thought, and he wondered what was coming next. As far as he was concerned, he and Jenny should be able to do what they wanted. If they wanted to marry they should but Jenny wanted her mother's blessing. She was an only child and Mrs Wallace had no one but her. She wanted to bring her mother with them. This was why he had agreed to come tonight to talk things over.

'Right,' said Nank, his tone cool, neutral.

'I don't believe in going round the houses,' said Mrs Wallace, 'but I'm not happy.'

He expected it was his criminal record that she minded, but it wasn't. It was the religious upbringing of any children they might have that worried her. Nank was a Catholic and it was her experience, she said, that in mixed marriages the Catholic partner usually insisted on the children being Catholic. That was one reason the Protestants were dying out and she didn't want to be seen to support a marriage that did that. She also said that the Wallaces had been Church of Ireland since whenever and she didn't want that tradition to stop. Then, her speech finished, she offered Nank a cup of tea.

A few minutes later, as they sat drinking out of fine porcelain cups (Mrs Wallace had put out her best delft) Nank promised to have any children he and Jenny produced baptised into the Church of Ireland. Mrs Wallace immediately shook his hand vigorously, like a farmer in the mart sealing a price.

73

THE CEREMONY TOOK PLACE IN MARCH 1982, with Nank's mother, Docker and Mrs Wallace the only people present. After the ceremony, Nank gave his name to the registrar as Stephen Gerard Declan Pearse Nank Melanophy.

'Nank ... that's an unusual name,' she said. She was a square, bulky woman enclosed in a tight-fitting tweed suit with purple in the weave.

'It's an old family name,' he said, 'on my mother's side.'

'Really,' said the registrar. She stared at the birth certificate he had provided. 'I don't see it anywhere here.'

'It's not on that but can't you put it in anyway?' he asked.

'No.'

'Why not?'

'If it's not on the birth certificate it can't go down on the marriage certificate.'

'Why not?'

'Because those are the rules.'

'Well, let's bend them today. Go on, live a little.'

'Nank,' said Jenny quietly. She caught his eye and shook her head. He nodded. He understood. He was to leave this alone.

The registrar filled in the certificate with black ink, blotted it and put it into an envelope.

'Nank can be a pet name known only to Mrs Melanophy,' she said.

Jenny took the envelope. 'Thanks. Come on, Nank,' she said.

74

FROM THE REGISTRY OFFICE THE NEWLY married couple went to their home at Grange Cross. There was a party in the evening, to which his five sisters came with their families, his mother, Jenny's mother and other relatives of hers. The only guest who was not a member of either family was Docker.

The next day, Nank and Jenny set off on their honeymoon. The plan was to drive down Ireland's west coast and stay in different places each night. On the fifth night, they were in a small bed-and-breakfast in the village of Greystones, Connemara. They went to a restaurant for dinner and came back at ten.

'I want a bath,' said Jenny, 'and you need a shave.' She touched his chin. She didn't like him to make love to her when he was unshaven: his bristles brought out a rash on her neck and shoulders, her belly and her thighs.

They went to the bathroom together and locked the door. She ran a bath and got in. He stood at the sink and shaved. When he'd finished, he carried his razor and shaving foam to the bath and sat on the edge.

'What do you want?' said Jenny, looking up at him.

'You know you told me you'd often wondered what it would be like?'

This had been the night before.

'Yes,' said Jenny.

'Well, now you'll find out,' he said.

He put his hand under her back and lifted her middle out of the water. Then he draped her legs over either side of the bath, sprayed her with shaving cream and shaved her slowly and carefully while she watched. Once the black hair was gone, a surprisingly white mound was revealed with the pink tongue-coloured slit running down it. They went back to their bedroom and locked the door. Nank pulled down the covers on the bed. Jenny put on a suspender belt and stockings, as she had every night. They lay side by side.

'Touch yourself,' he said, 'and tell me something dirty.'

He liked to watch her while she talked and she liked this as well.

'I've got a white dress on and it's summer and I'm driving,' she said. 'There's something wrong with the car and I go into a garage in the country. I get oil on my dress. There are four mechanics and one tells me to take it off and he'll bring it over to his mother. She lives behind the garage and she'll wash it. I pull the dress over my head and I start to feel excited ... '

Later they made love, and then they curled up together. Nank had his back to Jenny and she had her arms around him, her hands folded over his chest.

'You've seen everything there is to see of me,' she said. 'There isn't any more.'

'Isn't there?'

'I'd say not,' she said dreamily.

From the street below came a man's voice. He said, 'I don't know what Manchester United are playing at.'

'Yeah, what are they playing at?' said Jenny. She laughed. 'What are your secrets?' she said suddenly.

An image sprang into Nank's mind. He was beside the sheephouse at the top of Dermot's Field. His father had unbuttoned his flies and pulled out his penis. 'Now you rub it, son,' Father said.

He shuddered.

'You jumped,' said Jenny.

'Oh, it's nothing.'

'It wasn't nothing. What startled you?'

'Nothing.'

'That wasn't nothing.'

'It was.'

'In which case,' she said, 'tell me.'

There was a long silence. Finally he said, 'Something I'd rather not think about.'

'You won't have to once you tell me. Tell me and it'll go.'

She told him he would have to tell her. She said this emphatically. She said she wouldn't stop asking until he told her. He was in no doubt this was true.

So he started to speak. He was cautious. He was euphemistic. He was skimpy with the details. But Jenny wouldn't let him away with that. She pressed and pressed, and gradually, over the hours that followed, she drew out of him an account of everything that had happened, first with his father and later at Mulberry House with Mr Purdue. It was dawn by the time he finished. They made love again, and after they were done he did not withdraw but lay as he was and they fell asleep like that, arms and legs entwined, his cock inside her, shrinking slowly until it fell out.

75

ROBERT, THEIR ELDEST, WAS BORN IN 1983, in the County Hospital in Omagh, just as Nank was. After a couple of years they tried for another child but it was five before Emma was born in 1988, again in the County Hospital. His mother was in the hospital at the same time. She had heart trouble and was in for observation. He brought the new baby in to her and she held her for a few seconds. The next day his mother died. Nank inherited the farm, which was still rented to Martin Feeley.

Throughout these years Nank continued to work for Docker. Every two or three months he would go somewhere and move something. Jenny didn't like it, but they had come to an understanding. He did it and she didn't object, and when he got back he gave her the money he'd earned. She would put this in various bank accounts in the Republic or the Channel Islands. As long as she didn't think he was keeping money back for her, and as long she knew all the money he made was for the family, they could be happy. With the money going to her, she never got jealous or suspicious and life was good.

76

IN THE SUMMER OF 1989 NANK was in Amsterdam. He was staying in a hotel and he had a large sum of cash that Docker owed to someone called Terry.

He met Terry in an Indonesian restaurant. They ate satay with peanut sauce. He gave Terry the money in the Gents'.

Back at their table a third man joined them. Terry went back to the toilets and gave him the money.

Terry paid for their dinner and invited Nank to come with him to a café to smoke some hash. The place they went to had wooden walls and posters everywhere of Che Guevera and other revolutionary leaders.

Much later, early the following morning, Nank shook Terry's hand. He said he would find his own way back to his hotel. He knew how to get there, he thought, and if he didn't he'd ask. Everyone in Amsterdam seemed to speak English.

He set off. There was a canal on one side and houses with dark doorways on the other. The street appeared to be empty, and then it wasn't. Two men came from behind him, then ran round so they were in front. They had knives. One said something in Dutch. Nank replied in English. The speaker pointed at his watch with the knife, then at the pocket where his wallet was. It was a mugging. Two guys, both Moluccan he guessed from the colour of their skin, had jumped him

This was ridiculous, he thought. He wasn't a man who got mugged. And he wasn't a man who handed over his wallet and his watch meekly. He'd run back to the café, get Terry and they'd sort this pair out.

He turned. He found himself looking at a third man he had not known was behind him. This one didn't have a knife so he went to push past. The third man shoved him back and a leg, the third man's leg, he thought, he couldn't be sure, knocked his and he tumbled to the pavement. He felt a sharp kick in the small of his back, a couple more, and then he sprang up. This surprised them. Then he felt a slicing sensation at the back of his neck and knew, but vaguely, which was how you knew everything in a fight, that they'd cut him. That was bloody unbelievable. He'd felt detached before, intent on getting away and not letting these arseholes rob him. But now rage filled him. They'd cut him. He'd teach them a lesson they'd never forget.

He wanted a weapon. He hadn't one on him so he'd have to go and get one.

He surged sideways and spurted away, running down the middle of the street. He was aware of them behind him, then their footsteps falling away. He came to a side street that led off the road he was on and decided to risk looking back. They were about thirty yards away, standing together. One gave him the finger.

He turned into the side street and began to jog along the pavement. He saw a building with scaffolding outside and ran up to it. He tried a few scaffolding struts but they were all attached and he had no spanner to get them undone. He went to the front door, which was temporary, made of plywood and secured with a padlock. He kicked. The wood splintered and he was in.

It was dark inside and he could feel sand and grit crunching under his shoes. He began to feel around: there were planks, bundles of insulation and bags of concrete, then he felt something round and cold. He had a piece of scaffolding.

He ran out. His intention was not to retrace his steps but to go in a circle the other way and come out behind them where they wouldn't expect him. As he ran he thought of his father and Mr Purdue, but they didn't make him angry now as they once had. So he thought about the three men, the way they had tried to rob him, the cut they had made. As he ran, his rage grew into something murderous. By the time he got back to the road by the canal, he was ready to kill.

Then he saw them. They had their backs to him. He crept down the street keeping to the shadowy doorways until he was a few yards away. He broke into a run and came at them with the bar raised over his head.

He caught the first on the ear and the second on his face. The third tried to run but he smacked him, too, on the head and he fell. Now they were all on the ground trying to get up and he hit them ruthlessly, indiscriminately. And as he threw down the blows he felt their energy leach away and the idea crossed his mind that if he continued to beat them he'd end up killing them. Then he remembered that that was what he'd decided to do.

It was at this point that a passing police car braked. Two officers jumped out and grabbed him. He had nothing against them and knew better than to try to take them on. He let his rage flow away, dropped the bar and went limp. He was searched, cuffed and manoeuvred into the car. In the station later, in the presence of a British Embassy official, a police interpreter told him he was to be charged with assault. His victims had broken bones, fractured skulls and smashed teeth. This was a serious matter and he had better prepare himself: he was going to prison.

77

HE WAS REMANDED AT A JAIL in the centre of Amsterdam, a modern one. At first he was bewildered. He had no Dutch so he didn't understand the regime. Even something as simple as getting to know the weekly timetable was a struggle. But he found some prisoners who spoke English and explained things, and he learned a bit of Dutch. He kept busy. There was work: he was a cleaning orderly.

There was an excellent library with many English-language books so he read. He wrote letters home. And he watched television: many of the programmes had been made in Britain and were shown with Dutch subtitles with the English intact.

His trial, even though the proceedings were translated, was a bizarre, mysterious and confusing experience. He was perpetually trying to catch up as he followed the interpreter and, worse, though he grasped the sense of what was happening, the nuance was lost. About the conclusion, however, there was no mystery: he was found guilty. When the interpreter back at the police station had told him to prepare for a stint in jail he had been right. On top of what he'd already done on remand, he'd serve ten months.

78

ON THE EVENING OF THE DAY he was tried, he sat in his cell on the tenth storey of the jail and gazed out at the Amsterdam skyline. He felt as if something inside had torn and that dense, sticky silt was pouring in, clogging the mechanism inside and slowly filling him up.

Over the following days, the silt rose higher until, at last, he was choked with it. Its other effect was to exhaust him. His job was a struggle and he only managed to get through mopping the corridors and scrubbing the toilets by fixating on the thought of his bed, into which he would collapse at the end of each day. Everything else became impossible because he hadn't any energy. He stopped reading. He stopped writing letters. He stopped watching television. And then he stopped eating.

79

IN HIS DUTCH JAIL, MEALS WERE eaten alone in the cell. The Dutch frowned on association between prisoners; they knew it led to trouble. The meal orderly was Rolf, a driver from Hamburg who drove a refrigerated lorry. He'd buggered an eight-year-old Kurdish boy, then strangled him. For weeks he hid the corpse in the back of his lorry, until a meat inspector in Rotterdam found it in a holdall, hanging with the beef and lamb carcasses.

Rolf noticed Nank wasn't eating. He asked the prison librarian for a funny book in English and was handed *The Complete Nonsense of Edward Lear*.

On the next dinner run, Rolf gave it to Nank. The cell door closed.

Nank opened the book and turned the pages listlessly, reading stray sentences. He had not encountered Lear before and the poet's fanciful ideas made little sense to Nank and his drawings didn't look much good either. Then his eye fell on a pen-and-ink drawing of a man dancing with a cat while pouring tea into a hat. He read the words below:

There was an old man on the Border,
Who lived in the utmost disorder;
He danced with the cat,
And made tea in his hat,
Which vexed all the folks on the Border.

For the second or two, while his attention was engaged, Nank forgot his anguish. Then it came back, the dreadful stuffed feeling of despair. The relief was momentary but this, he realised, was the way to save himself.

He made himself read, and the more he read, the longer the intermissions of relief, and the shorter the episodes of pain. But it was weeks before his mind was scraped clean and the Swiss watch mechanism, as he imagined his mind, was free of silt and back in working order.

80

WHEN NANK GOT BACK TO GRANGE Cross, he found the kitchen table laid for a party. As he'd been in prison for his last birthday, Jenny had decided they would celebrate now. There were sandwiches and a cake with thirty-three candles and banner on the wall, which Robert and Emma had made, that read WELCOME BACK TO DADDY.

That night when he made love to Jenny she burst into tears. She clung to him, her face on his shoulder, and told him it had been the hardest time of her life and she had felt bereaved, widowed. In the morning she told him she had not worn her cap and nor would she any more. Their third child, Sarah, was born the following year, 1991.

81

THE NEXT YEAR, 1992, NANK DID no work for Docker. Jenny wouldn't hear of it in case something happened to him and he was taken away again. She wanted him at home, with her, at least while they had the new baby.

The next year, however, she felt stronger and less anxious

and also, she conceded, he needed to go back to work because by not working he wasn't raking in the money as he had been. They weren't poor—there was money in various accounts in the Republic, the Channel Islands and now the Isle of Man. But, of course, they were spending, they had to live, and she knew Nank would have to go back to work eventually.

After Sarah's first birthday she said he could resume but it had to be modest to begin until she had reacclimatised. He did a couple of small runs to England, then a big one to France. When he came home each time she was reassured that he could be away without mishap. He could go back to work properly, she said, and do as much as Docker wanted.

He did six more runs that year and the next, 1993, he made eleven journeys to England and the continent. As 1994 rolled on, he made another six. By the middle of the year he had two hundred and twenty-two thousand pounds in various bank accounts, some in his but most in Jenny's name. His shop, still managed on his behalf, continued to trade, selling groceries, confectionery, cigarettes, newspapers and petrol. He also sold, from his forecourt, a small number of second-hand cars. This part of his business was a most useful way of absorbing spare cash as well as providing transport for when he went to work. He never used his own car for a run but always one of those he had for sale, and he only ever took any of them once. That was his rule.

82

IN THE LATE SUMMER OF 1994, Docker asked him to do a job in Edinburgh. Nank selected from his stock a green Volvo estate. He chose it because he was taking second-hand books on this trip—the car was to be filled with them. Books, he thought, would sit well in a Volvo.

It was late August, with already a hint of autumn in the air, when he loaded the car with the empty customised cardboard boxes he had prepared, drove south and caught the ferry from Dun Laoghaire to Holyhead. On the sailing there was talk of an industrial dispute the following week on all the ferries between Wales and Ireland. When he arrived in Holyhead, he went to the ticket office to enquire. The woman at the desk confirmed what he'd heard.

'What about the Liverpool to Belfast sailing?' he asked.

'When?'

'Next week.'

'I think that could be down too,' she said. 'But the good news is you could go from Stranraer to Larne in Northern Ireland.' She inflected Northern Ireland in that funny way peculiar to the English—as if the very words were explosive and might go up in her face. 'And I think we'd be able to change your ticket,' she added.

While she examined it Nank pondered. The idea, in the event of a strike, of sitting in Holyhead or, worse, Liverpool, with a car full of what his would be full of was unappealing. He wanted to get to Ireland and pass the gear onto Docker as soon as possible. On the other hand, Stranraer to Larne wasn't a route he used often. He didn't like the thought of all the policemen on the other side. Of course, if they were looking for caches of Semtex and RPG launchers, they'd pay correspondingly less attention to himself and his cargo, providing his camouflage was good. It wasn't him and his type who were the primary focus: it was the bombers, the shooters and their hardware. This thought swung it for him. He made his decision.

'All right,' he said.

'When would you like to travel?' she asked.

'Last sailing next Tuesday.'

'What day's that?' She looked at her calendar. 'August the thirtieth,' she said. She fiddled with his ticket and scribbled. 'Ten-thirty,' she said, handing it back. 'Allow an hour for boarding.'

He drove to a suburb of Liverpool and collected a Ruger revolver with fourteen rounds of ammunition from one of Docker's contacts. He put the gun and the cartridges in a Quality Street tin and stored them under the driver's seat. He didn't like the thought of travelling on what was not his usual route home with the weapon, but he liked even less the idea of embarking on the journey he was about to make without it. No one would travel alone and unarmed with what he had to pick up. Without a weapon, he wouldn't have a chance if anyone decided to relieve him of his cargo.

He drove on to Edinburgh, booked into a guesthouse and spent a couple of days buying books in the city's better second-hand bookshops and packing them into the boxes he'd prepared and brought with him.

83

THE FOLLOWING TUESDAY, THE DAY NANK was due to sail home, he made his way across Stockbridge then turned on to a hill. The normal sound of tyres on asphalt gave way to the slap of cobbles. He was in Edinburgh's New Town. The suspension responded to the cobbles and Nank was jigged up and down in his seat. He turned into a street and drove slowly along. Gaunt, stone houses loomed on his left, while on his right there was a steep drop of several hundred feet to a park and a river, beyond which the southern suburbs of Edinburgh stretched to the towers of Fettes School.

As he drove, he scanned the parked cars and the pavement. The vehicles were empty and the only pedestrian was a window-cleaner with a ladder and a bucket from which wipers stuck up like arrows in a quiver.

After he had driven up and down three times, he parked and locked the car. He crossed the pavement to number eighteen. The stone steps leading to the front door were bowed like a butcher's chopping block. He felt the dips as he climbed up them.

At the top, he looked for a bell. There wasn't one so he lifted the knocker and rapped on the brass stud that stood proud of the wood.

He heard footsteps inside. The door opened. He saw a man with a long face and a droopy mouth. 'You must be Monty,' Nank said.

The face reminded him of Bill Ward, the drummer from Black Sabbath, whom he hadn't thought about since he was a teenager and read *NME*.

'Hello,' said Monty. His long hair was tied in a ponytail. He wore a waistcoat and a white shirt with no collar. He was about fifty. 'Can I help?'

Nank recognised the accent—half Edinburgh, half Home Counties—from their telephone conversations. 'I've come with the books,' said Nank.

Monty was staring over his shoulder. Nank turned and saw the window-cleaner putting his ladder into the back of a white van. 'Do you know him?'

'Aye, that's Alf,' said Monty. 'He's just done my windows.'

Nank turned back and squinted into the hall. There was a table the colour of old sherry. The bare floorboards and the stair treads were a dull black. The empty interior was unlike any he'd ever seen. Monty had told him on the phone this was because the house was exactly as it had been the day the builder finished in seventeen sixty-something. Nank had forgotten the exact date. Evenings and weekends, tourists, mostly Americans, paid to come to Monty's house for Georgian evenings at which their host wore eighteenth-century dress and read aloud after dinner from Boswell's *Journal of a Tour of the Hebrides*. Johnson and Boswell, it was said, had visited the house.

'Oh, yeah, the books, sorry,' said Monty. 'Take the lane and go round the back.' He pointed. A small blue swallow was tattooed on the back of his right hand. 'There's a gate. I'll be waiting.'

Nank drove round by the lane and reversed into Monty's yard. It had high walls topped with broken glass. While Monty banged the gates shut, Nank opened the Quality Street tin, took out the revolver and put it into his jacket pocket.

Monty came up from the gate wiping his hands. 'Nice back-up,' he said, a faint pulse of lechery in his voice.

I don't like this, thought Nank. 'What are you talking about?' he said.

'I like the way you back up a car.' There it was again, Nank noticed, the common-or-garden compliment mixed with an erotic undertow.

'I don't know what you're on about,' he said, 'but I do know this. I've twenty-four boxes of books in here need shifting inside. Let's get cracking shall we?'

Monty stared at him now as if he didn't understand or hadn't heard. So, not only was he as horny as hell, thought Nank, he was also stoned out of his mind. He never had liked old hippies, he remembered.

'I've twenty-four boxes of books,' he said, speaking slowly, as if to a foreigner, 'and I need help carrying them in.'

Monty shook slightly like someone who was just waking up. 'Oh, yeah, sure,' he said, in his normal voice.

Thank Christ they were through that little episode, thought Nank, and he made a mental note to talk to Docker about Monty's unsuitability as a conduit.

They carted the boxes into Monty's kitchen, a square room with a scrubbed table, several presses and a lead sink. Shining copper pots and pans hung on the wall. Embers smouldered in the black grate of an open fire.

'How long did it take to restore the house?' asked Nank.

'Eight years,' Monty said. I did most of it myself, keeping it period as far as possible. Of course, there is a bathroom.'

'What about electricity?'

'Oh, I've got electricity. How do you think I run the telly?'

'You have a telly? I thought this was a Georgian house.'

'I'm not giving up *Neighbours* and *EastEnders*, even for the eighteenth century. There are some things a modern boy can't do without.'

Abruptly, Monty turned his basset-hound face to the window and stared out. Nank turned and saw great white bundles of cloud with pale blue streaks behind.

'Do you ever dream you're on stage with nothing on?' said Monty.

'Never,' said Nank.

'Oh.'

'I don't remember my dreams,' said Nank. 'Shall we get to?'

He lifted the Walker's Crisps box onto the table and began to unload the books, including *Lord of the Flies* by William Golding, *My Family and Other Animals* by Gerald Durrell and *Seize the Day* by Saul Bellow.

'Good books,' said Monty.

'I went to a lot of trouble,' said Nank. 'I even put together a box of first editions. It's mainly English stuff—Barstow, Sillitoe, but quite collectable. They're all books I'd like to read in fact.'

'Is there an eighteenth-century box?' asked Monty.

'I've some Samuel Johnson, Richardson and some Swift. They're not first editions but you can keep them if you want.'

'I only try to live like the eighteenth century,' said Monty. 'I read from every century.'

The box was empty. The two men stared at the cardboard tongues laid over each other in the bottom.

'See anything?' asked Nank.

Monty shook his head. 'No.'

Nank lifted the flaps to reveal a slim cavity, its bottom formed by a second set of flaps identical to the first.

'Excellent,' said Monty. He opened a press and revealed twenty-four half-kilo wraps of cocaine stacked on a shelf like slices of mozzarella.

Monty took the top one and opened it. Nank took a dab and rubbed it on the gum above his front teeth. He got a bitter taste, then numbness. He nodded. Monty resealed the wrap and dropped it into the cavity. Nank closed the upper flaps, lifted the box upside-down and shook it. The flaps held. He put the box back onto the table and the two men repacked it. They repeated the routine twenty-three times more, then returned the boxes to the car. The job done, the Volvo looked like the car of the second-hand-book dealer that, in a sense, Nank was about to become. On Sunday mornings an informal market operated close to his garage on wasteland straddling the border between the Republic and Northern Ireland, and he intended to open a stall there, using these books as his start-up stock.

'That's that,' said Monty, closing the boot. 'Do you want a cup of tea?'

'Aye.'

The gas stove was hidden inside a kitchen press. The kettle went on the hob and the two men stood awkwardly, waiting.

'How's Ireland?' said Monty.

'Still there,' said Nank.

'Will it ever end, do you think? Will there ever be peace?' said Monty.

'If I'd a pound for every time I got asked that,' said Nank, 'I'd be a millionaire.'

Monty stared at the blue gas flame and lapsed into reverie until the kettle had boiled; then he snapped out of it and made tea. He put cups and milk on the table, laid out a couple of lines of cocaine, rolled a note and offered it to Nank.

Nank said, 'Ta,' and bent to the mirror. A few moments later, while they were sipping tea, Monty said, 'Can I ask you a question?'

'Go ahead.'

'Personal.'

'I don't mind.'

'Where'd this name Nank come from? Anything to do with wanking?' Monty stared at him, waiting for his answer.

'No,' said Nank. 'It was evening association. I was reading *The Pursuit of Love* by Nancy Mitford ... what a fucking dodgy book to read in jail but I was so desperate I'd read anything then. Armed robber comes up, takes book, cover's defaced, Nancy has become Wanky, from which he gets Nanky, which turns into Nank.'

'My first time in,' said Monty, 'I was eighteen, no watch, and every ten minutes, I'm at the screw, "What time is it?" And guess what name they came up with on the wing? I mean jail humour, subtle or what? Clock. A few years ago, I'm back in, haven't been in jail for ages and guess what? Within minutes it's "Hello, Clock, how are ye doing?"'

'What did they stick on you?'

'You mean on the last one?'

'Yeah.'

'Possession of an offensive weapon, possession of pornographic materials and possession of two pounds of hash.'

'How long?'

'Five and I did two-thirds—three years and four long months.'

'Fuck. Where'd you do it?'

'Kingsley House. It's a new jail between here and Glasgow. Fucking kip.'

Three lines of cocaine later, Monty tried to kiss him. Nank rebuffed him. 'Come on, Monty, don't act the cunt.' He finished his tea. 'I'd better go on,' he said.

'I'll open the gate.'

They went out. Monty walked to the gate. Nank got into his car and slipped the gun into the Quality Street tin, then drove down the yard and out between the piers. He turned and made his way back by the lane to the street, then set off, bumping on the cobbles. The route took him past number eighteen and, lo and behold, there was Monty on the steps waving. He waved back as he passed, relieved to be on his way. Monty was a header.

84

IT WAS SIX WHEN NANK LEFT Edinburgh.

He drove through industrial Scotland and down the long Ayrshire coast to the port of Stranraer. He arrived as it was getting dark. Now that it was the end of August, the evenings were shortening.

He stopped at the office by the gate and passed his ticket through a window. It came back to him with a boarding pass.

'Go on to Security,' said a voice.

He drove into a shed open at either end where a man stood in a Day-Glo tunic with 'Security' written in black on his left breast.

'Ticket? Boarding pass?'

Nank handed them to him.

'Larne?'

'Aye,' said Nank.

'Did you pack your car yourself?' From his voice, Nank could tell he wasn't a policeman: he was too polite, too trusting.

'Yes,' said Nank. 'I packed every book myself.'

The security guard shone his torch into the rear. Nank turned to see. The beam lit up the *Selected Tales of Chekhov* lying at the top of an open box.

Nank smiled. 'That one's a good box,' he said. 'They're all Russians. The Chekhov stories are fantastic.'

'I don't know him,' said the guard. 'I'm a Terry Pratchett man.'

'Oh, I never touch the hard stuff,' said Nank. 'Far too addictive.'

The guard laughed.

'Here's your boarding-pass and ticket. Don't lose them. Drive into the aisle marked B, would you?'

Nank did so and looked ahead. A line of dark cars led his eye to the huge bulk of MV *Kathleen Ni Houlihan*. The lights were on but no one was boarding yet. A breeze wafted the smell of diesel through his open window. Assuming the ferry left on time, he'd make Larne about two, Docker's by six and be home by ten. The kids would be at school. He would take Jenny to bed.

He rummaged in a box and came across *The Outsider* by Albert Camus. Rolf, the dinner orderly who had recognised his despair at the start of his Dutch sentence, had given it to him saying it was his favourite book. Nank had read it in a single sitting one evening. The story, as he remembered it, was powerful and gripping but he felt there was more under the surface than he had grasped. He had time now, he thought, to try to find that meaning.

He turned on the overhead light and started. *The Outsider* was about a man in Algiers called Meursault. He'd just reached the point where Meursault smells his girlfriend's smell on his pillow when he heard the engine of the car in front start up.

He put the book down, turned the key in the ignition and drove the car up the metal gangplank and on to the ferry. He parked and got out, taking *The Outsider* with him. The hold smelled of old fish, engine oil and wet rope. Men in overalls were guiding the traffic.

He went to the Motorists' Lounge and sat down. The harbour lights slid past the window as MV *Kathleen Ni Houlihan* floated out to sea. He bought sausages, beans and a fried egg from the servery and sat down at a table with an abandoned copy of the *Sun* lying on it. He idly turned to the *Sun* Stars Spot. Apparently, it was a good day for Aquarians to travel. He smiled. He was an Aquarian.

He tried the end of the sausage. It tasted of bread and old meat. The egg white was rubbery and the yolk watery. The beans were cold.

He carried the plate back to the counter.

'Didn't we enjoy that?' said the youth standing behind it, dressed in the company livery—shining polyester slacks and a black and white striped waistcoat. His red bow tie was spotted with grease.

'No, we didn't,' said Nank.

'Would you like me to stick it in the micro?' asked the boy.

Nank shook his head. 'No, thanks.'

'Can I get you anything else?'

'Just tea,' said Nank.

The boy filled a mug and pushed it across the stainless-steel counter. 'On the house,' he said.

Nank took two tiny ribbed cartons of milk, went back to his seat and pushed on with *The Outsider*. It was a strange story. In the middle Meursault went to a beach with a friend and killed an Arab, shooting him five times. He did this because of the sun, he explained, and because he was too hot.

When he came to court, Meursault pleaded guilty. He did not deny what he had done. Or try to excuse it. On the contrary, he embraced it. He insisted on taking responsibility for the murder. On the last page Meursault was described lying in his cell, not simply reconciled to his fate but gleefully anticipating his walk to the guillotine, surrounded by a crowd, jeering and hooting at him.

This puzzled Nank. How could the man be happy as he made his way to the scaffold? No one could be happy knowing their head was going to be cut off. Inside every human being there was a desperate fidelity to life. Apart from suicides that was, but they were unhappy, so they didn't count. No one in his right mind welcomed extinction or could possibly anticipate their imminent execution with the gusto and detachment of Meursault. Unless, of course, Meursault understood something that Nank had not grasped. He could see this was possible but he had no idea what it might be.

He fell asleep and didn't wake until the ferry was juddering into Larne. He opened his eyes and saw a derrick through a window and a few yellow streetlights. His sleep had been heavy and dreamless. He always slept like that after cocaine. He put it down to exhaustion. Cocaine made his thoughts race, so his exhausted mind needed deep, seemingly dream-free sleep to recover.

The PA crackled. Nank stood and, without listening, started for the door to the car deck. The people he passed all had perplexed looks on their faces.

'What is it?' he asked a man in a knitted sweater, realising he should have listened to the PA.

'Apparently, we're not allowed onto the car deck. We're to leave by the gangplank.' Although nothing had been said they both knew what they were talking about: there was a bomb on board, or the possibility of one at any rate.

'Oh,' said Nank.

'I always thought the ferry was off-limits to them,' said the man.

'They bomb the railway line to Dublin often enough, so why shouldn't they do the ferry to Larne?' said Nank.

'But all the people on board,' said the man. 'Think if it had sunk at sea—think of the loss of life.'

'It's probably only a hoax.'

'Probably,' the man agreed.

Yes, Nank thought, filing down a gangplank with all the other passengers while soldiers and policemen surged up another. It had to be a hoax. Friday afternoon rush hour in Belfast was regularly ruined with this sort of carry-on.

Nank and the passengers were put into a cold, unused waiting room in one of the port buildings. The door was locked and a guard posted. That was standard procedure, Nank guessed, in case there really was a bomb aboard the ferry and a passenger had driven it on, or armed it, or both.

After a two-hour wait, the door was unlocked. The passengers were informed they were free to go.

Nank reboarded and went down to the deck where his car was. He noticed a lorry in the corner, its entire load tipped out. He guessed this was the vehicle that was supposed to have had the bomb. It hadn't but its stones had had to be tipped out anyway, just to be on the safe side. Now they would have to be picked up again. The next sailing would be delayed. And, naturally, there was no Casey's Quarry driver around to help. He'd put the lorry aboard at Stranraer, then left. It was pathetic. Nank and hundreds of other passengers' schedules had been skewed and for what? If this ever

achieved a united Ireland, his name wasn't Stephen Gerard
Declan Pearse Nank Melanophy.

He made his way along the narrow space between two
lines of cars. The air stank even more strongly of fish, rope
and diesel than before. The ferry's engines had heated the
atmosphere, which had made the smell worse.

He reached his car, slipped the key into the lock, opened
the door, then made a sinuous corkscrew movement and
dropped onto the driver's seat.

He closed the door. After the hubbub of the car deck, it was
strangely quiet. It was like stepping out of a busy street and
into a church. The inside of the Volvo was cool as well as
quiet. He closed his eyes and smelled the wonderful aroma of
paper, glue and old book. He felt happy suddenly. He'd done
it. He would drive to Redhills, make the delivery, hand over
the gun, and receive payment. He would put the wad in his
Quality Street tin. He would drive home. He would take
Jenny to their bedroom. He would undress her. They would
lie down and he would climb onto her. He would bury his
face in her hair and inhale its apple and shampoo scent mixed
with her intimate musty odour. Then he would tug with his
teeth at her earrings and the metal taste he associated with
sex would prick his tongue. Finally, he would hold her under
her buttocks as she liked and he would pull her towards him
while he pushed down into her.

Afterwards, they would lie back and talk about what to do
with the money. She would decide. 'You make it and I'll
spend it,' she joked. It was a good arrangement. The money
usually went on the children or the house and rarely on her,
but if it did it never bought anything ostentatious. Jenny
loathed showing off. Her virtues were modesty, simplicity
and self-effacement. And saving. Jenny ran several savings

accounts where she kept money gathering interest, sometimes for years at a time.

The ferry doors opened. The rear lights of the car in front came on. Nank started his engine and turned on his headlights. A few moments later, he bumped down the ramp and followed the snake of cars in front of him across the dark tarmac. As he approached the gates, a man stepped forward and beckoned to him. He turned his car into a little covered bay. The man approached his window.

'Could you step out of the car, please?'

Customs and Excise, Nank thought. The official would poke around in his boxes of books, find nothing and tell him to go away.

'No sweat,' said Nank.

Nank got out. The Customs man asked Nank to open his boot. As Nank turned the key in the lock, two policemen rushed out of a door. One shouted, 'You're under arrest.'

Before he could react, they had his hands behind his back and a pair of handcuffs on his wrists.

85

NANK WAS TAKEN TO LARNE POLICE station. His clothes were removed for forensic examination and he was given a blue paper suit to wear. He phoned his solicitor and asked him to visit and to tell Jenny where he was. He was interrogated through the next morning. At lunchtime, he was taken to a small interview room used for legal visits. It was an airless box, lit by a humming neon strip and furnished with a table and two chairs. A large man in a blue pinstripe suit sat on one.

'Good afternoon, Stephen,' he said.

His solicitor, Harvey Golden, didn't use nicknames with his clients. 'It gives an impression of over-familiarity,' Harvey had explained to him once, 'and that gives policemen another reason to be nasty to me. And life's too short for that, isn't it? So, I keep things straight.'

'How are you?' said Harvey, as Nank pulled out the other chair and sat down.

The two had known one another fifteen years. Over that period, whenever Nank was summonsed, usually in connection with motor-vehicle taxation, fuel duty and VAT irregularities, Harvey represented him in court. There'd been only one serious problem in that time, but as the trial had been in Holland, Harvey hadn't been able to help. It was Nank's belief, however, that if Harvey had represented him, he might have got off.

'Oh, marvellous,' said Nank.

'Ah, the famous Melanophy sense of humour is intact.'

'Yeah, what else is there to do but laugh?'

'Smoke?'

Harvey Golden proffered a packet of Benson & Hedges. Nank took two. One went behind his ear and the other into his mouth. Harvey produced a lighter. It was gold and slim, and a tongue of blue flame appeared. Nank lit his cigarette.

'Would you like to know what happened on your ferry last night?'

'Do I have to?' said Nank.

'It seems some of our friends in the National Liberation Movement gave a coded warning.' Harvey always used sarcastic alternative titles for the paramilitaries. It was one of the reasons Nank liked him.

'I guessed as much,' said Nank.

'The ship was evacuated.'

'I know. I got to spend quality time in a lovely cold building.'

'The security services swept the hold. They found the lorry where the bomb supposedly was and found it clean. Everyone was ready to go home except one of the dogs couldn't keep away from your car. The door was opened and the animal was in like Flynn, I'm told. A box of books was unpacked and guess what they found in the bottom? Then they looked under the driver's seat and guess what was in the Quality Street tin? It wasn't chocolates. The rest I think you know.'

'How did you find out?'

Harvey Golden shrugged.

'Contacts,' observed Nank.

Harvey took a cigarette and lit it. 'Did you hear the other news?'

'What?' said Nank. 'That this has all been a terrible dream and I can wake up?'

'Our friends in the IRA announced this morning that as of midnight tonight they're on ceasefire.'

'You're joking?'

'Scout's honour.'

'That means?'

'That means no more war. Yes, it's over. Well, the other lot have yet to give up, but I'm sure that's coming.'

Nank stared at the wall. There were bits of old yellow Sellotape here and there that once held up a poster.

Of all the days in the year, he thought, he had to choose the last one before the IRA ceasefire.

Twenty-four hours later, and they wouldn't have been making coded telephone calls and leaving lorries on car ferries. He'd not have been caught and he wouldn't be staring at a lengthy jail sentence.

'I have to decide what to plead,' he said.

Harvey nodded.

'I suppose my fingerprints are everywhere?'

Harvey made one of his characteristic shrugs.

'I'll think about the plea,' said Nank.

'You do that.'

'Going for bail?' said Nank.

'Naturally.'

'Likely to be declined?'

'We'll see,' said Harvey.

That afternoon Nank was brought before the magistrate and charged with possession of a Class A drug with intent to supply, possession of a firearm and fourteen rounds of ammunition. His application for bail was refused.

86

AFTER HE HAD APPEARED IN COURT in Larne, the police took Nank to HMP Loanend and delivered him to the Tank, as the Induction Centre was known. It was an airless basement whose linoleum floor was pocked with cigarette burns.

'Name?' called the Senior Officer, who stood behind a high counter.

'Melanophy.'

The SO nodded at the escort. Nank held out his arms. The cuffs were taken off. They had slowed the flow of blood and left his hands cold and stiff. His committal warrant was checked, verified, stamped and signed by the policeman. A

Polaroid camera flashed twice and two squares shot out of the bottom. The SO flapped them in the air to dry them.

'I hope they turn out nice,' said Nank.

The uniforms ignored him.

'Sign.'

This was addressed to the constable, who scribbled his name on the back of the Polaroid.

A Body Receipt was written up, signed by the SO and given to the policeman. The other constable from the car appeared with a paper sack containing Nank's things, which had been taken from him at the police station. Both officers left. His property was listed on a Property Card, and his money on a Cash Card. His Golden Virginia, a packet of green papers and his Zippo lighter were returned to him.

'Right,' said the SO, 'off you go.'

He went round a corner and found himself in a room of booths.

'Come on,' called an officer, and he stepped into one. This man had dark blue eyes and a square black beard, like a spade. 'Unzip the suit to the waist and get your arms out.'

The Beard, as Nank named him, examined his torso for marks, peculiarities, tattoos, scars and deformities. He found the scar on Nank's palm from when he had cut himself escaping from Mr Heggarty through the broken window, the scar on his neck from the time he was stabbed in Amsterdam and two moles on his left elbow. The Beard noted all these details down.

'Okay, we leave the best till last,' said the Beard. 'Strip from the waist down.'

Nank pulled off the pants suit and his bottom half was scrutinised. He'd a couple of large scars on his knees from childhood falls and the Beard made a note of them too.

'Right, kit back on, hop up there.' The Beard pointed at a set of scales.

Nank dressed and stepped onto the footplate. The needle trembled and stopped. The Beard wrote his weight on an Index or I Card.

The Beard pointed at the height gauge. Nank stepped under. The pointer dropped heavily onto his skull. They were much gentler at school when they did this, he thought. But, that was the point. The staff were rough so the new prisoner was left in no doubt as to who was boss.

The Beard wrote his height on the I Card, then added the colour of Nank's eyes and hair, the shape of his face, and his build.

'Have you ever been in prison before in Northern Ireland?'

'Yes.'

'Of course you have,' said the Beard, who appeared to have found a piece of paper with this information. 'Your prison number was BC3232. You're still BC3232, Melanophy. Don't forget it.'

One of the Polaroids taken earlier was attached to the card. From now on, wherever Nank went in the jail, this card with his picture would go with him.

'You need some clothes,' said the Beard. 'Philip,' he called. An old man appeared. He had a large head and glasses that magnified his eyes. 'Get this prisoner some clothes.'

Philip measured him quickly with a creased linen tape, went off and came back with ugly black shoes and a pile of blue clothes.

'Anything in brown or black?' Nank said. 'Blue really isn't my colour.'

The Beard guffawed with delight. The clothing store, contained clothes the prison had acquired over the years on an ad hoc basis. These clothes were issued to prisoners who needed something to wear either when they came in or during the course of their sentence. Most prisoners had family or friends who would leave in what they wanted so most prisoners didn't have to rely on the store. The exceptions were the sex offenders who often hadn't anybody who'd leave anything in for them and so could sometimes be dressed for their entire sentence in clothes out of the store. Although it wasn't official prison policy, the clothes that came into the store tended to be blue or pastel and on account of this an understanding had evolved among the prison population that anyone dressed exclusively in blue or pastel was a root. Nank knew all about this from friends who'd been in this jail. He knew, therefore, that when he appeared on the landings in this get-up, it would be assumed he was a root and that it would be awkward until everyone knew that he wasn't and that he was waiting for his wife to visit and leave in something decent for him to wear.

'Oh dear, blue isn't your colour,' said the Beard. 'Well, you should have thought of that before you did what you done. That way then, you wouldn't be in the shit you're in now, fretting about your wardrobe, would you?'

The Beard led him deeper into the Induction Centre. There was a table piled with towels. The Beard handed him one. 'Time to scrub up.'

There were two rows of cubicles with grubby doors and gleaming brass locks. The Beard chalked 'Melanophy, BC3232' on one, then unlocked the door. 'I'll take the suit and plimsolls.'

Nank went in, undressed, handed over the plimsolls and the pants suit. The door closed. He wrapped the towel round his middle and sat on the slatted seat. The walls were covered with graffiti. He read one or two by the sickly light that leaked from above. I DIDN'T DO IT, HENRY 'KILLER' DIGBY, 19 AUG. 1977. FUCK JUSTICE KENNEALLY, JOHN MAGUIRE, 24 DEC. 1982. KILL ALL ROOTS to which AND CATHOLICS had been added. Perhaps he should write something himself. I LOVE JENNY maybe, with his name and date. But he had no pen.

He felt a sudden collapse of energy like the wavering of a torchbeam as the battery goes. To sleep and recharge, he thought, would be a lovely thing but that was impossible. An officer would be along shortly to take him to the shower.

He heard voices outside. More prisoners coming to be processed. He wasn't interested. Stephen 'Nank' Melanophy was gone, he thought. They had taken him away with his clothes at the police station. He was BC3232 Melanophy now.

As the thought crossed his mind, he felt something like a little rent. He knew at once what this meant. He'd been here before. Oh, yes, this had happened in Amsterdam and silt had poured in, and as day succeeded day, it had covered more and more of his mind. It had filled him to the brim and left no space for anything else. Depression, as he had often thought since, was imagined by those who'd not known it as emptiness, flatness but in fact it was a sensation of fullness. When it came he felt bloated with it. It was a true paradox that he never felt more full than when he was most miserable.

He breathed slowly. Oh God, he thought. A repeat of Amsterdam. He didn't want that. He must do something drastic himself. He began to whistle.

The key went into the cubicle lock and the door swung back.

'What's that then?' said the officer looking in at him. This new man, like the one who processed him, also had a beard (perhaps, thought Nank, the Induction Unit was a beards-only working environment) though this beard was white, neat and trimmed, not long, bushy and black.

'That tune seems familiar,' the new officer continued. He had a pipe in his mouth and blue clouds of smoke floated from the bowl, while behind the white shirt front, a little belly pushed forward.

Nank felt like saying, I can't remember and why does it matter? But what would that achieve? It would annoy the hell out of the man, no doubt about it. 'It's "Mary from Dungloe",' he said.

'Thought so,' said the officer, and started to sing in a quavering tenor:

'"Oh, then, farewell sweet Donegal, the Rosses and Gweedore, I'm crossing the main ocean, where the foaming billows roar."'

'McCarthy, shut the fuck up,' someone shouted.

McCarthy, thought Nank. He had his name.

McCarthy looked pained. He wasn't going to dignify the insult with a reply. In a nearby cubicle, a man was crying.

'My granddad would sing that,' said McCarthy.

'Would he?' Nank looked into the officer's face. He had brick-red skin, like a King on a playing-card, and the lines in his forehead were deep. He must be in his early fifties, Nank decided.

'Shower time,' said the officer.

Nank followed McCarthy into a steam-filled room. At the end there was a single shower head with water blistering down from it.

'Towel on the floor and get under it,' said the officer, lounging on a plastic stacking chair in the corner.

Nank put down his towel and stepped into the water. It was very hot. He stepped back.

'Very hot,' he said.

No reply from the officer. He ducked his head into the streaming water. He took a cake of jellied soap from the hole in the wall and soaped himself under the armpits. The lather that formed was thin and gritty. The noise and smell of prison hadn't changed and neither had the soap. It was White Windsor, the same as when he was in Borstal.

'Time's up,' said the officer.

Nank was hot and red-faced when McCarthy locked him back into his cubicle. He put on the clothes Philip had brought. The underwear was baggy. The blue jeans, shirt and jersey were roomy but not uncomfortable. The heavy shoes actually fitted.

He sat down. Beads of sweat broke out along his hairline and trickled down his forehead. Couldn't they even have the shower at the right temperature? They could, but they'd chosen not to. That was the point. They did the choosing.

Oh no, thought Nank. This way, depression. He began to whistle again, quietly this time.

Then he heard a scuffle and struggling. It was far away at first, but it drew closer and then it was outside his cubicle. A man was shouting, old by the sound of his voice, and officers were breathing heavily.

'Leave him alone,' Nank yelled.

His cubicle door ripped back.

'Have you a fucking problem?'

The speaker was a man in a brown boiler suit and a helmet with a visor. Behind him, three similarly dressed men had an old man and they were pulling down his underpants. The riot squad, Nank guessed.

'Because when we pull you out of here, squealing like a pig, you will have a fucking problem, won't you?' said the boiler suit.

The door slammed. Nank stayed on the slatted seat. Outside, he heard the old man being carried off and then, distantly, howling. They had him in the shower, Nank guessed.

His cubicle opened again. 'Let's be having you,' said McCarthy.

He was brought back to the Beard who asked, 'Have you a wife?'

'Aye.'

'Well, she can bring you new clothes.'

The Beard handed him *Guidance Leaflet for Prisoners Regarding Clothing in NI Prisons*.

'Read that, then tell your missus what's allowed. No suits, white shirts or ties.'

That, he guessed, was to stop prisoners impersonating officers.

'Read that too.'

Nank took *Sheet No. 1, Notes for the Guidance of All Prisoners*.

'You can read, can't you?'

'Aye.'

The Beard was filling out his door card. He saw his name, prison number, date of birth, religion and committal date. Three lines were left blank at the bottom, his Prison Work Station, his Early Release Date and his Long Release Date. When he finished, the Beard handed McCarthy his I Card and the door card and McCarthy led him to a bench at the front where Philip, the orderly, was sitting.

'Wait here,' said McCarthy.

Nank sat and McCarthy went away. Nank glanced sideways. Philip, thought Nank, had the air of a root, with his polite, deferential over-eager manner, though his clothes defied the sex-offender stereotype. Instead of blue or pastel, he wore black tracksuit bottoms and a T-shirt with Rage Against the Machine on the front. Perhaps he was a root who had friends or family after all.

'You're the orderly?' said Nank.

'Aye.'

Nank dropped his head. He wanted to say something confidential. Philip bent closer. 'What was all that about earlier with the old man?' said Nank.

If anyone could tell him, it was Philip.

Philip rolled his eyes. The old man was Ivor Jones, he explained, a hill farmer who, because he only ever watched the long-range forecast on his television, didn't see why he should pay his licence fee. The magistrate thought otherwise. He'd been brought to Loanend that afternoon and wouldn't shower. So the riot squad had been brought in to make him.

'And now they're going to lock him up, which is pointless,' said Philip, 'and you know why? All the cells in the main prison have televisions, but not a one has a licence. You see, Crown property, which the jail is, is exempt. I ask you, is the whole world mad or what?'

'Philip!' It was McCarthy. 'Would you like to go back to the metal workshop? Before you answer, remind me what those boys there wanted to cut off? Was it one of your fingers?'

Philip said nothing.

'If you want to stay here, stop shit-stirring.' He turned to Nank. 'Follow me.'

They climbed stairs and stopped at a grille at the top. On the far side, Nank glimpsed a wing lined with steel cell doors. It smelled of laundry and stale bread. This was the induction landing, McCarthy explained, and he would spend his first night here, before he was transferred the next morning, after he had seen the doctor, the governor and a welfare officer, to either Donard or Topped, the remand blocks.

'Do you think he'll make it?' said Nank.

'Who?'

'The old fellow. Ivor, I think he's called.'

'God knows.' McCarthy put his face to the bars and called, 'Grille key. New man for induction.' He turned back to Nank. 'You don't have to be mad to come here, or work here for that matter, but by God it helps.'

87

TWELVE MONTHS LATER, NANK WENT TO trial. He was charged with possession of a Category A drug with intent to supply, possession of a firearm and ammunition. At first, Nank's counsel, under instruction from the client, alleged that the narcotics and the weapon had been planted. 'It won't work,' the barrister muttered on the afternoon of the third day. Nank changed his plea to guilty. He was returned to court on the morning of Wednesday 6 September 1995, and sentenced by the judge to fourteen years for the drug offence and six for the possession of a firearm, to run concurrently.

The instant sentence was pronounced, he looked for Jenny and found her at the back of the court. She was wearing a white dress with a rose print. She mouthed something—I love you, he thought, or, perhaps, Be brave. He must remember her words of encouragement, he thought. They would sustain him in the bleak weeks, months and years ahead.

How strangely practical, he thought next. Shouldn't he be screaming? He didn't feel like that yet, though he had no doubt it would come. For now, he had to make certain that his wife and her words were in a place from which he could retrieve them long after the judgement, and the court with its green walls and its smell of baked radiator paint was gone.

Then he saw Jenny's face screw up. She bent forward and put it in her hands. She was going to cry. Oh, fuck, he'd really gone and done it now, hadn't he?

He felt the officer moving behind him. 'Let's be having you,' the man said.

He left the dock and went out into a corridor, then down a set of concrete stairs to the basement under the court. He was put in a holding cell, a large, square, bleak room with benches on which sat three other grey prisoners.

Later, he was taken to a consultation room where Harvey Golden and Jenny were waiting.

'You can appeal the sentence if you want,' said Harvey, 'but you don't need to decide now.'

'Should he?' said Jenny.

'We'll think about it. I'll leave you now.'

He shook hands with Nank and left. Nank said to Jenny, 'What was it you said in court?'

'Don't forget me.'

They sat then, saying nothing, holding hands, their skin where it touched growing hotter and hotter ...

Later again, an officer appeared, cleared his throat and said to Nank, 'Come on.' He was put back into the holding cell and the door locked behind. He slumped on the bench. He felt numb and there was nothing in his head at all, absolutely nothing. After a while, he became aware of a commotion in the corridor, men shouting, doors opening and closing, engines revving. He guessed the transport to the jail must have arrived in the yard. The door was unlocked.

'Right, you,' said an officer, pointing at him.

He stood up and stepped out.

'Wrists.'

He lifted his arms mechanically. The cuffs went on, and closed with a click. They were thick, heavy hoops connected not by a chain but a short rigid stem, and they were extraordinarily uncomfortable.

A different officer brought him out to the waiting blue transporter. 'In.'

He climbed the metal steps.

'That one.' The officer pointed at a cubicle.

He went in and sat on the metal slat. The door slammed. A key turned. There was a strong salty smell. He looked and, sure enough, there was a puddle in the corner. Prisoners, on the journey to or from court, sometimes pissed in the cubicles. They did it if they needed the toilet and couldn't hold on, or sometimes they did it just to annoy the officers.

'There's piss all over the floor in here,' he shouted, banging on the door.

'All right,' he heard.

A couple of minutes later, the door was unlocked and the officer who'd put him in there was back, a tall man with broad shoulders, a wide, flat face, and a head of thick white hair. His most prominent features were his strangely curved lips and small white teeth. His mouth reminded Nank of a fish.

'Here,' he said. He handed Nank a milk carton. 'It's just water but it'll take the curse off the smell.'

Nank tipped the carton. The water that came out was slightly white with milk. It was also hot and when it hit the floor and mingled with the pee, it started to steam.

The officer took back the carton and locked the door. Nank

lifted his feet and jammed them against the wall. He didn't want the slops on the floor wetting his shoes.

The engine trembled and the transporter began to move.

88

AT FOUR O'CLOCK, NANK STEPPED THROUGH the grille and onto his wing in Topped, the remand block.

'What did they stick you, Nank?' said a burly man in a cell doorway.

'Fourteen, Vincent.'

'Fuck the cunts.'

Vincent was an alcoholic. One night, pissed on vodka and cider, he had stabbed his drinking partner to death with a kitchen knife. When the police found him, Vincent was asleep by the corpse, his hand on the knife, which was stuck in the dead man's throat, and his clothes were soaked with the dead man's blood. He was woken by a policeman, sat up abruptly and said, feeling, his blood wet clothes, 'Have I pissed myself?' Everyone on the wing knew his story.

Nank moved on. When he had left there that morning, he had been on remand but now he was sentenced he was something else. A convict. He liked that term. It was much better than inmate, felon or prisoner. Convict had a ring. The men who went to Australia on the prison hulks, they had been convicts. A convict might have done wrong but he wasn't only bad. A convict was also a man to whom wrong had been done. Stephen 'Nank' Melanophy, BC3232, convict. He liked that.

He approached his cell. 'Keys. Cell three,' he shouted.

An officer left the office and sauntered up to him. 'Hello, Nank.' His name was Hogg. He was young with pebble-grey eyes and a mild expression.

As Hogg inserted the key into the lock, Nank saw that he was smirking and guessed he already knew his sentence and so did all the others in the office. Someone must have telephoned from the court. He remembered the officer with the strange mouth who had given him the milk carton of water. Perhaps at that moment of kindness the unkind call was being made.

'I should be out in seven,' said Nank.

'Course you will,' said Hogg.

He pulled the door back and Nank went in. The bed was stripped. Two paper sacks, filled with his possessions, lay on the mattress. He found a phone card and put it into his pocket. Then, having checked that Hogg had gone back into the office, he slipped across to the cell opposite. Inside, a slight young prisoner with black hair sat on the bed. He was a car thief called Milligan. He wore a Stone Roses T-shirt and shorts.

'Okay,' said Nank.

Milligan put his hand inside the filthy bandage round his knee and fished out a nub of hash wrapped in clingfilm.

'There you go, mate,' said Milligan. 'I didn't touch it.' Milligan, known as Tiny, was only five foot four and wouldn't have dared. That was why Nank had left his stash with him.

In one fluid movement, Nank squatted, put his hands down his trousers and slipped the hash up his behind, taking care to leave a small tail of clingfilm sticking out. He felt as if he was shitting of course. He stood and flexed the muscles. The sensation passed. It was amazing how the body adapted.

'Here you are.' Nank handed Tiny the phone card, the fee they'd agreed.

'Nice one.' Milligan slipped it under the bandage.

89

ABOUT SIX O'CLOCK, NANK WAS BROUGHT to the Induction Centre.

'Name and number?' The SO behind the counter was the same man who had been there when he was remanded.

'Melanophy, BC3232.'

The SO opened Nank's file, muttered, closed it.

'Now you're sentenced,' he said, 'new rules. One visit per week and two first-class stamps, but you can also buy your own stamps and you can send as many letters as you want ... '

The SO rattled on. In essence, now he was sentenced, Nank would have less of everything. Well, he thought grimly, prison was supposed to be a punishment. The only good news was that the pay for prison work was double what he'd been getting on remand.

'Round the corner, you know the drill,' said the SO when he'd finished his talk.

Nank went round and found that the only free booth was, of course, the Beard's.

'Well, look who it is,' said the Beard. 'What a nice surprise to see you again. How are you? Have you had a good day in court?'

'Lovely thanks.'

The Beard found a form and a Biro.

'Length of sentence?'

'Fourteen.'

'Oh, fourteen. Time on remand? A year, wasn't it? When did you come?'

'The thirty-first of August, 1994.'

'So you've been here just over a year. And I bet the time's flown, hasn't it?'

'Yes.'

Behind the questions lay two alternative sentences. His full sentence was fourteen years, which would have him out in 2008. But with remission for good behaviour he'd only do half, which was seven, less a year on remand, which left six, which would have him out in 2001. These details would go on his door card.

'You can't keep what you wore in court,' said the Beard. 'Have you something to change into?'

Nank indicated his sacks.

'Good lad,' said the Beard.

Nank was taken to the changing area. He could hear the shower running as he took a towel. The Beard chose the cubicle beside the one Nank had last time and chalked 'Melanophy, BC3232' on the door. Nank went in, undressed and handed his trousers, shirt and jacket to the Beard.

'These will go in your personal property,' said the Beard, 'and someone will take you on to the shower.'

He slammed the cubicle door and turned the key. Nank undressed, wrapped the coarse towel round his middle and sat down. So, here he was, back in the Induction Centre. First time round, dress rehearsal, he thought, and now the performance, the start of his sentence.

So, six years, if he could avoid adverse reports and not lose any remission. That wasn't such a long time, was it? Well, actually, it was a very long time. He'd miss his children growing up and he'd miss Jenny. Oh, Christ, six more years without her lovely fleshy softness ...

He could feel something tugging. That was the fabric inside, as he imagined it, threatening to tear. And if that happened it would start to seep in, the dense, heavy silty stuff of despair. Under no circumstances must he allow that to happen. And what was the way to stop it? He mustn't think about what he would miss. He mustn't think about his children growing up, their ages now and their ages in six years. Instead he must think about how to make the best possible use of the time that stretched ahead.

He must read, work, and involve himself in the life of the prison. He must live in the present with only occasional forays into the past and he must never let himself think about what he was missing.

It was the future to which he must turn his face and he must accent the positive. It was six he had to do—and he would remind himself of this every day, every hour, every minute, if necessary—and six was better than fourteen. Yes, a lot better and if he kept himself busy it would be gone before he knew it.

The key turned and the cubicle door swung back. 'Melanophy?'

From his slatted seat, Nank found himself looking up at an officer with a red face, a pointed nose and a pudding-bowl haircut. He was a Roundhead with a faintly bird-like appearance.

'Shower,' he said.

The Roundhead led him through. He put his towel on the floor and got quickly under the water, taking care not to let the officer in the chair see the little tail of clingfilm between his buttocks. As last time, the water was too hot. He found the bar of White Windsor soap, jellied as usual, and lathered himself, and rinsed himself.

'Out,' the officer in the chair shouted.

Nank took his towel and, sweating, followed the Roundhead, passing on the way a swaggering youth with a pale face, a mass of freckles and shaggy black hair, heading for the shower.

'You know who he is?' said the Roundhead, when they got to his cubicle.

Nank shrugged.

'That bad boy, Willie Mullen.'

The name meant nothing.

'Pretended to be delivering a birthday cake and shot the man who answered the door. It was in the papers.'

Nank nodded. He remembered now. It had been all over the press about the time he'd come in. The victim was a Catholic, middle-aged, sad and paunchy, and his killer, the boy who had just passed him, was one of a new breed of heartless young Loyalist diehards.

The Roundhead locked him in. He dressed in clothes taken from one of his paper sacks. This was how he had been, hot after a shower and waiting to be called, the last time he was here. Then there was all that shouting, he remembered when that fellow—what was his name? Ivor. Now it all came back. They were taking Ivor for a shower.

From this, Nank went to the next part of the story. It was a few days later. He was in Topped and a prisoner he didn't know came into his cell and said, 'Did you hear?' When there was some big piece of news prisoners would barge into one another's cells like that.

'No, what?' he had said.

'A fellow just topped himself over in Sperrin. Ivor someone or other.'

It was a few days before Nank got the full story. After he'd come in, Ivor's wife had had a heart attack. The night he heard the news, Ivor had torn his sheet into strips and hanged himself from the metal cover on the smoke extractor in his cell.

Don't think about it, Nank told himself now. Don't dwell on the bad. Think about the present. He was about to start his sentence. He must make the best of it.

The cubicle door opened.

'Let's go,' said the Roundhead.

He carried his sacks across the Induction Centre and up the stairs. Through the bars at the top he saw the Induction Wing and inhaled its laundry and bread smell. A year earlier, hadn't he stood here with McCarthy? Suddenly he was stricken by the sense that this was one of a huge number of repetitions that he would be obliged to suffer in the course of his sentence. He had six more years of them to go, he thought, and wondered if he had the strength.

He shook himself and sighed.

'Are you all right?' said the Roundhead, sounding startled.

'Absolutely,' said Nank.

He must never allow himself that evil thought again. It was forbidden. Of course, he had the strength. One year down, six to go, he could do it.

90

ON THE FAR SIDE OF THE grille George Boyd appeared. He ran the Induction Wing. Nank recognised him from the last time. He was a short man with a funny shuffling walk. He turned the key jauntily, and pulled open the grille. 'Welcome,' he said. He took the cards from the Roundhead. 'Ah, Melanophy. I knew the face. I just couldn't put your name to it.' He closed the grille and, behind the bars, the Roundhead began to go down the stairs. 'Follow me,' said George.

They moved towards the cells.

'What did you get?'

'Fourteen.'

George stopped at cell ten, the number painted on the lintel in postbox red. 'I think this'll do you nicely,' he said.

The door was grey, and so was the flap over the glass observation slit. Every cell in Loanend had one: they allowed officers to see what prisoners were doing before they unlocked. If the prisoner was seen, say, to be sitting on the toilet, then the door was not supposed to be opened. That was the theory.

George unlocked and pulled the door back. The cell smelled of tobacco and semen.

'In you go,' said George, and flicked the light switch.

Nank stepped in. It was a small square room, lit by a neon strip cased in a metal grille. The shadows from the grille crossed and criss-crossed the room. The effect was like a gigantic spider's web.

He was surprised to see bunk beds and, laid out on the top one, bedding, Bic razors, soap, towels, plastic cutlery, plates and bowls for two.

'I thought Induction was all singles,' said Nank, appalled at the thought of sharing. 'I thought we were supposed to spend the first night of our sentence alone, contemplating our crime.'

'I've heard about your way with words,' said George, 'and I'm not impressed. You act up in here and the Brownies'll have you down the SDC so fast your feet won't touch the ground.'

'The SDC?' said Nank, innocently. 'Is that Select, Delightful and Comfortable quarters?'

'Separation and Detention Centre, as well you know.'

Of course he did. But George, always literal-minded, had felt the need to explain and Nank had achieved a little victory in getting him to do so, not, of course that George knew that. Such minor triumphs were one of the superior pleasures of prison.

'Going to tell me who I'm sharing with?' said Nank.

'Everything belongs to Induction,' said George, ignoring his question. 'It's for your use for one night only. Make certain you leave it all here when you go tomorrow morning. Now make your bed.'

The door slammed.

For a second, he contemplated wrecking the cell—he'd certainly get a cell on his own that way—but then he asked himself would it be worth it? The S and D team, the Brownies, would cart him away and tomorrow he'd be in adjudication—in effect, a prison court. The charge would be read and a governor would pronounce. And the outcome— well, that was utterly predictable. He'd get several weeks in the punishment block. For a few days he'd be denied books or a radio and left to stew. Later, the regime would relax slightly, but there'd be no association, no education and he'd be locked up twenty-three hours a day. It would be incredibly boring and he'd be marked as a troublemaker. When he had first gone to HMP Kingsman he hadn't cared when he was sent to the punishment block for fighting. In fact, he'd relished it: it had given him a reputation as a tough nut. But now he was thirty-eight, he did care. He wanted an easy sentence and the way to ensure that was to stay out of trouble. So he wasn't going to wreck his cell.

He made up the bottom bunk then sat on the plastic seat by the rickety table. It was a smaller cell than the one he'd had on remand—these induction cells, like the ones in the punishment block, were intended to make prisoners feel hemmed-in and anxious—and there was no television, of course. The toilet had no seat, either. He thought about having a wank. He looked at the toilet-paper holder by the toilet. Empty. He felt in his pocket but found no tissue. He looked in the bin. No, he couldn't do it in there. So, what else was there but to lie down and let his mind go still? He'd become an expert at this over the previous twelve months.

He jumped up onto the top unmade bunk, lay back and let his mind empty. Time passed and then the flap outside banged up. Nank opened his eyes. He saw movement on the other side of the observation slit, then the door swung back.

'In,' said George.

A figure stepped forward. He had a white face, freckles and shaggy black hair.

'Hello.' Nank swivelled, and dropped to the floor.

'This is Nank,' said George. 'Cleverest talker in the place. And this is Willie.'

Willie Mullen. He must have been in Donard, thought Nank, while I was on remand in Topped. Hence, they'd never met. And now, for their first night as sentenced prisoners, they were to be banged up together. He could imagine the talk in the office as they'd planned this one. 'Let's double yer Loyalist up with the Fenian drug smuggler.' Ha-ha. A real rib-tickler. Jail humour wasn't basic; it was prehistoric.

'See you later,' said George and closed the door.

91

THERE WAS ONLY ONE WAY TO deal with this, Nank thought. Head on.

'They're having a bit of fun putting us in together,' he said. 'Fuck them.'

'They win if we fall out.'

'What do I fucking care?'

Oh, right hard, thought Nank. Willie probably thought he was a Republican and that he had to signal he was taking no shit. Fair enough. Still, best to get it out so there could be no misunderstanding.

'I got fourteen years for drugs,' he said.

'Fuck.'

Hard to know if this was, "Fuck, that's awful," or, "Fuck, you deserve it, you cunt." When it came to the expression of nuance, "fuck" didn't cut it.

Willie sighed. The trick, thought Nank, was to get the youth to talk about his life. The trouble was, paramilitaries were warned to be wary of friendly prisoners or officers. Nank might be a plant. For this to work, Nank had to suggest that although he was happy to talk he was just as happy not to, and either was fine.

'Good day?' he said with maximum insouciance.

'Best fucking day of my life,' said Willie.

'I was just thinking the same,' he said. 'Fourteen years away from the wife and the children, fucking marvellous.'

'It's really seven though, isn't it?' said Willie. 'With remission?'

'Yes,' he said. He felt uneasy, suddenly, as if he'd been caught boasting.

'Seven years, long and all I know, but you're lucky. I got life.'

Nank considered. Here was someone, he remembered, who was barely an adult when he'd dressed up as a delivery man and shot someone. It was probably the fault of the parents. They'd probably both worked and neglected him. He knew the sort. Well, no child of his would ever come home to an empty house. He and Jenny would see to that. Then he checked himself. Fruitless line of thought, no bearing on the conversation.

'My name's Stephen,' he said, 'but everyone calls me Nank.' He gave an account of how he'd got the name, laying heavy emphasis on his criminal career.

'They call me Willie,' said the other. 'I'm really William, of course, as Dad is, as Granddad was and so on, back to, God knows, the Boyne probably.'

For a Prod, that was quite elegant, thought Nank. Willie wasn't a fool. With any luck, he wouldn't be a bigot either.

'Very cold, isn't it?' said Willie. He sounded sad. He was still standing exactly where he'd stopped when he'd come in. It occurred to Nank he was in shock and it had only just hit him. This was it. He'd been found guilty and he was going to be locked up for years.

Poor shit, Nank thought, then rebuked himself. Willie had wasted a man and made a hole in a family. The victim might have been a Provo, he couldn't remember that detail, but even so, Willie deserved what he'd got. Besides, as it said on walls all over Loanend, "If you can't do the time, then don't do the crime."

Nank touched the heating pipe that ran above the window. 'There's hardly any heat in that.'

'Oh aye,' said Willie. 'This way, when we go up to the sentenced block tomorrow, it'll seem like a hotel.'

'Something like that,' said Nank. 'How are you feeling?'

'Och,' said Willie, 'I'll just get my head down. I'll get through.'

Down the corridor, a prisoner began throwing his body against his cell door making a dull booming sound.

'Shut the fuck up, you weirdo,' said a voice.

'Ah, the soundtrack of prison,' said Nank.

Feet sounded outside. Nank and Willie stared at their door. They heard a key turn. The banging stopped.

'Listen,' they heard George say, 'you can't have a doctor. I told you before. He's not here. He'll come later and until then, shut up. Otherwise you'll be sent to the hospital and they'll put you in a strip cell and you'll like that even less than here.'

A door slammed and there was no more thudding.

'I've taken the bottom bunk,' Nank said, 'but I'm easy. You want it I can go on top. Or you go on top. I'm happy, either way.'

'"On top",' said Willie, mock-mournfully. 'Words I won't hear from a girl till God knows when.'

'But you'll manage. See this?' Nank held up his right hand. 'That's how you do it.'

Willie chuckled. 'I'll go on top,' he said.

He made his bed. They both lay down ...

Later the door opened. It was George with Willie's two paper sacks, his name and prison number written on the outside. Interesting, thought Nank, that he had been allowed to fetch his own things but Willie wasn't. Was that because he was a paramilitary? George dropped the sacks and produced a roll of toilet paper.

'I forgot to leave in the regulation roll earlier,' he said, and put it on the side of the sink.

'That's very considerate,' said Nank.

George turned to go, then remembered something.

'You usually get tobacco when you see the governor tomorrow but seeing as I'm such a kind-hearted soul ... ' He fished rolling tobacco and cigarette papers out of a pocket. 'Can I interest either of you?'

'Never say no to free tobacco,' said Nank.

'No, never,' said Willie.

George handed each man a packet of papers and a pouch. Both were white and stamped HMP Only.

'Have you ever considered,' said Willie, 'that smoking is bad, yet the prisons dole out tobacco to prisoners?'

'Oh Lord,' said George. 'You haven't been ten minutes with Nank and you're starting to get clever too.'

'You're trying to kill us, aren't you?' said Willie, in an Ian Paisley voice. 'But you won't get far. I shall be going to the court of Human Rights about this. I shall take this right to the top.'

'Very good,' said George, laughing.

'What's the grub?' said Willie.

George was at the door. 'Fish-fingers, peas, chips. Lovely.'

'Now don't forget, will you,' said Willie, 'that I like my fish-fingers cold, the peas dry and the chips burned?'

'Ha-fucking-ha,' said George, and closed the door.

They rolled cigarettes and, with the bin for an ashtray, stood leaning against the bunks, smoking. Nank told Willie about his wife and children. Willie listened and puffed. Judging by his face, he was interested.

92

THE DOOR OPENED.

The orderly who stood in the doorway with the meal trolley was a sixty-year-old with a coconut-shaped head. He was from Belfast and once played cricket for an English county team. He'd met a girl at a disco, taken her to a wood, raped and strangled her, dumped her in a drain. Some Boy Scouts found her body two months later. The dead girl was fourteen, though he had claimed, at the trial, that she'd looked eighteen. Winky—the nickname came from his proper name, Winkworth—started his sentence in an English jail. Though a Rule 43 and kept away from the majority, he had worked in the laundry, where there was limited contact with other prisoners. One attacked him with two PP9 batteries tied up in a sock. Once he had recovered, he had been transferred home to Loanend where the authorities made him Induction Centre orderly. He never mixed with the rest of the population.

'Is there a vegetarian option?' asked Nank.

George sighed in the background. 'Oh, my God, not a healthy eater.'

'Stir-fry with rice,' said Winky.

'Or fish-fingers, peas and chips if you want something decent,' said George.

'That's a pretty convincing argument. I'll have that, then.'

'Me an' all,' said Willie. Each prisoner handed Winky a plate. He ladled out their food.

'Any vinegar for the chips?' asked Nank. He directed the question to George.

'What do you think this place is?'

'A hotel with room service,' said Nank, taking his plate back.

'Oh, fuck off,' said George.

Nank heard Willie snigger. Excellent, he thought.

'When you've finished, wash your plates,' said George, 'or you'll have rats in tonight. Hang on, what am I saying? They're in already, ba-boom.' He closed the door. From outside came the rumble of the wheels as the trolley trundled on.

Nank sat on the bottom bunk, Willie on the chair. The youth nibbled the end of his fish-finger. 'This is fish but not as we know it, Captain Kirk,' he said.

Nank took a forkful of peas. 'Aye,' he said. 'I know what you mean.'

After they finished they washed up, then took it in turns to pee while the other looked away. The lavatory wouldn't flush so they opened one of the narrow windows. As the colder air rushed in from outside, each took a duvet and draped it over his shoulders.

'What cigarette would you fancy if you could have any brand at all?'

'Lambert and Butler,' said Willie.

'Sweet Afton for me.'

'They don't have tips, do they?'

'No, but if you really want a hit, they're your man,' said Nank.

The door swung open. It was George. 'Washed our plates? Good. Phone time. One call each. Who's first?'

'Can I?' asked Nank, politely. 'I want to get the kids before bedtime.'

Willie nodded. 'You go ahead.'

'Thanks, mate,' said Nank, and rummaged in his sack. He found a phone card and followed George down the wing. The booth was a small box with smeared Perspex walls. When he got through Jenny said she felt numb and wanted to sleep, and they would all get through this. He spoke then to his three children, Robert, Emma and Sarah. His younger daughter cried and asked him when he would come home.

'When you've almost lived your whole life again,' he said. 'That's when I'll be home, darling. And as you're so very young, only seven, nearly living your life again won't take you long.'

'Won't it?' said Sarah.

'I'll be home very soon,' he said. 'Ask your mother to get a calendar and you can start marking the days off.'

93

NANK RETURNED TO THE CELL AND Willie went off to telephone. When he came back something about his face was different from before. It was like the expression Nank had seen on his children's faces after they'd taken an exam at school. It was a drained, tired, relieved look.

How long had they been together? A few hours. Yet already Nank knew Willie well enough to notice this. Obviously Willie had rung home. That was the most likely explanation for this change. Something was going on with the parents but what?

From here his thoughts ran to other, more general questions. He knew something of what the newspapers had said but what did Willie have to say about what he had done and why? And how did he see his future in Loanend? If ever there was a time to find out, it was now. Tomorrow they might be sent to separate blocks. They might never be in the same cell again with an evening to fill and nothing except talk to fill it. It had to be now. The trick, besides not asking direct questions or being pushy, was to create the right atmosphere. He had to put Willie at his ease and Nank knew how to do that.

Willie heaved himself onto his bunk and threw himself back. The mesh under his mattress squealed.

'Do you want some blow?' said Nank.

'Wha'?' said Willie, as though he hadn't properly heard what was said.

'Jazz Woodbine?' said Nank.

Willie smiled. 'What do you think? Oh, aye, skin up, mate.'

Nank reached down the back of his trousers, found the clingfilm tail and yanked. He dangled the brown square by the tail and said, 'Nice bit of Moroccan.' He threw the clingfilm into the bin and washed his hands, deftly glued three Rizla papers together and rolled a joint. Then he lay back on the bottom bunk, lit the end and inhaled. The smoke hurt as it hit his lungs but he pulled it deeper and held his breath for a count of ten.

'Here,' he said, exhaling, and holding out the joint.

'Cheers.' A hand came down and took it. 'Why'd you do it?' he heard Willie ask.

'You mean run cocaine?' said Nank. 'I wanted the money. Wife and family to support, and all that.'

He paused. With the first thing he'd said, Willie had given him the means to lead the conversation in the direction he wanted. All Nank had to do now was bat the question back. It was that simple. 'What about you?' he said.

The joint came back down. Nank took a hit.

'How long have you got?' said Willie.

The sagging shape in the mesh, made by Willie's body, vaguely reminded him of a chalk outline on the ground marking the position of a dead body in a black-and-white film. 'All night if you want,' said Nank without any trace of enthusiasm. On the contrary, his tone suggested, he was offering to listen if Willie wanted to talk. That was all. He passed the joint back up.

'It's a long story,' said Willie, 'and it starts in the seventies. Are you ready?'

When Nank had offered to roll the joint a few minutes before, he hadn't thought he'd get to this point this quickly. But, seemingly, he had. 'Okay,' he said, very carefully.

94

HIS STORY, SAID WILLIE, STARTED 1973. He was born in February and three months later, on what he imagined was a sunny afternoon, while he was home with his mother, two RUC constables, Adam Quigg and Sidney Cribben, went to a Loyalist drinking club to speak to a Hubert McVeigh about a driving offence.

Hubert and four other men overpowered Adam and Sidney and took their guns off them. They were feeling miffed that afternoon on account of the recent arrest of a local man for murdering a Catholic. What was the police hammering honest Loyalists for? The Republicans were the real enemy.

They took the two policemen into the toilets. It was a dank space that smelt of wet concrete and the disinfectant balls in the urinals. Hubert checked the stalls, found a turd floating in a bowl. He spiked it on a toilet brush, lifted it out and put it on the floor.

'Right,' he said. 'Eat up.'

Hubert and the others trained their guns on the policemen. Sidney started to whimper. Adam knelt on the damp floor, put his mouth over the end of the turd and bit off a small piece. The shit tasted vaguely meaty; its texture was gritty. In his mind he repeated, over and over, I must not be sick, I must not be sick ...

'Good boy,' said Hubert. 'You may wash your mouth out now.'

Adam stood, ran to the nearest handbasin, turned on the cold tap full and put his mouth to it.

At some point, as the water spurted out, and as he frantically rinsed and spat, he became aware that Sidney was at the next basin. So, they'd made him do it too, he thought.

A few minutes later, their hair and faces sopping, their mouths cold and tasting faintly of limestone from the local water, Adam and Sidney were thrown into the street.

'We won't say what happened in the toilet,' said Adam, pulling his handkerchief from his pocket and mopping himself.

'Never,' said Sidney.

At the police station, they told their sergeant that they had gone to the club and were overpowered by masked men who took their guns.

Two months later a disciplinary inquiry followed. Each man was reprimanded and fined for the loss of his weapon.

The next year Republicans ambushed them. Sidney Cribben was killed. Adam Quigg survived. He stayed in the police force and rose to the rank of detective inspector. His speciality, it emerged over the years, was the interrogation of suspects.

95

NANK ROLLED OFF HIS BUNK AND stood up. This was brilliant but he wanted to see Willie as he talked.

Willie was still stretched out on his back. On his eighteenth birthday, he continued, his present had been a surf lesson at Rossnowlagh beach in Donegal. When he'd got out of the sea, cold and tired, he could just about ride a wave. His father had bought him a cheap board on the spot.

That summer, the Mullen family went to Portrush as usual for their annual holidays. Willie spent all his time in the water. He got quite good. Willie inhaled and the joint glowed. The joint came back. Nank took a pull. He was down to the roach. He'd let it burn out.

'The October after I started surfing,' said Willie, 'this UDR man gets shot. His daughter's at my old school. Elaine Dunwoody they call her.

'I go to the funeral. Elaine has a broken leg. It got broken by the men who murdered her father, and there she is, at the front of the church near the coffin, this big white cast sticking out into the aisle. I can't keep my eyes off it. It's like an accident, when you keep staring.

'After the burial I go back to the wake house. I don't think Mrs Dunwoody likes smoking, so I go to the garden for a fag. I'm puffing away down the end, behind some willows where no one can see, and who comes out on her crutches but Elaine and hobbles up to this ornamental pond. I should have gone, "Hi, Elaine," but I don't. I'm smoking—well, that's the excuse. Actually, I don't know what the fuck to say to her.

'Next thing, she starts crying for her daddy. I get butterflies in my stomach, listening, and I feel this blinding white rage. What had Dunwoody done but join the UDR?

And what reward did he get? Some fucker plugged him having a quiet cider in a country pub. I wanted to get a gun and plug them back.

'So there I am and Elaine screams, "Daddy, Daddy." Then I see she's stood up on her good leg and thrown her crutches down. What's she doing? I don't get it. Then she topples forward into the ornamental pond.

'I pelt up the garden shouting and some other mourners run from the house and we fish Elaine out. One is this fellow Boreland, who's like the main man round our way, and the other's his mate, Hubert McVeigh, the one who took the policemen into the toilets in the club.

'I tell Hubert I want revenge. Over the months, we talk about commitment and loyalty. Hubert doesn't pull his punches. It's either jail or death. I start running wee errands for him, moving things, passing messages, hiding things, nothing really major, but I know I'm being tested and I make certain I don't fuck up. I want in. On my twenty-first birthday, Hubert gives me a beautiful surfboard.'

Willie's grey eyes roamed about the cell. Whatever he had done was just below the horizon and about to appear. Willie started talking again: his subject, the last moments of Patrick O'Neill of 28, Strabane Park, Tullyloan.

96

IT WAS ANOTHER SUNNY AFTERNOON IN May, Willie explained, in the same Ulster town twenty years later ...

Willie finished in the supermarket where he worked at four. He went to the staff toilets, put on the tracksuit bottoms, the Adidas trainers and the windcheater Hubert McVeigh had given him. He put his own clothes into a holdall and left the shopping centre.

Outside there was a car park with plastic drums for glass bottles and a covered skip for newspapers. As he stood waiting nearby, he smelled the fish smell that all skips seemed to give off no matter what they held.

A Nissan Sunny saloon drove up, Derek behind the wheel. Jesus, Willie thought. The world was filled with cars and what had Derek taken? A tin box with a balsawood engine. Willie didn't say anything as he got into the back. He just sighed.

'Stop it,' said Derek. 'We won't stand out in this.'

Derek was forty, with a vast forehead and a pointed chin. In their circle, he was known as Lady Penelope after the Thunderbirds puppet, though as he hated the nickname it was only used behind his back.

'Too bloody right,' Willie said. 'We'll blend in with all the other crap cars.' The closest he had come to a nickname was Wee Willie.

Derek released the handbrake and drove out of the car park and onto the ring road. Willie lifted the flaps on the Cadbury's Flake box beside him and peered in. A smell of gun oil and chocolate drifted out. There was a bundle of grubby crêpe bandage in the bottom and a pair of flesh-coloured plastic gloves. He pulled them on and lifted out the bundle. Even through the latex, the bandage was somehow oily.

Willie found the end and began to undo it. As he unwound the material he was reminded of the long scarves worn by Dr Who in the videos his brother, Lee, watched endlessly but which he'd never much liked, being a *Star Trek* fan.

He had come along ten years after Lee. As his mother would put it when she'd had a couple of drinks, he was the

Mullens' love accident, an idea that was reinforced in her mind by his being born on St Valentine's Day. And the poor lad, she would add, when the notion of her son's origins took hold of her, what had he ever known but the Troubles? Willie couldn't stand her when she was like that because she always wanted to kiss him.

Willie was still unravelling the crêpe but he could feel the hardness at the centre of the bundle now. Oh, yes. Just a couple of more turns, and he would have it in his hand. And he was right. For suddenly, there it was.

He let it rest on his palm. The barrel was black but not really black. Metal was never that dark. The handle was brown, cross-hatched with filigree lines to make it stick to his hand and vice versa. Lovely, he thought, a bonding mechanism to make flesh and metal mesh.

The bottom of the magazine jutted down from the handle a quarter of an inch or so. He pushed it home as Hubert had shown him, flicked off the safety and slid the top backwards then forwards. Inside, he felt the gorgeous mechanism engage and click. That was the first bullet in the spout.

Derek heard the noise. 'Careful,' he said.

'Don't worry,' said Willie.

He engaged the safety. They were passing Lemming's factory, which made the screw tops for plastic bottles. There was wasteland beside it. He saw a hand-painted sign propped against a lamppost that read, "Wood, please". There was already a pile nearby that included pallets, mattresses, and a brown three-piece suite. This was the beginning of the bonfire that would burn on Eleventh Night, surrounded by a happy, jeering, drunken crowd, the flames visible and threatening to the Tullyloan estate on the hill ahead. The next day, 12 July, some of the same crowd would watch the Orange lodges celebrating the victory of William of Orange over James II at the Battle of the Boyne.

It never ceased to amaze him how much was burned at the bonfires and now he found himself wondering, as the car went on, if this meant his people weren't as thrifty as they claimed. Perhaps, on the contrary, they were careless, treated their possessions badly, which explained why there was always so much to burn on Eleventh Night.

It occurred to him next that these were strange thoughts given what he was about to do. Then, unaccountably, he found himself remembering *To Catch a Thief*, which he had watched on television a few nights before, and the fantastic fireworks at the end that lit up the night sky.

'Are you ready?' said Derek.

'Aye.' He caught the other man's eye in the rear-view mirror. 'Aye,' he said, and then 'Aye,' again, this time with enthusiasm.

Derek's eyes flicked from the mirror to the windscreen. So did Willie's. He saw the Tarmac unfurling under the bonnet, ragged hawthorn hedges on either side with black plastic scraps from silage bundles trapped in the branches and, bang in front, he saw Tullyloan hill with the estate halfway up.

'Will you stop that with the safety?' said Derek. 'You're making me nervous.'

97

HE PUT HIS THUMB TO THE side and looked ahead. The Tullyloan estate comprised two dozen streets surrounded by a road that connected to the ring road along which he and Derek were moving. The houses on the estate had once been white but now they were grey, like old snow. The roof tiles were brick red and wet with the rain that had fallen earlier. Every house had a chimney and from practically every one a plume of smoke curled away into the air.

A sign flashed past reading VICTORY TO THE IRA, and suddenly there were Tricolours on the lampposts too, hanging limply because there was no wind to move them. The turning into Tullyloan was coming up. He sensed Derek slowing. He heard the car indicator. He noticed a girl with a pushchair on the corner. She looked puzzled. She didn't recognise the car and she didn't know him or Derek. He grinned at her. This was what Hubert had told him to do. Always act as if he were at home. And it worked, for, as Derek turned the car in and they passed within a few feet of her, she raised her hand automatically in greeting. Willie had got her to think he was one of theirs when, of course, he wasn't; he was one of the others. Her reaction was grimly satisfying.

Derek began to drive forward carefully, swivelling his head as he went, and Willie did the same. They were looking for cars with police or soldiers in plain clothes or, worse, some of their lot, but every parked car was empty.

They entered Tullyloan proper. Willie saw a girl playing hopscotch on the pavement, then a man in his vest on an upturned beer crate trimming a hedge. An elderly woman in a floral print dress was sweeping up the clippings.

Derek turned right and left and right again and Willie heard, coming through Derek's open window, applause from a daytime television programme, a radio jingle, and a child shrieking with delight. Then they arrived in O'Neill's street. The house was in view and at the end was the road that looped back to the ring road.

Derek indicated, pulled over and stopped. If O'Neill had

looked out at that moment, he wouldn't have seen them unless he'd squinted sideways.

Willie put the gun into the right-hand pocket of his windcheater. It was deep and the weapon would not fall out. That was why Hubert had chosen this jacket.

'In the boot?' he asked.

'In the boot,' said Derek.

Willie climbed out, went round to the boot and opened it. The white cake box rested on a piece of newspaper so it wouldn't get dirty, just as Hubert had said. He lifted it out and felt that it was weighted as if there were a cake inside, again as Hubert had promised.

The man he had come to kill had a daughter, Rita, and she was about to turn eighteen. Hubert had discovered these facts in the local paper. And O'Neill was always to be found at home at this time of the afternoon. Hubert had been told that by a contact in the British Army. From these two pieces of knowledge, he had constructed his plan.

Today, the day before Rita's birthday, Willie would appear during the afternoon in O'Neill's road with a cake box. If challenged, he would say he was from Moran's Cake Shop and he was delivering a cake for Miss O'Neill. He'd practised saying this with Hubert for days.

Willie would go to the O'Neill house. If O'Neill answered the door, he would know he hadn't ordered a cake. This wouldn't matter, Hubert said. He would assume someone else had ordered it for his daughter and it was only necessary that O'Neill believed this for as long as it took Willie to get the gun out of his pocket.

On the other hand, if it wasn't O'Neill who answered the door, Willie had to ask for him by name. Willie had practised this dialogue with Hubert as well.

He closed the boot and walked carefully along the pavement as if he really were carrying a cake. At the same time, he whistled the Nirvana song, 'Come as You Are'. Kurt Cobain had killed himself the month before since when the band's songs had been played incessantly on the radio.

He opened the garden gate and stepped onto the path. Now, into his thoughts, came images of the night before. He was with Alice, dancing. She was not a girlfriend but a girl he liked and a girl, he hoped, who liked him. Then he was in Alice's living room with the lights out, and he'd got her knickers down as far as her knees and he had a hand nestled in her surprisingly springy pubic hair. Then her father was shouting 'Alice,' from the top of the stairs, and then he was on the back step by the kitchen door. Alice was masturbating him vigorously. His semen shot across her hand and up her arm. 'Have you a tissue?' she whispered. He felt in his pocket. 'Sorry.'

'Men,' said Alice. She licked her wrist cheerfully. 'Never have what you need when you need it, do they?'

The memory vanished. He had reached the door. He pressed the bell. He heard a man calling, 'I'll get it.' Judging by the voice, it might be O'Neill.

The door opened back.

Yes, it was.

98

O'NEILL WAS ABOUT FORTY, WITH A red face and a broken nose. Willie recognised him from the photographs Hubert had shown him. They had come from the same soldier who had known when O'Neill would be at home.

'Are you Mr O'Neill?' asked Willie.

O'Neill looked startled, then puzzled, and finally wary.

'Who wants him?' O'Neill's eyes were fixed on the box.

'I have a cake here for Miss Rita O'Neill,' said Willie.

'A cake!' O'Neill turned. On the table in the hall there was a vase full of daffodils. 'Rita, do you know anything about a cake?'

Willie dropped the box, put his hand into his pocket, clicked the safety off and took out the gun. O'Neill turned back and saw the dark round O of the muzzle, his expression a mixture of surprise and alarm.

Willie pulled the trigger. The gun banged. There was a silver muzzle flash. His head rang.

There was a smell like solder and a tingling up his arm. Even though he'd had several test fires in a quarry with Hubert it was still novel and shocking.

The bullet hit O'Neill in the middle of his body. It was as if someone had pushed him hard with the flat of their hand. He went back a couple of feet. Willie pulled the trigger again and he was aware of a cartridge flying past his face. At the same time, he noticed a girl at the top of the stairs. He knew it must be Rita. She wore only a T-shirt with a bullseye on the front. Her pubic hair was fair and she had a plaster on her right knee.

Rita was staring at O'Neill, who was on the hall floor now. There were little splashes of blood on the skirting. She made a noise, more like a squeal than a scream, and now it had started it wouldn't stop. Willie knew this because Hubert had warned him of what to expect. He pointed the gun at O'Neill's head and pulled the trigger twice. Then he pointed the gun at O'Neill's chest and pulled the trigger once. Five shots in all. He had counted them.

He bent down and picked up the cartridges from the ground, one, two, three and four. He could smell their cordite-and-gun-oil smell. But he'd fired five. Where was the fifth? He lifted the wire cage where milk bottles went but found only leaves and a grey woodlouse. He lifted the doormat. There was just a coat of fine grey dust and the imprint in one corner of a key that had once been left there. He checked under the cake box. The fifth cartridge was nowhere.

Then he saw a drain beside the doorstep with no grille. So, that was where it had gone. He thought about putting his hand down and feeling around but decided there was no point. The cartridge case would wash away, wouldn't it? Only if there was rain, he told himself. It had rained earlier but now the sun was shining. Rain didn't seem likely.

Now he noticed the vase of daffodils in the hall again. He put the gun in his pocket, stepped inside and took it, then stepped back and closed the door so Rita wouldn't see. He pulled the flowers out and tipped the vase. The water hit the drain and made a sloshing noise. A smell rose up, a combination of pond and old brick, mixed with the sharp odour of daffodil stalks.

He put the flowers back into their vase, picked up the cake box, walked down the path and out of the gate, the sound of Rita sobbing and shouting behind growing fainter the further he got away from the house.

99

DEREK DROVE ALONG THE ROAD TOWARDS him, stopped and reached round. The back door of the car opened like in a film, and Willie saw the roomy back seat. He threw everything in, then himself and closed the door.

Derek drove to the end of the street, turned left and began to follow the loop towards the ring road. He did not drive quickly as that would only have attracted attention. In the back, Willie put the gun on the floor between his feet and the shell casings into the empty envelope stuck to the Cadbury's Flake box. Then he took off the gloves and the Adidas trainers, the tracksuit bottoms and the windcheater. He took his own things from his holdall and put them on. He'd practised undressing and dressing for weeks in the back of Hubert's car as Hubert drove him around and he was able to do this quickly.

Derek stopped on a bridge over the Bann. Willie tipped the casings into the water, got back into the car and put the bullet envelope into the Flake box. Derek drove on. Willie bandaged up the revolver. Derek stopped on a piece of unused ground behind the garages at the back of Willie's estate. The two got out, Willie carrying his empty holdall and the gun, and Derek set the car on fire, with the cake box and everything else from the murder on the back seat. Derek took back the gun in its oily scarf, got into a car that was waiting for him and was driven away. Willie walked home. He went in by the back door, as he always did. His mother was in the kitchen, shelling a hard-boiled egg under the cold-water tap.

'Good day at work?' she asked.

'Aye, not bad,' he said.

100

RITA O'NEILL TOLD THE POLICE THAT the young man who had shot her father had taken the vase of daffodils and a neighbour confirmed he'd emptied it into the drain.

The next day, in the sewer in front of the O'Neills' house, a police frogman found two weapons dumped there by the local IRA and the fifth cartridge.

The following Saturday, early in the morning, Derek was stopped at a checkpoint with the gun used to kill O'Neill in his glove compartment. He was on his way to Hubert to return it. He had used it the day before to rob a post office.

Later that same Saturday, in the afternoon, shortly after Willie had got home from work, two detectives in civilian clothes rang the bell. His mother opened the door.

'Willie about?' one asked gently.

'In the lounge.'

The detectives stepped into the room. Willie looked up from the rugby match on the television.

'Willie Mullen?' It was the one who had spoken at the door.

'Aye.'

'I'm arresting you for murder. You do not have to say anything, but I must caution you that if you do not mention when questioned something which you later rely on in court, it may harm your defence. And if you do say anything, it may be given in evidence.'

Willie blinked.

'Do you want to say anything?'

Willie shook his head. This felt unreal and faraway. He noticed that his mother, in the doorway, had started to cry.

They put all the clothes from his wardrobe in an evidence bag, then led him outside and put him into the back of a car. They sat on either side of him. A third man was in the front.

'Okay,' said the detective who had spoken inside. 'Let's go.'

The driver eased off the handbrake and moved away. Willie caught a glimpse of his mother at the door and then she was gone.

'You know,' said the talkative detective, 'I thought you'd be smaller.'

It was several seconds before Willie realised he had been spoken to. 'Did you?' he said.

This no longer felt unreal.

The car drove on. He saw his estate sliding past and later the shopping centre where he worked. He saw cars parked between white lines painted on the ground. He saw the trolley bay with trolleys in rows and abandoned trolleys in a cluster nearby. Then houses gave way to fields as they drove out of town. Willie felt anxious. 'Where am I going?' he asked.

'You'll find out,' said the detective who hadn't spoken.

101

SOME TIME LATER THE DRIVER PARKED the car at the back of a building. They'd brought him to a holding centre, Willie guessed. The detectives got Willie out and took him inside. He found himself in a room with a counter, a sergeant in uniform behind.

'Here he is,' said the talking detective.

Willie gave his name and address, his date of birth and his National Insurance number, which he had by heart. 'I want to ring a solicitor,' he said.

'You don't want one of them unless you're guilty,' said the detective who hardly spoke.

'You can do that later,' said the sergeant. 'Shall we deal with the formalities? Is there anyone you need to tell you've been arrested?'

'My ma.'

'She was present at the arrest,' said the talkative detective.

'We'll ring her and let her know you're here,' said the sergeant. 'Empty your pockets. I want your belt, too, and your laces.'

His lighter, handkerchief, wallet, keys, belt and laces went into a clear plastic bag. This was sealed and put into a locker. He signed the custody record. He was photographed in front of a grey roll-down screen holding a white card with his name and date of birth. His finger and palm-prints were taken.

Then he was led to a cell with a bottle-green mattress on a concrete plinth and a drain in the middle of the floor with a steel grate riveted across. While his escort waited he took off everything except his boxers and socks, and put on a light blue all-in-one paper suit, with a white plastic zipper running from crotch to neck, and a pair of plimsolls. The escort itemised his things and put them into a paper sack.

'If you want the toilet, press the bell,' said the escort. 'We generally answer in a few minutes, providing we're not distracted by some other cunt fucking around.'

He locked the door. Willie sat on the hard mattress and stared at the button in the steel frame by the door with the word "Call" in red underneath. He felt relieved. That was the worst over, wasn't it, until the interrogation?

The light went out. There was tittering and scuffling outside the door. The light came on. The light went off. The door opened. The light went on. He saw three policemen with batons drawn. The light went off. The light went on. The men were two steps closer. The light went off. The light came on. The men were closer still. The light went off. Willie scrambled for the corner. Something hit his shoulder. The light came on. Willie was manhandled onto the floor of the cell. The paper pants suit was ripping. The men were pulling it off. He was hit hard on the buttock. The light went off. The light went on. The paper suit was right off now. He saw its tattered remains flash past as it was thrown into the corner. He put his hand over his groin. The light went out. The blows fell. He hadn't imagined anything like this. This was the worst. No, it was worse than the worst. He mustn't think like that. He had to remember what Hubert had said. He had to imagine a golf ball. The golf ball was in the middle of his body. And this was his essence, essence of Willie Mullen. Everything else was peripheral. He had to concentrate on this golf ball. And he had to forget about everything else. If he could do that he could get through this. He could live. If he did not, he died.

At some point, as the blows continued to rain down on him while the light came on and went off, Willie the golf ball floated off and the pain flooded into the empty space it left behind. As more time passed and the light came on and went off again, the pain grew. After a while, the evil thought came as the light came on and went off again; they were going to beat him to death. There was nothing he could do to stop them. His life was over. He knew it.

No sooner had this registered than something happened in the deepest part of his being. He knew it was happening but he couldn't stop it. The turd slithered out of his boxers and plopped onto the floor.

'He's shat himself,' shouted a policeman. 'Oh, no! It's all over my shoes.'

The blows stopped. The light came on.

'What the hell is going on?'

He recognised the voice of the sergeant who had processed him.

'Pick that up and get out.'

He was aware of the torn pants suit wrapped around a hand, his turd being removed from the floor and the men walking out, silently.

'I don't know what that was about,' said the sergeant. 'I'll get you another suit.'

He closed the door. Willie climbed onto the mattress and curled up. His boxers were lightly soiled but he wouldn't take them off. The skid marks would dry. The door opened. The sergeant threw him another pants suit. 'Get that on,' he said.

He went off and came back with a mop and a bucket of hot soapy water.

'Get this place cleaned up,' he said.

Willie mopped the brown stains and left the floor soapy and faintly steaming. When he had finished the sergeant took the mop and bucket and locked the door.

102

HE THOUGHT IT WAS SATURDAY NIGHT, though he couldn't be certain, the first time he was brought to the interview room. It was a square, windowless space, and a little too warm. A table stood in the middle, one end flush to the far wall with chairs on either side. On the wall to the left as he came in, a flat, rectangular digital clock hung, mirrored, on the wall to his right, by a portable television and video-recorder. They put him in the corner on the clock side. Two strange men in suits took the seats opposite. They gave their warrant numbers, not their names. One was middle-aged, the other younger. The older was the talker. He explained to Willie that the interview would be recorded. He indicated the microphone in the wall above. He asked Willie if he understood.

Willie had prepared for what was about to begin by undergoing several mock interrogations with Hubert. He knew he must refuse to answer no matter what the question. This way he would deprive the interrogator of any opportunity to develop a relationship. And to help maintain his silence, the best strategy was to think about something else. He looked down at the tabletop and imagined a big blue wave with a white cap rolling towards land.

'Willie Mullen has had the conditions explained to him under which the interview will be conducted,' said the talker, 'but has declined to respond.' He cleared his throat. 'What were you doing last Tuesday?'

Willie remained immobile as he had been trained to do.

'Did you go to twenty-eight Strabane Park, on the Tullyloan estate?'

The tabletop was white melamine. Willie wished it was wood with grain and whorls he could lose himself in. He tried to imagine the sound of the wave as it hurtled towards the shore.

'You were at twenty-eight Strabane Park, last Tuesday, weren't you? You were driven there by Derek Donaldson.'

He felt certain that the one who hadn't spoken was staring at him, watching for a reaction to Derek's name. He knew from Hubert that was what they did. One always spoke, the other always watched. Once they got a reaction, the police would press relentlessly at the same point hoping to break the suspect down.

At the same time as he remembered his training, he realised his position was hopeless. The police knew. They would charge him, bring him to trial, and he would be found guilty. He felt queasy, and swallowed. He must not think thoughts of this kind. He must stare at the table and refuse to answer. When the worst happened, and it would, he knew that, he must be able to hold his head high and say he hadn't cracked.

'Patrick O'Neill lives at twenty-eight Strabane Park, with his daughter, Rita. Did you see Mr and Miss O'Neill, last Tuesday afternoon, about four thirty?'

The talker asked him variations of these questions for a long time. Then he was taken back to his cell. He ate a cheese sandwich and drank a cup of milky tea served in a blue plastic mug that smelled of washing-up liquid.

103

LATER, HE WAS BROUGHT BACK TO the interrogation room and the talker asked him the same questions as before while the watcher stared. This was his second interrogation. It might have been Monday now. Or Tuesday. He was disoriented. He tried to read the wall clock in the interrogation room but the numbers didn't make sense. All he could do was count the times they had him out of the cell. He was up to six when his cell door opened and a policeman he had not seen before looked in.

'Move it.'

He shuffled out and turned left for the interrogation room.
'Other way, pal.'

Willie turned right and his stomach pulsed with dread.
Was there another beating coming? As he trod along one
unfamiliar passage after another, the terror rose. 'I need the
toilet,' he said.

'When we finish. This won't take long, what we've got to do.'

The escort brought him into a long room with men lined on
one side and a mirror on the other. It was the identity parade,
he realised, with a rush of relief. He took his place and stared
at the mirror. He had no doubt that Rita O'Neill and other
witnesses were standing behind.

The parade over, he followed the escort back the way he
had come. The escort was silent but his step was jauntier. The
police had got a result. Willie was certain of it. He'd been
identified.

The escort opened a door to reveal a small room with a
white toilet and handbasin. 'Don't try anything funny. The
door doesn't lock and I'm standing here, listening. Got it?'

104

HE WAS TAKEN BACK TO THE interrogation room. He was
put in his usual seat in the corner. The talker and the watcher
sat opposite. There was a brown cardboard box between them.

'This interview will be recorded,' said the talker. 'Willie
Mullen has had the conditions under which the interview
will be conducted explained to him, but has declined to
respond.'

The corner of the cardboard box fluttered at the edge of Willie's vision. He dreaded to think what was inside.

'What were you doing last Tuesday?' said the talker.

Silence.

'Did you go to twenty-eight Strabane Park on the Tullyloan estate?'

Silence.

'Patrick O'Neill lives at twenty-eight Strabane Park, with his daughter, Rita. Did you see Mr and Miss O'Neill, last Tuesday afternoon, about four thirty?'

Silence.

The talker went on asking variations of these questions for a long time. Finally, he said, 'I'm going to take the lid off this box and I'm going to show you what's inside.'

Willie couldn't stop himself looking up. He found the two detectives staring back at him, both on the verge of smirking. They had him. He'd reacted.

He dropped his gaze to the melamine tabletop. He heard the something coming out of the box. Two plastic envelopes appeared in front of him. In one, he saw a nine-millimetre gun with cross-hatching on the handle. In the other was a single spent brass nine-millimetre cartridge. It was the lost one, he was sure, the one he'd tried to flush down the drain.

'The gun and the cartridge casing match and a bullet, that matches this casing, was dug out of Mr O'Neill's chest at his autopsy,' said the talker. 'This gun, using that bullet, killed him. Have you got that, Willie Mullen? Now all we need to know is who used the gun. Well, we know, don't we? That's why you're here. You murdered Mr O'Neill last Tuesday. Don't try to pretend you didn't.'

He couldn't stop himself shitting when they'd beaten him, and now he couldn't stop the tears. That was the body for you, he thought. It always let you down. He had this thought in the detached part, the part that monitored what was happening, but in the part where he was currently located, he had only emotions, the predictable mix of pain, misery and hopelessness.

'Gotcha,' said the watcher, the first word he had spoken so far.

Willie felt more tears come out in great hot gouts. He was weeping like a boy.

'We have a witness,' said the talker, 'who not only saw you kill Mr O'Neill, but who also saw you pour water from a vase down the drain outside the O'Neills' in the hope of washing away the spent cartridge.'

Willie touched the little puddle of tears that had formed on the white melamine in front of him.

'This has got to be the clearest case I've come across in all my years on the police.'

Willie looked up and stared across the table at the talker. The detective picked up the gun and the cartridge and put them back into the box.

The other detective reeled off the charges against him. These included murder, membership of a proscribed organisation and taking and driving away.

'Interview with Willie Mullen is now terminated,' said the talker.

Willie put his wrists to his eyes and tried to stop his tears. It was over.

105

HE WAS WITH THE SERGEANT, THOUGH he had no idea, he was now so confused, how he came to be with him again.

'Your copy of the charge sheet,' the sergeant said. It was yellow and flimsy, like a page from a Bible. 'Give that to your solicitor.'

Still in the paper suit, he was cuffed and driven to the courthouse in his town. It was an old Victorian building, surrounded by blast-proof walls.

Inside, the cuffs came off and he was put into a holding cell, a twelve-foot-square room lit by a single bulb with fixed wooden benches. The walls and ceiling were covered with names, dates and slogans.

At some point, he was taken to a consultation room where Napier Conway, his solicitor, was waiting. He handed over his charge sheet.

'Do you understand what's happening?' said Napier.

He nodded.

'They're going to remand you into custody. I'll go for bail, of course, but I suspect you'll go to jail.'

He nodded again.

'Guilty or not guilty?'

He shrugged.

'We'll say not guilty for now. In court, confirm your details and don't say anything else. Leave the talking to me. Understand?'

'Aye,' he said.

He was taken back to the holding cell and sat, numb, on a bench. There were three other men with him but they ignored him.

He was cuffed again, brought into the court and put into

the square wooden dock. He was aware of the magistrate sitting above him. He saw his solicitor and the talker, the detective who had done all the talking during his interrogation sitting at separate tables below.

The hearing began. He confirmed his name and date of birth. The charges were read out. He had heard them before and paid no attention. Then the talker went to the witness stand. He swore an oath on the Bible and gave his name as Adam Quigg. As soon as he heard this surname, Willie's memory stirred. Hubert had warned him. Quigg was a dangerous policeman who had a particular interest in Hubert. Willie had to watch out for him.

He decided to listen. He heard the magistrate ask Quigg if he could connect the accused to the charges. Quigg confirmed that he could. Then he heard Napier Conway apply for bail on his behalf. The application was denied.

He was returned to the holding cell and the cuffs were removed. Then he remembered who Quigg was. He was one of the young policemen who went to the club to talk to Hubert and was taken to the toilet. In which case, Willie realised, he was part of something between this policeman, Quigg, and Hubert, which explained the beating and all the other things he'd noticed, like the escorts' elation after the identity parade. Everything that had been done was supposed to strike at Hubert. There was some comfort, he thought, in having understood.

106

HE WAS LED BACK TO THE consultation room where Napier Conway was waiting.

'Listen, ' said the solicitor, 'you're not going to Culcavy.'

This was where all the paramilitaries were and where he had expected to be sent, his organisation having claimed him.

'Why not?'

'Your mother has had a word.'

'My mother?'

'You're going to Loanend, with the ordinary decent criminals.'

'Loanend?'

'And one day, believe me—because where you're going is far better than Culcavy—you'll thank your mother for this ... '

Willie paused. Nank threw the old roach into the toilet and pushed the button.

'Have you a picture of your mum and dad?' asked Nank.

'Aye.' Willie jumped down and pulled a white frame out of a sack.

'That was taken on their thirtieth anniversary.'

The picture showed the couple on a sofa holding hands. Willie's father was a bald man in a suit. His eyes were dark. His mother was a good-looking woman in a red dress. He wouldn't want to admit this but he'd have known they were Protestants. How did you know these things? There was no answer except that you did. Anyone looking at a photograph of his mother and father on their anniversary would have known they were Catholics. Of course, there wasn't such a picture—they never had done anything together, his mother and father—but the truth remained. You could tell. You weren't meant to but you could.

'They look like a mum and dad,' he said.

'They're that all right,' said Willie. He put the photograph away.

'Were they at the trial?' said Nank.

'They had me tortured. It was the worst part of the whole trial, worse than the cross-examination, the two of them sitting there, Ma with her red eyes and my father like this.'

Willie jumped back up onto his bunk and assumed a stern, disapproving, almost ferocious expression. 'He never said anything to me, but I knew what he was thinking. "We brought you up good, you never wanted and then you go and do this."' He spoke in what Nank presumed was his father's voice. '"Why, son? Why'd you do it? You've broken your mother's heart, do you know that?"'

Willie lay back.

'He's worked in a drapery shop all his life,' said Willie. He was back to his own voice. 'Drapery shop. That says it all, doesn't it? Open the shutters at ten to nine, Monday to Saturday, half-day Wednesday, two weeks holiday every July in a caravan in Portrush, five cigarettes a day, two pints of Guinness on Friday night but never more, sherry on Christmas Day and whiskey only at a funeral. Day after month after year, like clockwork.

'But if the parents were bad, the older brother was worse. He sent me a letter in remand, said I'd disgraced the family and he wanted no more contact. He wouldn't even come to the trial.'

'What about the relatives?' said Nank, blandly.

'Who?'

'The relatives of the dead man.'

'They didn't come,' said Willie. Nank couldn't tell whether he was angry, miserable or blank.

'Shall I skin up again?'

'Fuck, why not?' said Willie, 'I'm not going anywhere.'

'Is everything all right at home?' said Nank. 'I imagine it's home you just rang.'

'Everything's all right,' said Willie slowly, sounding stoned. 'Well, actually, it's not.'

'Oh.'

'Of course it isn't. I'm here, aren't I? But at least I'm not in Culcavy.'

'Actually, now you mention it,' said Nank, 'why are you here?'

He had all his smoking things on the end of Willie's bunk and he was gluing two papers together. Willie sat up and dangled his legs over the side.

'From day one,' said Willie, 'my parents wanted me here. They reckon, in here, I won't be running around with the paramilitaries. I'll just do my time, my heart won't harden and I won't get bitter or, worse, political.'

Nank sprinkled tobacco along the paper, then began to tease it apart to ensure there were no knots.

'Soon as I'm arrested my ma goes straight to see this fella Boreland. He's the main man at home. Remember him? I met him at the Dunwoody wake I was telling you about. He runs a furniture shop in our town. Soon as Ma comes in, he takes her into his little office and closes the blinds and the door. He thinks she's going to eat the face off him, on account of me being in his organisation, although actually, because I was Hubert's, I'd never had much to do with him.

'He says, "Look, Mrs Mullen, I'd nothing to do with your son."

'She says, "I don't care. I'm here because I don't want him down Culcavy. I want him in Loanend." Boreland owes her, so

he says he'll sort it. My ma tells the solicitor to tell me I'm for
Loanend, not Culcavy, which he does and I'm told that soon
as I'm charged. When I get my first visit, I say, "Ma, what you
done?" She says, "Don't worry, Boreland owes me".'

That was the second time Willie said "owe". How could
someone like Boreland, thought Nank, possibly owe
something to a woman like Willie's mother?

'She must have some powers of persuasion, your ma.'
Nank held the nub of hash carefully between forefinger and
thumb. 'Did they ever go out, she and Boreland?'

'Don't be daft. The only man my ma's had is me da.'

Nank got his Zippo going and began to roast the edge of
the hash furthest from his fingers. As the flame played over
the bumpy brown surface, the hash went black and a coil of
blue smoke rose up. He breathed this in and the taste of hash
spread over the back of his throat.

'So what's her secret then?' said Nank.

'Here's the story,' said Willie.

107

WILLIE STARED AT THE WALL, GATHERING his thoughts.
'Okay,' he began. 'Boreland's got three daughters and Vicki's
the youngest. She works in the same factory where my ma is
part time. The factory makes toilets and cisterns. Vicki's on
the floor, my ma's in Accounts, Mondays and Fridays.'

Nank gingerly touched the blackened edge of the hash. It
was still hot. He blew on it to cool it.

'Vicki's wedding's coming but she hasn't told no one in the
factory. She doesn't want any pranks because she knows they

won't be nice. She thinks no one likes her because of who her daddy is. In fact, no one likes her because she's always acting big because of who her daddy is. So, she isn't far wrong.'

The hash had cooled. Nank broke the burned edge off the lump, crushed it between his fingers, then sprinkled the granules onto the tobacco.

'Anyway, it's discovered Vicki's getting married, and Friday afternoon, just before clocking off, some girls run her in the toilets, get her clothes off, take her down to the front of the factory and tie her to the flagpole. This isn't the works entrance. That's at the back. The flagpole is at the front where the clerical staff and the management go in and out. Vicki's marrying some management fellow and this is meant to be a surprise for him when he comes out; Vicki tied to the flagpole, wearing next to nothing, covered with flour and eggs.'

What was this to do with Willie's mother? Nank was confused. He lifted the open joint off the top bunk and started carefully to roll it. 'Was your mother one of these ones playing the prank?'

'Don't be daft, of course not.' Willie sounded outraged. 'She'd never do a thing like that to anyone. I'm coming to her, just wait. Imagine the flagpole, glass doors, entrance hall and stairs leading up to accounts. Got it?'

'Yep.' Nank folded the paper in on itself.

'Now, under the stairs, you've got a cupboard where the cleaner keeps his stuff. The factory girls have tied Vicki to the flagpole when one of them remembers the cupboard and thinks there might be a bucket of water in there to tip over Vicki before they plaster her with flour and eggs.

'So this girl goes inside and opens the cupboard and, happy days, isn't there a bucket and it full of water? She carries it out, tips it over Vicki. Only it isn't water, is it?'

'Isn't it?' Nank licked the gummed edge and, with a final twist, a cigarette appeared.

'No. The cleaner, who isn't called Wally for nothing, always mixes up a solution of caustic soda on Fridays to do the drains Saturday mornings and that's what they've poured over her. Caustic soda—it's acid. Course Vicki starts roaring. The girls think Vicki's just carrying on, and they laugh and tell her any moment her fiancé will be down and she'd better have a nice smile ready for him. You know the sort of carry-on.'

Nank did and it disgusted him. In his mind's eye, he imagined Vicki, small breasts and heavy thighs, rope looped around her and the white flagpole at her back.

'At that moment,' continued Willie, 'out comes Ma on her way home. She sees Vicki screaming her head off and she sees the bucket. She looks inside. She sees crystals in the bottom. She thinks, Wally, cupboard under the stairs, drains on Saturday morning. It isn't hard to work out. She's in Accounts. She knows Wally gets caustic soda. She pays the invoices.

'"It's caustic soda, not water," she shouts.

'She gets the fire hose from the hall and turns it on Vicki and the girls think this is hilarious, my ma hosing Vicki down. And by now there are clerical staff hanging out the windows upstairs, laughing and clapping.

'But my ma carries right on screaming, "Cut her down. Cut her down," and then someone upstairs suddenly sees what my ma's saying makes sense and Vicki isn't putting it on, she really is in agony. And this one shouts, "Cut her down," and then other ones upstairs join in and the factory girls cut her down and an ambulance is called and takes Vicki away. She's burned, badly, but she wasn't burned near as bad as she would have been if my ma hadn't come out. So now, you see, when my ma said to Boreland after I was arrested, "I don't want Willie down Culcavy", what could he say?'

'I see that,' said Nank. He lit the end of the joint, inhaled and passed it to Willie. 'So are they saying they want you down Culcavy now you're sentenced?'

'You got it,' said Willie. He pulled on the joint. 'It was sorted at the start. I could do it here. But then the complaints started, and at the trial they said that once I was sentenced I had to go down there.'

'So are you?' All Willie had to do, as Nank knew, was tell an officer and he'd be taken down the next morning.

'No. Ma's been back to Boreland. I stay here.'

'Oh.' No wonder he'd seen something in Willie's face when he got back from the phone. It was all this. 'She's some woman, your mother,' said Nank.

'Oh, aye.'

'What's her name?'

'Edith—Edith Mullen,' said Willie, handing him the joint.

'Boreland must love her.'

'Oh, aye.'

'So is that it?' Nank inhaled deeply and passed the joint back.

'I hope it is. I've finished now. I've done my bit. I don't want to have anything more to do with anything. I'm here, I'll get through this and then we'll see what happens. At least, that's what my ma says and I agree with her. She's a terror so of course I do. And she's only five foot nothing. She's tiny, but you don't want to get on the wrong side.'

Willie took a pull and handed the joint to Nank. 'Very good gear,' he said.

108

SOME TIME IN THE NIGHT, NANK woke. The neon light had come on. He realised it was the night guard. Every hour, the guards turned on the lights in every cell (there was a switch outside as well as inside each one) and checked the sleeping prisoners.

The flap over the observation slit banged down, and the light went out again. He listened as the guard went to the next cell and the one after. Then he became aware of another sound. It had an animal quality. Could it be a rat? They were known to dive under U-bends and get into the cells that way.

He strained his ears, his heartbeat accelerating. He heard the guard put his key into the recorder at the end of the corridor, which registered that he had done his round. Every wing in Loanend had such a device.

The guard retraced his steps to the office. Nank heard the door close. There was silence outside. But the noise inside his cell was still there.

He stared upwards. He could just make out the bottom of the bunk above, the supporting metal mesh and the sag in the middle where Willie's body pressed down. The mesh trembled and he identified the noise now. Willie was crying.

Nank felt shame mixed with embarrassment. He shouldn't be hearing this. He shouldn't even know about it.

He rolled sideways, moaning theatrically like someone deep asleep and pulled the covers right over his head. Inside his cocoon, his ears were filled with the magnified roar of his breath and he could no longer hear Willie.

After a few minutes, he fell sleep.

109

THE NEXT MORNING, THE DOOR WAS unlocked at eight. Nank got out of bed and Winky passed him their breakfast, plus two mugs of weak tea and two cartons of semi-skimmed milk. Every prisoner got a pint each day. The door closed.

'What have they give us?' asked Willie, lifting his head from the pillow.

His eyes were bloodshot. It was the crying, thought Nank, and he felt a twinge of sympathy.

But no sooner had he felt this, than he had a counterbalancing thought. Willie had murdered a man. Willie might have cried for the dead man, Nank didn't know, but he'd cried mostly for himself.

'Cold toast, butter, marmalade, cornflakes,' said Nank.

They ate in silence.

Later, George appeared. 'Mullen,' he said, 'Doctor, governor, welfare.'

Willie went off. Nank fished Conrad's *Heart of Darkness* from a sack and started to read. He was on board a steamer on the oily black Congo river when Willie came back.

'Fucking welfare,' he said. 'I'm supposed to address my offending behaviour. That's what I'm here for, the woman said.'

'Which woman?'

'The welfare woman, the probation officer.'

'Good tits?'

'She can go fuck herself.'

'Oh, please, can I watch? And can I take some pictures too?' said Nank.

Willie threw himself on his bunk. 'They have you here but that's not enough for them. Oh, no.' He tapped his forehead. 'They want to get in here and fuck with your head.'

'Think of this as a play,' said Nank, quietly. 'You are the convict. She represents society. You have your lines. She has hers. Turn in an Oscar-wining performance. That's what you're here for.'

The door opened. It was George again. 'Right, Nank, you now.'

George brought him to a small room where a doctor examined him, then announced, 'That's enough, I'm finished with you.'

He was brought to another room where a man in a suit sat at a desk.

'I'm Governor Black,' he said. 'Everything all right?'

'Aye.'

'Have you read the *Notes for the Guidance of All Prisoners*?'

He nodded. He'd read it the day he was remanded.

'Any questions?'

He shook his head.

George brought him next to a dusty interview room where the welfare woman was sitting. She asked some biographical questions and then said, 'Will your marriage survive?'

'I hope so,' he said, 'but of course it might not.'

'How do you feel about that?'

'Awful.'

'Is your wife surprised you're here?'

'She's always known what I did and accepted I might get caught and that was fine as long as I was out.'

'And now it might not be?'

What did he know? He hoped it would be fine but he didn't know for sure.

The woman talked blithely about the importance of maintaining links, after which George returned him to his cell. Lunch was at midday.

In the afternoon, George came back. 'Gather your things, tidy the place, strip the beds,' said George. 'You're both for Sperrin.'

110

A PAPER SACK TUCKED UNDER EACH arm, Nank, Willie and their escort—it was the officer McCarthy—entered a courtyard of blue asphalt with raised flowerbeds and rounded concrete benches known as Blue Square. There were blocks on three sides, Topped and Donard for remand prisoners, and Craignamaddy for sentenced prisoners. These were all barrack-style buildings with concrete bars, while on the fourth side of the square there was a long red-brick structure with no bars on the windows, which housed Education, Welfare and the tuck shop.

There was a tunnel through the middle of this building. McCarthy led them along it and out into a courtyard of yellow asphalt known as Yellow Square with three more barrack-style buildings, Gullion, Belmore and Sperrin. Every block in Loanend was named after a local mountain so no prisoner could claim the names were politically inflammatory or take offence.

They turned right and came to Sperrin. The grass under the cell windows along the front was littered with cereal slops, balls of crumpled newspaper, bread crusts and chicken bones. McCarthy rang the bell. There was an electronic click and he opened the door.

Inside, McCarthy handed their I Cards to the officer in the tally lodge then brought them to the main circle. On one side was the control room, from where all the downstairs grilles could be opened electronically, and on the other the office of the principal officer of Sperrin, Ernest Gilloway. He came out into the circle now. He was a small man with straw-coloured hair, from which he got his prison nickname, Thatch. He looked at the two new arrivals and then, without a word, went back into his office.

'He's talkative,' said Nank.

'Don't you know that silence is golden?' said McCarthy.

He led them through another grille, across the dinner hall, which smelled of marmalade, passing a prisoner eating toast, his false teeth in his hand, and up a greasy stairwell to a hallway on the first floor. There were two grilles here at right angles. On the lintel above one, the figures '3' and '4' were painted, while above the other, '5' and '6'.

'Straight ahead,' said McCarthy.

Nank began to pad forward along the threes. Todd Terry's "Back from the Dead" was playing somewhere. A fat man in a tight-fitting Rangers shirt stood in the doorway of the first cell. His head was shaven. Nank felt his stare as he passed.

Inside the next cell, there was someone on the bed. He, too, was staring out. Nank did not look back. The trick was to pass unnoticed. At least until he had friends.

He went on, his gaze locked on the circle at the end. He was almost there when someone bolted out of the last cell on the right—cell one—and cannoned into him. He recoiled and Willie banged into him from behind.

'What the fuck?' The speaker was an enormous man with very blue eyes, dressed in an immaculate starched white vest that stretched tightly over the huge muscles of his shoulders and chest, blue Adidas tracksuit trousers and a pair of very new, very white trainers on his huge feet.

'What's the big rush for, Flip?' This was McCarthy.

Ah, a good start, thought Nank. He'd collided with Flip McCausland. "A legend in his lifetime though not one you'd want to meet," as prisoners said. Flip was a lifer. He had killed a sub-postmaster and his wife during a raid to raise funds for his organisation. He was in Loanend because his fringe Republican group had feuded with the Provisionals for years and was now banned from Culcavy.

'I didn't see,' said Flip, churlishly.

'Is that what you say when your car piles into the one in front? "Oh, sorry, I didn't see"?' said McCarthy.

'Naturally,' said Flip. 'You think I'd accept responsibility, if I were driving, which, incidentally, I'd love to be doing. Just give us the key and I'll fuck off right now.'

Flip's hair, coarse and black, sprang from his crown and fell in an even circle. Nank thought of a monk and was puzzled that a man of Flip's reputation should wear his hair in this ludicrous style, though presumably it was because of his reputation that he could.

'Just watch where you're going,' said McCarthy, 'or you'll hurt someone. Now go back to the fives where you come from.'

'Yeah, yeah, whatever.' Flip hurried away. Nank's heart-rate, he noticed, had accelerated. He passed through the bottom grille and entered the space that connected the threes with the fours, the corridor that went off at a right angle. This was Upper Circle One although, like all such areas in the prison, it was square not round.

On one side, there were telephone booths, and a table with steaming water-boilers and a sooty toaster. On the other was the office, with its huge observation window. The officers inside were staring out at them. One got up, opened the door and came out. The little hair he had left was dark and wiry. This was the senior officer on the threes and fours, Cyril Lowry.

'Mac,' he said to McCarthy, 'what have we here?'

'Melanophy and Mullen.'

A handwritten notice was stuck on the back of the top half of the office door (it was in two halves, like a stable door), "The answer is No. Now, what is your question?"

'Remind me where they're going,' shouted Cyril.

Through the observation window Nank watched another officer go to a whiteboard screwed to the wall and covered with names and cell numbers. 'They're on the fours,' he shouted. 'Melanophy's in eight. Mullen's in fifteen.'

'Oh, number fifteen,' said Cyril. 'Ivor Jones's cell. Sad what happened with him.' He sniffed and paused to allow the remark to sink in. 'Well, Mac, show them down, would you?'

McCarthy led them along the fours.

'Mullen,' he said, when they were halfway along, 'that's you.' He pointed to a cell on the side that didn't overlook the yard.

Willie went into fifteen. McCarthy slipped the door card into the holder.

Prison	HMP Loanend
Reg no.	DA8373
Name	William Howell Mullen
Date Committed	11/5/94
Sentence	Life
Long date	
Remission	
Date of birth	14/2/73
Religion	Presbyterian
Employment in Prison	

'And you, Nank, you're in here.'

McCarthy slotted the Door Card into the holder over number '8'.

Prison	HMP Loanend
Reg No.	BC3232
Name	Stephen Gerard
	Declan Pearse Melanophy
Date Committed	31/8/94
Sentence	14 years
Long date	1 September 2008
Remission	1 September 2001
Date birth	11/2/57
Religion	RC
Employment in Prison	

Nank went in. His cell was six foot wide by eight foot long. There was a basin with a notice screwed to the wall above, NOT FOR DRINKING, and above that a plastic mirror. The water in the cells was brown and gave you diarrhoea. The water for drinking was up in the circle and came out of the water-boilers, piping hot. Every evening, prisoners filled their Thermos flasks to make tea or coffee in the night. There was a toilet in the corner, and a narrow bed along the wall, with bedding laid out for him. There was a tiny rickety table, some small shelves and an open cubicle for clothes. Wedged between here and the bed was a chair.

Nank dropped his sacks and went to the window. The concrete bars were three inches wide and four inches deep.

He looked through to the exercise yard below. Two men walked in a circle, one kicking an empty milk carton. A couple of crows pecked and fought with much flapping of wings over a piece of bread.

'Who's Ivor?'

Willie had come in.

Should he lie? Willie was bound to find out soon, Nank thought, and wasn't it better he told Willie carefully, rather than someone else nastily?

'Ivor was a guy,' he said, 'who hanged himself.'

'And they've put me ... where he ... ? They wouldn't have?'

Nank nodded.

'Bastards.'

'They're trying to wind you up. Tomorrow, nice as pie, they'll start. "How'd you sleep, Willie? We've had a lot of complaints about that cell. Do you think there's anything in this idea that the spirit of someone who kills himself hangs around the place where he did it?" And you know what you're going to say?'

'I slept like a log.'

'That's right.'

'Was that Flip McCausland you ran into just now?'

'Yes.'

Willie's face was so pale his freckles looked to Nank like tiny brown circles of felt floating in milk.

'Don't worry about Flip. You're not going to be his favourite person but we'll just keep out of his way.'

'We?'

'You don't think I'm going to run with Republicans, do you? Not with them being the reason I'm here.'

Nank described the hoax bomb call that led to his arrest at Larne after he came off the ferry.

'Oh,' said Willie, when he'd finished.

'I'm so fucking pissed off with the Republicans,' said Nank, 'that the very first thing I'm going to do tonight, after I'm locked, is write a letter. "Dear Gerry Adams, Thank you very much for making that false call regarding the lorry on the Stranraer boat. That was fucking magic. I'm now doing fourteen, you cunt, and I'm one of yours. I thought you were supposed to get us out of jail, not put us in. Anyway, please pay my missus forty grand a year until I get out. Yours, very sincerely, one fucking aggrieved Taig. (That's 'Catholic' to you Gerry).'''

Willie had an expression of intense gratitude on his face. 'Why are you helping me?'

'When I first went to jail somebody helped me. I'm just doing the same. Someone does you good, you do someone else good later. What goes around comes around, blah, fucking blah.'

'Mullen, Melanophy,' a voice shouted from the direction of the office.

'Come on, we're wanted.'

111

'THERE YOU GO,' SAID MCCARTHY. HE put two sets of prison issue plastic plates, bowls, mugs and cutlery on the shelf on the office door. 'You'll be getting televisions in a couple of days. Sure, this is the finest hotel in the western world. Now get your grub.'

Nank and Willie set off down the threes.

'You know why the televisions?' said Nank.

'No.'

'To sedate us. Works with the rest of the world, so why not us? Plus, it's a way to control us. They threaten to take away the TV, we cry like babies, we do what they say.'

'So you won't be taking yours, then?' said Willie.

'Oh, very droll. Course I'm going to have it. I'm not an idiot.'

The dinner hall was a long room filled with men. Their cries rang from the walls. The shutter over the servery was down but a queue had formed. Willie and Nank joined the end. Flip was at the front.

After a few moments, the shutters were flung up to reveal prisoners in white overalls, the dinner orderlies, and an officer. The food was in a line of dixies with boiling water below to keep the food warm.

'Sausages and mash, boys,' one of the orderlies shouted.

Flip was served first. His plate was heaped with mash, cabbage and sausages, and two ice-lollies were tossed into his bowl. He strolled to a table in the middle of the room and sat down. Two big men joined him.

The queue shuffled forward. There was now just one prisoner between Nank and his meal. Nank saw he was in his fifties, with a baggy, sagging face, and a single buck-tooth that snagged over his lip.

The prisoner held out his plate and lumpy mashed potato was carelessly thrown on it. Cabbage and two black sausages followed and one of these tumbled back into the dixie it came from. The orderly pretended not to notice, picked up two more sausages and plopped these onto Nank's plate beside his mash and cabbage. The man with the baggy face scuttled on. An ice-lolly was slung into his bowl. Then, watched by Nank, he scuttled across the dinner hall, keeping as far from Flip as he could, before vanishing through the door at the end.

'You want your ice-lolly?'

Nank turned back to the orderly who had addressed him, a man with long dark hair tied in a ponytail. 'Is it any good?' The ice-lolly was in a plain orange wrapper with no brand name.

'What do you fucking think?' said the orderly. 'Look at it. Who made it? Where did it come from? It doesn't say. Doesn't even have a name. Bound to be crap.'

'How could I decline?' said Nank. 'I'll have it.' The ice-lolly was dumped in his bowl.

'Could be a frozen goldfish,' he said. With its orange wrapper and white stick, there was a resemblance.

The orderly chuckled. 'They ain't killed your funny side. More power to you, mate.'

Nank began to walk back across the dinner hall with Willie just behind. Flip clocked them as they passed which made both feel uncomfortable.

They were silent until they got back to the start of the threes. 'Gangsta's Paradise' by Coolio was booming in a cell.

'All right, Willie?'

'Aye.'

In cell twenty, the first on his left, Nank saw the man who had got one sausage, bolting his food. A root, thought Nank. He reminded himself again, how it always paid to be alert. From the tiniest details, he could learn so much.

112

IT WAS MORNING, THE NEXT DAY, Friday. Nank woke as his door was swung back and locked into the keepers.

It was exactly the same start to his day as it had been on remand except that his new door squeaked. Also, there was less daylight because this cell faced south and the old one had faced east.

'Did we sleep well?' said the officer in the doorway.

Sarcasm, already, thought Nank. It was only bloody eight o'clock.

'Is everything all right?'

Nank sat up and peered over.

'Don't you remember me?' said the officer.

It was the officer who had given him the carton of water in the transporter vehicle. He recognised the fish-like mouth and the white hair.

'Aren't you on courts?' said Nank.

'Was. When I got in this morning though, I was told to come here.' His manner was brusque yet sad. 'I may be gone tomorrow,' he went on, 'or I may still be here in three years' time. That's what it is to be an officer. I'm Jumbo Johnson.'

'How do,' said Nank.

Jumbo disappeared. Nank heard the next cell being unlocked.

At nine o'clock Nank and Willie were by the water-boilers in the circle with Cyril Lowry.

'Did you sleep all right?' said Cyril.

'Dead to the world, me,' said Willie, 'from the moment my head hit the pillow.'

Cyril was watching Willie closely and Nank was watching Cyril.

'Really,' said Cyril.

'Best kip I had since I came into jail.'

Cyril nodded and Nank guessed that Ivor Jones, his death or how well Willie was sleeping, would not be mentioned again.

'How'd you fancy being circle orderlies?' said Cyril. He put his hands into his pockets. 'You work morning and afternoon, every day including Sunday, at forty-five pence a session, that's ninety pence a day, which is £6.30 a week, each.'

Add on the £3.15 every prisoner automatically received from the state, Cyril continued, and they'd pull £9.45 a week.

Cyril then outlined their duties: they would have to clean the office, mop and polish the corridors and circle, the laundry room and ablutions area, the gymnasium and the recreation room. They would also, on occasion, have to clean cells and make beds. If required, they also had to prepare the officers' breakfast in the office's little kitchen.

'Well, what do you think?'

'Yes,' they said.

Cyril led them into Ablutions. He showed them the buckets and mops, the cloths and the great drums of disinfectant and polish. 'You might as well get started now,' he said.

At that moment, Nank noticed that the sink was clogged with Shredded Wheat and toast. 'Don't they know how to use a bin?' said Nank. 'That's disgusting.'

'Just clean it up,' said Cyril.

There was something worrying in Cyril's tone so, while Willie started on the mess, Nank nipped into cell nine, the one beside his. Here he found Davy Tate, known as Lyle, the dinner orderly with the ponytail.

'Hello,' said Lyle.

Lyle had been caught in a flat in Stoke Newington with eighty thousand ecstasy tablets, got ten years, and was transferred home. During five minutes together after tea the previous evening, Nank had found he and Lyle knew a lot of the same people in the drugs business. On this basis, Nank felt, he could ask Lyle a few questions.

'Listen, mate, food slops in the bathroom?'

'All over the place, are they?'

'Just the sinks.'

'Not the toilet seats?' said Lyle. 'Well, that's something.'

A photograph of a girl with earrings and a sentimental pencil copy lay on Lyle's table. Lyle was the Sperrin artist. He charged fifty grams of tobacco per portrait.

'Right, what's the story?' said Nank.

'It's Flip. He doesn't like Crafty, the orderly.'

'Crafty?' said Nank.

'He's an old guy, sagging face, looks like a crumpled bag.'

'Oh, yeah.' He was the one Nank had seen bolting his tea.

'Any chance he gets, Flip comes round from his cell on the fives and chucks food into Ablutions here for Crafty to clean up.'

'Why don't the screws stop it?'

'Because they all fucking hate Crafty. He's a bad bollocks. Father dead, lived at home with his mother, shed at the back, did it up like a bedroom, Winnie-the-Pooh wallpaper, fish-tank, got these young girls in, eight and ten, got them pissed on cider, bucked them. At his trial he asked for another hundred-odd offences to be taken into account. It was in the papers.'

'Well, I'm the orderly now ... well, me and Willie.'

Lyle put on a baseball cap then pulled his ponytail out of the gap at the back. 'Here,' he said, 'I've an art class to get to.' He turned to go. 'A word of advice: however you sort this, don't get on Flip's bad side. Not worth it. See you.'

They left the cell. Lyle headed for the stairs. Nank went to Ablutions and helped Willie finish the sinks.

Later, when the morning's work was done, Nank and Willie reported to McCarthy in the office.

'Good day, boys?'

'Aye,' said Willie.

McCarthy ticked their work sheets. 'You're now forty-five pence richer, lads. It's official.'

113

LUNCH WAS BEEF STEW AND BOILED potatoes. At two-fifteen, when Nank went to Ablutions, he found spuds and gravy smeared on the taps. He and Willie cleaned up the mess. When they'd finished they got the machines out and polished the linoleum in the circle and along the wings.

Later, McCarthy ticked their sheets again and then, from the servery, they collected battered cod with peas and chips, plus a choc-ice on a stick. They were about to head back across the dinner hall together when Nank whispered, 'I want to have a word here.' He nodded at Flip and his two friends, seated at the same table as the day before. 'You go on.'

Willie slipped away. Nank went over. Flip was eating so he had his face down, and his hair fell like a curtain over his face.

'How do?' said Nank.

Flip lifted his heavy head slowly to show his broad, flat face, very white, like dough, and somehow childlike too.

'I'm the new orderly on the threes and fours. Well, I am and so's Willie Mullen. We're doing it together,' said Nank

'Oh,' said Flip. 'So what?'

'It isn't Crafty any more.'

There was a long pause. 'Oh,' said Flip. 'Crafty's not the orderly no more.'

His eyes reminded Nank of a gas jet, they were so very blue, hard and unyielding. 'Fucking brilliant,' he said, 'and who are you mate?'

'I'm Nank.'

'Nank,' said Flip. 'You taking the piss?'

'Oh, no.' Nank told his story about HMP Kingsman, Nancy Mitford's *The Pursuit of Love*, and Higgins.

When he finished, Flip pointed his plastic knife at the man

on his right. 'This is Big John.' He pointed at the other man. 'This is Big Jim. The two Bigs they're called, aren't you, boys?'

'Or Large and Large,' said John. He was older than Flip, grey, balding. Jim, on the other side, was younger and leaner. His bare arms and shoulders were covered with tattoos.

'Well, nice to meet you, ah, Nank. We'll have a yarn some time, okay?' said Flip.

That's it, thought Nank. Dismiss: He walked off quickly and did not look back.

Lockdown was at four-thirty. At five-thirty, Nank was waiting at his cell door. As soon as he was unlocked, he rushed down to Ablutions. There were no peas on the floor, chips in the urinals or batter crumbs on the toilet seat.

Suddenly Cyril was in the doorway. 'I hear tell Flip put his slops in the bucket after tea. Nank, I'm impressed. You do have a way with words.'

114

THE PHONES, WHICH HAD BEEN OFF the previous evening, were on during association and he rang Jenny.

Each started by asking the other how they were. Their replies were bland. Then they made plans. Jenny would come to visit him on Saturday afternoon in a week's time, without the children. That was the preliminaries over.

'How's things, really?' he said.

There was a pause.

'You know Mrs Lyons?'

He couldn't quite picture her. 'Mrs Lyons?'

'Drives a Fiesta ... corduroy shopping bag.'

'Oh yeah.' He remembered it, with red piping and a red handle. It was funny what stuck in the mind.

'After school, car full of kids, I stop at the Spar, buy a few things, rush back to the car. Then, remember kindling, rush back, just in time to hear Mrs Lyons say to Linda on the till, "De da de da de da, the jailbird's wife." Then Linda spots me and says, "You're back, Mrs Melanophy." You could have cut the atmosphere with a knife. I get my kindling, pay and leave, heart pounding but it doesn't show and I have myself under control. As we drive away, Emma pipes up, "You look like you're in a pickle jar. Is something the matter, Mummy?"'

'Oh God,' said Nank.

'You were in the Belfast papers,' said Jenny, 'and you'll be in the *Tyrone Constitution* tomorrow—LOCAL MAN, FOURTEEN YEARS FOR DRUGS. I'll be the talk of the parish. What am I saying? I already am. Why wouldn't I be? But it's the kids I really feel for.'

'Yeah,' said Nank.

A prisoner tapped on the Perspex side of the booth and pointed at his wristwatch.

'Okay,' said Nank.

'What did you say?' asked Jenny.

'There's someone wanting the phone. I'd better say goodbye. I don't want to get known as a phone-hogger, not starting a sentence.'

'I don't suppose you could ring again?'

'There's a queue and only two phones between forty.'

'Why don't they have more?'

'Because it's prison,' he said bleakly.

'I love you,' she said.

'I love you too.'

Back in his cell, he stared at little buttons of dried

toothpaste on the wall above his table. Prisoners used it to stick up their posters as it was forbidden to use Sellotape or Blu-Tak. It was one of the worst things about jail, he thought, the inability to intervene in a crisis at home; pure torture. Suddenly he heard an officer call, 'Goodnight,' and looked up to see his door swinging shut. It was evening lock-up on the third night of his sentence.

115

IT WAS SATURDAY, 16 SEPTEMBER. HE came through the door and into Visits. It was a large room with chairs and tables scattered everywhere. The walls were green and the floor was covered with brown carpet tiles. There was a playpen for children at the end and the plywood cubicles used for boxed visits—for prisoners who didn't want anyone seeing them or their families—were on his right.

Nank saw Jenny sitting in an easy chair, another beside hers. She was smoking. She uncrossed her legs. For an instant, he saw the area of shadow that lay under her skirt and was filled with desire.

She dropped her cigarette into the ashtray on the floor, got up and hurried towards him. They threw their arms forward and embraced. He folded her into himself and buried his face in her neck.

'Don't get me started,' she said, and stepped back. He looked at her long face with its large strong nose, then at her eyes, very dark and brown, and finally at her mouth.

'Are you all right?' he asked. He kissed her and felt her lipstick on his mouth.

'I'm all right, Nank,' she said. 'Are you?'

They sat in the chairs she had taken. He heard the rustle made by her tights as she crossed her legs. His eyes flickered down to the hem of her skirt. It came to about an inch below the knee.

'You'd better have a cigarette,' she said. He looked up and saw she was holding out a packet of Benson & Hedges. Behind him, he saw that a woman was sitting on a prisoner's lap, watched by an officer a few feet away.

'They're having a good time,' he said.

Jenny glanced at the couple and turned back to him. He took one of her cigarettes.

'No, they're not,' she said. 'They're torturing themselves.'

She lit his cigarette and one for herself. They smoked and talked. She told him about each of the children. She told him about the shop. She said she collected the takings every evening and banked them every morning after the school run.

When her news was finished, Nank started on his. He described his cell. He mentioned Lyle and Willie. He described his cleaning job. He joked about the ordeal of ironing his clothes. He had done it the night before, he explained, but come that morning he had found everything was still creased and he'd had to iron them again.

She closed her eyes and laughed, her hand on her neck, her head rolled back. He wanted to kiss her. He touched her chin. She opened her eyes. 'I want to hold you,' he said.

She put her cigarette in the ashtray and leaned forward, putting her head chastely against his chest. 'Are we going to manage?' she asked.

'We'll have to,' he said.

'I'm sick with missing you. I'm heartsore,' she said.

'You have to make friends and go out and ... '

'And?' she said.

'Have a social life.'

'I don't want a social life. I want my husband.'

Up to this moment, he had felt excited. Now that feeling vanished with bewildering rapidity. He sensed it was the same with his wife. He heard her sniff and her body trembled. She had begun to cry. A few moments later he felt her tears soaking through the cotton of his Fred Perry shirt. His throat hurt. This was what happened when he was about to cry. He mustn't let it happen. He had to send her home happy.

'Would you like to hear a joke?'

'What?'

'About the bishop and the actress.'

'No,' she said.

They separated and she pressed her eyes with the heels of her palms. 'I promised myself this wasn't going to happen and I still make a show of myself,' she said. She looked at him directly. Her eyes were so dark they were almost black. 'Will we get through this?' she asked.

'We have to,' he said.

She nodded, as if she were agreeing with herself rather than with him. 'Yes, we must,' she said. 'We must.'

116

BACK FROM VISITS, HE FILED INTO the main circle. He sniffed the air and smelled the curry and rice that had been served the day before, mixed with floor polish, sweat, tobacco and toast. He felt the pleasure that comes with recognition of the familiar.

It was incredible. Didn't he hate this place? Well, he did. He'd give anything to be out. Yet he felt safe. Everything was predictable. He had his cell and his job. With his salary, and what Jenny sent in, he could buy tobacco and phone cards from the tuck shop. He was fed three times a day. There was a library. He had a television in his cell. Two videos were shown every night on the internal system. In here, he didn't have to look at his wife crying. In here, his throat was never sore because he was about to cry. In here, there were no troubling feelings. It was remarkable how quickly he'd got used to it.

He felt exhausted even though the visit had lasted less than an hour. It was hard to believe. From the moment it was planned, he couldn't wait for the visit to come. Then it had come, it had gone, and now he was back in the world of Sperrin and it felt good.

Would it be the same next Saturday when Jenny was bringing Robert? Would he ache and yearn all week, and then, when the visit was over and he got back, would he feel relieved? Yes, he thought, for Sperrin was already his home. Nank felt guilty now at what he felt and what he anticipated he would feel. He would never tell Jenny about this, of course.

The escort gave him a pat-down, and he sidled through the grille into the corridor at the back of the dinner hall. The door to the exercise yard was on his right, wedged open with the cardboard tube from a toilet roll. He could see a prisoner on a chair leaning against the wall on the far side.

Nank slipped out. The yard was a square of asphalt. Lyle was striding around the edge, as he did every day before his orderly duties. The yard orderly was sweeping up with a wide brush—orange peel, cigarette cartons, Styrofoam trays and cigarette butts. On the far side, a crowd of prisoners had gathered. He recognised Flip, in his huge gleaming white trainers, John, Jim and Sulky Stewart, a housebreaker and tie-up artist, out of whose cell Flip had bolted the day Nank had entered Sperrin for the first time.

'Good visit?'

It was Willie, sitting on the ground behind the door, which was why Nank hadn't seen him until now. Nank hunkered down beside him. 'The best,' he said. 'Jenny's left a box of oranges into my personal possessions.' The peel would be examined for puncture holes in case LSD had been injected and then, once they were judged clean, the fruit would be sent up. With luck, he'd get them in a day or two. 'We'll have a vitamin C fest when they arrive.' He talked about his visit and then said, 'How was your afternoon?'

'You could eat off the toilet bowls. They're gleaming.'

Willie had cleaned in Nank's absence. Nank would get paid, though. Orderlies received pay if absent in Visits or Education up to a maximum of three sessions a week.

'It's getting rough, boys,' said Lyle, approaching. He pointed at the men in the far corner.

'What's going on?' said Nank.

'It's those two roots that came in last night,' said Lyle, hurrying off.

Two newly sentenced prisoners, who should have gone to HMP Limavady, the Category C prison on the north coast, but hadn't because it was full, had been brought into Sperrin. They were both called Shilliday, they were related, and they had both got four years for offences against their young nephews. This information had come from the previous day's evening paper, copies of which had circulated around the prison the night before and as a result everyone in Loanend now knew about the pair and their crimes.

The Shillidays were doubled-up in the corner cell closest to the office on the ground floor and, Nank guessed, had opted for twenty-four-hour lock-up for their own protection. Since they wouldn't come out, Flip and the others had come to shout through the window at them.

Nank shifted on his heels. He felt queasy. The Shillidays were shits but their tormentors were no better. Not, of course, that he was going to express his views. He didn't want to be classified as a "root-lover".

'Haven't they read their Bible?' said Nank. "He that is without sin among you, let him cast the first stone against her."'

'No, of course they haven't,' said Willie. 'They can't fucking read.'

The orderly prodded his rubbish. Lyle continued his circuit. The sunbather moved his chair. Flip and his friends shouted up at someone on the first floor.

'Look at them,' said Willie. 'You'd think they were at a rock concert.'

Lyle came round again and this time he stopped. 'Oh, they're getting serious now,' he said. He lifted away the long hairs stuck by sweat to his forehead. 'That's some heat.' He wiped his face with the hem of his T-shirt.

On the other side of the yard, a mop was squeezed out through the bars of a first-storey window. 'That's one of ours,' said Willie. It tumbled and was handed to Flip, who jabbed the end between the bars of the Shillidays' cell. The faint tinkle of breaking glass sounded across the yard.

'No screws about of course,' said Nank. He fished out his tobacco tin and began to roll a cigarette. 'They're never around when you want them.'

'And yet they're always around when you don't,' said Lyle.

'Just as well, though,' said Willie. 'They'd only stop it, and the roots deserve it.'

Nank licked the gummed edge of the Rizla paper and stuck it down.

'Give us a loan of your tin?' said Willie.

Nank lit up. 'Course.'

As Willie rolled, Nank watched Big John pick a milk carton out of the orderly's rubbish pile and disappear back into the crowd.

'What are they doing now?' said Willie. He lit his cigarette.

'Pissing in the carton, I'd say,' said Lyle. 'Can I have a fag?'

'Sure,' said Nank.

Lyle took the tin.

The crowd parted. Flip had the carton and Big John had the mop now. The head had been snapped off to leave a sharp, splintered end of white wood. John stabbed his spear through the bars while Flip reached through with the carton. There was a moment of tension, then everyone fell back laughing uproariously.

'Did you see?' shouted Flip. 'Covered them with my piss.' He threw the empty carton on the ground and kicked it away.

'Well, kids'll sleep safer in their beds tonight, won't they?' said Nank quietly.

'They're roots. That's what happens.' Lyle lit his cigarette and gave Nank his tin back.

The mob was moving away from the corner. They'd had their fun, thought Nank, or perhaps they'd calculated that if they made any more noise, an officer would come to see what they were doing. They glided across the yard, laughing and chattering, their happy voices echoing off the walls. John twirled the mop handle, threw it into the air, and caught it, then tried to repeat the trick and dropped it.

'Well done,' said Willie. 'Good hand-eye co-ordination.'

Flip and his group were almost at the door where Nank and the others were sitting.

'What are you looking at?' said Flip. There were beads of sweat across his forehead and his white singlet was wet in places.

'Nothing,' said Nank.

'I was talking to the Orange toe-rag.' Flip pointed at Willie.

'I wasn't looking at anything,' said Willie. He spoke quietly and he looked at the ground submissively.

Flip swept through the door, the others following.

'Except your fucking ugly face,' said Willie, as soon as they were out of earshot.

Nank and Lyle began to laugh, softly at first, then hugely.

A few minutes later, Nank and Willie were in the queue waiting for tea.

'Those roots won't come here to collect their tea, will they?' said Willie.

'Not likely.'

'How do they eat then?'

'The screws bring them their food,' said Nank, 'if they remember that is.'

117

THE NEXT MORNING AFTER BREAKFAST MCCARTHY brought Nank the box of oranges Jenny had left.

'That was quick,' said Nank.

'We aim to please.'

The officer sloped away.

Nank laid out a dozen oranges between the prison bars to ripen in the sun. The box with the rest went under his bed. Willie bounced in.

'The oranges came,' said Nank.

'They did.'

Willie stood scratching his hand and pondering. 'Could I have a couple?' he asked.

'Help yourself.'

He took two from the window and put one in each pocket. 'I'll be back in a moment and we'll get stuck into the cleaning,' he said, and left.

Ten minutes later, Willie returned from his mysterious errand and they began the cleaning. When they'd finished Nank felt groggy. He'd take a walk, he thought. The air would revive him.

He slipped down to the yard. Once again, the orderly was there, patiently sweeping up the rubbish thrown out the night before. Nank began to walk round the edge of the yard, hugging the wall. As he drew close to the Shillidays' cell, he noticed orange peel on the ground beneath the bars.

He stopped. Could it be? Had Willie passed the oranges to them. The why wasn't hard to work out: he'd done it, even though he hated roots, because Flip would have hated it and that gave Willie more of a kick than anything.

Nank squinted through the glassless windows. He saw the Shillidays, one on each bunk, both asleep. One was blond, and the other had a paunch. The salty, brackish smell of pee hung in the air.

The following morning, Willie bounced again into Nank's cell.

'Can I have another couple of oranges?' he asked.

'Aye,' said Nank. Willie pocketed two as before and went off.

For the next few days, Willie continued to take oranges. He stopped the day the Shillidays were shipped out to HMP Limavady.

118

HIS FIRST CHRISTMAS INSIDE IN 1994, when he was on remand, Nank had survived by believing it might be his last. It wasn't. He got fourteen, which meant seven, but with one done, that made six.

He knew that the surest way to make a sentence worse was to sit in his cell and brood, so he established a routine. He got up every day at eight, regardless of how tired he felt. He shaved every day without fail. He changed his sheets on Monday. He cleaned his toilet and sink on Tuesday. He polished the cell floor on Wednesday. He cleaned the toilet and sink again on Thursday. He wiped and dusted the cell on Friday. He polished the floor again on Saturday. He went to Mass on Sunday.

He got busy. He had the orderly's job. He started English, Craft and IT classes. He went to the gym three times a week. He dealt a little dope that Jenny brought in to Visits and passed from her mouth to his when they kissed. The life he shaped was bearable. As long as he could stop himself thinking about certain things—home, wife, children—he was cheerful in the day and he was able to sleep at night.

And mostly he managed except at certain times. Christmas 1995, his first as a sentenced prisoner, was one. He got through by telling himself that once it was done he'd be two down and there'd be only five to go. A feed of ecstasy tablets helped. He spent his time dancing when he was locked in and once 1996 had started, he felt better. He believed he could do his sentence.

Christmas 1996 was much better than the last. He'd done it twice now so his third would be no problem, he thought. He spent Christmas Day stoned, watching television and working his way through the bag of chocolates with which the governor provided every inmate. When 1997 started, the search team found two LSD tablets in his cell and he lost ten days' remission but his optimism was undented. He'd three done and once he got through Christmas 1997, his fourth, he'd be over halfway through. His release date, with remission, taking into account the ten days he'd lost, was 11 September 2001. Oh yes, he had it licked.

119

IN LATE AUTUMN 1997, EACH BLOCK including Sperrin, was assigned a slot in Visits for their Christmas party. It was a high point of the Loanend calendar. In the weeks following, which also happened every year at this time, there was a rumour in Sperrin that somebody was making hooch. The prisoners, though they didn't know who was involved, or even if it were true, were so delighted by the possibility that they took to humming the UB40 song, 'Red Red Wine', whenever staff were nearby. It really pissed them off.

The party was on Tuesday, and when the day came, Nank woke when it was still dark and sat up. By the light coming through the bars he saw his family's Christmas presents piled on his rickety table. He'd made everything in craft class. For

Emma and Sarah, leather chokers and bracelets: for Robert a card box with a handmade set of cards inside: and for Jenny a mock Fabergé egg, marbled in gold and blue, hinged at the back, mounted on a plinth, and with a message written in gold inside, "Nank & Jenny for ever" and the names of the children below. They were all wrapped in gaudy paper but each parcel, as regulations required, was open at one end so they could be checked by staff before they left Loanend. Jenny would seal them at home before they went under the tree.

He turned on the light, washed and shaved with great care at the sink, then dressed and made his bed. McCarthy opened his door just before eight and handed Nank his daily pint. The Tetrapak was cold and wet. He bolted two Shredded Wheat, then he and Willie hurried off towards Ablutions. The party was in the afternoon, so they had to do in a morning what they normally did in a day.

Nank opened the door of Ablutions and stepped in, Willie following. The room reeked of alcohol. There was a puddle of vomit in the bath. It was red and streaked with cabbage and phlegm.

'Oh, no,' said Nank.

At that moment, Jimmy Phoenix appeared. He was a red-faced officer who grew award-winning roses in his spare time. 'Horrible smell,' he said and vanished.

'Oh, Jesus,' said Nank, 'there'll be trouble—and today of all days. Off you go, Willie, I'll do this.'

He cleaned the bath and was mopping the floor when McCarthy appeared. 'Lock-down,' said the officer.

'You're joking,' said Nank.

'Nope.'

'But I've got to get everything sorted. Christmas party this afternoon, in case you've forgotten. I can't clean if I'm locked.'

'Someone's vomited in here and it's drink. Now, you know the drill. Put the mop down. In your cell now.'

All over Sperrin, doors were slamming and keys turning.

120

HALF AN HOUR LATER, NANK SAT reading JP Donleavy's *The Ginger Man*. He was passing under the arch of the back gate of Trinity College when the flap clanged and his door swung open.

McCarthy stood in the doorway with a man in a brown boiler suit and black lace-up boots. Officer Duncan, of the S and D team, was six foot four and weighed sixteen stone. 'Size does matter' was his catchphrase.

'Melanophy,' said McCarthy. 'Sorry to disturb you.'

McCarthy could be a sarcastic so-and-so, thought Nank, when he wanted.

They stepped in and Duncan's eyes fell on the presents.

'Take the paper off,' said Duncan, pointing at Emma's.

'It'll tear if I do. Can't you just look in through the open end? It's just a leather—'

'I want the paper off all of them,' interrupted Duncan. 'Now do it.'

He did and when he was done and his presents were lying spread across his table, and the paper was all torn, Duncan stomped off, McCarthy followed him, and the door closed.

Bloody marvellous, thought Nank. All his presents would have to be rewrapped and he'd no Sellotape left.

At midday the search team left without having found the hooch and Sperrin was unlocked. Nank, all thoughts of cleaning forgotten, went to the office. He found Cyril Lowry writing at the counter.

'Any Sellotape?' he asked.

'No, sorry,' said Cyril.

Nank went from cell to cell along the fours and then the threes but no one could spare him any Sellotape. On account of the hooch, the search team had devised a particularly inspired form of collective punishment that morning: they had made every man do what Officer Duncan had made him do and unwrap their gifts. The result was that every man needed what Sellotape he had to reseal his presents, or had promised what he had to someone else who needed to reseal his presents do so.

Now there was only one cell left on the fours where he could ask, the one at the end by the top grille, after which he'd have to try the fives and sixes. Nank went through the door.

Inside he found Crafty on the bed, his legs crossed, his sad, baggy face angled towards the door. A traditional gypsy caravan made of matchsticks sat on his table. It stood over a foot high.

'You made that?' said Nank. He was impressed.

'For my mother,' said Crafty. He had a lovely, precise voice.

'It's too big to wrap,' said Nank, 'which means you might have some Sellotape.'

Crafty pulled a roll from under his pillow.

'You need to look inside the van to appreciate it,' said Crafty.

Nank bent forward and peered through the open door at the back. Inside, he saw a range, a table, chairs, crockery, beds, a dresser, four figures modelled out of dried bread, and painted, a mother and three girls in long skirts and shawls.

'No father,' said Nank.

'He's here,' said Crafty, smiling.

It took Nank a second before he understood.

'Don't forget to bring it back.'

Nank bolted out of the door and ran straight into Flip from behind.

'What the fuck?' said Flip, and turned.

He wore a white beard attached with elastic and a red hat. He was playing Father Christmas at the party and this was part of his outfit.

'Sorry, didn't see you,' said Nank.

They began to walk up the threes towards the circle.

'Any more trouble out of you, Nank, I'll set the reindeer on you.'

The joke felt old but Nank laughed anyway. It always paid to humour Flip.

'What were you doing with that cunt Crafty?' said Flip.

'Getting the loan of some Sellotape,' said Nank. 'Got to redo my presents. Fuck, there's so much to do.'

'Tell me about it,' said Flip. 'But at least Sulky's got me Santa suit ironed, haven't you Sulky?' he shouted.

'Course I have,' Sulky roared back from inside his cell, the last one on the right before the circle.

Flip shot through the doorway and Nank stopped to look in. The red suit hung from a nail in the wall. Sulky, a small stocky man with a protruding lower lip, was sitting on the bed. He was doing eight years for burglary with violence. He'd broken into a farm occupied by an old man and when he wouldn't say where he'd hidden his money, Sulky had taken off the old man's boots and emptied a kettle of boiling water over his feet.

'See you, Flip, Sulky,' Nank called, and hurried off across

the circle, heart pounding. It was Flip. He had that effect. Nank reached the fours. He must calm down, he told himself. Nothing must spoil the afternoon.

121

HE ARRIVED IN RECEPTION ON THE prison side of Visits and handed in his presents. Once the officers had examined them, they'd be passed to the visitors' side and Jenny would collect them. There was some paperwork and then he was told to go into a sweatbox for his search. It was a small, grey, windowless cubicle with an officer on a chair. He stripped to the waist first, turned a circle before the officer, his arms over his head so his armpits could be seen, redressed, stripped from the waist down, and turned again in front of the officer.

'Lift your bollocks.'

He did to show he had nothing hidden.

'Go on,' said the officer. 'Have a good party.'

When Nank got into Visits his children rushed up to him, wanting to be picked up and shouting questions. Nank said he would answer them all in time, and they had to wait their turn. He had no sooner said this than he saw their expressions change. For weeks they had been filled with excitement. For weeks, they had lived for the moment when they would see their father at the Sperrin children's Christmas party.

And with one sentence he had punctured them. The delight that filled them drained away and they deflated.

Then he saw Jenny watching him. Her eyes were brown

and clear and they told him that, yes, the joy had emptied but they would rally. They were children, after all. Everything might have gone wrong all morning but he was in this now, he told himself grimly. The curtain had parted, the play had begun. He'd fumbled his entrance but he couldn't start again. He had to get through the best he could.

Out of the corner of his eye, he saw Flip taking his seat on the throne in 'Santa's Grotto'. A little girl in a velvet dress wriggled onto his lap.

'Yo-ho-ho,' shouted Flip, and the little girl, Nank knew it was Sharon, Flip's seven-year-old daughter, shrieked with laughter.

He felt a hand slide behind his neck and Jenny was pulling him towards her.

'Come here, stranger,' she said, and he felt her lips on his, her small pointed tongue touching his tongue.

The Melanophy family sat and conversation began, the children gabbling about Christmas and gifts, school and friends, Jenny throwing in explanations when the talk was of people or things of which Nank knew nothing because he was in jail and out of touch.

Minutes passed. Nank felt himself enveloped in the domestic life of his family. It felt warm, safe and good. The part that looked after his personal safety, however, that stayed separate from the proceedings. It was turned out towards the room and it paid particular attention to Flip.

With this part of him, Nank saw Flip as he took one child after another onto his knee, including Nank's youngest, Sarah. As the afternoon wore on, he noticed Flip's face growing redder, and that the period each child spent on his lap was growing shorter. Then he saw Flip, duty done presumably, stand up. His wife came towards him. Sandra was a wide woman with an ample chest. Her hair was crimped and wavy.

Nank watched as Flip pulled his beard to one side and went to kiss her with open lips. He guessed Flip was expecting her to push drugs into his mouth.

Flip and Sandra clinched and then, a moment later, Flip broke away. Now he and Sandra stood opposite one another. Flip was angry and his mouth was moving fiercely, to which Sandra responded by folding her arms and shaking her head.

Sharon, Flip's daughter, was on the floor dressing a doll. She jumped up and ran to her parents, the petticoat under her dress swinging as she ran. Her face was tight. Then she was crying. Sandra said something to her but Sharon wouldn't stop. Sandra spoke to Flip. Flip sat on a chair: Sandra sat opposite and took Sharon onto her lap. Neither adult was speaking now.

At this point, Nank noticed Crafty, an old woman—Crafty's mother, he guessed—and an officer passing. Flip must have said something because the officer stopped and spoke, his finger raised.

Then the officer, Crafty and Crafty's mother crossed to the boxes, the plywood units for those who wanted privacy or were under threat.

Middle-class prisoners and sex offenders mostly used them. There were twelve boxes and they had no ceilings, so officers could look in, yet the walls were high enough to shield whomever sat inside from the rest of Visits.

The escorting officer opened the door to one of the boxes. Crafty and his mother went in and the officer shut the door. Then the officer went back to Flip, spoke to him again, then left, and Flip looked furious. What a scene, Nank thought.

First, Flip didn't get his drugs, then he lashed out at Crafty, because it made him feel better, and finally he was rebuked by an officer.

Jenny squeezed his thigh to get his attention. He hardened immediately and had to cross his legs.

122

BACK IN HIS CELL—AND AS usual, it was heartening to be back amidst the familiar—Nank sat on his bed. He felt happy because he had seen his wife and children for a whole afternoon, and sad because the party was over and there wouldn't be anything like it again until Sports Day in the summer.

Were the two feelings at war, he wondered, and if so which would win? Sad always won out over happy, he thought, and he saw he must distract himself.

He looked around and noticed the Sellotape and what was written inside the cardboard centre: THIS BELONGS TO CRAFTY CORRIGAN. GIVE IT BACK.

As Nank stood, Willie came in. 'I've got us a little treat,' he said. 'It's about four inches long, and it's in a king size Rizla.' He had scored some hash from a dealer on the ones and he measured the length of the joint in the air.

'Got to whizz this round to Crafty first,' said Nank, waving the Sellotape.

Willie walked round to the fours with him and was right behind when Nank hurried into Crafty's cell and collided with someone, which caused Willie to bump into him from behind.

'Sorry,' said Nank. The prisoner he'd run into wore a vest

and he saw muscles like ropes under the skin and great dips filled by shadow. It was Jim, Flip's friend, he realised.

'Crafty, here's your Sellotape,' he said, peering round Jim's torso.

'Put it on the table,' said Flip. He was sitting on Crafty's bed in his Santa suit, his hat on the back of his head, his beard round his neck, and John beside him. Crafty sat on the chair, his baggy face looking baggier than ever, angled towards his palms. There was something on each one. It was bread, wasn't it? It reminded Nank of bait pellets for a fishhook, only bigger and more disturbing.

'Good visit, Crafty?' said Nank, as he put the Sellotape where the caravan had stood earlier.

Crafty didn't say anything so Nank said, 'Are you all right?'

'He's all right,' said Flip. Then he added, 'Aren't you?'

'I'm all right,' said Crafty.

'He said he's all right,' said Flip. 'Now, Nank, do us all a favour and fuck off, would you?'

Jim turned and brought his face to within inches of Nank's. His breath smelt of spearmint and toothpaste ... and what? Alcohol? Of course, thought Nank. Flip and the two Bigs were the hooch-makers. Now that he knew, he saw it had been obvious all along and he should have guessed it was them.

Jim shunted him with his huge chest towards the door and he, in turn, pushed Willie back. Then they were in the corridor and Jim's bulky body blocked the doorway.

'Bye-bye,' said Jim.

They went back to Willie's cell.

'The bell will be going any minute. It's hardly worth it,' said Nank.

'Nah,' said Willie, 'a couple of puffs, better than nothing.'

He put his lighter to the twist at the end of the joint and sucked in the flame.

'Do you know what was going on back there?' said Nank.

Willie inhaled deeply and shook his head.

'Razor blade, halved lengthways, inside bread pellets, it slips down easy, apparently, a Root's Supper.'

Willie, appalled, coughed and handed the joint to Nank. 'Shit,' he said.

Nank got two hits before they heard the alarm bell go and prisoners all round Sperrin jeering at it, as they always did. The deed was done, Nank guessed. Crafty had swallowed the bread pellets, each with half a blade inside, and Flip, John or Jim had hit the bell as they left his cell.

Nank heard the bulkhead grilles slam shut. In a few minutes, the Separation and Detention team would be in Sperrin, and they would cart Crafty away to the ambulance that would take him to hospital.

'Better get that out,' said Nank.

'Aye.' Willie nipped the end off the joint and threw it into the toilet, then stowed the rest in the hidey-hole he'd made behind his mirror.

Nank crossed the corridor to his own cell and lay down. The whole block was locked.

Thirty minutes later McCarthy unlocked him. 'Excitement over,' said the officer.

Nank took his plate and bowl and went down to the dinner hall with Willie. Everyone was talking about Crafty and everyone had the same story. Unable to face the misery of Christmas in jail, the cunt Crafty had taken the coward's route and swallowed a blade to get a fortnight in hospital. There was no mention of Flip or his friends.

Dinner was chicken in lumpy white sauce with sweetcorn and chips. There was also an ice-lolly.

They ate in silence in Nank's cell, then Willie went off to play pool and Nank sat in his chair staring at the skin that had formed on his leftover white sauce. He heard a noise and saw Flip in his doorway.

'Your little friend Willie had better not tout.' Flip modulated 'little' in a vile way.

'What are you on about?'

Flip stepped into Nank's cell. 'He's a root-lover.'

Nank shook his head. 'No, he isn't.'

'The Shillidays? Don't make out you don't know.'

'What?'

'The business with the oranges—I let him away with it because he was new but now it's no more Mr Nice Guy. I get one whiff he's opened his gob to the screws about Crafty, I'll tell everyone he's a tout, he'll be finished, and you, his friend, you'll be finished too. Got that?'

Flip left. Nank trembled and his thighs felt watery. He smoked three roll-ups in a row.

123

THE NEXT MORNING, WHEN HE FOUND Willie in Ablutions filling a bucket, Nank gestured he wanted to talk. Willie left the tap running and followed him to the window.

'I'd Flip in my cell last night,' Nank whispered. 'He thinks you might tout to the screws about Crafty.'

There were men shouting in the corridor outside as they left for the workshops or education.

'I won't.'

Nank shook his head. 'I know, but if he thinks you have, he'll tell everyone in here you're touting for the jail. You'll be finished.'

'You too,' Willie added.

Nank nodded. He was relieved this had been said. It showed Willie had grasped that the situation didn't just concern him.

'I could be a rule twenty-seven, I suppose,' said Willie. This allowed prisoners to be temporarily quarantined in the Separation and Detention Centre for their own safety.

'You don't want to do that,' said Nank. 'You'd go nuts over there.' The boiler suits like Duncan were far stricter than the uniforms.

'I'll have to go to Touts Hole, then.'

Officially known as the Special Centre, it was for those who informed or gave evidence against other prisoners. It was located inside the compound where the S and D team did their riot training but the year before some men on the garden squad had started a small fire there, and tried to burn it down.

'Or I could go down Culcavy,' Willie continued. 'I'd be off-side then.'

Nank thought this was a good idea, but for the sake of friendship he had to argue against it. 'What would your parents think about that?' he said.

'It'd kill them if I went there now, I know. Look at what me ma did to get me here.'

'Then you're going to have to be the invisible man.'

Willie closed his eyes. 'You can't see me, can you? When I was a kid and I closed my eyes I thought no one could see me.'

'Your bucket's full.'

Willie opened his eyes, crossed the room to the tap and turned it off.

'Everything'll be all right,' he said. 'Flip won't even know I'm here. Trust me.'

124

THREE MONTHS HAD PASSED, AND IT was March 1998. Nank was in Ablutions scouring the sinks. He could see Willie through the open door, mopping the floor of the corridor outside.

McCarthy clicked up and, as he passed Willie, he muttered, 'You done well. PO Gilloway knows—he'll be shifted,' and swept on.

At midday, Nank and Willie went to the dinner hall. They were served grey roast beef and crumbling boiled potatoes with black marks on them, like the scuffs rubber-soled shoes made on wooden floors.

'Let's go to mine,' said Nank.

As they climbed the stairs, they passed an officer coming down with Colin, a good-looking paedophile from the fives who carried two bulging paper sacks. According to the newspaper reports, and everyone in the jail had seen them, the twelve-year-old girl he'd raped was so badly torn she couldn't ride her bicycle for months. Because of this detail, an appeal judge had recently increased his sentence from ten to fourteen years.

'Colin's shipping out,' said Nank, when he reached the landing at the top.

'Yeah, I know.'

'You don't sound surprised,' said Nank.

'No.'

McCarthy's words returned. "PO Gilloway knows—he'll be shifted." 'You knew?'

'Let's talk about it in a minute,' said Willie.

They turned onto the threes and passed Crafty's old cell. Crafty, who came round from his operation claiming he couldn't remember what had happened, had been sent to HMP Limavady, and Henry now occupied his cell. Henry was doing ten years for manslaughter. He had stolen a car, when high on drugs and alcohol, and killed a schoolboy. His nose pointed down and his chin pointed up: he looked like a malevolent Punch. He was popular. Henry was standing in his doorway. 'Lads,' he said.

'Henry,' they said, and hurried on.

When they came into Nank's cell, Nank took the chair and Willie the bed. He forked a piece of potato into his mouth. 'Why is the spud always cold?' he said. 'Why can't they find a way to keep it hot while they bring it over from the kitchen?'

'How did you know Colin was going?' said Nank.

'I told McCarthy to get him moved.'

His heart pumping, Nank watched Willie put a piece of beef into his mouth.

'This beef,' said Willie. 'It's not off but it tastes old, like it's been refrigerated for years, don't you think?'

'Why did you tell McCarthy to move him?'

Willie put his fork down and swept the hair off his forehead. 'In the gym, a couple of days ago, I heard the Two Bigs in the shower talking about Flip giving Colin what Crafty got. Soon as I heard I thought, I'll see about that, and first chance, I told McCarthy.'

He smirked. Nank felt a churning sensation behind his solar plexus, close to his spine. 'You hate roots,' said Nank.

'Yeah, but Flip pisses me off more.' The smirk turned into a broad grin. 'Now I'm going to sit back and watch him running around crying, "What have they done with my root? He was supposed to eat a blade."'

'And I'm going to piss in my pants,' said Nank. He looked into Willie's deep grey eyes. 'You have an argument with McCarthy, you know what he's going to do? He's going to let the whole block know you're a tout, starting with Flip.'

'McCarthy's sound.'

'But that's what happens in here. Things aren't meant to be found out but they are and then there's shit to pay.'

'Did I do wrong, then?' said Willie.

Nank shrugged.

'It's wrong, isn't it?' said Willie. 'Flip shouldn't be allowed, should he, to do that? No. We're sent here as punishment, not for punishment. What else could I do?'

'I don't know.'

Willie picked up his fork again. 'Think of it like this. Today, for the wrong reasons, a good deed has been done. Hold on to that and eat your dinner. You haven't touched it.' He popped another piece of potato in his mouth and chewed. 'I hate cold spuds,' he said, 'but if they got them to us warm, you know, I think I could be quite happy in this shit-hole.'

125

IT WAS A WEDNESDAY MORNING AND Nank was in Education for his creative writing class. Squinting through the pane in the door of the classroom, he saw Flip at the filing cabinet with the top drawer open. The filing cabinet was off-limits to prisoners. Nank's other creative writing classmates—there were three of them—were seated round a big table. One was Sulky Stewart, who was watching the door.

Nank turned the handle and went in. 'Hello,' he said.

'It isn't Nanko, is it?' said Flip, without turning.

'What is it, Flippo? Aren't you pleased to see me?'

'Oh, always pleased to see you.' Flip's was the distracted tone of someone reading.

'And have we done our homework?' said Nank. Each man had to write a recipe and a short narrative that used it.

'I don't fucking cook,' said Flip. He was fibbing. He was a wonderful cook and his Spaghetti Bolognese was famous in Sperrin.

'Where's Deirdre?' asked Nank.

'Photocopying,' said Sulky.

Prisoners were banned from the office where the machine was, so all copying was done by staff.

'Photocopying what?' asked Nank.

'A story,' said Sulky.

'Yours?'

Sulky pointed his thumb at Flip. 'His.'

'His recipe story?'

'Nah. Something else.'

The starting bell rang, a high, tinkling sound, quite different from the deep, clanging alarm. Flip locked the cabinet and muttered, 'Jumbo Johnson's a gimp.'

'Why do you say that?' said Nank. 'He's all right.' He had not forgotten Jumbo's kindness when he got into the cubicle of the transporter after he was sentenced and found the floor awash with pee.

'Just.' Flip was at Deirdre's desk. He put the filing cabinet key back with the paper clips where it lived, shut the drawer and sat down.

Deirdre came in holding the photocopies. She was a small woman in her mid-thirties with a sharp nose and brown hair pinned behind her head. She wore a pink cardigan and a long black skirt. 'Here's your story, Flip.' She sat and passed the copies round.

'Were you able to read it?' said Flip.

'Didn't, no,' said Deirdre. 'Only got a peek but it looked interesting.'

A copy landed in front of Nank. It was about ten pages, stapled. The title was at the top, underlined: The Journey. 'Did you do this as well as the recipe story?' asked Nank.

'Sure did,' said Flip. 'I'm full of stories. I love writing. I can't wait to get behind the door at night and start.'

Nank let his eyes roam over the first page. 'Who typed it for you?'

'Me.'

'I didn't know you could type,' said Nank.

'I learned at school.'

'I thought typing was a girl thing.'

'So?'

Nank looked at Flip on the other side of the table, with his large powerful body, shovel-like hands and enormous head. It was hard to imagine him in a class of schoolgirls, learning to touch-type.

'My mother said I'd always have work if I typed,' Flip continued. His blue eyes radiated friendliness and pride.

'And can you do it properly, using all the fingers on both hands?'

'Course,' said Flip, wriggling his fingers.

'And how did you get a typewriter?' Usually it was only Open University students who were allowed computers or typewriters in their cells.

'Went to the governor. Said I was doing creative writing. Deirdre here supported me. Bingo. Permission granted. Wife got a manual for a tenner in a car-boot sale plus a box of ribbons, and Bob's your uncle. Flip McCausland, writer, was in business. I hope to get a computer next.'

Nank looked back at the typed pages. He felt envious. Why hadn't he written an extra story to give to Deirdre? Why hadn't he a typewriter—and why couldn't he type for that matter?

'Okay,' said Deirdre. 'Flip, we'll do your story later. First, homework.'

Flip pulled a sheaf of pages from his folder. Nank saw these were typed too, and Flip saw him looking.

'Bet you wish you could type like me, don't you?' he said.

126

ONCE EVERYONE HAD READ HIS OWN recipe story, and next week's work was set, Deirdre read out Flip's story. The journey of the title was the one he had made from his home in north Belfast to and from school. All his routes passed a Loyalist estate that was home to a Tartan gang. In his Catholic Grammar uniform, Flip was an obvious target, and the gang attacked him endlessly. The story ended with Flip stabbing the gang's leader in the eye with a chisel he had stolen from his school's carpentry workshop. Everyone, even Nank, applauded at the end and they were still clapping when

Maggie, the secretary, put her head round the door. 'Deirdre, phone.'

'Oh.' Deirdre got up. As she left, the bell rang.

An officer came in. 'All out,' he said.

They filed into the corridor. The other classrooms were emptying too. Nank drifted with everyone to the hall at the end but the escorts to take the prisoners back to the blocks hadn't turned up yet and, in the meantime, an officer was checking everyone against their I Cards. Nank caught his eye. 'Melanophy, BC3232,' he said. 'I left something in Deirdre's class. Mind if I go back for it?'

The officer nodded. Nank melted into the crowd and, once he knew that Flip and Sulky weren't watching him, slipped away. Inside Deirdre's classroom he found the key, opened the filing cabinet and pulled open the top drawer. As well as creative writing, Deirdre taught basic literacy, English and a personal-development class for officers. The drawer was full of folders with nametags attached. He saw his own name, then McCausland and Stewart. He saw the names of several other prisoners. Finally, right at the back, he saw 'James Johnson'. Jumbo. Eureka.

He took out the folder and inside found two stapled bundles, both titled 'Dirty'. This had to be what Flip had been reading, he thought. He stuck a copy down the front of his trousers, locked the cabinet and put back the key. A minute later he was milling with the rest of the waiting prisoners. No one seemed to have noticed his absence.

127

AS SOON AS HE WAS LOCKED after lunch Nank got Jumbo's manuscript out from under his mattress and started to read:

Dirty

I wake. No slow drift from sleep to semi-consciousness to wakefulness for me. One moment I'm asleep; the next I'm awake; eyes open; mind alert; dreams behind me; the day ahead.

I look up at the ceiling. White, no cracks, bumps or lumps but that's a new house for you. I sense the covers rising and falling as Maureen breathes beside me.

I reach out. My nail snags on her nylon nightdress. I've often said, 'Why won't you wear cotton? It's so much nicer.' But she won't. 'Nylon dries so much quicker on the line,' she says, 'and it doesn't need ironing.'

I find a thigh and stroke her, more from habit than anything else. She sighs and murmurs. It isn't "Yes" but it's not "No" either. Maybe tomorrow, her murmur implies, just not now.

I withdraw my hand. There's no point complaining. That is how it is with us—day following night following day of quiet physical estrangement. Maybe tomorrow, I think, just as I do every morning. My nail snags on the nightdress again. I sit up.

Our bedroom is square, with a large picture window at one end. We don't use curtains. We use net. I don't like net. I like a dark room with heavy curtains because then intimacy is much more likely. The rare occasions when we do it nowadays are usually in winter when the nights are blackest and longest. If we had heavy curtains, I often think, my life might be so different.

I peer at the net and try to judge the day outside. The sun lights up the net from behind. It's a nice bright morning in May.

I lift the hand I touched Maureen with and smell the ends of my fingers. I smell Cusson's Imperial Leather and Squeezy washing-up liquid. But that wasn't how I always smelt, seemingly ...

In 1981, we lived in a small house, suburban, detached, on a private estate outside Moira. Good enough house but not that nice. We had dreams. We wanted a better house, out in the country. And I had promised Maureen when we married that she would have one.

I had just bought the land for the new house but I couldn't afford to build it yet. Then came the dirty protest, the Republicans smearing their cells with their dirt, and the request for volunteers to clean the blocks for great money. Maureen joked, 'It's a dirty job but someone has to do it,' and I signed up.

Then, one afternoon, a few weeks later, when we sat in the kitchen of our old house eating tea with the kids, I saw her sniff the air. She could smell it, she said. 'What?' 'You know,' she said. She didn't want to say with the children there.

Later, I told her that was impossible. We wore overalls and gauntlets, helmets with visors and heavy-soled boots. Furthermore, after we finished, it was off to the changing rooms, overalls in a bag for the laundry and then a long hot shower. But she wouldn't budge and over the weeks that followed, she became more convinced. She said she smelt it under my nails, in my hair, between my toes. I washed myself fastidiously, covered myself in lotions, deodorants and aftershave, but no matter how much effort I made, Maureen could smell it. Sometimes I thought I could even smell it myself.

All physical contact stopped of course. I could see Maureen's point. Who would want to make love to a man who smelt like that? I told myself it was just temporary. It would only last until this thing blew over, and the prisoners stopped their dirty protest, and Culcavy reverted to normal conditions. That was my mistake. I should have stopped. But, I didn't, did I? I was greedy. "I'll just build the house and then stop." That's what I told myself.

So I stuck it out. The new house was built. The family moved in. The protest ended. Culcavy went back to normal. I was transferred over to Loanend. But our married life was never what it had been again. Oh, if she'd had a couple of drinks, or if it was a special occasion, Christmas or my birthday, and providing it was dark, she'd lift up her nightdress and call me over. I could do it but that was all, no kissing or touching. And it would be over in a couple of minutes. I would roll away. She would pull her nightdress down. She would call, "Goodnight." I would call, "Goodnight" back. We might hold hands. We would fall asleep. Weeks would pass before she would lift her nightdress and call me to her again.

And that's how it still is. This morning's touch and Maureen's sigh are part of something that started ages ago and hasn't changed since.

Ah well, another day, I think. Maybe this one will be different. I stretch my arms over my head. The dog will be waiting, I think, with her nose against the back door, anxious to get out.

From the top of the stairs, I can hear her moaning faintly.

'Coming, Lucy,' I call.

A few moments later I come into the utility room. Lucy, a Jack Russell, jumps at me. I feel her warm tongue touch my hand. I love her excitement, the way she leaps like a fish. I open the door and she rushes out barking and disappears into the garden.

I will have a shower and put on my uniform. I am due at the prison at eight. I wonder what's for tea. Maybe we could have lamb chops with mint sauce and new potatoes. I must remember to ask Maureen.

At the bottom Deirdre had written, 'Encore, well done, sir. (Or shall I call you James?) This is real writing. You have taken painful personal experiences, brought them to life and, more importantly, turned them into art.'

Nank burned each sheet in turn in his metal bin, flushed away the charred pieces, then lay on his bed. Something nasty would come of this. Jumbo was weak and Flip knew it. Of course it would. Nank was sure of it.

128

OVER THE WEEKS THAT FOLLOWED, THE air got warmer and the days got longer. Nank and Willie gave up their orderly jobs. Willie joined the painting, and Nank the garden squad. It was a pleasure, after boring indoors cleaning the threes and fours for so long, to be outside, under the sky, every day.

One Monday morning, early in June, Nank and Willie stood in the dinner hall. It was filled with prisoners waiting to be called to Education or work.

'Painters,' an officer shouted.

'That's me then,' said Willie.

He went through the grille in paint-spattered overalls, followed by Sulky, who was also in the painting squad, and disappeared.

A few minutes later, an officer shouted, 'Garden squad.'

Nank went to him and lifted his arms.

The officer ran his hands down him. 'Okay,' he said.

Nank stepped away and, to his surprise, Flip took his place. Even more surprisingly, instead of his usual white singlet and trainers, he wore a sweatshirt and boots.

The officer ran his hands down Flip. 'Okay, McCausland.'

Flip came up to Nank. 'I'm on gardens,' he said, 'starting this morning.'

'Oh,' said Nank. 'I thought you were in Braille?' This was the unit where prisoners typed printed texts up as Braille.

'Was, mate, but summer's here and I fancied a change. I've opted to do a few months in the open, then back to Braille in October.'

Nank was amazed. Prisoners couldn't normally move between jobs so easily. 'How did you manage that, then?'

'Charm,' said Flip.

Outside, a thin white haze lay across the sky and the concrete path below their feet was covered with a slick of dew. The escort brought them round to the works at the back of Belmore. Several acres square, it was once the centre of the old Second World War army camp on which Loanend had been built. There were several old Nissen huts, now used as stores, and many new buildings. These included the laundries (one for staff, the other for inmates), the tailor's, carpentry and metal workshops, the kitchens, the gymnasium, the chapel, the Separation and Detention Centre, and the S and D training compound with the Special Centre inside for informers.

The base from where the garden squad operated was also here. It was situated beside a manicured lawn, and consisted of greenhouses, some huts and two bins made of railway sleepers for grass cuttings and compost. These were so close to Belmore they blocked out the light from the last cell before the corner on the ground floor.

The escort gave the instructing officer their I Cards. Mike was a fierce-looking man with green eyes and golden hair. He gathered the squad together. 'Right,' he said, 'today we start on the pitches. We're going to get them ready for Sports Day.'

This would happen on the last Saturday of the month. The pitches were on the far side of the works.

'I love Sports Day,' said Flip, as he helped Nank load tools into a handcart. 'It's even better than the Christmas party. You're outside, you've the races, the barbecue, the kids have masses to do—I love it to bits.'

Nank, who had attended each Sports Day since he came, wasn't so sure. If your child won a race, they were delirious, but if they lost their mood plummeted.

'It's all right,' he said.

'Oh, Nanko,' said Flip, 'try and show a bit more enthusiasmo.'

129

ON THE MORNING OF SPORTS DAY, Nank and all the Loanend prisoners with children were escorted to the pitches. The grass was short, with neat white lines painted everywhere. There were poplars planted along one side of the pitches and a soft breeze stirred the leaves.

The families arrived, Jenny and his three children among them. Nank ran a three-legged race with Sarah and came third. Emma, who was not sporty, managed a decent fourth in her category in the egg-and-spoon race. Robert came second in the hundred yards for those under sixteen.

Jenny did not participate in anything. She was pale, and more reticent than usual.

'Something wrong?' asked Nank, while they stood at the bouncy castle, watching their two youngest jumping and falling around. Robert was away, watching the tug-of-war.

'I've got my period.'

'Ah.' That explained it. 'That's a relief,' he said.

'Why?'

'Thought you were going off me.'

'What?'

'You just don't seem, you know, as friendly ... '

'What?'

'As usual.'

'I am friendly—what do you mean?'

Her tone was sharp. This conversation, he thought, could escalate into an argument. He mustn't let that happen. 'I don't know what I meant,' he said.

'Then why did you say it?'

'I don't know,' he said. 'Sometimes I say things and I don't know why.'

'I don't,' said Jenny.

'I know. You're perfect.'

'I am,' she said bleakly. 'I look after three children on my own, no help, and it's a struggle.'

'Three years this September I walk through the gate.'

'I'm worn out,' she said, 'but I don't mind that. That isn't the hard part. Robert's coming sixteen. Have you any idea what it's like trying to handle someone that age?'

'I was sixteen once. I can imagine.' This was lame, but it was all he could manage.

'I don't see where my life's going,' she continued. 'I feel time is slipping through my fingers and one day soon I'm going to wake up, grey, old, and that'll be it, children gone, my life over.'

'Can I put my arm round you?'

'No.'

'Don't you want a cuddle?'

'No, I don't.'

'You don't, right.'

'I don't, that's right,' said Jenny, 'and why do you think you can just fix everything by putting your arm round me?'

'I don't think it'll fix everything,' said Nank, 'but I thought it would be better than talking.'

'We're not talking, we're arguing,' she said.

Nank's eye fell on Flip, with his wife, Sandra, sitting on the grass. She wore a long loose skirt and it was spread out around her. She and Flip were smoking, and their daughter Sharon was running in circles nearby. The scene looked perfectly normal except that Sandra had her hand stuck down the front of her skirt and was ... He looked down, feeling ashamed, and then he heard Jenny say, 'I'm sorry.'

He turned and stared at her.

'We mustn't spoil today,' she said.

'No,' he said.

'But that doesn't mean you can ignore what I said.'

'Oh no.'

'It's horribly hard and lonely. Don't get me wrong, I don't mind the work, it's the emptiness I hate.'

'What do you miss most?' he asked.

'What do you think?'

'I suppose ... ' he began, but didn't finish.

'Not the act,' she said, 'but the closeness, the intimacy. That's what I miss the most.' A tear welled in each of her brown eyes. 'Christ, the kids mustn't see this. Have you a tissue?'

Nank pulled one out of his pocket. 'I miss just what you miss,' he said, as Jenny took it.

She dabbed her eyes, then turned her face towards him and lowered her eyelids. 'I spent ages putting on mascara. I don't want it to run.'

'It hasn't,' Nank said.

'Here,' she said.

He took the tissue back. There were two dark wet patches on it.

'Remember when we met in that pub in Bundoran,' she said, 'after you'd been in prison in England? You were with that friend ... '

'Smiler.'

'If you'd taken me in a time machine to now, here, Sports Day, Loanend jail, I simply wouldn't have believed this was how my life would turn out. I'd have said it was impossible. But now, standing here looking back, I can see it was absolutely logical and I wonder how the hell I could have thought it might go any other way.'

He nodded.

'You can't do this again.'

'What?'

'Come to jail.'

'I've no intention of it.'

'No more runs.'

'I've already agreed that, haven't I?' They had discussed this and he had.

'I'm just saying.'

He looked back at Flip and his wife. Her hand was out of her skirt and under her husband's singlet. She was rubbing his back. He felt a surge of resentment. Flip and his wife were having a good time, and he and Jenny weren't. As he wondered about this, he felt his elbow squeezed and turned back to his wife.

'You can put your arm round me now,' said Jenny. Then she added, in her nice voice, 'Please. I blame my period.'

'Yeah, what timing,' he said. 'Today of all days.'

130

IT WAS EARLY SEPTEMBER, AND HE stood in the dinner hall with Willie. They were waiting to be called to work.

'Painters.'

Willie sloped off towards the grille, followed by Sulky.

'Morning, Nank,' he said.

'Morning, Sulky.' Sulky had shaved his head. 'New haircut?'

'Easier to manage.' Sulky darted through the grille. Nank watched as Willie and he were patted down and led off. He rolled a cigarette and lit the end. He should give up, he thought.

'Gardens.'

Nank nipped off the glowing end and put the roll-up behind his ear. He climbed the steps and went out through the grille. The escort was waiting. It was Jumbo, with his shock of white hair and funny mouth. 'Morning,' said Nank. He lifted his arms up for the pat-down.

'Listen,' said Jumbo. He looked strained. 'You've been bumped, Nank.'

'What?'

'You're not on garden squad any more.'

Nank dropped his arms. 'Of course I am.'

Jumbo angled his clipboard so Nank could see the list of names. His name had a black line through it and beside it was written 'No longer required'.

'When did this happen?'

'Look, Nank,' said Jumbo. 'I don't make the arrangements. I'm just given the list and told to collect the prisoners from Sperrin whose names are down and take them to the garden base. Your name isn't on the list. Go back inside and ask your PO to ring the base. That's all I can suggest.'

Nank turned and found Flip waiting behind him. 'Where you going?' Flip asked.

'Back to my cell.'

'Aren't you coming to gardens?' Flip sounded incredulous.

'I've been bumped.'

'What's going on, Jumbo?' said Flip, raising his arms and stepping forward. 'Nank's in the squad.'

'Don't ask me,' said Jumbo, patting Flip's huge ribcage. 'For some reason gardens don't want him.'

'Get a screw upstairs to ring over,' shouted Flip. 'There must have been a mistake.'

Nank went back upstairs. McCarthy telephoned the base. He had a brief conversation with Mike, the instructing officer, put the phone down and turned to Nank. 'Mike says it's not down to him,' said McCarthy. 'He said someone rang, he can't remember who, and told him you're off the garden squad.'

'Oh.'

'You'll have to apply for a new job. In the meantime, take it easy. You like reading—go and find a book.'

'I just don't understand,' said Nank.

He rang Jenny and told her what had happened.

'It's not the end of the world,' she said. She sounded uninterested and tired. He wished he hadn't rung.

131

EIGHT DAYS PASSED. IT WAS TUESDAY, early, just before work and everyone was getting ready to go off. Nank wished he was going too. He'd applied for a job in the kitchens but hadn't heard back.

Willie came into his cell. 'Can I have a bit of tobacco?' he asked.

As Nank watched Willie transfer the crinkled brown tobacco between tins, he said, 'Where are you for this morning?'

'Belmore,' said Willie. The re-painting timetable followed the same unchanging pattern, and Belmore was always done at this time of year.

'And how is it?'

Willie explained that because the jail was so full the wings couldn't be cleared of prisoners. Instead, one side of a corridor doubled up with the men from the other side, and the empty cells were painted. Then everyone doubled up in the newly-painted cells and the other half was done.

'Yesterday we cleared half the ones, and today we start painting,' said Willie. He snapped the lids onto the tins. 'Pity you're not still with the garden squad. We're doing the cells on the garden side this morning. Could have waved to you.'

Willie went off. Nank cleaned his cell. The sun rose outside and the air grew warm. Nank heard the mowers going behind Belmore. The garden squad, he guessed, were cutting the grass all over the works. He went up to the circle and was standing at the urn filling his Thermos with boiling water when the alarm bell went off, loud and menacing. Officers tumbled out of the office, one of them McCarthy. 'Back to your cell, Nank,' he said. He snapped the tap on the urn shut.

As Nank screwed the top on his Thermos, McCarthy was physically hurrying him across the circle and down the fours. Nank could hear doors closing and keys turning all over the block.

'What's happened? Somebody pressed the bell for fun?' Nank ducked under the lintel and into his cell. 'Are we going to be locked for long?'

'How the fuck do I know?' McCarthy slammed the door and turned the key.

Nank stood just inside his cell. That was the first time in all the years he had known him that he had heard McCarthy swear.

132

HE MADE TEA, AND WHILE HE waited for it to cool, he listened. He heard the alarm and running feet. He heard officers' voices, frantic and impatient. He heard doors around him being locked hurriedly but not Willie's. When he heard Lyle's door slam, he got onto his chair and brought his mouth close to where the heating pipe went into the wall just below the ceiling.

'Lyle?'

He heard a chair scraping, then Lyle's voice coming back through the tiny gap round the pipe. 'I'm here.'

'What's happening, mate?'

'I'm fucked if I know. I was in Education, in the art room. Suddenly the screw runs in. "Right, everyone, back to the blocks." And we're all marched out. As we're going across Yellow Square there are screws everywhere and the boiler-suits are going into Belmore. So whatever went off, it happened in there.'

Nank registered this last piece of information. 'That's where the painting squad were this morning.'

'What—Willie too?'

'Yeah, and he isn't back.'

'Try Sulky,' said Lyle.

Nank went to the bars and opened the window. 'Sulky!' he shouted.

He was competing with many other voices but eventually he got through and Sulky yelled back, 'Yeah, what's up?'

'Where's Willie? He's not in his cell.'

'He's hurt.'

'What?'

'That's all I can tell you, mate.'

Nank got back up on the chair and shouted along the pipe: 'Sulky says he was hurt.'

'How hurt?'

'He doesn't know.'

Outside, the alarm stopped. Lyle agreed to ask around and come back if he heard anything. Nank got off the chair and sat down. There were many reasons to hate prison. There was no freedom. There was no privacy. There was no autonomy. There were no women. But of all the things he hated about prison, this was what he hated most: the not-knowing after something had happened, the prisoner's dependence on gossip and rumour.

133

AT HALF TWELVE, MCCARTHY UNLOCKED HIS door and said, 'Dinner?' He had a battered trolley piled with mustard-yellow Styrofoam boxes.

Nank handed him his plate and glanced at Willie's door. He'd heard it being locked a few minutes earlier but Willie hadn't gone in. The cell was empty, he was sure. 'Are you going to tell me what happened to Willie?'

'You probably know more than me,' said McCarthy. He plonked a styrofoam box with roast pork, two roast potatoes and cabbage on Nank's blue plate.

'Was he taken to hospital?'

'Yep.'

Nank exchanged the plate for his bowl. It came back with a box holding a portion of apple crumble and very yellow custard.

'All I know,' said McCarthy, 'is that he was found collapsed in Old Choky.'

Nank knew the cell. It was the one in Belmore behind the railway-sleeper compost bins on the corner, and it was always dark. When he'd worked at the garden base, he'd often talk to whoever was in it.

'Why did he collapse?'

McCarthy shook his head sadly. 'I don't know. You'll be locked now. We'll let you out in pairs through the afternoon for hot water, okay?'

'How long are you going to keep us locked?'

'No idea,' said McCarthy. Officers never told the truth about lockdowns. It led to rows and men refusing to go into their cells. It was better to let them find out gradually.

'Are we talking days?'

'I said I don't know.'

'What about visits?' Nank nodded at the envelope stuck to the lintel marked MAIL OUT, inside which was another envelope, unsealed, as the prison censors required. 'That's for my wife.'

'What day are we talking?' McCarthy took the envelope and saw the colour of the form inside. 'Oh, Saturday coming. Should be all right. I'll see it goes off.' He shut the steel door. The key turned.

Nank heard the dull rumble of the trolley's wheels as McCarthy pushed it to the next cell. He put his plate on the table and sat down. He didn't feel in the least like eating.

134

NANK LAY ON HIS BED AND didn't move until some time in the afternoon when he and the prisoner from cell sixteen were let out. He threw his dinner into the slop pail, went to the urn and started to fill his Thermos with boiling water.

He ached now behind his solar plexus and in his throat, exactly like he had before he cried when he was a boy. If word spread that he had been seen crying, prisoners would offer him their handkerchiefs and sing 'No Woman No Cry' for months to come. On the other hand, if he let the officers see how affected he was, they might be considerate. They might tell him. It was a risk but he decided to take it.

His flask full, the top screwed tight, he crossed the circle slowly to the office. The notice he had seen on his first day was still there. "The answer is No. Now, what is your question?" Someone had since scribbled in the corner, "I want my wife." Inside the office, McCarthy was digging in his pipe bowl with a screwdriver and Cyril was waiting for the kettle to boil.

'What's the film?' Nank asked.

'*Mad Dogs and Englishmen*,' said Cyril. 'It's got Liz Hurley.'

'Willie is my best friend in here,' said Nank, his voice breaking.

'We know,' said Cyril.

'He was taken to hospital. What's happened to him?'

'That's all we know,' said Cyril. 'Isn't it, Mac?'

'Aye,' said McCarthy.

'But we hear anything we'll let you know first, promise,' said Cyril.

135

THE FOOTSTEPS STOPPED OUTSIDE HIS DOOR. He swung his legs off the bed and sat up.

The door swung back and Nank saw McCarthy. The officer had combed his hair, straightened his tie and tucked in his shirt. It was a bad sign, Nank thought, that this tidy man had spruced himself up.

'Can we have a word?'

He nodded. The officer came in and pulled the door to. This was an even worse sign.

'Cyril's sent me down,' said McCarthy. 'It's going to be on the news, probably tonight, tomorrow for certain.'

'The news?'

'He died. Willie died,' said McCarthy. 'We heard a few minutes ago.'

Nank had already thought he might be dead. Until now, though, part of him had hoped Willie would cheat death. Now he knew he hadn't and he felt a rushing feeling in his head.

'He was shot.'

At first, Nank couldn't understand the words. Then, as the seconds rolled on, they became clear.

'He was shot? But this is a prison.'

'I know. And before you ask, no, we don't know who did it.'

McCarthy spoke then of his own mother and father's deaths and the importance of allowing feelings to be felt. Nank was dimly aware that advice was being given. He was grateful for it. They must be worried about him, he guessed.

Then, suddenly, McCarthy turned. The visit was over, Nank realised. He wanted McCarthy to stay. He had liked hearing his voice talking soothingly. But what could he say?

"Please stay"? No. He'd had his few minutes of kindness and it was time to say goodbye.

136

FIVE MINUTES HAD PASSED AND NANK was up on the chair with his mouth at the pipe. 'Willie was shot,' he said.

'You're joking.'

'I'm telling you. McCarthy said.'

'Are you sure?'

'That's what he said. Why wouldn't it be true?'

'Fucking incredible. You wouldn't believe it in a book, would you?'

'You don't need to tell anyone. They'll all find out soon enough.'

'No problems.' Then Lyle said, 'You must be gutted.'

'Yeah, you said it.'

137

MCCARTHY CAME WITH THE TEA.

'What is it?' asked Nank.

McCarthy lifted the lid off one of the boxes. Inside there was stew and rice.

'No thanks,' said Nank. 'Not hungry, but can I get some hot water?'

'We're not meant to ... Oh, go on,' said McCarthy, 'quick as you can, and don't tell anyone or they'll all want out.'

Later, he lay on his bed, a mug of tea cooling beside him. His television was on. The flicker from the screen bathed the walls and ceiling in its strange television light. He knew that the news was coming and, with it, something about Willie. McCarthy had said so.

Did he want to watch it, though? As he pondered he remembered funerals, specifically those at which the officiating priest hadn't known the dead person. They had always left him feeling dishonest and disappointed with himself for having gone along with what he knew was wrong. If he watched this now, wouldn't it be the same? The reporter, standing outside the gate with the HM Prison sign in the background, and a stranger to Willie, would never be able to say what he was really like or what a loss he was. And if he listened to it, wouldn't it leave him feeling grubby and annoyed because he had gone along with what he knew was a sham? Yes, it would. He would be better off without it.

He pulled the remote from under his pillow and pushed the button. The image on the screen collapsed and the little standby light came on below. That was better.

He stared up. His neon light was on and he heard its low, insistent hum. Beyond this, he heard the drone made by the television sets that were on in every cell, as everyone in Loanend waited for the evening news. He had made the right decision.

138

'NANK,' HE HEARD LYLE SAY.
He got up on the chair. 'Yeah.'
'Did you hear the news?'

'Nah.'

'Oh, sorry, mate. Yeah. They found the gun and a homemade silencer, a lemonade bottle stuffed with cotton pads, in a compost bin.'

Far away, a dog barked.

'How are you feeling?' This was Lyle.

'Not too good.'

'Yeah,' said Lyle. 'He was your friend. But imagine his mum and dad tonight.'

He saw what Lyle was trying to do and even if his line wasn't the most original, he couldn't fault him for trying. 'It's always worse for someone else,' said Nank. 'Listen, I just want to lie down and think for a bit.'

'You go on, mate,' said Lyle. 'Sorry to have brought you such bad news. Now remember, if you want me, I'm here. All right? Just knock or call. Any time. Middle of the night, four in the morning, you'll get me. I'm a light sleeper.'

'Thanks, Lyle.'

'No worries,' Lyle called back.

Nank lay back on his bed. Voices drifted in through his window. Now they had seen the news, prisoners whose cells faced the yard were talking to one another about what had happened. For a while, they would be excited, even exhilarated, by the drama. Later, when they were alone, their mood would change as what had happened sank in. Men in jail felt a death more keenly than any other group he knew. There were so few opportunities for distraction and, besides, they were powerless to do anything about a death except think about it.

139

HE TURNED OFF THE LIGHT AND fell asleep, then woke with a jolt. It was the middle of the night. Sperrin was utterly still. Before he had fallen asleep, he'd been bloated with pain. Now that feeling was gone. His mind was clear too. But he knew he had to think quickly, if he wanted to work the story out, because this wasn't going to last.

He drew little bits and pieces together, and after a while he had an entire story. He'd turned it over in his mind like a pebble. He didn't know if it was right, but it was a story and it made sense. It explained who had killed Willie and how it had been done.

Next he needed to talk to someone, not a principal, someone on the fringe, who could confirm if his story was right.

And suddenly he knew exactly who that someone would be. All he had to do now was wait for this lockdown to end and then they could have their chat.

While he'd been thinking he hadn't felt any pain. But now he'd finished he felt something like a balloon swelling inside, squashing his organs and filling him so he felt sated again.

Of course there was no way to escape what he felt. But suddenly he knew the pain wouldn't be quite as bad as it might have been because now he had his story and, more importantly, he had his plan. If he could remember that, he could stop his feelings overwhelming him.

140

IT WAS FRIDAY, EIGHT O'CLOCK IN the morning. Rain was falling and a seagull was screeching in the yard. Nank had washed and shaved, and was sitting with a tepid mug of tea, made with water that had been in his Thermos all night. At the end of the corridor he heard a key turn, then the sound of a door being pushed into the keepers that held it open. That hadn't happened since Tuesday. Hallelujah, he thought, at long last unlock.

A few minutes later McCarthy opened his door. 'Morning, Nank,' he said.

'Is that it?' asked Nank. 'Normal routine today? Work, education, no more of this being locked twenty-four hours?'

'That's the plan,' said McCarthy, 'unless some joker has other ideas.'

Nank peered across the corridor. On Willie's cell card, someone had scrawled 'Rest in Peaces' with 'Peaces' scratched through and 'Pieces' written underneath. The illiterates, he thought. They didn't even know how to write a grammatical insult.

He dumped the tea in his sink and washed his mug. There was someone he had to talk to. He just had to get himself ready and then he could go.

141

HE SLIPPED ACROSS THE CIRCLE AND glanced down the threes, with the gleaming green linoleum floor, neon lights in protective covers and cell doors locked open. Everything was back to normal, as men got dressed, got breakfast, or sat in their cells waiting to be called for work or education, except that the grille at the far end was locked to stop prisoners from his side and the fives and sixes socialising. Prisoners were always angry after a long lockdown, so it was prison policy to stop them mixing afterwards. It reduced trouble. Normally Nank would have resented this but not today. With the grille locked, Flip and his friends round the corner couldn't surprise him.

He stepped into the threes. Cell One was on his left. Nank ducked under the lintel and found Sulky on his bed, watching television.

'Nank,' he said, and the colour left his face.

A good sign, Nank thought. 'Can I talk to you?'

'Talk's free. Why not?' said Sulky, with a put-on swagger. He pressed mute on the remote.

'Mind if I sit down?'

Sulky shook his head.

Nank sat on the end of his bed. 'So,' he said.

'So?'

'Awful week.'

'Yeah,' said Sulky.

While Nank waited, staring every now and then at the silent screen, Sulky burbled about the lockdown, and how he had missed work. He wouldn't be paid because he hadn't gone to work and he thought that was an injustice because he had been willing to go.

'Yeah, maddening, isn't it?' said Nank, 'Willie getting himself killed like he did. What a lot of trouble he caused us all.'

Sulky's face reddened. 'I didn't mean to, ah, sound like I didn't care,' he said.

'No, no, don't worry,' said Nank. 'Being locked since Tuesday was horrible. I understand.'

Sulky looked relieved. 'Were you interrogated?' he asked. The police had been in on Wednesday and Thursday, getting statements, so it was an obvious topic. Nank felt a thrill of delight. Sulky was heading exactly where he wanted without his having to direct him.

'Yesterday,' said Nank. 'Complete waste of time. I was here. What could I tell them? Of course, they asked if Willie had any enemies.' He let the statement hang.

'What did you say?' said Sulky.

'Nothing.' Nank shrugged. 'I mean, I have my thoughts but who'd believe an old lag like me? What about you?'

Sulky's eyes flicked to the door, then back again to Nank.

'Are you expecting someone?'

'No,' said Sulky, too quickly. He was rattled, no doubt about it.

'So what did you say to the police?'

'I'm with the painters, Belmore,' said Sulky. 'Willie and me are down the ones. We're doing the cells on the garden base side. I start in the bottom cell, Willie's in the top one ... '

'Willie's in Old Choky?'

'Yeah. I'm painting away. Suddenly, alarm goes, Kevin, the instructor, starts bellowing. I run down and there's Willie, face in a fucking pool of blood. I don't know what the fuck's going on. No one tells me. I'm brought back here and locked like everyone else. Then yesterday I spend an hour going over what I just told you. Pointless, but there you go. That's the police.'

'That is the police,' said Nank. 'Always asking their questions, aren't they? But do they get the truth? Very rarely, I'd say, and I can't imagine in this case they've got a snowball's chance in hell of finding out what happened.'

'You think?' said Sulky.

'Oh, yeah,' said Nank. 'I'm sure of it.'

He put his hand inside his cheek and pulled out a lump of hash, then a second. He put them in the middle of his palm and showed them to Sulky. There was about an ounce altogether. 'What do you think of that?'

He studied Sulky's face. Up to this moment, Sulky had been nervous, anxious. Now that he had produced the drug, Sulky was surprised, relieved and even mildly excited. He had stopped flicking his eyes at the door, was focused on the two brown lumps on Nank's palm and smiling. Sulky wanted what he saw. That was obvious. He wanted it very badly. Now Nank had him, and it was time to strike.

'Would you like this?' asked Nank.

Sulky snorted. 'How much?'

'As a gift.'

Sulky furrowed his brow. The offer didn't make sense. 'I don't know,' he said. 'Is this for real?'

'I'll give it to you, yeah,' said Nank. 'You just have to listen to something and tell me what you think.'

'What exactly do you want me to hear?'

'A story,' said Nank.

'What story?'

'I want you to listen to a story and then I want you to tell me if it's any good, exactly like you would in Deirdre's creative writing class.'

'And what's this story about?' said Sulky.

'It's just a little something I made up. All I ask is you listen and tell me what you think and then I'll give you these.'

'And that's it?'

'Yes.'

'And what if I don't like your story?'

'I don't mind,' said Nank.

'I can tell you I hate it?'

'You can tell me you hate it,' said Nank.

On Sulky's face the battle between the part that wanted to say yes and the part that wanted to say no continued. Then he smiled and Nank knew which side had won.

'All right,' said Sulky, 'tell me your story. I'm all ears.'

'Funnily enough, it starts in Deirdre's class. You're sitting at the table and Flip's at the filing cabinet. He's reading something. Afterwards he says, "Jumbo's a gimp." Now a gimp is weak and vulnerable. A gimp is someone you can use and abuse. Hold on to that. It becomes important later.

'Same class, just a few minutes later, Deirdre appears, with Flip's story, typed. He's got a typewriter, it appears, because he's doing creative writing. Hold on to that as well. It's important too.

'With the next part I'm a bit hazy. I know Jumbo's in it and there's a girl outside, someone Flip knows. She's willing, and Jumbo's lonely. She fucks his brains out and once he's snared, Jumbo starts talking and Flip finds out Willie had Colin moved. He's very annoyed. He hates touts. He wants Willie dead because that's what you do with a tout. You kill him.

'How is he to do this, though? There's stabbing but it doesn't always work and it's messy. Blood gets everywhere, and with modern forensics, one spot on your shirt is enough to convict.

'He decides shooting would be better. It's got a bit of style about it and it's pretty foolproof. I think Flip's wife brought it in, on Sports Day actually, up her you-know-where, and slipped it under a flap of turf, I think I actually saw her doing this, and Flip, who was on the garden squad, retrieved it and brought it here. Then he broke it down and put it in his typewriter. Remember the typewriter? The search team, looking inside, would just see bits of metal, wouldn't they? They couldn't tell the typewriter mechanism from the gun parts. What he couldn't hide were the bullets but I think he kept those up his shitter.

'Monday, week before last, I find I'm off the garden squad. And who breaks the news? It's our old friend Jumbo. He's had me bumped, not mind you that he knows what's coming.

'Go forward now, to Tuesday, this week, the painting squad is in Belmore, the ones. You've cleared the cells, now it's time to paint them. This is where you play your vital role, Sulky. You say, "You go in there, Willie, into Old Choky, and I'll start at the other end," or something like that. Willie doesn't know you're setting him up, so he says, "Yeah, okay," and into Old Choky he goes.

'A few minutes later, Flip comes to the window. Bang, bang. No one hears because the mowers are going full belt. No one sees because he's behind the bins made of railway sleepers. Then he chucks the weapon in the compost. The end. So, what do you think of my story? How Flip killed Willie and how you helped. Good, isn't it?'

Sulky dragged his upper teeth over his lower lip. His eyes flicked to the door and back to Nank. He screwed up his face. 'What?' he said. 'What are you on?' Then he paused. And then he said, 'Where did that come from?'

'You don't like?'

'It's crap.'

'I was lying when I said it wouldn't matter if you didn't like it. It does.' Nank closed his fingers over the two blocks of hash. 'I didn't know if I had it right, but the way your eyes are going and the way you're eating your lip, I know I am.

'Now you're worried, Sulky, understandably, that I'm going to tout. You needn't worry, I won't tell a soul. I'm sure you don't like that but do you have an alternative? You can hardly go to Flip and say, "Nank knows everything," because he's going to say, "How come he knows?" and are you going to tell Flip, "Oh, I told him"? I don't think so. So, we can leave it there. This can be our little secret. I won't tell. You won't tell.'

He put the cannabis back inside his cheeks, left Sulky's cell and returned to the circle. He would go down to his cell, and stash the blocks behind the smoke-extractor cover.

He set off towards the fours and was halfway across the circle when he heard, 'Nank.'

Oh, no, he thought.

He turned.

McCarthy was standing in the office doorway. 'Come here,' he called.

Oh, Christ. Nank hoped the bulge in his cheeks didn't show. He walked over. 'Yeah?' he said casually.

McCarthy leaned forward, indicating he had something confidential to say. Nank leant forward. 'Your wife called. Wanted to check Visits were on. I said yes. Told her what a week we've had. Anyway, she wants a boxed visit tomorrow.'

'What?'

'She wants a boxed visit.'

Nank was appalled. He wasn't a rapist or paedophile who had to keep out of sight in case of attack by other prisoners. He was an ordinary decent criminal. 'I've never had a boxed visit in my life,' he said.

It was true, and he didn't want to start now either.

McCarthy smiled. 'The lady wants a boxed visit, so the lady gets one. I phoned the request through to Visits already.'

142

AFTER HE WAS LOCKED THAT NIGHT Nank lay on his bed with the light off and smoked a joint. His thoughts came slowly, but they were precise.

First, he'd have to get back on the garden squad. He'd have to work like mad but he could do it if he pushed hard enough. Also, Flip said he was going back to Braille in October, so he wouldn't be there in the background, whispering to Jumbo, pulling strings and blocking his reinstatement. Yeah, he'd do it. He'd get back on the garden squad. He had to. Everything depended on it.

Then he'd ask Docker to get him a gun. His friend wouldn't want to. He'd come out with his old spiel that violence didn't work because someone tougher would always come along.

Nank had his counter-argument marshalled. His inaction would be seen as a sign of weakness. It would invite further attack. He had to strike. If he didn't put Flip down, Flip would do for him.

Then there was the matter of how to get it in. He'd copy Flip but he'd have to have Jenny's help. It would be a very small weapon and she'd bring it in next Sports Day. It was nearly a year away, which would give him plenty of time to work on her. On the day they would sit on the grass while the children ran a race, she with her long skirts spread in a circle around her. When no one was looking she would pull it out and slip it under the turf that he would have cut in advance.

The day after Sports Day, because he was back on the garden squad, he'd be on the pitches for the clear up. He'd retrieve the gun, take it back to his cell and store it in the typewriter he'd get for his creative writing. After that, it was just a matter of time and place.

143

FROM THE PRISON SIDE, HE PASSED through the door into Visits. It was packed with prisoners and their families and a cloud of cigarette smoke had already collected under the ceiling.

He saw Jenny at the other end of the room, alone, without the children. He waved. Jenny waved back. He moved down Visits towards her and she moved towards him. They met in the middle.

'Hello,' he said.

'Hello.'

She wore a loose grey dress and a short black jacket and she carried her purse with cash for the tea-boat, cigarettes, a lighter and her visitor's pass. He leaned forward to kiss her. She offered her mouth firmly closed. He touched his lips to hers. They separated.

'Where's the kids?'

'No kids today,' she said.

'Why? They were on the pass.'

'Yeah,' she said, 'but I didn't want them with me today.'

And why was that? he asked himself. Had she come to say something unpleasant? Was that why she had asked for the boxed visit?

Instead of an answer, a new thought swam forward. He needed Jenny's help. Without it he couldn't do what he was determined to do. This was no time for the marriage to go wrong. His stomach lurched. 'Have you got something awful to tell me?'

'Just wait,' she said.

'You know I don't like surprises,' he said. 'Could you not have given me a hint of what's coming? Said something on the phone?'

'No, I couldn't,' she said.

'Give me a hint now, then.'

'No,' she said.

'A bit of a hint?'

'Not even a bit of a hint,' she said.

'Why not?'

'Just wait until we're inside the box.'

'You know who the boxes are for, don't you?' he said. 'They're for roots. It's not good for me to be seen going into one.'

'I know, but once we're in, you'll understand.'

Perhaps she'd asked for the box so they could be private, so he could express his feelings about Willie's murder without anyone looking at him, he thought. Behind the plywood, he could talk more frankly than he could on the Visits floor. So maybe the box was a good thing.

They went to the officer in charge of allocations.

'Melanophy,' said Nank. 'Boxed visit.'

'Number?'

'BC3232.'

The officer looked at a list. 'Three.'

They crossed the floor to a door marked '3'. The box walls reached just below his shoulder. Inside, he could see chairs with cushion seats and backs covered with brown plastic and a low Formica table. They went in quickly and he closed the door. The air smelled of perfume, sweat and cigarette smoke.

'All right?' An officer with popping eyes was staring in at them over the plywood wall.

'Yeah,' said Nank.

The officer vanished. Nank sat in the corner and put his tobacco tin on the table while Jenny shunted the seat next to his towards the door with her knees.

'Don't you want to sit beside me?' he said.

'No.'

'Why not?'

'Because I want to sit on your lap,' she said.

This he had not expected. 'Oh.'

'It's allowed,' she said.

In Visits, a partner or wife was permitted to sit on a prisoner's lap. But, if there was kissing or touching, the officers would ask the couple to sit apart. If they refused and carried on, the prisoner was removed and the visitor asked to leave. They would not be allowed back for twelve months. The severity of the punishment ensured that the rule was obeyed.

'Come on, then.' He patted his knees. She lifted her skirts and sat sideways onto him, her knees pointing towards the box door and her face in profile to his. She smelled of shampoo, make-up and perfume, and under these he detected her unique Jenny smell, the one he associated with intimacy.

'You've had a terrible week,' she said. She rolled her pelvis back and forth. 'And I'm going to make it up to you.' He felt himself harden.

'This is not a good idea,' he said.

'Don't you like it?'

He really should ask her to get off, he thought, and glanced up, half expecting to see the officer with the popping eyes looking over the partition and to hear him saying, 'Get off him at once, Mrs Melanophy. That is an order.'

'I didn't say that,' he said.

In his head, he marshalled his thoughts. He must explain about Willie. How important and good a friend he had been. And what had been done. And how he proposed to retaliate. And the help he needed from Jenny. And why she must do this for him even though it was a great deal to ask.

'You know this isn't a good idea,' he said. 'They check the boxes every few minutes.'

What would be best, he thought, was that she get off but that he stay hard and then, when he got back to his cell, he could wank into a sock.

'Don't you like me sitting on your lap?'

'What do you think?'

'And don't you think I like it too?'

She bore down on him now, pressing rhythmically. Between his legs, he was starting to ache.

'I'm not wearing tights or knickers,' she said matter-of-factly. 'I took them off in the toilets. I left them in my handbag.'

Visitors were forbidden to bring bags into Visits.

'I'm going to turn and face forward,' said Jenny. 'I have an article in my purse here. It's from *Homes & Gardens*.'

She opened the purse, pulled out the glossy pages and opened them on the table.

Visitors were forbidden to bring in magazines, papers or books.

'We're going to look at this together and we're going to talk about my new kitchen,' she said. 'And if an officer comes, we'll look perfectly innocent. He'll see us looking at a few pages cut out of a magazine. I'm going to get up for a second now and let you get into position.'

She stood. This was wrong, he thought, and reckless.

But, his hand moved to his zip, undid it and pulled his cock out.

She turned her back on him and lowered herself. She was seeking him and then she found him. She sat down then very slowly and he felt himself sliding up until, at last, he was enclosed.

'Now,' said Jenny. Her knees were parallel with his and her weight was on his lap. He began making small, careful, upward thrusts. She flattened the pages on the table, smoothing away the lines and bumps that had formed when they were folded.

He glimpsed a headline: THE LUCK OF THE IRISH. Below this there was a picture of a house. It was white, obviously Georgian. It had casement windows and french doors. The front door was black. There was a fanlight with coloured glass above and two honey-coloured Labradors on the step below. It was a classic *Homes & Gardens* photograph.

'"Over the years,"' Jenny began, reading from the top, '"a two-storey Georgian shooting lodge in County Laois, Ireland, has been turned into a glorious family home, the charming decorating scheme blending artfully with the soft Irish light that pours in through the many large windows."'

Jenny turned the page. There was a picture of a kitchen with a cream Aga, some painted cupboards and a sink.

He must focus. Once he'd said his piece, she'd talk. What if Flip's organisation retaliated, she would ask, by coming for her or, worse, the children? What could he say to that?

'"During their years in residence,"' Jenny read, '"the owners have gradually redecorated the house. As they have done this, they have tried to maintain and in some cases to recapture a sense of the Georgian style of the original building."'

And then there was the risk of what he wanted her to smuggle in. What if she was caught bringing in the gun, no matter it was hidden deep inside her, where he was now? She would go to prison. The children would be without two parents. What could he say to that?

'"In the summer,"' Jenny read on, '"the oil–fired Aga goes off, and the family switch to a gas stove, but the open fire in the kitchen burns every day. It never goes out, ever".'

If he was going to have any chance of persuading Jenny, he thought, he'd better pull out now, and come on her thighs. But even as he had this thought he knew he couldn't stop. Not now.

'"There's something about that open fire, according to the current owner, that says more emphatically than anything else does what the house is. It is a living, breathing organism,"' read Jenny.

The rush that had started was gaining momentum. That moment, the moment, was coming.

'"It's the heart of the house, and when it goes out, we always say, then the house will have died."'

His excitement was mounting. He no longer heard Jenny's voice as she read. He no longer heard the hubbub of the visitors on the other side of the plywood walls. He was almost done, he was almost there and then ...

'"It also means,"' Jenny said, her voice switching on like a radio, '"that whatever the Irish weather does, and the Irish weather can only ever be relied upon to rain, she never has any difficulty drying the considerable amounts of laundry generated by her large young family ... " Can we have an open fire in our kitchen?' Jenny asked.

'Whatever,' he said. He was full of that lovely still feeling that always came after.

'And an Aga?'

'Absolutely.'

'How are we doing?'

He looked up and saw it was an officer. This one, different from the last, had a huge nose and glasses that magnified his eyes.

'I'm fine,' said Nank. 'We're discussing home improvements here.'

'In my kitchen,' said Jenny, 'I want an Aga and an open fire.'

'I hope you're not being greedy,' said the officer. With his great eyes, he was staring down, looking for signs of improper contact.

'I'm never greedy,' she said.

Nank felt Jenny clenching and unclenching around him.

The officer nodded. 'We'll be calling the end at half three.' He looked at his watch. 'You've got the guts of half an hour.'

'Thank you very much,' said Jenny. She clenched again but he was smaller now. He would fall out of her soon.

The officer turned and went.

'My knees are a bit sore,' he said.

'I'll stand so.'

She got up slowly and he put his hands under her skirt, folded himself away and zipped up the fly. Then Jenny stepped away, smoothing her skirt, and sat on the other chair.

'We'd better agree a code,' said Jenny. She stuck her belly out and held it. 'I know. The eagle has landed. Isn't that a popular one?'

He hadn't thought about this until now, and now he wondered why not. What an idiot he'd been. How could he possibly ask for the help he needed if that happened? 'Oh, fuck,' he said, 'I thought ... '

'What?'

'I thought ... aren't you ... using something?'

Jenny shook her head.

'Oh, Jenny,' he said.

'I can't wait for you to come out,' she said. 'I'll be too old. It has to be now.'

'But I won't be at home.'

'I'll manage and the kids'll help. My mother too.'

'Anyway,' he said, 'it's not necessarily ... '

'No.'

'I mean ... it mightn't ... '

'We'll see,' she said.

They talked then about the children, but he never mentioned Willie or his plan—he didn't feel he could under the circumstances—and soon the officers were calling time outside and the one with the popping eyes put his head over the partition again.

'Come on,' he said. 'Time's up.'

They stood. Popping Eyes opened the box door and went off.

'Today's the best day of the month for me,' she said, 'but if it doesn't work I'll have another boxed visit and I'll go on taking them until it does.'

She walked out before he could speak. He followed her. Outside, on the floor of Visits, prisoners waving and calling goodbye were flooding towards the door to the prison side, while families also waving and calling goodbye, were moving towards their door at the opposite end.

'I can't believe what you've just said,' he told her.

'Cheer up, it's not the end of the world,' she said, and kissed him.

144

TWO WEEKS LATER AT EIGHT IN the morning, McCarthy opened his cell door. 'Night guard took a message,' he said. 'Did you get it?'

'No,' said Nank.

McCarthy handed him the yellow Post-it and Nank read what had been scrawled in Biro: "Message from Mrs Melanophy for BC3232. The eagle has landed."

He still hadn't told her about his plan and the help he needed. He saw it was impossible now. That night, when he thought things over while he lay waiting for sleep, he saw it was for the best. He was never going to beat Flip and he must have been mad to think he could.

145

A YEAR LATER, ON THE SECOND Saturday in September 1999, he had a visit from Jenny, Robert, Emma, Sarah, and his three-month old son. As far as the prison was concerned, he was Nank's nephew. The baby had his mother's colour and smelt of milk. He had been christened the previous Sunday in the same Melanophy christening robe Nank had worn at his christening. Jenny showed him the photographs: the baby in her arms, the priest dashing water onto his head, and Willie's parents, Mr and Mrs Mullen, holding him afterwards in the good room in their house where the christening party had been held. The baby, in memory of their son, was named William and they were his godparents.

146

IT WAS JUST AFTER FOUR WHEN Nank got back to the main circle in Sperrin. It smelt of aftershave from the men who had passed through to Visits, and the chips that the dinner orderlies were unloading in the servery.

'Next,' said the officer. Nank stepped forward and, smiling broadly, he raised his arms. The officer began to pat his body. 'What are you smiling for?' he said.

'What am I smiling for?' said Nank. 'Well, you know how it is.'

The officer reached his ankles, straightened up and looked into Nank's eyes. 'No, I don't. You tell me.'

Nank wondered how to proceed. On the one hand, the world was a rotten place: Jumbo had been promoted, and Flip was back in Braille. On the other, he had a new son. He had to smile about that even if he couldn't talk about it.

'Had a visit,' said Nank, 'saw the wife, saw the kids, good chat. On top of which, I'm out this time year after next. So, all in all, yeah, it's been a good day.'

'A good day?'

'Yeah, a good day for a dog.'

The officer laughed. 'A good day for a dog. That's a new one on me. Go on, fuck off.'

'Woof, woof,' said Nank, and sailed through the grille.